Final Belongings

a novel

Sarah Beauchemin

Copyright © 2022 Sarah Beauchemin

Final Belongings is a work of fiction. Any references to historical events, real people, or real places are used fictitiously. Other names, characters, places, and events are products of the author's imagination, and any resemblance to actual events or places or persons, living or dead, is entirely coincidental.

All rights reserved. No part of this book may be used or reproduced in any manner whatsoever without express written permission of the publisher except in the case of brief quotations embodied in critical articles or reviews.

ISBN (eBook) 979-8-9865499-0-3

ISBN (Paperback) 979-8-9865499-1-0

ISBN (Hardback) 979-8-9865499-2-7

Cover Design by Damonza.com

For Bart

Chapter One

My job interview is at one o'clock, so I need to start sobering up by noon. I glance at my phone. Eleven-thirty. There's still time for another Bloody, as long as I cut the vodka back by half. Just a little something to take the edge off my nerves, to hone my focus. Like those business-class passengers I'd see on early flights when Matt and I used to travel. Important people doing important work. Sipping an icy screwdriver to temper their steaming coffee, their laptops open with DocuSigns and emails and Slack threads awaiting their decisions. If they can enjoy a morning bracer, why not me? Plus, I'm not even drunk right now. I'm just in that perfect warm zone where I feel alive again.

I roll back from the antique desk in our study, maneuvering around its titanic leg just in time before I stand up. After six months of bashing my knee almost daily on this walnut graduation gift from Mom, I finally learned my lesson. You'd think the regular dose of blinding pain would've been enough to spark a clever idea to write about. Or, really, any idea at all.

You'd think.

I go to the kitchen, yank open the freezer door, and unscrew the Grey Goose. The vodka clouds the tomato juice into plasma as I stir. Snippets of my old life stare at me, held fast under fridge magnets. There we are, Matt and me outside that retro ski lodge in Tahoe; sitting with plates scraped clean in that euphoric Anthony Bourdain recommendation in Thailand; tearing open our stocking gag gifts on Christmas morning. Matt's eyes, clear and assured, fixed on me. The safety and warmth of that steady gaze.

But then I remember. My stomach lurches like it's drowning in sea water. Briny, bitter cold. Boundless.

I whisk my drink off the countertop and into the living room where our stuff sits in respective piles on the floor—his and hers. This room, our entire home, was once my sanctuary. But now it's just another place I can't wait to escape. To where, though, I have no idea yet.

Was. Is there a more poisonous word? See, I've learned that the expanse between *was* and *is* is so much greater than I could've ever imagined. Think about the inevitable we all face: "I was young, now I'm old. I was beautiful, now I'm just another monochrome face in the background. I was in love, now I dread each time I hear the key turn in the lock."

On the list of terminal illnesses, *was* ranks up there

with the worst of them. That moment you realize you've moved from one state of being to the next without your permission. When you notice you're a stranger in your own skin. It's staggering, really. The unfairness of it all. If you're lucky, it'll smack you all at once. You won't feel it slipping away little by little, like I did.

Downing the rest of my drink, I drop onto the West Elm sofa I decided I'm taking with me to my next abode, wherever that may be. I've only got two more weeks to find an apartment. So far, every option in my price range is roughly the size of a placemat and sits two feet from a roaring freeway. The damn couch probably won't fit anyhow.

I sigh and let my eyes close. I just need a minute to rest. Before I know it, my phone trumpets from somewhere in the house. What time is it? Did I fall asleep? I prop myself up on my elbow, squinting and disoriented, cold with the creeping panic of something I've forgotten. Then it hits me—the job interview.

I leap up and run to the study, stabbing at my phone to silence the alarm while opening my laptop. Of course, it takes forever, and I curse the little rainbow spinning wheel to the fiery depths of hell. Scooting into my chair, I smooth my hair and swipe at my eyes, praying I can pass for a functioning adult. Maybe this guy will be just as casual as me.

To my dismay, an impeccable man in his fifties appears on screen with a tight smile. The room sways around me, and I realize that in addition to being late for the interview, I'm more drunk than I thought. For a second, I consider clicking off and going back to sleep. Would it really matter?

"Juliet?" he says.

"Hi, Scott, sorry I'm running behind." I feed him the line about how it's the weirdest thing; today technology just doesn't want to work.

"No worries," he says. "Let's just dive in."

I straighten. "Sure."

He recaps the essence of the job, which is a remote position managing communications for a law firm marketing agency. And this is the least bleak of the three job interviews I managed to snag.

"Your resume's solid, and so is your deck," he says, referring to my work portfolio I sent him. "It looks like most of your stuff is from your time at Hummingbird, right? That's a marketing agency?"

"Yes. They mainly do branding and content for tech start-ups. But other industries, too."

"Mm. Any experience with law firms?" he says. *You mean besides currently paying them thousands of dollars to finalize my divorce?*

"Not directly, no. But I'm really well-versed in agency life. You know, switching gears fast, juggling multiple projects, interfacing with all types of clients. That kind of thing."

Oh, God. I want to crucify myself for using *interfacing*. The only thing worse I could've said is *synergizing*. Better yet, *synergizing industry verticals*. I wish I could pinpoint exactly where, along my line of grave missteps, I turned into someone who talks like this.

"Great. We're looking for that. Agency life isn't for everyone, you know."

"Right," I say. I squash down the little voice screaming inside me that I belong to that very group of folks.

"Can I ask, then, why you left Hummingbird?"

I pause, hoping the heat in my face isn't visible "Well, actually, I was laid off."

"Really?" His eyebrows shoot to his manicured hairline. "I'd think there'd be no shortage of work when it comes to tech start-ups." True, but it turns out there is a shortage of work for people who hate working for tech start-ups.

The last project I worked on before I got laid off was for this dating site that's in beta called FoMo. Let me describe it like this: If you combined all the worst traits of humanity and put them into words, you'd have something that still stood head and shoulders above FoMo. Some twenty-year-old jackass in Palo Alto thought it would be awesome if an algorithm could complete your entire dating profile for you, just by uploading your photo. No need to waste thought describing oneself. If you have a certain kind of smile, for example, the program already knows you're an extrovert. Or if you've got brown hair, you're more likely to be sensitive. It actually worked most of the time. But that won't cut it with venture capitalists. FoMo hired Hummingbird to help with content, and that's where I came in. Day in and out, I wrote hollow copy that could fill in the program's gaps so kids could get laid. Not exactly curing malaria, but damn close.

After a few more questions that illustrate just how mind-numbingly dull this job will be, Scott asks me if I have any of my own.

"Yes, about compensation," I say, "the post just said 'competitive.' Can you give me a range?"

He tells me, and my gut turns to ice. I force my expression to stay neutral as I swallow an expletive. Way less than I made at Hummingbird, and definitely not enough to justify this position's level of responsibility. Even worse, the abysmal pay is exactly in line with the other jobs I interviewed for. I'm doomed.

"Sounds good," I horrify myself by saying. He says he'll let me know about next steps, and we say our goodbyes.

I've barely had a minute to process this conversation with Scott when my phone rings. I throw it a weary glance. Mom. Who else would it be? If you were to scroll through my call history, hers is the only name there. I know she's only trying to help with her daily check-ins. But I have no energy to dodge questions about why and how my life is tanking, especially after our last blow-up where I told her that she, like all tenured history PhDs, is a pompous elitist. I'd pointed out how I would never have been that way, had I gotten my professorship.

The call ends and my phone screen goes black. Guilt scuttles across my chest. It's fine, I'll call her later. But as soon as I get out of my chair to refresh my drink, she rings again. Huffing, I grab the phone and hit decline.

But there's something else behind my adrenaline surge, an uncanny needling at the back of my mind. It's not like her to call twice in a row. I stare at the phone. Nothing.

I move two steps toward the kitchen before the phone rings again. My hands tingle. I slowly turn back and pick it up.

"Juliet." It's a strangely flat voice that doesn't belong to my mother, and I immediately know everything is wrong. It takes a second for the voice of Mom's closest friend to register in my mind.

"Colette, is that you? What's going on?" The words sound viscous and slow to me through the roaring that's begun in my ears.

"I'm at your mom's house," she says. Then she's going on about how she doesn't know how to say this and asks if I'm sitting down and I hear walkie talkies in the background and all the other cliched, disembodied noises of despair fill my head until I think I'll never hear anything else again.

And there it is, just like that: I was a daughter, and now I am not.

Chapter Two

"I can't do this," I say. "I thought I could, but I can't." Colette holds me tighter, her arm secure against my damp back. We're standing in Mom's hallway in front of the closed door to her study. It hasn't been opened since the coroner removed her body four days ago.

By some grace of the universe, when Colette found Mom, they say she'd only had the stroke a few hours before. She hadn't been alone very long. But she *had* been alone.

My mother died alone.

The thought tears through me, ripping open the protective sutures I tried in vain to stitch around my heart.

"You're stronger than you think, Jules," Colette says, pulling me to her. I try not to wince. I'm so limp, I feel like one more squeeze from her will send all my insides erupting through the top of my head. "I promise you can. We'll do it together."

"Oh, God," I whisper through chattering teeth. The hallway bends around me. It can't be possible for me to cry any more, but nonetheless, tears start to burn my retinas like acid. How can anyone live with the persistence of loss? How will I?

Colette turns me to face her. Her eyes are loving but firm. They pull me back to the present.

"Look. We're just in and out today, okay?" she says. "Just to get the photos. We'll deal with the rest of the stuff another time."

Mom's funeral is in three days. I'm running out of time to put together the celebration of life collage for her wake. I know the box of old family photos is in the study's closet somewhere, among heaps of other stuff. There's no choice. I have to go in.

"Okay," I say, running a hand through my greasy hair. "Right. Okay. Just the photos."

I grip the doorknob in my sweaty palm, turn, and push it open. My eyes clamp shut as Colette leads me stiffly over the threshold and a few paces into the room. *What if Mom's still in here?* I think crazily. *Lying dead on the floor, waiting to ask me why I didn't come for her?* A flash of our final phone conversation explodes in my mind. Me, exasperated: *I can't make it over today, Mom. I'll let you know when it's a good time.* Now I have forever.

"You with me?" Colette says. With a feeble nod, I open my eyes.

Yes, Mom is still here. In a million different ways. The smell of warm chamomile lingers. I can hear her off-key humming over the steady click of the keyboard. I still see her, with furrowed brow and twisted mouth, massaging her eyeglass lenses with that fancy cloth that never got them all the way clean.

These are the things will haunt me—not her ghost, or any other. Just the loose ends, the fingerprint remains of a life cut short, answers that will never come.

Against my will, my gaze darts to the floor next to her desk where she was found. I've always thought that a person's knees buckling in response to trauma was hyperbolic, but now here I am, dropping to the floor myself, my legs like two deflated accordions. Colette kneels beside me.

I let go, and so does she. An ungodly sound reverberates all around me, like a cat screaming in pain. It takes me a second to realize that I'm hearing my own elongated, choking sobs, so guttural I taste copper mixed with bile at the back of my throat. Saliva sprays from my mouth in ribbons and my lungs gasp in staccato breaths. And then I know just what I sound like, because it's exactly what I am: a lost girl crying out for her mother.

Colette and I stay on the Persian rug like this for what feels like hours. The waning sun paints stripes on us through the slatted blinds, and dust particles dance all around. When I was little, Mom used to tell me this was fairy dust. Proof there was magic all around me. But I never saw it.

When we both begin to quiet, I raise my head and look around with eyes as hot and dry as the sands of Egypt. I'm in that wrung-out, post-grief state where exhaustion temporarily cauterizes emotion.

I force an empty laugh and blot at my face with my t-shirt.

"Should we look for those photos, then?" I say.

Colette's eyes are steeped in sympathy behind those round Parisian rims. They're offering me comfort I don't deserve, and I look away, embarrassed.

"I think that's a good next step," she says, and we help each other to our feet. Her fingers are slender and dexterous and lovely, a reflection of a sane and disciplined life. I push my own rough hands with bitten-down fingernails into my back pockets. Then I take a deep, shuddering breath and shake out my limbs. *Just in and out today. I can do this.* Putting on my invisible blinders, I stride over to the closet and swing the door open.

At one point, it was actually a sizable walk-in. But now you can't get more than three steps in before stubbing your toe on the old-school metal filing cabinets brimming with academic research or spraining your ankle on the monstrous books tiling the floor. How we're ever going to be able to find that box with family photos is beyond me. My heart collapses. So much for getting in and out quickly.

Colette comes up behind me, blowing her nose. She's carrying a tissue box she must've found somewhere and offers it to me. I thank her and take one, wiping at my snot-encrusted face.

"Wow," she says, lifting her glasses and dabbing a

Kleenex under her eyes. "This thing is packed. Any idea where we should start?"

"Those," I say, pointing to the boxes lining the top shelf. If I remember right, that's where they were the last time Mom and I looked through them ages ago. Reaching up, I wrestle down the first stack of boxes above my head. I catch a whiff of my underarms and grimace. When was my last shower? I honestly can't remember if I've had one since I got the news about Mom.

Box after box comes down. I take a quick peek in each, then push them over to Colette, announcing their contents as I go. Receipts and paid bills. Folders of graded student papers from fifteen years ago. Even though none of this stuff is embarrassing, I feel a vague tug of shame as I expose these long-buried items to the light of day. I half expect them to cringe and wiggle away, back into the darkness and safety of the closet like worms.

"It's gotta be one of these," I say, before grabbing the next box, which is sagging with extraordinary weight. It tangles briefly in the overhead light's pull chain and I groan.

"Careful, Juliet!" Colette says, the calm in her voice fracturing for the first time today. I maneuver it down over my head and drop it to the floor like an anchor, then straighten up and wipe my forehead. I open the tattered box's cardboard flaps, then stop. Adrenaline floods my hands and feet.

"Found it," I say. I move back so Colette can see for herself the stack of dusty framed photos and vinyl-bound family albums, thick as bibles. She peers in and raises her brows at me.

"Looks like the jackpot."

"I haven't seen any of this in, like, twenty years," I say, kneeling. "Ugh, I can't believe I'm old enough to say something like that." Colette shoots me a wry look. I half-shrug an apology.

I start to sift through the few pictures on top, and an ache tugs at the back of my throat. I remember Mom showing me these before. There she is when she's about ten, in stone-cold concentration, sitting at an ornate mahogany piano; at the beach, squealing with her tiny hands shoved into the wet sand; hugged into Nana's torso as they stand on a sprawling front porch, a huge weeping willow looming behind them.

Jesus. Nana. I nearly forgot she was here at the house with us.

"Oh, man," I say. "Do you think Nana heard us in here wailing?"

She grimaces. "I don't know. She's all the way in the living room. But if she did, I'm sure she understands."

"Yeah. I just don't want to upset her even more."

Nana, Mom's mother, is my last living relative. She's been staying here for the past few days with Colette and me and will stay a while longer after the funeral. Although Nana is here under the least desirable circumstances possible, it probably still beats her "suite" at the assisted living home. She's sharp, that one, even though she's in her nineties. If you say something stupid, her eyes narrow and lock onto you right away. Just like Mom used to. Not me, though; I never could master that glare. What happened that I missed out on all the useful genes in the family?

Rummaging deeper into the box, I turn over a photo and my breath catches hard in my throat. This one I haven't seen before. A gold-plated frame boasts an early family portrait of Nana, Pop-Pop, Mom, and Henry—Mom's dead brother. The air goes out of me.

Henry. He died years before I was even born, and neither Mom nor Nana ever talked about him. They'd made it clear to me that the topic was off-limits. It was almost like he'd never existed at all.

But that's not the part that's thrown me so hard. It's the fact that in this photo, he looks exactly like me.

"Colette. You've gotta see this."

Henry and I could be twins. He's a teenager in the photo, and darkness shrouds everything about him—hair, eyes, and mood. The downward slope of his eyebrows, the pooched curve in the middle of his bottom lip, the easy tilt of his chin. It's uncanny. I can't stop staring.

"Oh, my God. Is that Henry? You two are nearly identical."

I whip my head around. "You know about him?" Did Mom tell Colette everything about Henry and leave me here in the dark?

Colette hesitates, seems to read my mind. "Not a lot, but your mom gave me the gist," she says slowly, her eyes on the photo. "I knew she had a brother who was estranged, and that he was killed in this horrible car accident in Italy. She said it happened back when she was just starting at Northwestern, in the early seventies. But by that time, no one in your family had talked to Henry in years. If I remember right, up until he died, they didn't even know he was in Italy. He was so young when it happened, too. The whole thing sounded ghastly."

My body relaxes a notch. "Yeah, that's all she told me, too." I'm reassured that Mom hadn't excluded me from any privileged information. As I gaze at the photo, I can't shake the absurd feeling that Henry and I see each other. I put the picture aside and reach into the box with renewed determination.

The next thing I lay my hands on is an old manila envelope. *Henry*, it says in Mom's handwriting. I definitely haven't seen this before, either.

I fumble with the rusted metal clasp on the back and carefully release the contents onto the floor in front of me. It takes me a few beats to understand I'm looking at Henry's personal effects—whatever he had on him when he died, returned to our family by the Italian coroner. In addition to the death certificate, there's a key ring with a calcified door key, a half-empty pack of European cigarettes, and a wallet.

"I take it she never showed you any of this?" I say to Colette. If she says yes, I'll probably start bawling again.

"No. Never."

"Me either." I pick up the death certificate. It's simple and brief:

Prenomi/Cognomi: Barton, Henry Anthony.
Data di nascita: 18/10/1943, Philadelphia, Pennsylvania, U.S.A.
Data di morte: 08/07/1971, Rosanera, Italia.
Causa di morte: Incidente stradale.

At the bottom, there's an official seal and the signatures of the mortician and filing clerk at the records office.

I grab my phone and Google *incidente stradale*. Sure enough, "automobile accident."

Next, I pick up the wallet and peel it open—literally, as the sides are stuck together with the adhesive of age. Nothing. I sigh and put it aside. What must it have felt like to have only these scant remains of your own brother or son randomly returned to you one day? After no communication for years? There's not even one personalized item in here, absolutely nothing that would set Henry apart from any other man on the planet.

All this focus on death and tragedy makes me want to crawl into bed and sleep forever. Colette sees I'm starting to flag.

"Why don't I give one last look to see if there's any other boxes with photos in here?" she says. "If not, let's take this box into the other room and we can go through it more after dinner, or tomorrow morning."

"Yeah, fine," I say, slouching against the oversized leather armchair behind me. As the fog of grief starts to lift, I'm aching for my daily liquid remedy. I had Bailey's with my morning coffee (and subsequent refills), but that was hours ago, and the warmth has long worn off. I toy with the ancient cigarette pack from Henry's things. It's been ten years since I quit smoking. But with them right here in my hand, lighting up is all I can think about.

"How bad do you think these things taste after this long?" I say, dangling the pack in the air. Colette leans out of the closet to see and makes a face.

"I wouldn't want to know. A fresh pack tastes bad enough. Can't believe I smoked those things for decades. We were all idiots back then."

How "back then" differs at all from today in this context, I fail to understand, but I don't bother voicing my sarcasm. Instead, I open the pack and run my fingertips over the coarse ends of the fifty-year-old rolled tobacco sticks. They're unfiltered. Little squiggles of tobacco poke out like saffron threads from the ends of the rolling paper. Was Henry smoking one of these when his car crashed? I suddenly want to feel what it's like to hold one between my fingers.

I reach in to grab one, and something sharp slices the tip of my finger. I inhale sharply and yank my hand back. Blood rises into the tiny red slash on my skin. It looks like a paper cut. How could a cigarette give me a paper cut? Holding the pack up to eye level, I give it a careful jostle to separate the cigarettes from the pack itself. Then I see the offender. There's something folded and tucked into the box between the cigarettes and the pack. What the hell?

I gingerly loosen the folded paper from the side of the

pack that's been closed for more than five decades. Once it's free, the paper flutters out along with something else that was folded inside it. I pick this up first, unfold it and smooth it out.

It's a photograph. Of a grave.

No, wait. *Grave* isn't the right word. A mausoleum. It's a tall, narrow stone structure that looks to be a century and a half old. A wrought-iron double-door, speckled with rust, sits in the center. There is a kaleidoscope of cracked stained glass embedded in each panel of the door. The left one is closed, and the right one sits slightly ajar, revealing only darkness inside. On either side of the doors is an intricately carved, life-size granite figure wrapped head to toe in a hooded robe. The statues are mirror images of one another, each of their faces buried in their hands, as if weeping.

I grab the yellowed paper that the photo was wrapped in and open that too. The faded ink reads *Giovanni, 57 Via della Servi, Rosanera*.

"Colette," I say, getting to my feet. "Look what I found. It was in the cigarette pack."

She puts down a box in the closet and comes over to me. I hand her the photo and note. She frowns.

"What do you mean it was in with the cigarettes?"

"It was folded up and shoved down in the pack. I wouldn't have even found it if I wasn't trying to fish one out." She gives me a sideways look, which I ignore. It's not like I was going to actually smoke it. Pretty sure, at least. "Where is this, do you think?" I say.

Colette studies it for a minute. Only one of us here

is a tenured history professor, so I'm thinking she'll have more insight about it than me. As she's doing that, I pick up my phone and Google the address written on the note. Within seconds, I've pulled up a map and street view of the location halfway across the world. It's shocking to me that humans ever got anything done prior to the invention of the search engine.

The house on Via della Servi is a nondescript abode that looks like all the others on the street. Two-story, squat, beige and grey stone, closed shutters in need of a paint job. I pull up Google again and type in the address plus "Giovanni." No results found. I click absently on the first few search results just to make sure, but there's no more info about the property, at least not any that's publicly available.

"Well, it's definitely European, I can tell you that much," Colette says. It takes me a second to realize she's talking about the mausoleum photo.

"How can you tell?" I look over her shoulder.

"The twin statues," she says, tapping the photo. "They were quite the popular feature of European tombs starting around the late eighteenth century up until the end of the nineteenth century. Particularly in Italy, Spain, and France." Colette is an expert in early modern history, and even though this falls a little past that, I trust her knowledge.

"Hmm." I pause. "But how do we know this isn't somewhere else, like right here in the U.S., but just designed in that European style?"

Colette tilts her head. "It's possible, but unlikely. First off, mausoleums in American cemeteries are very rare. We bury our folks right in the ground with a headstone because there's such an incredible expanse of land compared to Europe. There, mausoleums for multiple people, or even multiple families, are par for the course. The closest to that kind of thing here is New Orleans, but even still, I think it's a long shot. Also, see how close together all the tombs are?" I move closer. The photo doesn't give much in the way of a panoramic view, but she's right—the surrounding tombs that are visible are packed together. Almost one on top of the other.

"That's the hallmark of a very old cemetery that serviced a very dense population," Colette says. "And the fact that this photo is paired with that address in Italy"—she points to slip of paper in my hand—"tells me you can bet that it's European, most likely in Italy. Too bad we can't see the name anywhere in the photo. It looks like it's just out of view here." She points to the top of the photo, where the very top of the mausoleum is cut out of the photo and indeed where the family name would be.

Was that intentional on the part of the photographer? And to that point, who was the photographer? Was it Henry? And why was it hidden in a cigarette pack with this guy's address? A thought occurs to me.

"I bet you Mom and Nana have never seen this," I say. "If they had found it, why would they put it right back in there? Makes more sense to just leave it out with the rest of the stuff in the envelope."

Colette exhales. "You're probably right."

"Well, that sucks. What if they know where this grave is, or who Giovanni is? What if it would've helped them figure out what Henry was doing in Italy? All this time they were left wondering with no idea."

"Yes. That is unfortunate."

I chew on my thumbnail. Of course, it's possible for me to ask Nana about the photo and note. But after all the hush-hush about Henry for decades, can I really bring it up now? Four days after Nana has lost her *other* child?

"I don't know," I sigh. "It's still bizarre to me that this was hidden away in a cigarette pack, but I guess nothing—" I stop abruptly as I flip the photo over. There, someone's penned a note: *If I don't make it back—third tomb, lower left.* The skin on my arms grows taut.

"What?" Colette says, concerned. I hand it to her without a word. She blinks rapidly for a moment and then she looks at me.

"And what in God's name do you think *that* means?" I say. "'If I don't make it back?' Back where? Did Henry write that?"

Colette gives her head a tiny shake. "I haven't the faintest."

Was this supposed to be a message, a directive, to whoever found this photograph? *Third tomb, lower left* sounds like the X on a macabre treasure map. Is there something in this mausoleum Henry wanted someone to recover in the event of his death? Maybe that's why he hid it away in the cigarette pack—as a safeguard. And what about this Giovanni guy? Was he involved somehow?

It sounds far-fetched, and I know it was forever ago, but I don't care. The whole thing is weird and creepy. What actually happened to Mom's brother?

"What does the inside of a mausoleum look like?" I ask Colette. Stupid question, but I don't think I've ever been inside one.

"It varies. Basically it's just a large room. It can hold single crypts, ones that are side-by-side, or the crypts of an entire family sealed on top of one another in the walls."

"So there could be three tombs in there, side by side?" *Third tomb, lower left.*

"Sure."

"And if it was this old, kinda dilapidated mausoleum, there's a chance that no one's visited it for a very long time?"

Colette gives me a soft smile. "I'd say that could be the case."

I glance down and catch Henry's dark eyes staring up at mine from the framed family photo on the floor—searching for answers that never came.

It's time I talked to Nana about her long-gone son.

Chapter Three

Philadelphia
July 1954

THE SUNSET LOOKS all wrong. For one thing, the sky is far too red. It reminds Henry of a bloodbath. Where are the delicate purple tufts creeping in above the horizon? And why does the sun look like a rotten orange? Henry scowls, mashing his paintbrush into the rinsing cup next to his foldable easel and watercolor set. He slides back in his chair and compares yet another one of his pathetic attempts at art to the actual majesty unfolding outside the living room's bay window.

It's becoming increasingly apparent that watercolors are just another pursuit he'd be better off abandoning. He should cross it off the list of artistic possibilities and move on. By now he's also tried colored pencils, oil paints, and acrylics. It doesn't matter. He's bad at all of it, and he doesn't need another grimace from his mother telling him as much. Henry's eleventh birthday is just three months away. Time is running out for him to get good at something, like all the other kids already are. He sees how their metal lunchboxes have been swapped out for instrument cases, or duffel bags packed with cleats and uniforms. But much to his parents' sustained anguish, Henry doesn't care about trumpet lessons, or tee ball, or after-school clubs. He only wants to do art, the thing he's not any good at.

It all started on that class field trip to the Philadelphia Museum of Art last year. Henry had walked in a stupor through the massive Greek columns at the museum entrance certain that he'd been transported to another place, a different era. Surely nothing this grand could fit, was meant to fit, into the confines of his small life. He'd followed his classmates and teacher inside and up the sweeping marble staircases, down palatial halls displaying centuries of textiles, ceramics, and paintings.

It was the latter that stole Henry's breath. Those striking pockets of life frozen forever on canvas, each so different from one another. The same delicate brush strokes, but so many different realities. Excitement flooded his veins. What if he could also do this—capture life just as he saw it? With painting, it didn't seem to matter how accurate you were. As the museum's guide had pointed out, some of Monet's stuff just looked like swirls of color, and they were hanging in museums all over the world. But Henry had wanted to make sure. Mainly so that his mother couldn't argue with him later about it.

"How do we know if the painting actually looks like what the artist saw in real life?" Henry asked the old docent conducting the tour.

"Well, we don't, necessarily," the elderly man said. Eyeglasses loomed as large as jack-o-lanterns on the bridge of his nose. "But it's the artist's interpretation, and that's good enough."

The artist's interpretation. The phrase had dominated Henry's mind for weeks afterward. Life could exist outside of right and wrong? Where your own interpretation of the world could be good enough? He had long dreamed about creating a world that was all his—not as it was dictated to him by his mother. What if that could be his talent?

Henry soon dove in, experimenting with every possible medium of color and paint, but it was one disappointment after the next. He hated everything he set his brush to. Nothing ever translated onto the canvas how he saw it in his mind. And certainly none of it, in his estimation, was "good enough" like the museum man had said.

So instead of becoming the best young artist in the Northeast as he'd planned, Henry has let his painting episodes dwindle to almost nothing, and instead slid back into what he knows. It is familiar, if nothing else. He spends most of this summer hiding out under the thick branches of the enormous weeping willow in the front yard. Mom is always on him about not getting too tan, so he might as well kill two birds with one stone. He invites Matt Benson over from down the street, who is allowed to come over on the days he doesn't have football practice, and together they flip through the *Mad* comic books they stashed under the tree branches. Or practice shooting craps in the old cardboard box so they could get good enough to play with the older kids downtown. Or, between snorts and giggles, trade cuss words out loud—the same ones he wants to scream at his mother during the speech lessons she gives him four days a week.

Her words bounce around inside his head. *You have to learn to enunciate your words, Henry. No one will ever take you seriously in this world unless you speak clearly and properly. You sound like some foreigner.* Henry can't wrap his head around his mother's bizarre preoccupation with speaking perfect, grammatical English.

Or her obsession with him staying out of the sun. *How many times have I told you? Stay in the shade, for God's sake! You're already brown, you don't need to get even darker. It's not a good look, Henry.* Her narrowed eyes and twisted mouth endlessly surveying him from the front door.

Why can't he ever just be left alone? Henry shoves himself back from the easel, scraping his chair hard as he gets up. Then he looks out the window and freezes.

A heavyset man is lumbering across the sprawling front lawn toward the house. He's in a dusty white undershirt with thick, brown suspenders over top, fastened to shabby black workpants. An oily green newsboy cap is tucked under one arm. He looks like what Mom calls *grunts*—men who toil away outside all day.

Henry inches closer to the window and watches the man stop halfway to the front door and look around. He quickly licks his fingertips and passes them over the top of his balding head to smooth down the remaining strands. His eyes flick to the window where Henry is, and Henry's heart shoots up his throat and lodges there, rattling. The man's gaze continues over the front of the house, and Henry realizes with relief that he didn't see him.

The stranger makes his way onto the front porch, heavy boots clomping on the pristine white wooden planks. A brief pause hangs in the air before a slow, loud knock.

Henry holds his breath. Mom never likes him to answer the door, and she really wouldn't want him to answer it now, for this grunt. But even saying the word now in his mind sends a pang through Henry's chest. Unlike what Mom always says about these types, the man at the door doesn't look dangerous or moronic. Just poor. Old and worn through, more so than his actual age probably warrants.

"Henry, was that the door?" Dad calls. Henry runs to the bottom of the stairs and looks up at his father.

"Yeah. A man is here."

Dad frowns and comes downstairs, his lanky frame outfitted in a crisp shirt and ironed slacks. Even after the workday ended, he always still looked like he was going right back to work.

"Probably just a salesman," he says, patting Henry's shoulder as he passes. Henry scurries back to the living room and squeezes against corner of the window, which gives him a clear view of the porch.

The door opens and Henry sees the man straighten.

"*Allo, Signore. Desculpe*, no speak good English. Livia is here?" Henry watches his dad look the man up and down. It's as if he's just opened the door to a rabid wolf.

"Sorry, what is this regarding?"

The stranger shifts in his creased, dusty boots. He wipes his glistening brow and mutters something Henry can't make out. Henry's father stares at him.

"Ed, who's there?" Mom calls. Henry leans back from the window to watch her come downstairs in a bright flowered sundress with Ellen on her hip. When she hits the last step she halts, mouth agape.

"Livia?" the man at the door asks incredulously. "*Non ti avevo riconosciuta.*" He lets out a short laugh, which goes unreciprocated.

"Well, you look the same to me," she says curtly.

The man smiles at Ellen. "*E questa mia nipote?*" He flutters his calloused fingers at the staring baby. Henry's eyes widen. Now that he can see the man better, he sees they share the same black hair, russet eyes, and nut-brown skin. This is the first time anyone dark like him has ever come to their house.

Mom stiffens. "I'll handle this," she tells Dad. "Take Ellen, please?" The baby gurgles and whines as she's passed to her father, and the two retreat into the house. Mom lets the screen door smack shut behind her as she steps out onto the porch.

Henry creeps to the front door and strains to hear them talking. He rises up barely an inch, just high enough that he can peer through the screen at them. The man is gesturing, hands flying all over like a cartoon clock in fast-forward, as he speaks that foreign language. French? Spanish? Henry can't make it out but he realizes, with great surprise, that his mother can. He can tell by the rapid rise and fall of her slim shoulders. The way her cheeks are growing red as overripe tomatoes, like they always do when she's mad.

Who *is* this guy, and why is he here?

Suddenly Mom cuts the man off with a scathing torrent of words in the same foreign language. Henry slaps a hand over his mouth.

"There's nothing for you here," she finally hisses to the man, in English. "Go back to the city. Stay there. And for God's sake, make something of yourself."

She turns to come inside, and Henry scrambles back to the living room window. He hears the front door slam and the bolt slide home.

Through the glass, he watches the man on the porch reach for the doorknob, then stop. His hand drops and shoulders collapse. He starts to leave, glancing once more at the living room window. This time he locks eyes with Henry. Henry gulps air and goes rigid. But the man's feverish expression softens. Henry raises his hand, gives a small wave. After a moment, the man does the same. *It's like looking in a mirror,* Henry thinks, his heart quickening. Surely the man must also see it. Henry waits for more, for this acknowledgement from the man, the way grown-ups take the lead on such things, but it doesn't come. Instead, the stranger turns and makes his way back to the darkening road.

Henry feels an urge as old and earthy and deep as time itself to run after him. But his mother's certain wrath restrains him. He hears his parents in the next room and leaves the window to join them.

"Who was that?" Henry says in the doorway, arms crossed.

"No one," Mom says automatically. Her tone tells him the subject is closed, but Henry's having none of it.

"That's not true. You know him," he pushes. "And why didn't you ever tell me you speak another language? What was it anyway, French?"

Mom sniffs and sets Ellen down in the bassinet next to the custom-built china cabinet. The baby looks at Henry and erupts into a wet giggle. In spite of himself, Henry's heart swells. His sister is already shaping up to look nothing like him, towheaded and blue-eyed with pudgy fists as white as the Wonder bread on their kitchen counter, and on some level, despite the unfairness of it all, he is glad for her.

"Just drop it, Henry," Mom says, ignoring the question. "It doesn't matter who he is. He won't be back. It's late. I need to get dinner on the table."

"Mom," he insists, looking up at her. She hesitates on her way to the kitchen, as if she might disclose more, give Henry the explanation he needs to move past this feeling, but she brushes past him into the kitchen with averted eyes.

She can't even look at me, he thinks. *I look just like him—dark and wrong, and so she hates me too.*

"That was your Uncle Pietro," Dad says quietly, startling Henry. He feels unsteady and wants to sit down, but he knows then the tears will come, and he can't let that happen yet. Not in front of them.

"What?" he says.

"Mom's brother," his father tells him. "He's from Italy, like Mom, but he doesn't speak much English. This is the first time I've met him, too."

Henry stares. The fact his mother even has a brother is jarring enough. But this is a double whammy. She's Italian? To him, his mother looks like the painted women in the Museum of Art. The ones who wore fancy ruffled collars and sat unsmiling against cold, stone backdrops. He can't imagine his own mother relaxing in the warm Italian sun, *turning brown*, laughing and eating pasta like the women in the magazine ads for Ragu spaghetti sauce.

"What did he want?" Henry asks, and he hates that his voice quivers when he speaks.

"A job."

"Like, at your store?"

"No. Here at the house. He's a mason. That means he fixes sidewalks and walls, things with stone and brick."

"What did you tell him?" Henry says. His father's eyes dart to the kitchen.

"We told him we don't need his help," Dad says, taking Henry's arm and walking them both further into the dining room.

"But we do," Henry says, yanking his arm back. "The

stone wall over by the pond is falling apart. He could fix that, for starters."

Dad straightens up and sighs. "Your mother just doesn't want him here, Henry. End of story."

"Why? And if he doesn't have a job, how's he gonna survive?"

"He'll get a job in the city. There's plenty of work there, trust me. He's just not our kind of people. That's enough now. We don't want to upset your mother any more than she is."

Not our kind of people. Henry is convinced that in a quarter of an hour, he's found and lost the one person who might ever understand him. Was he really doomed to never knowing his own uncle?

Henry walks trancelike back into the living room. Outside, the sun hovers low on the horizon now, eking out the last light of day. A purple stillness has settled over the front lawn. He gazes at the painting on his easel and chews his lip. Drying streaks of water have turned the canvas's blood red sky to fleshy pink in spots, tinted the sun a brash, desperate orange.

Henry picks up the paintbrush and, after a few tries, steadies his hand enough to wet it and dip it into one of the hardened paint circles on the watercolor palette. With as much precision as he can muster, he paints two brown figures on the canvas, headed toward the road together.

It doesn't look so terrible anymore.

Chapter Four

THE TV IN the living room blasts political commentary on how the world is falling apart and we're all fucked. Nana is on the sofa with her arms crossed, hands cupping her elbows, frowning at the screen. She's wearing a cream silk blouse and charcoal skirt cut just right for her tiny frame, and her feet are tucked into fashionable Dior suede flats. Around her neck hangs a modest, woven gold strand with a tiny pendant. Her thready hair falls into a soft silver bob around her narrow face. She looks a thousand times better than me—a woman a third of her age.

"Hi, Nana," I say, walking in and sinking down into the sofa next to her. "How're you doing?"

She looks at me and a tiny smile creases her tissue-paper thin cheeks. "Better now that you're here," she says, gesturing to the TV.

We'll see about that, I think. My hand goes damp around the photos I'm holding, which of course includes the mausoleum. I tossed and turned all last night, questioning my decision to bring it up with Nana. I know it'll be dreadful for her to talk about Henry. But what if the photo and address I found finally brings her closure on his death? They might be the missing pieces she's needed all these years to understand why her son was in Italy.

I pick up the remote and mute the supercilious rant on the TV screen. A gaunt man in a paisley necktie is roasting a young blonde with resting bitch face about the military industrial complex. Breaking news of no consequence runs in perpetuity along the bottom of the screen.

"Thank you," she says, shaking her head. "Garbage, but nothing else was on." I wonder why old people always seem to put up with whatever program is on TV, even if it drives them mad. Maybe the prospect of silence is worse.

"Remember how Colette and I were looking through photos yesterday?" I say. She nods. "I picked out a few that I thought you'd really like to see. I'm going to add them to the collage for Saturday." *For Saturday* sounds better than *for the funeral*. For a minute, I almost even fooled myself.

"Oh?" Nana says. She reaches for her eyeglass case on the couch cushion next to her. Once she's gotten her frames on and situated, I hand her the first few photos I found in the box—the ones of Mom as a child. Nana holds them an inch from her face, her feathery eyelids pitched into tents, cycling through them carefully. As she does, I study her. What must it be like to revisit these memories six decades later? To re-experience your own daughter, who herself grew old and is now buried underground, as this innocent being?

"It's hard to believe any of this ever really happened," she says, as if in response to my thoughts. "It feels like another lifetime." She lifts the photo higher, a wistful smile spreading on her face. "Ellen loved playing piano. And going to the beach." Her thin finger taps the picture of Mom in the sand. "We used to spend every July in Ocean City, you know. Ed rented us the same little beachfront cottage every year."

That much I did know. Mom told me the beach was one major reason she'd been so thrilled to get a tenure-track position here in San Diego.

Nana moves on to the photo of her and Mom on the front porch. "Oh, that porch," she sighs, relaxing into the couch. "And that house. It was magnificent. The homes back east are so different from the ones here, you know. They were made to stand the test of time. Not like the plywood nonsense they charge millions for out here. Collapse like cards as soon as the ground shakes a little."

Ridges of contempt rise in her lips. When Nana moved from her house in Philadelphia to the assisted living home here a decade ago she'd made it clear to both Mom and me that it was the worst decision ever. But Nana couldn't live on her own anymore, and Mom couldn't give up her full professorship here. So, that was that.

"Was that the first house you and Pop-Pop lived in?" I ask.

"The only one," she says. "We were married July 12,

1942. Ed bought it a month later." She pauses, reflecting. "I was only sixteen when I met him. Seventeen when we got married. I worked full-time at his father's department store. That's where he first saw me."

"Full-time? What about school?"

She looks at me and sniffs. "Not back then. Not when you're the oldest of three, with parents who need your help, too. And certainly not after just arriving from Italy."

I'm amused by her choice of words. "Immigrants" must've been those other huddled masses that arrived at Ellis Island. Nana, on the other hand, had "arrived from Italy," like a jet-lagged starlet reclining in the back of a Bentley while her sweaty assistant deposits suitcase after suitcase into the trunk.

But Nana bringing up the old country gives me the perfect inroad to broach the subject of Henry.

"What was Italy like? Do you remember much?" I ask, easing in.

Her hands fidget in her lap as she studies something invisible in the distance. "Italy was a horrible place then. Mussolini had almost all the businesses under his control. My father's masonry business went broke. We had no choice but to leave." A wrinkle of scorn cuts between her eyes.

"You lived in Bologna, right?" I say.

"Just outside. A small town called Albero."

I summon all my courage. "Nana," I say, voice wavering, "I also found this in Mom's things." I hand her the framed family portrait—the one with a teenaged Henry.

She takes it from me and inhales. After almost a full

minute, she lets it slide from her hand to her lap. Her mouth opens and closes, but nothing comes out. I rest my hand on her arm, which is thin and coarse as wire. My heart's going. I feel like a royal asshole. Like so much in my life, this was a mistake. What right do I have to upset an old woman about her dead son? What right do I have to even know about Henry? Maybe none at all.

"It's been so long," she croaks, eyelids fluttering. I get up and grab a tissue box from the other side of the room and pull out a fistful, handing them to her. She takes them but they stay balled up in her hand.

"This was the last family picture we ever took," she says, looking down at it. "Henry must've been sixteen." The air in the room stirs and shifts when she says his name, as if trying to resettle around something that just entered. My spine tingles.

"Everyone tells you to have at least two children," she says, running a gnarled, shaky hand over her mouth. "That it's cruel to have only one, because then they will be all alone someday." Her lips twist into a lopsided bow. "But what people don't understand is the risk that comes along with that. What you have to face when you've *had* two, but life reduces you to only one."

My stomach drops, and I feel dizzy. What a positively devastating truth. I wonder if Mom thought the same thing. If that's part of why I'm an only child.

Nana wipes at her tired eyes again. "You look just like him, you know." Her gaze lingers on my face. "The dark hair, dark eyes, dark skin. Dark *everything*."

The scornful way she says the last part throws me. It lacks gusto, but the derision is there—even if it's eroded and smoothed around the edges, like a well-worn stone. *Dark everything?* This is Southern California in the twenty-first century, not Ellis Island in 1890. Is she really bothered by my darker Italian skin? And if so, it stands to reason she'd have felt the same way about Henry's appearance. Was that ever a point of contention between them?

"Nana," I say, pushing on, "can you tell me a little more about Henry? I'd love to know what he was like." *Was he like me?* is what I really want to ask but can't bring myself to.

Nana fixes a blank expression on the corner of the room and thinks.

"Henry was headstrong," she finally answers. "Had a mind all his own. Always. Thought he knew best about everything, even as a child." Her hands begin smoothing out her skirt as she talks.

"Ed and I tried to steer him right, but Henry resisted at every turn," she says. "And there *is* a right and wrong way of doing things, Juliet, I assure you. You live as long as I have, and you know not everything is this 'grey area' people like to make it out to be."

There's that icy harshness creeping into her voice. When she gets this way, it's like a warning shot: *Don't you dare contradict me.* Or else what, I never cared to find out. I wait obediently until she's ready to go on.

After a moment, she calms and continues. "Aside from that, he was smart. Thoughtful. Had a good sense of humor. Rode his bike, played with the neighbors' children. He loved animals, especially cats. Henry would bring them home from all over. We had seven or eight cats, and they lived quite well outside on our property. It was twenty acres, after all."

I smile as Henry begins to take form as a real human being in my mind. I fantasize about what it would be like if he were my own brother instead of Mom's. How it would feel to share a house with a sibling, to rely on their protection.

To mourn Mom together.

"He loved books, too," Nana says, looking at me with a shadow of a smile. "Not so much that he would go to graduate school for literature like you. But he liked them well enough."

Ah, yes. Grad school. I'm thrilled to be reminded of yet another life trajectory that has come to nothing.

"But above all with him, it was pictures," she says, her voice suddenly plummeting. Her jaw tightens, and I straighten up.

"Pictures? Like, drawings?" I say.

"No. *Photographs*. Henry became completely obsessed with cameras." My chest surges. It's almost a given, then, that Henry was the one who took the photo of the mausoleum—and wrote the note on the back.

"It all started when he was about twelve," she says. "Ed bought one of those little Brownie movie cameras for the family one Christmas." I make a mental note to Google the thing later on. "After that, cameras took over Henry's life. It ended up getting him in a mess of trouble."

Now we're getting somewhere. "What kind of trouble?" I ask, edging closer to her.

Nana scowls. "Getting into all kinds of radical political nonsense," she says. "Interfering in people's lives where he had no business." I can't help but wonder how much of this statement is colored by Nana's own concept of propriety. Regardless, this depiction of Henry as a bookish, artsy revolutionary has me hooked. I'm liking him more and more.

She closes her eyes and shakes her head. "Henry was always trying to find meaning in everything," she says. "He was never satisfied with things the way they are. He always had to dig and *dig*, convinced that it was his"—her bony fingers flutter in the air—"*duty* to uncover the truth about life, whatever that means. Making problems where there are none. I never understood it. Life has enough trouble without trying to make up more on your own."

My mind darts to the mausoleum photo and that strange note written on the back. *If I don't make it back—Third tomb, lower left.* Was this another thing Henry was digging to uncover truth about?

"It's what he ended up coming out here for," Nana says.

"Sorry?" I say, momentarily confused.

"The film program at UCLA. By that time Ed was finally as horrified as I was about him. It was one thing that Henry had no interest in taking over the department store for Ed. But becoming a *movie director*? Absurd!"

This floors me. Mom did share with me that Henry went to UCLA, but I never knew for what. Their film school is world-renowned. He must have been really good. I can't help but feel irritated with Nana for not supporting him in pursuing his passion. I wonder if Mom shared this irritation. But I'll never know. It hits me that I'm pitifully lost in the vast expanse of what I don't know about my own mother, and I feel like I'm going to be sick. I swallow.

"Did Mom miss Henry when he left for college?" I ask.

"Oh, yes," Nana says, softly. "Terribly. Henry was almost ten years older than Ellen. I had some...trouble conceiving. With that age difference, it's not easy for siblings to be close. But Henry was always so kind to Ellen. And she adored him. She was still in primary school when he left for college." She pauses. "That was the last time any of us ever saw him. June 1962."

It is still inconceivable to me how this could be the case. How does a person go away to college and never see his family again? Nana and Pop-Pop just continued to pay Henry's tuition for four years even though they never saw or spoke to him? They didn't come to his graduation. Didn't have a single clue as to what Henry did for the five years after college up until his death. They weren't even aware *he was in Italy* until he turned up dead, for Christ's sake. My mind spins. It's difficult to fathom what kind of cataclysmic event would have ever brought this bizarre situation into being. But I'm going to try to find out.

"Nana," I say, taking her hand, "what exactly happened?" Her eyes dart to mine before sliding away.

"There was an incident." The color drains from her

face and she falls silent. I wait with bated breath for her to continue. She seems to be choosing her words carefully.

"When he found out my brother Pietro died, Henry was inconsolable," she says. "There was no reason for it, because he never knew Pietro—just knew *of* him. He saw him one single time in his life, when he came to the house looking for work. Henry was just a boy. To this day, I don't know how or why Henry latched onto him. He must've imagined some kind of…kinship…between the two of them. But it was all in his head. I would never allow it to be anything else."

"Why not?" I ask.

"Pietro was a monster," she says. "But Henry never believed it. He just wanted to know as much as he could about him. Wouldn't let it go."

I sit back, dazed. Henry had also been digging for info about *his* uncle? This whole thing is officially getting very weird.

But it's also extremely confusing. Why would the death of his Uncle Pietro—a supposedly monstrous man he didn't even know—cause Henry to cut all ties with the whole family? It didn't make any sense. *There was an incident*, Nana said. Was she referring to Pietro's death, or to something else that happened afterwards? Something is missing. I'm dying to know what it is, but at this point the sheer exhaustion in Nana's face is evident. I need to wrap it up. Sweat stings every pore under my arms.

"I just have one more question, Nana. Do you recognize this photo?" I hold my breath as I hand her the mausoleum photo. She takes it from me, eyes scanning from beneath crinkled lids. Is this it? Will it finally dawn on her why Henry was in Italy?

"No," she says. "I've never seen this before. Whose grave is this?"

My diaphragm deflates, and I exhale. "That's what I was hoping you'd know."

"Me? Why would you think I'd know?"

I pause. "Nana, I found that photograph in Henry's things."

She stares at me, uncomprehending.

"In Mom's closet, I also found the envelope of Henry's personal effects that were returned to you," I say.

She holds my gaze, shakes her head. When she speaks, her voice is small and far away. "But we would have seen it."

"It was tucked inside the pack of cigarettes. That's why you never found it. It was folded up in there along with the address of someone named Giovanni in Rosanera."

"Giovanni?" she says, brows pinched together. "I don't know any Giovanni, and certainly not in Rosanera. I'd never even heard of the place until Henry—" She doesn't finish. Her pain is so palpable I can feel it coursing through my own veins. I delicately take the photo from her limp hand. There's no way I want her to see what's written on the back. It would only add to her distress.

"But you're sure the mausoleum in the picture isn't a family tomb?" I ask.

"Not one I know about. Both my parents' families were buried in Albero. And not in mausoleums."

I pause. "And it's not Pietro's, right?"

"No," comes her curt reply. "He was buried in Philadelphia, where he died."

Hope drains out of my chest. I take one more look at the photo and think about Giovanni's address. There's something here, some connection between them. I don't know what, but I can feel it. It's as if it's long laid dormant wanting, needing, to be resolved.

"I spoke to him the day he died, you know."

I jump, as much at the sound of Nana's voice as what she said. "You what? How?" I sputter.

She's now trembling so much that I think she might vibrate right out of the room. I take her palms tightly in my own and peer at her.

"I've never told anyone this before," she whispers. "Not Ed, not your mother. After all those years of not speaking to each other. You can imagine what I felt when I heard his voice."

"Oh, Jesus, Nana—"

"It was less than a minute," Nana says, her words like sandpaper. "He called me from a pay phone. He was upset, that much was clear, but the connection was so terrible I couldn't make out everything he was saying. Only one thing in particular."

"What did he say?"

She is whiter than paste, almost transparent. One more shade and she'd fade away completely.

"That he was coming home."

Chapter Five

Philadelphia
February 1959

"Let's go back to right before we picked you up, Henry," Officer Lockley says, settling back in his chair. The aluminum legs groan under the policeman's girth in the drab interview room. Henry thinks the man is probably only in his thirties, but the extra pounds make him look at least fifty. The push-broom mustache doesn't do him any favors, either.

"What were you doing taking pictures in Heller's yard?" Lockley says, lifting Henry's Minolta off the table in front of him. "And I swear to God, don't say 'just for the atmosphere' again. There's six inches of snow on the ground. No one's outside right now unless there's a damned good reason to be."

Henry slumps in his seat and glares at the cop from

under his eyelashes. His arms are crossed, hands jammed into the armpits of his grey wool sweater. He'll be damned if he lets the cop see them shaking.

"Ambience, not atmosphere," Henry mutters.

"What did you say?"

"I said I was there for the ambience, not the atmosphere," he says. "Their place has the old barn, the pines, deer. It's got nice composition." He's smug as the last word rolls off his tongue.

It's true, though. The Hellers' sprawling property is a photographer's utopia, especially today—the way the delicate light and shadow of a snowy day breathed life into the frosty winter stillness. A stark contrast to the horror that goes on inside the Hellers' house, which Henry had hoped to get evidence of this afternoon. Of course, his plan was derailed after that idiot neighbor looked out her window and called the cops on him for trespassing and "indecent photography." *Meddling old biddy*, Henry stews.

Lockley sniffs and turns to his partner, who leans against the interrogation room wall behind him. "'Composition,' he says. You believe this?" The other cop shakes his head and stirs his coffee, hiding a smile.

"I told you," Henry says, chin jutting up toward the ceiling. "I'm a photographer. I was just out there looking for inspiration."

"Oh, yeah? Inspiration like Heller's wife?" Lockley says.

Henry feels his face burn crimson. Well, yes, actually. But not for the salacious reason Lockley is implying.

A self-righteous grin spreads across the fat cop's face. He reaches into his shirt pocket for a packet of cigarettes and shakes one out.

"That Judy sure is a looker, isn't she? In fact, she's not much older than you," he says. "It's normal you would take a healthy interest in her."

Henry glowers at him. It's so much more than that for him, but he doesn't expect the imbecile in front of him to understand. Judy's true beauty is embroidered into the way she gets lost in whatever she turns her attention to. The way he finds her kneeling in the fresh-cut front lawn, her dexterous gloved hands cupping the delicate damask roses, pruning their cranes at the precise forty-five degree angle, watering can at the ready.

Henry never announces himself as he approaches along the sidewalk, but instead waits for her to come back to herself. She studies each blossom with curiosity and intention, as if seeing it for the first time. When she finally does notice Henry, she's all beaming apologies, flush rising high on her cheeks. "Don't mind me, Henry, I just vanished again," she'd say. Henry wonders where she goes, and if he'll ever be able to find his own way to disappear on command like her. She'll ask him what he's shooting today, and no matter what he tells her, she always sighs, "That sounds perfectly gorgeous."

Judy adores photography, but claims she's no good at it, which Henry finds hard to believe given the natural grace with which she does everything. "Did you know 'photography' is Greek for 'drawing with light'? How magical is that," she once said. Judy treats Henry like a peer; she sees him, legitimizes his passion and talent for photography in a way no one else does.

But there was also something tragic about her. For the longest time, Henry couldn't put his finger on it. It was as if she was always suppressing the urge to look over her shoulder.

He didn't have to wait long to find out why.

Henry witnessed it for himself through the Hellers' back window a few months ago while scouting scenes. And when he saw it happen, he was so overcome with horror that he had to choke back vomit.

"You don't get it," Henry says to Lockley. The cop arches an eyebrow at him, lights his cigarette, and inhales. Henry's nostrils flare. "Look, am I under arrest?"

"We just want to ask you some questions," Lockley says.

"Doesn't that mean no?" he asks, cursing the pubescent break in his voice at the end. Nothing better than sounding like an eight-year-old Boy Scout in front of two cops.

"That's right, you're not under arrest yet." Henry's eyes flick to the officer standing by the wall, who answered him. "But that depends on what we find out here. And if Mr. Heller wants to press charges."

Henry's blood scalds his veins like magma. Heller pressing charges against *him*? That's rich. But unsurprising. Bill Heller has staggering clout in this town. The guy isn't just a businessman. He's a paragon of the American

Dream, owning everything from prominent real estate to lucrative auto dealerships to bustling restaurants. Not to mention, he runs the massive annual fundraiser to feed the hungry every year. Everyone champions the indubitable moral constitution of Bill Heller. That's why Henry needed proof. He knew no one would believe him otherwise.

"I didn't do anything wrong."

"Well, maybe you'll have something more to say when your parents get here," Lockley says, smashing his cigarette butt into the ashtray in the middle of the table.

Henry shoots upright in his seat. "You called my parents?"

Lockley looks amused. "Of course we did. You're a minor. We're required to notify your parents that you've been taken into custody." He jerks a thumb at his partner. "Why do you think Potts asked for your name and address? He phoned them. They're on their way in now."

Oh, no. No, no, no. Henry goes limp with consternation. Up until now, he'd thought this was just an informal questioning, that he'd be able to go home and his mom and dad would never know anything about it.

Before Henry can say anything else, the metal door to the interview room scrapes open. Henry's mother is right in front of him in her cream tailored pea coat, burgundy leather handbag hooked on her forearm. Her blonde hair falls in sculpted curls around her narrow face, and her smooth cheeks are tinged pink from the blustery outdoors. She glares at Henry, and a cold sweat seeps out of all Henry's pores. Lockley pushes his chair back and stands. Potts straightens up from the wall.

"Mrs. Barton?" Lockley says, extending his hand. "I'm Officer Brian Lockley and this is my partner Officer Darren Potts."

"Officers," she says, giving them a curt nod and shaking hands. "Please call me Livia."

"Okay, then," he says. "Will your husband be joining us, Livia?"

"No, he won't be. He had to stay home and look after our daughter," she says. Lockley and Potts exchange glances.

"Please, have a seat," Lockley says, pulling a chair up to the table from the shadows. He helps her out of her coat, and she thanks him as she sits down. Lockley offers her a beverage, but she waves him away.

"Someone just explain to me what happened, please," she says.

Lockley gives her the rundown. The neighbor saw Henry in the Hellers' yard with a camera pointed at their windows. She called the police, thinking the teen was taking surreptitious photos of Judy. Lockley and Potts responded, took him into custody, and here they are.

Livia turns a wild expression on Henry. "Henry, explain yourself right now, for the love of God."

"It's not what you think, Mom," Henry says, fervor mounting. "I was only out taking pictures. Judy—Mrs. Heller gave me permission to use their property to do that anytime I wanted. It's so scenic there, like a painting."

"You like paintings so much, maybe you oughta take

up painting," Lockley grumbles before Henry's mom can answer. "A hobby that's not bothering anybody."

A hobby. Henry wishes the cop would have a heart attack right here on the spot. "Already tried painting, actually. Not for me," he sneers.

"Well, explain to us what *is* 'for you'?" Lockley erupts. "Taking snapshots of a man's wife inside her own home? Son, you're lucky he didn't kick your ass clear across town."

"Well, then I guess Mrs. Heller and I would have something in common," Henry shoots back. It comes out before he can stop himself. Lockley's face drops.

"What did you just say?"

"I said, Heller is a piece of garbage who pounds on his wife," Henry says. "I've seen him do it. I wanted proof. I was there to get the proof. Okay? Does that explain it good enough for you?" His mother touches her throat and gapes at him.

Lockley's eyes narrow to such a degree that Henry thinks he could blindfold the man with dental floss.

"Young man, that is a very serious allegation," Lockley threatens in a low voice. "Bill Heller is a close friend of the Department and many others in this community. And I can tell you right now I am not fond of *pervert kids* talking badly of upstanding fellas like Bill."

"I'm not a damn pervert!" Henry shouts, slamming his palms down on the table.

Lockley leaps to his feet and jabs a finger in Henry's face. "You watch your mouth, boy, and don't you dare get loud in here with me!"

"That's enough!" Livia thunders, rising from her seat. Lockley looks stunned, as if he'd forgotten she was even there.

"If what Henry is saying is true, then the film will support it," she says to Lockley. "We just need to develop the film."

If? Henry screams inside his head. What a surprise that his mother doesn't believe him right off the bat.

"Oh, believe me, ma'am, we are way ahead of you," Lockley says, grabbing the camera off the table. "We're confiscating the camera and the film. If there's so much as Mrs. Heller's bare shoulder in here, Henry's in for a world of trouble."

"Go ahead," Henry spits. "You won't find anything."

"Including any evidence of Heller being violent."

"I told you, the lady next door called you guys before I could get it."

"A likely story," Potts offers helpfully from his sentry post against the wall.

Lockley lets out a long exhale and shakes his head. "You know, Henry," he chuckles hollowly, "I think there's something your mother really needs to see. Maybe then she'll understand what her son is really all about. And why your story doesn't hold much water with us." His eyes flick to the floor next to his chair, then back to Henry. Henry blanches.

"What are you talking about, Officer?" Henry's mom asks sharply.

Lockley snatches Henry's bag from the floor next to

him. He makes a big show of dumping the contents out on the table in front of all of them.

Livia leans forward, scanning the paperbacks in front of her in disbelief. *On the Road, Howl and Other Poems, Tropic of Cancer,* and *The Well of Loneliness.*

"Ma'am, were you aware that your son had these indecent materials in his possession?" Lockley says. Henry eyes his mother with dread.

"No, I was not." Her voice is barely audible. She turns a cold stare on Henry.

Henry pulls his clammy hands through his hair. The room is stifling, an iron chamber devoid of oxygen.

"Look," he begins, his heart slamming against his ribcage. "They're not 'indecent,' alright? I know that's what people think, but no one's even giving them a chance. Even the judge in California ruled that they had no right to ban *Howl*. That it was a socially important work." He had memorized that from the *New York Times* article. "It's just different from what everyone's used to, so they assume it's bad."

"Is that so?" Lockley says. He picks up *Howl* and pages through it, then stops, clearing his throat. He proceeds to rattle off, in extremely poor form, Henry notes, the whole part about drinking turpentine in Paradise Alley and purgatoried torsos and drugs and waking nightmares.

Lockley trails off with disgust. "I am not going to pollute the ears of the decent folks in this room with what comes next." *Cock and endless balls,* Henry thinks, using all his willpower to crush an emerging grin. That line always gets him going.

Lockley flips through more pages and stops again.

"Oh, here now," he says. "Let's not forget the commie 'socially important work,' *America,* where this genius poet spouts leftist propaganda blaming *our great nation* for the Cold War." He turns his blazing eyes on Henry.

"Where did you get this filth?" His mother says tonelessly.

Henry shoots a quick glance at her. "Does it matter?" A twenty-minute bus ride from his suburban home into the heart of Philly, and the world was your oyster.

"This is revolting," she says. "I don't even know what to say. After all your father and I do for you, Henry. I can't begin to understand what's wrong with you."

"Mom, they're just books," Henry says, exasperated. "That's it. There's nothing is wrong with me." But the pleading edge in his voice comes out stronger than he means it.

"You're fifteen years old, Henry," Lockley says, tossing the book on the table and resting his hands on his generous hips. "You need to think about your future, about what kind of life you want to have. You start getting indecency charges on your record, well, they can really trip you up. Peeping in windows, reading obscene books. Take my advice: leave it all alone and get your head on straight."

Get *his* head on straight? Henry is fuming. Goddamn imbeciles. These cops, his parents, Heller, the whole damn town. None of them can see past their own tiny, useless lives, not even to help a woman who will probably die one of these days by her husband's hand. All because the kid relaying the information to them reads "filth." He can't conjure up anything more pathetic.

"I already told you I was *not* peeping in windows. This is unbelievable!" Henry stands up and shoves his chair back. "Doesn't anyone here care about what's happening to Mrs. Heller? You're not even going to investigate, or talk to her to see if I'm right? It doesn't bother you that an innocent woman is getting beaten up?"

"It's not your business!" His mother cries, standing up. Henry stares at her, stomach plummeting into his shoes. Is she seriously implying he should've turned his back on a woman being assaulted?

"You shouldn't have ever been over there in the first place, commiserating with an older, *married* woman," she continues. "She's got some screws loose in her head, if you ask me, for spending time with a teenaged boy."

"I was only trying to help, for Christ's sake!"

"It's their own private matter, between a husband and wife. Stay out of it!"

"I cannot believe what I'm hearing," Henry seethes. "I'm the good person here, and I'm being treated like a criminal. Why?"

"Because you are fifteen years old!" she yells. "You should be out playing baseball, or reading comic books, or doing *anything else* that a normal teenage boy does. I'm sorry to say it, Henry, but you're just not normal. These books! This obsession with photography and the damned Brownie camera! It's like you're completely detached from the world. Either you don't know what's right and wrong, or else you're plain refusing to see it, which is so much worse."

The room goes silent and Henry feels the air being sucked out of his lungs. He drops back into his chair, breathless. Which is just as well since he has no breath to talk anyway. Lockley inhales and turns to Henry's mother.

"I think we've got everything we need for now, ma'am," he says. "We'll develop the film and be in touch after that. We'll be sure to return the camera to you. He's free to leave now."

"Thank you, Officer," she says huskily.

"What do you want to do with the books?"

"Sorry?"

"The books," Lockley says, gesturing at the table.

Her delicate nostrils flare. "Just get rid of them, please," she says.

"My pleasure."

"Let's go," she says to Henry, pulling on her coat. As if in a dream, Henry hobbles to his feet on peg legs. Lockley holds out his empty bag to him. He says nothing and takes it, following his mother out of the odious room.

"Remember what I said, Henry," Lockley calls. "Think of your future." As he hears his books clang into the metal trashcan behind him, Henry vows to do just that.

Chapter Six

SOCIAL MEDIA IS a cesspool of garbage humans, but in rare instances it can be helpful. I'm hoping this is one of those times. From the leather armchair in Mom's study, I review my post to the UCLA Film School 1960s alumni Facebook group: *Super random question, but does anyone here remember a student named Henry Barton? He started in 1962. If you knew him, please DM me. Any information is greatly appreciated! He's my uncle, and I'm working on a family lineage project.* Straightforward enough.

UCLA is the only angle I can work to try to get more info on Henry. It's the last thing Nana knows for sure about him before he evaporated without a trace and showed up dead halfway across the world years later. Google gave me no results for my Henry Barton, even when adding in the terms UCLA, Philadelphia, Rosanera, Italy, photography, film. Nothing. It's as if he never existed at all.

But Henry had existed. For twenty-seven years. And

something went very wrong at the end of that time. After no contact forever, Henry called Nana out of nowhere and said he was coming home—on the very day he died. *He was upset, that much was clear,* Nana had told me. Add that to the note on the mausoleum photograph: *If I don't make it back…*

And he never did, did he?

I reach for my third glass of wine on the teak table next to me. It's filled to the brim, and I down it in a few gulps. Before I came across the box of photos, Henry was a buried footnote in my mind. Now he might as well be right here in the room with me, passing the bottle back and forth between us like old friends. He's here for good now, all twisted up inside me.

There's a knock on the door, and Colette pokes her head in. "You busy?" she says.

As I adjust in my seat to look at her, the room slants and grows dim around the edges. My stomach plunges, and I go clammy. Is it the alcohol? No, can't be. I switched from bourbon to wine an hour ago. Come on. The day I can't handle a Pinot Grigio is the day I hang myself.

"Come on in," I mutter, trying to shake it off. It's fine. Everything's fine. Colette walks in with a smile that drops from her face when she sees me.

"My God, are you alright?" she says. "You look blanched."

"I'm fine," I say, doing my best to straighten up. Then I remember. Must be the Xanax. Sure, I took a double dose tonight. But I just buried my mother yesterday. Don't I deserve to do whatever I want?

Colette keeps her worried eyes trained on me as reaches for the pull-string on the table lamp next to me.

"Do you mind? It's pretty dark in here," she says. Before I can respond, one hundred watts of additional light blast through the room. I wince, feeling like a crazed owl, huddled deep inside a tree's knothole, fearful of exposure to photons.

"That's better," she says, settling into the less comfortable linen armchair opposite me. She points to my laptop. "What are you working on?"

My head pounds, and I wish I didn't have to talk. "I just posted to that UCLA alumni group asking about Henry. Never know. Maybe I'll hear something back."

Colette's shoulders relax. She seems pleased by my rare optimism. "That was a great idea, Jules. People connect the dots through social media all the time. Might take a while, but still."

I sniff. "Well, that's perfect. Because I've got nothing but time now."

Her eyebrows tighten. "Oh, yeah?"

I nod and refill my stemmed glass a fourth time, vertigo be damned. "Got an email today from that lawyer guy I interviewed with a couple weeks ago. They decided to go with someone else." *Thank Christ*, I want to add, but abstain. May as well have Colette think I'm still a real go-getter and all that.

"Oh. Sorry to hear that. But there's plenty of other stuff out there. You'll find something."

Neither of us states the obvious, which is that at least for the foreseeable future, I don't have to. Mom's death auspiciously spared me the burden of job-hunting and finding a place to live.

What it won't save me from is my well-worn path to nowhere. It won't make Matt love me again, or turn me into a writer, or give me any reason to peel open the blinds in the morning. If anything, it'll just allow me more time to feel all the little pieces of what went wrong bleeding through.

Panic sears my insides as a new thought dawns on me. Now that Mom's funeral is over, Nana and Colette will be leaving the house soon. How will it feel to be back here in my childhood home, alone, all day every day? The same four walls, the silence. Nothing to do, no one to see. The few friends I still have came to pay their respects for Mom, assuring me I could call any time. Polite lip-service, of course—we hadn't seen each other in over a year. And it would have been even longer if it weren't for my dead mother. I try to take a deep breath and coax my diaphragm back down from my throat to my chest.

"Look, I've been thinking," I say, willing my voice to be steady. "What if I just go to Rosanera myself?"

Colette considers me, seems to be choosing her words carefully. I can read her thoughts. How would a direction-less loser who manages to fuck up everything in her life figure out a fifty-year-old mystery?

"Okay," she says slowly. "But to what end?"

"To the end of finding the mausoleum and this Giovanni guy," I say, more irritably than I mean to. "To figure out what message Henry left." Across from me, Colette nods and recrosses her slender legs, and regards me with inquiring eyes. I half-expect her to get out a notebook and ask me how it made me feel to say that just now.

"But isn't that why you reached out online?" she asks. "If Henry's got any old friends in the alumni group, maybe you'll have your answers. I think you should at least wait until you hear back, don't you think?"

Wait. That's all I've been doing for as long as I can remember now. What happened to me? To the person whose laptop screen was crowded with open browser tabs for writerly research, future travel bookings, interior design mood boards? Who struggled to respond to an overwhelming volume of text messages? One day she just vanished, like so many other girls who go missing all the time. Sometimes they're found again. But usually not alive.

"That could take forever," I say. "Who knows how many people are actually active in that group, or will even read my post?"

"True. But maybe give it a couple weeks. You just posted it."

I shake my head and get up, begin to pace the room. In my inebriated state, it looks like a Dali painting. But I force myself to stay standing.

"Nothing about this makes sense, Colette. There's a

reason Henry hid the photo and address in his cigarette pack instead of just putting it in his wallet. Obviously he didn't want just anyone finding it. Then Nana tells me he calls her, upset, to say he was coming home, but died later *that same day*? It feels wrong."

"I hear you, and I agree it doesn't quite square."

"He wrote 'If I don't make it back' on the back of the photo. Back where? To Philly? To L.A.? To wherever the picture was taken?"

"As I said, I admit that—"

"It's got to have something to do with his estrangement from the family," I mutter. I ping pong around the room as I talk, sawing at my thumbnail with my teeth.

Colette stops and peers at me, her forehead scrunched up. "You mean his death?"

My thoughts are all over the place. "No, I mean why he was in Rosanera at all. Maybe the whole estrangement drove him somehow to go to Italy. Maybe to find other relatives?"

"Well, perhaps."

"Nana said the reason they stopped talking was all because her brother Pietro died, and Henry was devastated over it; furious at Nana for not allowing him to have a relationship with his uncle. But Henry barely knew the man. So, why would that have caused such an explosive rift?"

"It wouldn't," Colette says quietly. My eyes jump to hers. "I agree that there's information missing. We don't have the full story."

I gape at her, buoyed by this validation. If someone as

whip-smart as Colette agrees, maybe I'm on to something here.

"But," she quickly counters, sensing my anticipation, "your grandmother clearly doesn't want to talk any more about it. I know it's frustrating, Juliet. But some things are too painful for people to relive. You need to respect her staying silent on the issue."

"That's exactly why I posted to that Facebook group, Colette. If Henry's got any old friends in the alumni group, maybe he told them why. That might be half the answer about the photo and Giovanni right there."

"And even if he did, you have to consider whatever he told them might not have been the truth," she says, folding her arms. "He was a teenage boy moving across the country to start a new life. Not exactly a demographic known for being the most forthcoming, especially about embarrassing family circumstances."

I stop pacing. Why hadn't that occurred to me? Henry could've been quite the unreliable narrator. That means anything I might learn about him from the alumni group people could be just plain wrong, leading me even further astray. The benzo mist in my mind is thickening, and with it my thoughts intensify.

"Fine, I might never know find out what really caused the estrangement," I say. "But the mausoleum photo and the Giovanni address? Those are real, actual things that can't be disputed. Maybe someone in the group knows something about *those*. Which would pretty much be the key to everything."

Colette stands up and studies me for a minute; an emotion I can't make out flickers in her face.

"I understand you're upset, Jules, and you have every right to be. But it's the day after your mother's funeral, for goodness' sake. You need to be kind to yourself, and get some rest. All of this can wait."

"It's already waited fifty years, Colette!" I explode, and she jerks back. "I told you what Nana said: Mom adored Henry, and she was absolutely devastated when he died. I know for certain that she never found that stuff in Henry's cigarette pack. If she had, she would've gone straight to Rosanera herself. I am telling you that she would."

Colette nods, but says nothing.

"I need to figure this out for her sake." My voice sounds like tires spinning on gravel. "And for Nana's. She's still here, still alive. And she deserves to know what happened to her son. To get closure. Doesn't she?"

"To be honest, Juliet, I've lived a long time, and I don't know that I believe in closure. At least not what it means in the conventional sense. Our demons, our fears, our sense of what was supposed to happen versus what did, that doesn't ever get packed up and sealed away. You may gain a deeper understanding. But sometimes, that can be even worse. The more you learn, the more it begs the question of other things: the coulds and shoulds.

"That all said, however, I do understand your need to pursue closure. All I'm asking is that you consider your own needs before making a decision. Because you need to prepare yourself for the very real chance that you may not be able to resolve this. Or that whatever you find out still won't bring Nana, or you, the closure you anticipate. Could you live with that?"

Her words wash over me, and I slump under the weight of her message as it creeps into my bones like lead. She's right. This could all turn out very badly, in so many ways.

"Okay," I say, biting back tears. "I need to think about it, but right now I need sleep more." The cumulative exhaustion I feel right now is like that of someone riding out a lengthy virus. There's a low-level sickness in me that never retreats.

I wrap my arms around her and tell her I love her. And as I say it, I imagine she's Mom.

"Love you, too," Colette says, squeezing my hand as I pull away. My feet are two anvils as I trudge up the stairs. It feels like space and time could swallow me whole. I'm tired, so wretchedly tired. When I collapse into my mother's unmade bed, where I've slept ever since I got here, terrified to wash the sheets because her scent will then be gone forever, my mind goes utterly blank and I fall into a fitful, empty sleep.

Chapter Seven

Philadelphia
June 8, 1962

THE BUS DOORS whoosh open, and Henry exits the stifling aluminum vessel. It feels good to be out of there, even though the air still hangs heavy and humid outside.

As the bus roars away, Henry puts on his sunglasses, lights a cigarette, and smiles as he starts for home.

Only eleven weeks to go now. What will it feel like to walk down Hollywood Boulevard for the very first time? He imagines the outlines of palm trees falling long across his face; passing shops and bars and restaurants, their doors propped wide open, offering everything you could ever want. The eternal summer breeze blowing a crazy part in his hair and ruffling his shirt collar. The hustle and bustle, the impropriety, the pure vitality of existence. A life actually worth living. He can't get there soon enough.

As he reaches his house, Henry ditches the cigarette and grinds it into the dirt with the toe of his scuffed black engineer boot. He opens the front door and hears the evening news in the living room, which means his parents are in there, so he creeps up to his room. Once inside, he dumps his bag onto the floor and kicks off his boots into the heap of clothes and records that are strewn everywhere. Roy Orbison, Muddy Waters, Otis Redding, and Bob Dylan form a winding path to the Magnavox record player by the dresser. He switches his oscillating floor fan on high, points it squarely on him, and falls back on the bed staring at the ceiling. Then comes a knock on his door.

"Who is it?" he says sharply, up on one elbow.

"It's just me," a little voice answers. Henry relaxes.

"Come on in, Ellen," he says. His nine-year-old sister creaks open the door.

"I heard you come home and just wanted to say hi," she says. "I haven't really seen you all week."

"Yeah, I know. I've been working extra hours. Trying to save up as much as I can before I go. Come in. And close the door behind you."

She shuts the door and marvels at the sea of relics in front of her. Records, clothes, cameras, and books. Her plaid jumper and white Keds are spotted with dirt, and her long blonde hair falls in tangles halfway down her back. She probably just came in from under the weeping willow. Henry noticed she's started hiding out there too, just like he used to.

"Are you going to take all of this with you to California?" Ellen asks, sitting down at his desk chair.

"Not all of it. There's no way it'll all fit in my dorm room. Especially since I'll have a roommate."

"So, what are you going to take?"

Henry shrugs. "Obviously the cameras. Some books. The records and probably my record player, unless my roommate has one."

"What about those?" she asks, pointing behind him. Henry turns to look at the Brownie film reels and framed black-and-white photos that had won awards in regional art shows.

"Ehh, I don't know. Why, do you want some?" he says. Her cheeks flush and she grins, dropping her eyes to the floor.

"I dunno, maybe," she says.

"It's okay if you do. Consider them yours."

Ellen nods, still looking down, but her smile turns into a trembling frown.

Henry sits up. "What's wrong?"

She draws a shaky breath and wipes her eyes with the heel of her hand. "It's just going to be weird here without you," she mumbles. "I'm really going to miss you."

"I'm gonna miss you too, Ellie," he says, getting up and hugging her. She clings to him, her damp face on his shoulder. He thinks she still feels like a baby, and realizes that nine years old is almost the same thing. "But everything will be fine. Really. I'll come back and visit on holidays and over break and stuff." Guilt slams over him like a tsunami. Even as he says the words, he knows they can't be further from the truth. He doesn't see himself coming back here more than once a year for a few days, at the most.

"Here," he says, pulling away from her, smiling. "Take anything you want in the room. Do you want the record player? You can have it. I can buy another one." Her shining eyes search his.

"Don't go, Henry," she pleads. "Please. It just won't be good without you."

"Ellie, it's college," he says gently. "I have to go. It's what people do. You'll go someday, too. The time will come sooner than you think."

Just then, he hears the hum of an engine and the crunching of pebbles under tires outside his window. When he looks out the window, his breath stops. Two police officers are getting out of the black-and-white parked in his driveway.

Henry leaps back from the window, his mind racing. *Did someone turn me in for grass?* He can't imagine who would do that. But why else would the cops be at his house?

"Why are the police here?" Ellen echoes from his side, her wide eyes watching his panicked face. He grabs his camera bag and rips it open, locating the little wooden box inside and shoving it under his mattress. A pathetic attempt at hiding, he knows, but what else can he do at this point?

The doorbell rings. Henry squeezes his eyes shut as

he hears his mother open the door. *I'm going to prison. I'll never get a chance to leave this hellish place after all.* Muffled voices exchange words and Henry braces himself, waiting for someone to come storming up the stairs for him, but nothing happens. After a few minutes, he opens his door and listens.

"You're listed as next of kin, so we needed to notify you," one of the officers is saying. "I'm very sorry, ma'am. Again, we aren't completely sure what happened, but we'll let you know as soon as we get the results from the Medical Examiner's office. It shouldn't be longer than a week or two. But we will need you to come down to the station as soon as you can to positively identify the body."

Now certain this has nothing to do with him, Henry walks to the landing. Ellen follows him. The two officers and his parents all turn to look.

"A body? What body? What's going on?" Henry asks. His mother's face is whiter than usual, and she's leaning into his father.

"My brother is dead," she said.

A high-pitched ringing begins in Henry's ears. "What?"

"You heard me. My brother, Pietro. He's dead."

Henry's mouth tastes like metal. "How?" he says.

"We'll talk about this later, Henry," his dad says.

"I just want to kn

ow what happened," Henry insists. He walks down to middle of the staircase. Uncle Pietro is dead. That's it. He would never see him again, never know anything about him. He would simply be forgotten now, forever.

"Oh, go ahead, then," his mother says roughly, to the officers. "Tell him."

The officer clears his throat. "Mr. Palumbo's body was found in an alley behind Samson at 19th Street today. Witnesses say he'd been working construction at a job site nearby. The cause of death is still being determined, but the initial conclusion is severe dehydration. With this heatwave, and him working outside…well, sadly, it's more common that you would think. You work ten, twelve hours without much of a break, and forget to drink water. It happens, even to younger fellows like him."

Dehydration? Henry thinks. *He died because of lack of water? Like someone living in a third world country?* All these years later, Henry can still conjure up that awful image of Pietro trodding across the lawn, back to the road. Disappearing in the shadows of the growing night. Because of *her*. Because nothing is ever good enough for her.

"We'll leave you to your evening," the officer says to Henry's mom. "Again, we're very sorry for your loss, ma'am. The County will be in touch after the autopsy is complete."

"I understand," she says. "Thank you for coming. Good night." The officers leave, and she closes the door behind them.

"Well, at least he's out of the picture for good now," Henry says. "You know, no need to worry about him coming around here, bothering us, looking for work and stuff. Or God forbid some water."

"Henry, I am warning you," his father says, in a low

voice. Henry ignores him. He can barely conceive of anything less threatening than his own father. *What are you gonna do except scamper to Mom's side like always?*

"How could you?" Henry continues, glowering at his mother. "He died on the street, keeled over in an alley. Think about that. You let your brother *die in the street*. How does that feel? Just because neither of you wanted 'his kind' here."

"Henry!" His father slams his fist down on the hallway table. Henry flinches in spite of himself. "Don't you dare speak to your mother like that!"

His mom storms up the stairs, stopping one step below Henry. She matches his glare, her narrowed blue eyes lit up like gas flames on a stove.

"You want to know the truth about your uncle?" she says. "He was a murderer. He killed a woman." Henry grips onto the oak banister for support.

"Why?" she continues. "Because he owed 'someone' a favor. See, that's how they work. The Black Fist, the 'brotherhood,' that made it all the way here from the old country. I might feel bad for some people getting mixed up in it, but my brother? He knew better. It was the whole damned reason my father made us leave Italy. They're like a disease, infesting the government, families, everyone. The very people who are supposed to protect you suddenly want you dead. It sickened my father. He talked about it every night to us when we were children. Pietro *knew* better. He ruined his own life, and I certainly wasn't going to let him ruin mine."

Henry feels like he might hyperventilate. *Bullshit*, he thinks wildly, *she's just trying to make more excuses for why she didn't want to help him. To ease her rotten conscience.*

"I don't believe you," Henry says. "That makes no sense. If he was connected to the Mafia, he'd be rich. He wouldn't need to slave away working in construction. You think I'm that stupid, do you?"

His mother lets out a slice of a laugh. "So, all your precious movies taught you about that, did they? *On The Waterfront* gave you everything you need to know about how it works? Is that right? You don't know a damn thing about life."

"I know you're full of it," he fumes. "That you hated your brother because he doesn't live up to this pathetic American dream you think you're entitled to."

Ellen is crying at the top of the stairs. "Please, stop it," she moans.

"This has gone far enough," his father says, coming up the stairs. But Henry's mom holds up a menacing hand to him, and he stops in his tracks.

"This 'pathetic American dream' has saved you from a desperate, dark world," she snarls at Henry. "But you're beyond hope. Going around with those cameras, looking for all the ugliness life has to offer. We gave you a life where you could do anything, but you end up wanting to go to Hollywood, a cesspool of the lowest common denominator of people, to *film* them."

"Stop making pathetic excuses," Henry threatens. "This has nothing to do with me going to UCLA. The fact is, I have never been good enough for you. You've never been proud of anything I've done. And not you, either!" He pointed at his father. "You think the world is ugly? Nothing has been uglier than living with you two!"

Henry starts down the stairs. He has to get out of the house, right now. But his mother moves to stop him, grabbing his shoulder. Her fingernails sink like talons into his flesh.

"You're not going anywhere until we talk about this," she says.

Henry shoves her off of him, harder than he means to. It throws her off balance and her arms begin to windmill. Before his brain can register what's happening, his mother tumbles face first down the flight of dense oak steps. Ellen shrieks.

"Livia! Livia?" Henry's father runs and kneels beside her, cradling her head in his lap. She groans and turns her head to one side. Her left arm hangs at a crazy angle and blood is quickly darkening her nose and lips. "Call an ambulance!" he shouts.

Henry's feet are glued to the stairs. His body starts convulsing with fear as reality sinks in. Ellen thunders down the stairs past him to the telephone on the hall table, and through her sobs begs the Operator to send an ambulance.

"Da-ad?" Henry says. "It—it was an accident. You *know* it was an accident. I didn't mean to. Dad? I didn't mean to. Daddy?" No one seems to hear him.

His brain is a short-circuiting electrical grid. Is she

paralyzed? Brain damaged? Will she die? Henry takes a couple feeble steps down the stairs like a toddler. He's overcome him with utter dread when he sees what is in front of him.

As his mother weakly tries to adjust herself on the floor, her hands go to her lower abdomen and she lets out a guttural wail. Dad's face is ashen. He puts his hands on top of hers, protecting her midsection.

"Oh, Jesus," his father chokes. "Ellen, grab me some towels. Now!"

He needs them for the rapidly growing red puddle that's spreading through the seat of her pants.

Chapter Eight

I'M REPLAYING MY recent conversation with Colette in my head when the girl and her dog suddenly appear in front of me as a screaming, horrified blur. I slam on the brakes with both feet, nearly pitching myself through the rental truck's windshield. By some miracle, I've managed to stop before flattening this pedestrian and her terrier. I'm so lost in my thoughts that I blew right through the stop sign. The stench of burning rubber mixed with the crashing tide of adrenaline threatens to make me pass out.

She smashes her fist on the truck's hood and shouts. The dog, having shot up into her arms seconds earlier, lasers a malicious glare at me. I stammer an apology from behind the wheel, raising a trembling hand. She gives me the finger, still scowling as she crosses to the safety of the sidewalk.

For the love of Jesus. I take a shaky breath and steer the vehicle into the far-right lane so I can continue on to my house at a vigilant, grandmotherly pace. Clearly, I'm not in the best frame of mind right now to undertake the move-out process from my house. But it needs to happen. Matt's work in Dubai is almost done, and he'll be home in a week. I want to have all my stuff out of there and back at Mom's house long before I have to see him again.

And maybe I won't have to see him for even longer, if I go to Rosanera.

It's still nagging at me, despite all of Colette's logic for me staying put for now. It's been three days, and no traction in the Facebook UCLA alumni group. My post got some likes and care emojis, along with a few "sorry, wish I could help!" comments. Dead end. But was I really going to travel six thousand miles from home to search every cemetery? What if the mausoleum *wasn't* in Rosanera. What then? Or, how about the fact that Giovanni, whoever he is, is probably long gone from that address—or likely dead by now. Which always brings me back to the fact that this happened so insanely long ago, and what is the point.

I slow down at the next intersection and turn right, pulling up in front of my house. I turn off the ignition and get out. Then I immediately freeze. The blinds in the living room windows are open. I know for sure I left them closed, since the house would be empty while I stayed at Mom's. My heart's thudding as I walk up the lumpy brick sidewalk to the front door.

I slide the key into the lock and turn it, the familiar squeak of the door welcoming me. "Hello?" I say, peering into the living room. There, among the piles of Matt's and my stuff stand five suitcases. I recognize three as Matt's.

Quick footfalls from down the hall, and then Matt is standing right there in front of me. My purse slips off my shoulder, and I catch it just before it hits the floor.

"What are you doing here?" I say, breathless. I fall against the arm of the couch for balance. This can't be happening. How is he home already? I'm going to have to pack and move the rest of my stuff out while he's *here*? I won't even get the privacy to say a proper good-bye to my home.

"Hey," he says, shifting. He looks different. He's thinner, tan, and he's wearing clothes he never wore when we were together. They're weirdly metrosexual and he looks like an asshat. I would tell him that if I had any air in my lungs.

"I was going to text you," he says. "We—I just got home a few hours ago. We wrapped up the project a little early, so I thought I might as well come back now."

"It's just, I wasn't expecting you," I say stupidly. Of course I wasn't. "I wanted to move my stuff before you got home, so we wouldn't have to awkwardly see each other. You know, like right now."

How can it be that we're standing in the same room we'd torn each other's clothes off in right after we closed escrow? Now we eye each other like wary strangers, all traces of familiarity gone. I hear a noise come from the study. The place where I was sitting when Colette called me about Mom centuries ago.

Matt whips his head over his shoulder, then back at me.

"What?" I say. He licks his lips.

"Look," he says, "plans have changed a little. I was hoping you and I could set a time to meet up and talk about it over the weekend."

"'Set up a time?' What is this, a business meeting?"

His jaw twitches. "I'm jet-lagged, Juliet. I haven't even thought through what I need to say."

What he said to me a few minutes ago finally sinks in. When he caught himself saying "we." The two extra suitcases. My blood drops into my boots.

"Is she here?" I say, standing up. "Is she here in this house right now?"

"Juliet, please. I was going to tell you. I didn't want you to find out this way, but—"

"You brought her back with you? *To our house?* You really are fucked in the head, you know that?"

I push past him and I'm down the hall into the office before he can stop me. I throw open the door, and there's Lauren. Ten feet tall, blonde, sunny. She's frozen in front of the bookcase (*my* bookcase), her tawdry, fuchsia-painted lips in a big round O. Her shoes are kicked off next to the ottoman, right where I used to leave mine. They're sparkly gold flats. The type of shoe I wouldn't be caught murdered in. I hear the faint hum of the clothes dryer from inside the closet.

"I see you're making yourself right at home." My voice is thin and sharp as wire. And from the way she's shrinking back from me, I must also look positively sinister.

"Listen," she says, hands up, "I'm just here for a few

days. For a job interview." She looks desperately past me over my shoulder, and I whirl around to see Matt standing there with arms crossed.

"She's interviewing for jobs *here*?" I say. This isn't happening.

Lauren's eyes ricochet between me and Matt. She stuffs her feet into her shoes and grabs her phone off the chair.

"I'm going to leave you two alone," she mumbles, brushing past me. Moments later I hear the front door close. I am incandescent with rage. Roaring, all-consuming white noise fills my head.

"Juliet, I know you've been through a lot," Matt starts. "I can't even imagine what you've been going through with your mom, then the divorce too. It's horrible. And I feel God-awful and guilty about everything. I know I've put you through a lot. We've talked about this so many times over the past few months. But how many more times can I say I'm sorry?"

We'd exchanged perfunctory emails and phone calls, it was true. Fleshing out the terms of the divorce with some back-and-forth about what went wrong between us. My emails were mostly drunken, drugged-out prose, while his were a series of infuriatingly rational responses.

"Yeah, you're right," I say. "There is no point in saying it again. Let's see. You had an affair while on a work assignment—an assignment I had no say in, by the way—and you left me here alone to deal with all of the logistics of a divorce and my mother's death. Does that about sum it up?"

"You made it super clear to me that you didn't want me back here for your mom's funeral."

"Why *would* I?" I cry. "Rely on my cheating husband for trusted support while coping with the death of my mother?"

"It wouldn't have mattered anyway!" he says. "Even if we were still together, it wouldn't have mattered. Juliet, nothing is good enough for you. *Nothing*. It never has been. You think you're the only one who's had it bad? Yeah, I did a shitty thing with Lauren. I've apologized for it a million times now. But you made me feel so lonely for so long." He runs his hands through his hair and turns his back on me, collecting himself. I'm running through a laundry list of retorts, all of them without teeth.

"You talk to me about career?" he says, facing me again. "Your obsession with grad school and with *getting noticed* was off the charts. After you found out you didn't get into PhD programs, you spent the last year of our marriage holed up in this room with a bottle of scotch. Applying to hundreds of adjunct jobs, sending out endless writing submissions, whatever you were doing. You quit everything else—your hobbies, your friends, me. Come on, Juliet, we didn't have sex for five months. The only time I saw you was when you were drunk, high, or completely miserable."

The room tilts. Was that true? No, that can't be right.

"I was just trying to cultivate a career, Matthew, like you," I say, syllables hanging in the air like icicles. "When you do it, it's fine, but when I do it, I'm suddenly abandoning my marriage and friends?"

"Juliet," he says, sinking down on the ottoman. "I'm done arguing. What's happening is this: Lauren's moving here, regardless if she gets the job or not. And I want to keep the house. I'll buy out your half."

I'm floating above myself, watching the sails of reality unfurl. Sour acid coats my tongue.

"You want to keep the house," I say tonelessly. "And have her move in here. We agreed that we'd sell it." Is this all I am to him? All I've ever been? Something that can just be swapped out and replaced? She'll hang her clothes where mine once were, shower in the tub that I refinished by hand, sleep in the bed against the wallpapered accent wall with the design I picked out, and it'll be like I never existed. What kind of person finds that acceptable? Who are these monsters?

Everything's coming apart, ripping at the seams. I try to take some deep breaths to keep from fainting. *Four, three, two, one...*

"It's just easier," he says. "And it's not like I'm leaving you out in the cold. You have your mom's house now."

"You're right, Matt. What a great trade-off for my mom dying unexpectedly!"

"Jesus, that is not what I—"

"You know what? Keep the house. I'm done." Something suddenly clicks in me, deep and cold. I don't recognize anything here—in this house, on the streets outside, the face reflected in the mirror.

I push past him down the hallway back into the living room and get my purse. It's all clear now. I know what I need to do, about everything. Matt's following me, feet scuffling like a dog.

"Wait, you're leaving? What about your stuff?"

"It's staying here until I get back." I turn the knob on the front door.

"Get back? From where? What are you talking about?" I finally turn to look at him. His eyes are clear and blue, and a memory flashes of us together somewhere I once felt safe.

"I'll let you know when I'll be picking it all up."

He's saying something else, but don't hear what it is. I'm already out the door and getting back into the truck.

I'm leaving for Rosanera first thing tomorrow. And I'm not coming back until I find what I'm looking for—even if that means coming back the same way Henry did.

Chapter Nine

Italy feels different from the last time I was here. Of course it does. That was four years ago, and I was in love. Matt and I were all entwined fingers and shared secrets and overdosing on the prosecco-laced newness of our marriage; we were that nauseating couple who marveled at the wonder of every object in our eyesight, living and inanimate, beginning the moment we stepped off the plane in Venice and continuing without cessation for the next pasta-and-wine-and-sex-immersed (not necessarily always in that order) two weeks.

Now I'm sitting alone in a Fiat the size of my palm, parked in front of a B&B in the unremarkable town of Rosanera, my head throbbing from the treacherous two-hour drive from the Florence airport. I'd imagined my journey here would be a scenic tour through the pastoral Tuscan countryside, and I couldn't have been more wrong. Instead, the GPS took me down a roaring highway packed with cars whose dour occupants looked like they subsisted solely on cigarettes and peevish verbal exchanges. The trip culminated in a particularly windy stretch of road into Rosanera along the cliffs, where I white-knuckled my way along at fifteen miles an hour. Every time I glanced in the rearview, I was met with the enraged face of a local driver gritting his teeth and ripping his steering wheel straight off.

I get out of the car and haul my suitcase from the backseat, slamming the door shut with the toe of my black Frye motorcycle boot. They were my last splurge—a graduation present to myself. Tufts of dust and rocks kick up off the gravel onto my black skinny jeans as I make my way to the arched stone entrance of Il Magari B&B. It's actually much nicer than the sparse photo gallery online had me believe.

Inside I'm greeted by a short, stout older woman wearing a polite smile. I find out she's Lucca, who owns this quaint seven-room B&B with her husband. She does the usual check-in stuff, runs my credit card and makes small talk, before leading me across the Tucsan-tiled lobby and up a narrow staircase to my room. "It's steep, yeah?" She huffs to me over her shoulder as we ascend. That's an understatement. I feel like I'm climbing straight up a ladder. Okay, so maybe there's a reason they didn't include *all* their photos on their website.

On the landing, we regather our breath and Lucca unlocks the first door on the right. I take a quick look around. There's a double bed with a crocheted white quilt, a small bedside table with lamp, and a secretary desk with a chair in the corner. A worn, red Persian rug partially covers the wide oak floorboards. Above the bed hangs a painting of an empty barn. The drab color scheme and deserted landscape give me the creeps, and I wonder at the choice to hang it up at all.

But it'll do. I thank Lucca and she nods, closing the door behind her. Plopping down on the bed, I unzip my backpack and whip out the giant bottle of Four Roses I bought in the duty-free shop on my way out of Florence International. With no VAT or tax, it's a better deal to get the 1.5 liter. My hands shake as I unscrew it and start guzzling like it's Evian. I close my eyes and sink back into the goose-down pillow behind me as the predictable warmth floods my veins and I go all heady. Just like any good dose of medicine, I feel well again.

Should I get some food? Find a bar? Go to sleep? I don't know what to do next. I'm filled with that jet lag buzz that can either propel you through the streets of your new destination for five hours, or knock you right out until tomorrow night. Through my room's modest tilt-and-turn window, the broad horizon is deepening into a dusky maroon. Crows dart from the teetering heights of nearby cypress clusters, screaming to each other. It suddenly hits me that I'm actually here in Rosanera, where my uncle Henry spent his last moments on Earth. A part of my own DNA once looked at the same sky I'm seeing right now. My fingertips prickle.

I take another few gulps of bourbon before it dawns

on me that I forgot to text Colette. I told her I'd let her know I got here okay. I pick up my phone and barely start scrolling through my contacts to find her before I stop abruptly, my thumb hovering over one particular name.

There he is, just lying in wait. He's been like a splinter in my mind ever since I booked my flight here. Yeah, he's in Paris, but that's only a couple hours' flight from Italy. Maybe I could just drop in for a quick visit when I'm done here? *No, idiot, you can't. Just stop it.* It's been five years since we've seen each other. But we have kept in touch ever since. The annual happy birthday email. The occasional "did you see this?" meme or news story or just-because text. Doesn't that mean something?

"Screw it," I murmur, brimming with eighty-proof courage and first-rate ideas. I open a new text thread with Bastian: *Hey, guess what? I'm in Italy on a work assignment. Thinking of you bc we're practically neighbors right now. Hope all is well, xx J*

I hit send before my brain can identify a reason to tamp down the tenuous excitement swelling in my chest. Then I move right on to Colette and let her know I'm here in Rosanera—safe and perfectly put together, as always.

Now revived by drink and nervous energy, I reach into my backpack and pull out the manila envelope with Henry's personal effects and my notebook. Might as well review the game plan. I open my notebook to the first page and review the meager list of Rosanera leads I've compiled as to finding the mausoleum's location:

> GIOVANNI – 57 VIA DELLA SERVI
> CHECK ALL 10 CEMETERIES IN THE REGION
> ROSANERA LIBRARY – MICROFICHE/ARCHIVES?
> CONTACT DR. BOLLA – M.E. WHO SIGNED DEATH CERTIFICATE

Giovanni is the obvious place to start since his name and address were folded up inside the mausoleum photo. I am dying to know who this guy is and how he's connected to Henry and this photograph. But I refuse to get my hopes up. I know the odds are extremely low of Giovanni still living at the same address he presumably did in 1971. And depending on how old he was back then, he could very well be dead by now.

If that's the case—and I'm *really* hoping it isn't—then I'll have to move on to the second bullet point: the grueling process of searching the ten cemeteries in the Rosanera region. All but one of them is on the outskirts of town, a testament to the old country's pervasive superstition of centuries ago. They didn't want the dead coming back, so it was best to bury them far away.

The third option, the Rosanera library, might also prove to be helpful. Their antiquated website claimed they have microfiche archives of local newspapers and magazines, none of which are online. Maybe Henry's car crash was covered in the news, with precious details I need about where it happened and why.

And finally, there's Dr. Fabrizio Bolla, the medical examiner who signed Henry's death certificate. For once

I got lucky, Googling him. He's still alive at age eighty seven-eight and lives right here in Rosanera. Aside from Giovanni, Bolla is one of my best shots at getting info on Henry. Bolla examined Henry's body and also put his final belongings into the envelope that sits in front of me now. Maybe Bolla knows exactly where the mausoleum is and its significance.

I put the notebook aside and check my phone. Colette has texted back, saying she's glad to hear I made it safe and that she passed along the message to Nana. She's graciously agreed to stay with her at Mom's house until I get back. No response yet from Bastian.

I'm just about to click the screen off when a Facebook Messenger notification pops up. *You have a new message from David Sherman. Accept?* I frown. Who the hell is David Sherman? Probably spam, but I open Messenger anyway. My heart flutters as I read:

> *Hi Juliet, I just saw your post in the UCLA alumni group. Man, it brought me back! I actually do remember your uncle Henry. We both started the same year and had some classes together. I don't know how much help I can be but I'm happy to chat with you. Let me know.*
> *— Dave.*

I re-read the message just to make sure I'm not imagining it. Here is an actual, living person besides Nana who knew Henry. Whatever this man can tell me, no matter how inconsequential, I'll gladly take. There's a green "active now" dot next to his name, so I begin firing off a response.

> Thanks so much for reaching out, Dave! I'd be thrilled to hear whatever info you have about Henry. I see you're online right now. Any chance you're free for a quick video chat?

I jump up off the bed and pace the room, too excited to sit. For the first time in recent memory, I'm smiling—nay, grinning. I feel giddy. Maybe Dave knows more than he thinks. He could have all the answers: the connection between Henry and Italy, the mausoleum photo, Giovanni. Everything. What if I could have this whole thing solved tonight?

My phone pings, and I leap over to it. *Fine with me,* Dave responds. *Whenever you're ready.*

I give myself a quick once-over in the bathroom mirror, smoothing down my hair and finger-scrubbing away the eyeliner that's made its way under my eyes during my twenty-hour trek from home. I palm cold water into my mouth and give it a good swish, then spit. Good enough.

I hit the video icon in Messenger, and it's ringing Dave. This B&B has surprisingly strong Wi-Fi. Moments later, an older man's face appears on my screen. He's got to be in his late seventies, but he's aged remarkably well. His skin is relatively unlined, and he's got a thick head of curly auburn hair. Kind, blue eyes smile at me.

"Juliet, hi," Dave says. "How's it going?"

"I'm great," I say, and for once I mean it. "I can't thank you enough for messaging me, and for hopping on a chat out of the blue right now."

He laughs. "My pleasure. At my age, you don't have much else to do." He peers closer into the camera. "It looks dark out wherever you are. I take it you're not in California?"

I take this opportunity to tell him no, I'm actually six thousand miles away from California, and here's the totally normal story of why. I fill him in as quickly as I can on everything, from discovering Henry's personal effects to my conversation with Nana and how I came to be sitting in this B&B right now. He listens patiently, raising his eyebrows at the appropriate intervals.

"So," I conclude, "that's about it. You're the only person who responded to my post. But now, you probably wish you didn't."

He chuckles again. It's a reassuring sound, and I'm grateful for it.

"It's totally normal to want to know more about your roots—especially when you've got a small family like yours," he says. "And on that note, I'm really sorry to hear about your mom's passing."

"Thank you, on both counts. And I know it's a long shot, but does anything I just told you about Henry ring a bell? The mausoleum photo, Giovanni, coming to Italy, anything at all?" I hold my breath, as if that will force Dave's memory.

"I'm afraid I'm going to be a big let down there," he

sighs. "As I said in my message, Henry and I were only acquaintances. I know nothing about him going to Italy or this Giovanni guy. But can you send me the photo? There's a chance I could recognize it."

"Of course," I say, and message him a digital copy.

"Got it," he says after a few beats, peering closer at his computer screen. My hands wrestle each other in my lap as I await his answer. *Please, please.*

"No," he says slowly. "I'm sorry, but I've never seen this before. It does look European, though. So good news is you're probably on the right track being over there now. Say again what he wrote on the back?"

"'If I don't make it back, third tomb, lower left.'"

"Huh."

"Sounds ominous, right?"

"It's unsettling for sure. I can see why you think something's stashed there. And you found the photo in with his smokes?"

"Yes. Folded up in there with the address."

Dave shakes his head and bites his lip, stares into middle-space. I wonder what's on his mind.

"Can you tell me a little bit about him? How you two met?" I ask.

That brings Dave back to Earth. "Well, as I said, we both started in '62. God, I feel ancient saying that out loud. There were only about forty of us in the class, so we all kinda knew each other. Henry and I were both in Dykstra—our dorm—and hung out in that larger circle together. I do remember he had a killer record collection. Hauled it all the way from Philly. It was damn impressive."

Movies, art, books, music. Why did I never get the chance to meet my uncle? We would've hit it off so well.

"He also had, like, five or six cameras," Dave continues. "Which was a *lot* for back then; that stuff was expensive. Home movie cameras and regular film. But he didn't flaunt it, you know? You could tell it was just part of who he was. The kid was truly passionate. More than most of us in the program. Hell, I came from Woodland Hills, a twenty-minute drive from Hollywood. I mostly wanted to go to film school just 'cause I grew up so close to where movies are made. Don't get me wrong, I had a real interest. But not like Henry. You could tell film was, like, *his thing*. You know?"

"Yeah," I say. I do know. A thousand years ago, I used to feel that way about writing.

"Aside from that, he was a friendly dude. Kept to himself a lot. Never left the dorm without a camera. I do have one particular memory of him, though. It was this student dinner we went to our first semester at the Formosa Cafe."

"Isn't that place pretty famous?" I say. Images of 1950s Hollywood stars clinking martini glasses in red booths float up in my mind.

"Oh, yeah," Dave says, waving his hand. "Used to be a big-time celebrity haunt. It's still there, but the heyday has long passed. Anyway, the film school dean—Jacobs was his name—took some of us students out to dinner there at the end of our first semester. It was kind of like this celebratory, inaugural thing. Both Henry and I won awards for our final semester projects.

"But I'll never forget Henry brought his girlfriend to that dinner. Can't recall her name, but she was a mini Marilyn Monroe. No joke. An absolute knock-out. We were all jealous as hell of him."

My head spins. Is this really my uncle we're talking about? "Was this girl also in the program with you?"

"No, but she did go to UCLA," he says. "I want to say she was sociology or something. You know, I might even still have pictures from that dinner. If I can dig 'em up, happy to send them to you."

"That would be fantastic, thank you," I say. "All of this info is super helpful. I just have one last question. Did he ever talk about his family at all?" Will I be so lucky as to learn anything about the estrangement?

Dave massages his mouth with his hand. "Not that I can remember. Sorry. All I knew is that he was from Philly. He came a long way to be in L.A., and didn't seem interested in talking about his life back home. I lost touch with him after sophomore year. We had different class schedules and found our own groups to hang with. But there's one thing I can tell you for sure—he didn't graduate. At least not with our class."

I nearly drop the phone. "What? Are you sure?"

"One hundred percent. Like I said, our class was tiny. I remember everyone who was there. He might've stayed on a fifth year and graduated after me, in '67. But I have a feeling he split."

Though I had no good reason why, I'd always just assumed Henry graduated UCLA. Neither Nana nor Mom ever said anything to the contrary. Did they even know he dropped out? It seems impossible to believe they didn't. But if true, this changes things.

For one thing, it alters the possible timeline of when he came to Rosanera in the first place. He could've been here years before he died, which means shouldn't there be some local record of him living or working here? And secondly, why did he abandon film school? Hadn't it been his dream? I relay these thoughts to Dave, and he thinks for a moment.

"As I said, I wasn't close with Henry, but I always sensed there was a deeper reason for why he was in L.A.," Dave says. "More than just for school."

I lean in. "What do you mean?"

He thinks for a moment. "It seemed to me like he was trying to prove himself—which he didn't need to do, his art spoke for itself—but that doing so was always just out of reach. I remember thinking that even L.A. wouldn't be enough for him eventually. It doesn't surprise me that he might've said the hell with film school and went after something else, something he believed was more profound, more personal. L.A. is a lot of things, but profound and personal it is not. And I say this as a born-and-bred Angelino."

I turn this over in my mind. If Henry valued purpose above all else, then it's clear he was in Rosanera for a good reason. He came here on a mission, not as a shiftless wanderer. For the first time, I feel justified in my decision to come here.

I've kept Dave long enough, so I thank him again profusely for his time.

"Not a problem," he says. "Meantime, I'll look for those photos. If I find anything, I'll send them your way." I gratefully accept his offer, and we say our good-byes.

Okay. So I found out exactly nothing about the mausoleum in the photo, why Henry came to Italy, or anything about Giovanni. That sucks.

I did, however, learn he was at UCLA at least through 1964, was a talented filmmaker, and that he seemed to be running away from, and towards, something huge. I file it all away for later.

I chew my thumbnail and open the Maps app on my phone. The blue dot, where I currently sit, pulses just two miles from the pinned location at 57 Via della Servi. It's a stretch. But Rosanera seems like one of those small towns where everyone is connected in one way or other. Or remembers. I'm convinced that even if Giovanni isn't at the Via della Servi house now, someone around there must know something. The past never evaporates in places like this. It clings with belligerence to every shadowy corner, hibernating. Waiting to be reawakened.

At least that's what I'll be counting on when I knock on Giovanni's door tomorrow morning.

Chapter Ten

Los Angeles
December 1962

THE CAB DROPS them off at the iconic restaurant on Santa Monica promptly at seven-thirty. Henry doesn't feel the ground as he walks up to the Formosa Cafe's entrance with a gorgeous California-bred blonde on his arm. Is this really happening?

"I can't believe we're really here," Cherie breathes in Henry's ear, which sparks a tingling that begins in his legs but doesn't end there. "Do you think we'll see Natalie Wood?"

"Maybe," Henry replies, "but I wouldn't even notice with you here."

Cherie giggles and slaps his arm, leans into him with her breasts pushing against his shoulder. His head goes fuzzy.

The doorman greets them with a practiced nod and bow, and sweeps open the mahogany door. Henry takes Cherie's damp palm and leads her inside, where they're quickly immersed in an ambient cocoon of jazz and spirited talk. At the crowded bar, a group of men in crisp dinner jackets, unfailingly sharp and sleek, erupt into laughter and clink their martini glasses. On the wall above the bar hangs a "Meet Me At Formosa!" sign, surrounded by black-and-white signed headshots of all the A-listers who are regulars here.

"Henry! Over here," calls a towering man in a deep charcoal suit. Dr. Everson, Henry's Introduction to Motion Pictures professor, is standing up at one of the two plush red booths reserved for their group. Henry waves and guides Cherie over to the table through the richly decorated restaurant, using all his restraint not to stare at the faces in the booths as he goes. Candles flicker in dusted-gold centerpieces on every table, enhancing the subtle Oriental decor. More black-and-white stills of Hollywood stalwarts cover the dark wood-paneled walls in the dining room, leaving space only for the ornate wall sconces throughout. Strings of Christmas lights with colorful bulbs as big as grenades hang throughout the room, and someone has tossed a Santa hat on the Buddha statue in the corner. It's fourteen days until Christmas.

"Have a seat, you two," Everson says, slapping Henry on the back. "And who is this magnificent specimen of female beauty you've graced our presence with?" Cherie turns raspberry red and trickles out a nervous laugh.

"This is Cherie," Henry says to the table, hugging her with one arm. From the second booth, Dean Jacobs and the three other film students and their dates turn and smile. Henry wishes he had his camera to commemorate the exact look on all the guys' faces.

"Very pleased to meet you," says Dave Sherman, shooting up from their booth to shake her hand. Henry bites his lip to hide a smile as he and Cherie scoot into the booth next to him. Dave's probably got the strongest eye for composition among all the students in the cohort. He's damn good. But his subject matter? Not so much. He's in the same trap most filmmakers are, trying too hard to make shit into Shinola, Henry thinks. Everson and Jacobs see it too.

"So, how about a glass?" Jacobs calls to Henry and Cherie, wiggling a bottle of French red in the air. Cherie shoots Henry a look. *We can drink?* Jacobs catches her eye and winks. He's warm, lively, acutely interested in what aspiring filmmakers a third of his age want to do. Basically the opposite of what Henry ever expected from a former motion picture studio executive.

"Absolutely, sir, thank you," Henry replies, raising his empty wine glass and squeezing Cherie's thigh with his other hand.

"So," Everson says, leaning into the table with a conspiratorial grin, "what does everybody think?" He spreads his hands out around him.

"Pretty damn incredible is what first comes to mind," Dave laughs. "I grew up twenty minutes from here and have never been. I can't believe it, really. Trying not to stare too hard at everyone around me."

"Cheers to that," says Mike Carlson. His sculpted plume of shocking red hair trembles as he hastily raises his glass. Everson fills Henry's and Cherie's glasses with the Malbec passed over from Jacobs, and they all toast. Now that the whole group's here, they pass around the menus. The waiter comes, jots it all down with a curt nod, and hurries back to the kitchen.

"So, Cherie," Everson says, lighting a cigarette. "What's your story? How'd you meet Henry?"

"Oh," she says, dabbing red wine dots from her lips onto a napkin, "we're in Intro to Sociology together. Our professor makes us all sit alphabetically, strangely enough. So, you know—me, Atkins, him, Barton—we're right next to each other. We became quite well acquainted." Henry loves the lightness and lilt of her laugh, like wind chimes.

"Is that all it takes?" Dave cackles. "Did I tell you I just signed up for that class and my last name's now Banner? Guess that bumps you back a spot, Barton."

The table erupts, another round of wine is poured. Emptying half the glass in one sip, Henry gives himself over to that perfect warm zone where he feels alive again. The waiter returns with their food and everyone digs in. Cherie nibbles on her baked halibut, linen napkin folded just so on her lap, elbows the appropriate two-inch distance above the table. She stays mostly silent with a polite smile, listening to the men chatter and nodding in agreement.

Henry's first bite of mouthwatering steak au poivre turns rancid as Mike asks, "What's everyone doing for the holidays?" Why does the conversation have to turn to family?

"Grandparents are coming down from Santa Barbara," Dave says, picking up a bottle of Malbec and shaking it. He puts it back and motions to Mike to pass him a full one. "They always stay with us for Hannukah. What about you guys?"

"Back to my folks' place in Whittier," Mike says. Cherie's eyes light up.

"My family lives in Whittier, too. What part?"

"Oh, really? We're in Friendly Hills. You?"

Henry smirks. He bets the posh families there, like Mike's, are real friendly. Just like his own parents are.

"Lovely area," Cherie says, taking a sip from her glass. "We're in East Whittier. My father is a police officer. There are lots of fellow police families, and the Fraternal Order is there too, so we're right at home."

Henry shifts in the booth, rankled, and gulps another glass of wine. *Right at home.* He shoots Cherie a sideways glance. How much does she really know about her father? What he does in interrogation rooms? How often does he help, say, women whose husbands give them the belt? Or is he just another mindless authoritarian, hell-bent on protecting the select few he actually serves?

"What about you, Henry?" Everson asks, dragging on his cigarette. "Are you flying back to Philadelphia to be with your folks over Christmas?"

He feels everyone's eyes on him, and wonders if they can all see through him, into his brain, into the truth and the bleak consequences. He picks up his napkin and wipes at his mouth and damp upper lip.

"Air travel is too expensive, so we just planned for me to come home in the summer after the first year is done," he lies. Everyone nods and murmurs in understanding. Cherie tilts her chin and gives him the tight, sympathetic smile that anyone would deserve in this situation, had said person not pushed their own mother down a flight of stairs and caused her to miscarry her child, thus effectively ending all communication between said person and the rest of the family. It wasn't so much that Henry's dad was paying his tuition as he was paying for him to stay away.

"Yes, it's very costly," Cherie agrees. "So Henry can come to my house for Christmas Day instead." She breaks into a huge grin and kisses him fast on the cheek. How does he tell her that he's fine, alone in his dorm room? It's a conversation for another day.

As if on cue, Dean Jacobs rises and clinks his glass from the other booth, putting an end to the family conversation, much to Henry's immense relief.

"First, I'd like to congratulate each of our six contenders here tonight for our annual Bright Media Award," he says, looking around the table with a warm smile.

"Out of your talented class of thirty-six, each of you have shown particular promise in your first semester at UCLA's Theatre, Motion Pictures, and Radio program." He motions to both booths with his wine glass and everyone applauds. Cherie winks at Henry. Now it's her turn to squeeze his knee.

"Believe me when I say it was a very tough choice, but Dr. Everson and I selected a winner from your final projects. Each of you deserves superb recognition regardless of who wins." Henry's hands are on his thighs, still. Everson couldn't stop complimenting his project after he turned it in. Henry smiles, hovering in that wine-washed haze that tells him he's won.

"So, without further ado, I would like to offer my sincere congratulations to… David Sherman for his short film, 'In The Reeds.' Congratulations, son!" Dave makes a champion's fist, and scoots past Henry and Cherie to get his award from Jacobs. Henry is capsizing in a sea of clapping and whistling and clinking glasses and swirling smoke from dozens of burning cigarettes.

"*But*, we have another award," Jacobs says. "Now, it was only supposed to the one. But Dr. Everson and I were so impressed with the technique of another student's project, that we've created the Emerging Director Award. And this one goes to Henry Barton, for his short film, 'Another Day.' Excellent work, Henry! We're thrilled to see what's yet to come."

"That's amazing!" Cherie cries, throwing her arms around Henry's neck. But when she pulls back and sees his face, her smile drops like an anchor. "What?" She asks in a low voice. "Henry, what's wrong?"

He gives a little shake, and swigs his wine, hoping the

alcoholic warmth will pump color back into his face. He forces a smile and stands to accept the award from Jacobs.

"Thank you, Dr. Jacobs, much appreciated," he says. His brain commands his hand to become steady as iron as he raises the award to the group and sits back down.

Poison thoughts crash down on him in waves. Second place? Might as well have just actually called it "the consolation prize." What's the problem? Is he just not as talented as he thinks? Maybe he held back too much on this one. Yes, that must be it. After giving it a think, he had left out the whole thing on skin color and the perception of success, thinking that it would be too "heavy" for this project, overkill. What was he thinking? Won't make that mistake again. By leaving it out, he'd lost to Dave Sherman and his movie about the old woman at the ecological reserve or whatever. Pathetic.

"Okay, everyone, group photo!" Dave calls, waving his Kodak in the air. He calls over the waiter who, with some irritation at being summoned by an eighteen-year-old nobody, reluctantly agrees to take the picture.

Dave rushes back over to the booth and squeezes back in beside Henry and Cherie. Henry feels the flash once, twice, a third time. He just needs to *think*, and frantically counts the seconds until he can get outside and walk the entire six miles back to campus. Winding through the retreating shadows of endless neon boulevard lights, alone.

Chapter Eleven

By the time I finally park the rental Fiat on Via della Servi, I'm sweaty and flustered. I was driving up and down this godforsaken road for nearly twenty minutes, my cell reception cutting out and repeatedly losing its GPS signal. Now here I am, in my dubious parking spot that's half on the street and half on the sidewalk. A true Italian parking job.

I crack the car window, taking a deep breath of the fresh morning air and looking down the narrow cobblestone street ahead of me. Rows of charming homes made of stone and brick line either side of the road, some with decorative wrought-iron balconies only large enough to hold plants. Down a few houses on the left, an old man smokes a cigarette and reads a newspaper on his front step, a skinny black cat sprawled out at his feet.

Does this all look the same as when Henry was here? And how many times did he walk up and down this street?

I'm about to trace his very steps—into what, exactly, I have no idea. Maybe in matter of minutes, Giovanni will answer his door, take a look at the mausoleum photo, and direct me to the exact location a couple miles away. I could be standing in front of the mausoleum today, ready to uncover whatever Henry noted half a century ago.

The house number directly outside my passenger window on the right says 33. I lean forward to look to the next house and see a 35. The numbers are going up; I'm facing the right direction. Giovanni is number 57.

I'm ready to get out of the car when my phone vibrates from my bag. A pump of adrenaline jolts through my chest as I root for it. Did Bastian finally text me back? No point in pretending I haven't been eagerly awaiting that response.

No. But something equally interesting: a new email from Dave Sherman, subject "photos."

Juliet, Went on a scavenger hunt after our call. Finally found the old boxes from my UCLA years after going through every closet in the house and the attic (wife wants to kill me for the mess I made. Worth it, though). I spent the rest of the night reliving my college days, listening to records, etc. Won't bore you with an old Boomer's life, so I'll get to the point...found not one but two photos of Henry! One from the Formosa dinner I mentioned but also one where he's handing out flyers on campus for Students for a Democratic Society aka SDS. It was one of the first "lefty" college groups (wikipedia for more info).

Kind of a predecessor to the anti-war stuff. UCLA didn't have an SDS group on campus and Henry was trying to get one started I think. Had forgotten all about it. Seems like another lifetime now. Anyhow, enjoy the photos and hope they prove useful in some way. Take care—Dave."

I'm now wide awake, zooming in on the Formosa JPEG Dave sent, which is in color. There's a group of fourteen people taking up two huge horseshoe-shaped red corner booths. The empty plates in front of them signal that it's a post-meal capture. Two important-looking men in their fifties wearing sleek grey suits are craning their necks to smile at the camera, cigarettes burning between their fingers. One must be the dean Dave mentioned. The other, maybe a professor.

Squeezed into the booths around the men, twelve students and their guests, who all look like they're exactly twelve years old, also face the camera with varying degrees of grins. Smack in the middle of the second booth is Henry and his girlfriend. I enlarge their faces until they both bleed into a mirage of pixels. Dave's right, the girl is stunning. She looks like 1950s All-American sweetness personified. Petite, blonde, a tiny upturned nose. Rosy full lips pulled into an eager smile.

Henry's no ogre, either. Although he's only a couple years older than he was in the family portrait I found in Mom's closet, his features here are sharper and more defined. He's got that strong jawline and a hint of those shadowy cheekbones that casting directors across L.A.

stake their careers on. But on his face is just a ghost of a smile, unlike like everyone else around him. Why? If I were him, treated to dinner at a celebrity haunt in Hollywood with a gorgeous girlfriend, I'd be over the moon.

I swipe to the next photo. A black-and-white Henry stands in front of a campus building, handing a flyer from a stack to another student who's reaching for it. He's much more animated here than in the Formosa photo, mouth open in mid-sentence, eyes alight. Two other male students with flyer stacks stand around him, one looking straight at the camera in a candid shot, the other with arms crossed and head turned over his shoulder.

So Henry was an activist. Maybe Nana wasn't exaggerating when she told me Henry got into "radical" stuff. But was she also right about how it got him into trouble? Was it some kind of activism thing in L.A. that made Henry come here to Rosanera? I can't see an obvious connection, but I'm more anxious than ever to find out.

And there may be someone who lives on this very street that can tell me.

With renewed vigor, I get out of the Fiat and huff up the *strada* to number 57, my mind and pulse racing. When I stop in front of the house, it looks just how it did on Google Earth. A brown stone structure with a faded red door—paint chipped and splintered, hinges lined with cobwebs, a tattered brown doormat in front. Above the door hangs a black iron lantern speckled with rust, its dim lightbulb still glowing from the night before. There's a chipped ceramic bowl of water on the ground, presumably for a cat. The fresh liquid inside appears to be the only thing about this property that has been updated in the last five decades.

I ball up my sweaty fist and knock before I can talk myself out of it. What am I going to say? What if Giovanni answers? What if he *doesn't*? I don't have much time to think about either scenario because the door creaks open to reveal a man squinting out at me from a dark hallway. His rumpled, striped pajama pants and crinkled white undershirt lead me to understand that he was asleep about two minutes ago. He wipes his mouth and says, "*Si, che cos'è?*"

One thing is immediately clear: whoever this is, it's definitely not Giovanni. The guy looks to be around my age, which would make him nonexistent when Henry died in 1971. I don't know if I'm relieved or disappointed.

"*Buongiorno*," I say. "*Mi chiamo* Juliet. Umm—do you speak English?" He narrows his eyes.

"You are lost?" he asks in a thick accent. "The main street is that way." He points over my shoulder back the way I came.

"Oh, no, not lost," I say. "I actually have a question for you. Probably a very strange question, but— " He just keeps staring with those squinted, sleepy eyes and brow furrowed. *Oh, just say it already!*

"Is there a Giovanni who lives here? Or maybe did years ago? I'm asking because I think he may have known my uncle." I blurt it all out in rapid succession and feel so idiotic that I want to turn and run. But he straightens and opens the door wider.

"Giovanni is my father." The fatigue falls from his face, replaced by curiosity. "You say he knows your uncle?"

I stare, unbelieving. I'd expected him to slam the door in my face, leaving me to trudge back down the street past the deflated old man and cat.

"Ye-es, I think so," I say.

He smiles ruefully. "You came at bad time," he says.

"Oh, it's too early. I'm sorry, I can come back later—"

"No, not that," he says. "He go yesterday to fishing. With his friend. Every year they go to sea, but mostly to drink. No fish." He makes the bottle-tipping motion with his hand and grins.

Seriously? By some unimaginable stroke of luck, Giovanni is still alive and lives at this address, except he's out in the middle of the ocean.

"I see. Do you know when he'll be back?"

The guy screws up his face and thinks. "*Domenica.* Sunday. Five days."

"Great, I'll just come back then," I say. "No big deal." Though of course it's a big deal, and five days might as well be five years. I turn to leave.

"No," he protests, reaching out. "It's okay. I am happy to talk with you. You came all the way from America, obviously. Maybe I can help. *Mi chiamo* Alessio, by the way," he says. We shake hands, and he seems to suddenly remember he's standing in his pajamas.

"*Un momento*, okay?" he holds up a finger. "Give me one moment to switch clothes and I return."

Before I can reply, he disappears into the house and I stand awkwardly on the front step. I'm sure Alessio's a real peach, but there's no point in talking to him. I know he isn't going to have a clue as to what I'm talking about. I just want to ask Giovanni himself.

Alessio comes back fully dressed a couple minutes later. I notice he's wearing those European sneakers, fashionable and sleek with a thin sole, so unlike the giant white monstrosities that American men strap onto their feet.

"Please, come in," he says, opening the door all the way. He sees my uncertainty and gives a comforting smile. "Or if you prefer, we can talk outside."

"No, it's fine," I say. "Thanks." I feel like a fool. What's he going to do, murder me?

I follow him into the living room where he goes from window to window, opening the heavy brown curtains, which look like they haven't been parted since Moses did the Red Sea. He turns on a tacky crystal lamp with a shade as big as a beach umbrella. I scan the room. What I see is very likely the exact same layout Henry witnessed half a century ago.

Rigid furniture, a worn thatched recliner, beat-down sofa, and faded wallpaper peeling at the top corners. The smell of ancient cigarette smoke possesses the room like a demon. Then it hits me what's really missing—a woman's touch. The place has a distinct bachelor feel, and I get the sense it's always been that way. Where is Alessio's mother?

Alessio turns to me and shrugs. "Okay?" he asks, as if nothing could possibly be done to improve the room.

I sit on the sofa, Alessio in the recliner across from me, and I begin my story. His expression shifts from intrigue to surprise to confusion as I talk.

"Wow," he says when I'm finished, like anyone would. "First I must say my father has never told me about any American friends at all, including someone named Henry." Alessio must see my shoulders slump because he continues on quickly: "But this is not surprising, as he don't talk much. He is—how you say—very private."

Well, that's great to hear. If he barely speaks to his own son, what the hell is he going to tell me, a perfect stranger? Either way, Giovanni is a dead-end until he gets back from his fishing trip. That being said, I'm anxious to move on to Plan B—starting my search for the mausoleum at the local cemeteries.

I get ready to thank Alessio for his time and make my exit when he asks to see the mausoleum photo. It didn't even occur to me to think Alessio might recognize it, but why not? I take it out of my bag and hand it to him. He scrutinizes it for a few seconds, turns it over to read the bizarre inscription, then flips it over again.

"I don't know it, but could be here," he says, running a hand over his morning stubble. His chin is a little too short and nose a little too long for him to be considered handsome in the conventional sense, but he's not altogether unattractive. "It is a very European design, like your friend say. This was in with my father's name and address?" He looks up at me.

"Yes. Do you think he'll know where it is? What it means?"

"I honestly cannot say. There is a chance."

Time to get out of here. "We'll see, I guess," I say, rising from my seat. "Thanks for your help. I'd better get started making my rounds at the cemeteries. If it's okay, I'll come by again on Sunday after your dad gets home—that is, if I haven't already found what I'm looking for." My smile feels too wide and bright, and Alessio picks up on it.

"But you are really going to search for this all by yourself?" He rises to meet me, eyebrows knitted together.

"That's the plan. Why, you think I can't handle it?" He's not sure if I'm teasing or not. To be honest, neither am I.

"I'm only saying there are thousands of *tombe* at these cemeteries. It might be good to have someone to help you. It will go double fast. You try one area, I do the other, no?" He points quickly back and forth between us, as if we're already a long-standing team.

My first instinct is to shut this down right now. I only met Alessio ten minutes ago, and among literally everything else I don't know about him, I have no idea how keen his sense of detail is. What if he just walks right past the mausoleum? I, on the other hand, have studied this photo so many times that I could find it in my sleep.

But I have to concede that this mausoleum search is going to be a huge solo undertaking. Maybe it wouldn't hurt to have someone help out, at least for the first couple cemeteries. If he turns out to be super weird or pisses me off, I can always tell him to get lost and finish on my own.

"You honestly have nothing better to do?" I ask him. "What about your job?" I have a vague hope that he's employed.

"I am a waiter. I work in the night shift, not until later," he says, spreading his hands as if that's that.

I sigh. Something tells me I'm going to regret this, but the words spill out before I can take them back.

"Fine," I say. "Let's go."

Chapter Twelve

Los Angeles
Thanksgiving Day 1963

"Jimmy, go in the kitchen and bring me out another beer, would you?" Cherie's father says to his son.

The boy leaps up from the floor, where he was laying sprawled on his belly, chin propped in his hands, watching TV. "Sure, Pop."

"And ask your mother if she needs any help while you're in there," he adds.

From the sofa next to Cherie in her family's living room, Henry sips a glass of Coca-Cola. He watches Jimmy obediently trot into the kitchen and remembers when he'd tried that with his own parents years ago—to anticipate their needs, to do whatever they asked of him, to make them believe he mattered.

In the end, it never worked. Which is why he is here,

on the opposite coast, having dinner with his girlfriend's family on Thanksgiving Day. People his own parents will never meet, or even know exist.

"You okay, sweetie?" Cherie smiles at Henry, patting his thigh. A little too high up on the femur for her father's liking, Henry can see.

"Never better," Henry says, nonchalantly trying to move her hand back to her own lap. Michael Atkins' glare shoots knives at him from across the room. Henry knows Cherie's dad doesn't like him. Whether or not it's personal, though, he's not entirely sure. Does it really matter?

Jimmy comes back to the living room with his father's beer. "Here you are, sir," he says. Michael cracks a stiff smile and ruffles the boy's blonde hair.

"Thank you, Jim," he says, sipping the foam. Henry wants to yank it out of his hand and guzzle glass after glass. It feels like the suburban living room is digesting him alive, one tiny inch at a time.

"Does your mother need any help in there, Jimmy?" Cherie's grandmother says. She's on the loveseat on the opposite side of the room. Cherie's grandfather is slumped next to her, a silent, crumpled man with an oxygen tank resting at his feet.

Jimmy looks flustered. "I forgot to ask," he says.

"Oh, well, that's alright, I'll go see for myself," the grandmother says, starting to get up. Before anyone can protest, Cherie's mother Alice comes into the room. She wipes her damp brow and tightens her stained apron around her tiny waist. It's obvious who Cherie gets her petite, shapely figure from.

"No, no, Mom," Alice says hastily to the old lady, "don't get up, everything's almost done. I'm just coming in because Johnson should be on TV soon."

It's only been six days since President Kennedy was shot dead in Texas. And in that dizzying span of barely a week, Johnson's been sworn in, Kennedy buried, his supposed killer murdered (it's so obvious to Henry that Oswald's nothing but a fall guy, *come on*), and the Warren Commission created. *So obviously*, Henry thinks, *it makes total sense to follow a mindless tradition of cramming turkey, stuffing, and wine down our throats like nothing's any different.*

"Sit here, Ma," Cherie says, and scoots over closer to Henry on the sofa. Alice sits down and gives her daughter a warm smile and kiss on the head. Henry can't conjure up a single instance where his mother would ever do the same to him.

"Oh!" Alice says. "The Vice—the President is coming on right now." Sure enough, the solemn black-and-white face of Lyndon B. Johnson fills the television screen.

"Tonight, on this Thanksgiving, I come before you to ask your help, to ask your strength, to ask your prayers that God may guard this Republic and guide my every labor," Johnson is saying. "All of us have lived through seven days that none of us will ever forget. We are not given the divine wisdom to answer why this has been, but we are given the human duty of determining what is to be, what is to be for America, for the world, for the cause we lead, for all the hopes that live in our hearts."

When Johnson's speech concludes minutes later, Alice and the grandmother are pushing crumpled Kleenexes into their eyes. Cherie gives her mother a sidelong look, and Henry looks down at his hands to hide a smile. Finally, she's starting to get it. To look at her parents in a different light, and notice the cracks in the Americana facade.

No doubt Kennedy's death is horrific. But is it really any worse than the violence, lies, and exploitation that so many people unjustly suffer from at the hands of this cold, capitalist machine called America? Is everyone to believe that human lives aren't worth more than the relative profit they generate for the country's GDP?

"May God help us all," Cherie's grandmother moans. Henry prickles with irritation. Alice stands and wipes her eyes.

"Alright, everyone," she says, "let's get the food on the table. Kids?" Cherie and Jimmy get up and follow her into the kitchen.

"Want to give me a hand over here, son?" Cherie's father bellows across the room at Henry, gesturing to his in-laws on the loveseat.

"Of course," Henry says, crossing over to help the grandmother up as Michael offers his arm to the grandfather.

"Oh, thank you, dear," the old woman says to Henry, patting his arm. "Aren't you a gentleman."

Michael glares at Henry, and Henry tries not to flinch.

Cherie's father is only a couple inches taller than him, but at least forty pounds heavier—all muscle. A razor-sharp part cuts through the right side of his black, gelled hair, making his square jaw and clean-shaven face even more severe looking. Here in his own living room, Michael appears only marginally less threatening than the first time Cherie introduced him to Henry, when he was clad in his LAPD inform, enormous hands resting on his shiny black belt decorated with weapons.

After all the food makes its way to the table, everyone sits down and bows their heads while Alice says grace. Michael carves the turkey, and plates and bowls circulate the table. Henry passes the Betty Crocker boxed scalloped potatoes and Ocean Spray canned cranberry sauce to his left.

"Henry, we're certainly glad you could join us for Thanksgiving," Alice says from one end of the table. "Going all the way back to the East Coast is very costly, I'm sure. I bet your parents miss having you there today."

Henry's throat constricts, turning the potatoes in his esophagus into cement as he chews and swallows.

"Thank you for having me, Mrs. Atkins," he says. "Everything's delicious." Then he recites his memorized script: "And yes, air travel is too expensive during the holidays, so I stay here."

"That, *and*, he needs to stay here over break to finish his fantastic film for Cinematography class before it's due," Cherie announces, nudging Henry's elbow. "He's the best in his class, you know. Everyone in the Motion Picture department talks about Henry's movies."

"I don't know about that," he says, although he feels like it's true. But is it really? He knows he's talented. His professors and other students tell him all the time. But ever since Dave Sherman won that award last year, Henry can't allow himself to be fully convinced of anything.

"So, what kind of pictures do you make, Henry?" Cherie's grandmother asks. "Westerns? Detective films?" Henry stares at her. Seriously?

"Uh, no, ma'am," he says. "I try to stay away from the more mainstream films. I like to make things that are a bit more interesting—you know, that show the reality of life. Not so much the glitzy glam of typical Hollywood. For instance, I'm really influenced by Federico Fellini." Everyone at the table besides Cherie stares at each other, then back at him.

"What I mean to say is," Henry continues, "I think that films aren't meant only for entertainment. They should also be enlightening, you know? Leave the audience thinking about something they haven't considered before."

"Well," the grandmother laughs, "Not me. I simply like to be entertained." *Of course you do*, Henry thinks. He inclines his head, shifts in his seat.

"Yes," he ventures, "but I think that there's a lot of interesting, new things going on in the country that people should pay attention to."

"Like what?" Michael asks sharply from the other end of the table.

"Well, for one thing, music," Henry replies. "If you

think about it, Elvis was really just the start. Now you have other songwriters like Bob Dylan. Or that English band, The Beatles."

"Oh, nonsense," the grandmother says, waving her hand. "I heard of that 'Beatlemania,' or whatever they're calling it in over there in England, on the morning news last week. Just a ridiculous fad. Don't young people have anything more pressing to think about than rock and roll music? Our President was killed, for heaven's sake."

"Yes, but why is that a bad thing?" Henry asks. Mouths are agape. Even the barely cognizant grandfather seems to snap to attention. Cherie's father drops his fork onto his plate and leans forward on his elbows. His eyes are narrow, simmering slits. He reminds Henry of that officer back in Philadelphia, the one who humiliated him about Judy Heller a thousand years ago.

"Excuse me, son?" Michael says.

"Of course it's not good that the President was killed," Henry rushes to say. "I just mean, why is it a bad thing that people are thinking of rock and roll music? Looking toward the future? Trying to find better ways to express themselves? Music, films, painting, what have you. That's why art exists. What's the point of just doing it to be *entertained*? People should be thankful that these new ways of thinking are coming out."

"I hardly think so," the grandmother huffs. "If you ask me, the country is going to hell in a handbasket. Just look at that Malcolm X—an odious man. Not to mention all that uprising in the South. Now, I understand colored folks haven't had it the best. But this is all too much, too soon. Everyone, colored or not, is getting too outspoken, in my opinion. I'm even afraid to go downtown these days. You never know when some trouble may start."

"Okay, but I hardly think that—"

"Who pays your tuition at UCLA, Henry?" Michael interrupts. Startled into silence, Henry feels his face blossom with heat.

"My—father does."

Michael's eyes bear into Henry's like steel rivets. "Then maybe a bit of thankfulness for the 'old way of doing things' is due."

Cherie throws down her napkin on her plate and crosses her arms. "Oh, please, Daddy. Give it a rest already."

Henry turns to her, shocked. Is she really standing up to her father?

Michael goes still, his eyes on her like a lion's locked onto prey. "What did you just say to me, young lady?"

"Look, what Henry's saying isn't out of bounds," Cherie says. "New ways of thinking *are* coming out. Especially on campus. It's what the SDS is trying to do."

"And please enlighten me as to what the SDS is," her father says.

She rolls her eyes at him. "Students for a Democratic Society. It started at Michigan last year, and all the big campuses are doing it." A muscle twitches in Michael's jaw, but it doesn't stop her. "They make some good points, alright? They say that America doesn't work to achieve international peace or economic justice. Instead it puts money and profit above everything else. And also, until *everyone* has a say in this country—that means people like Malcolm X, and *all* colored folks"—she shoots a pointed glance at her grandmother—"then it's not really a democracy at all, is it?"

Henry is floored. A year ago, Cherie called her father "sir," and now she's arguing the merits of the SDS with him.

"Cherie, they're nothing but *Communists*," her father emphasizes. "It's how they rope in nice girls like you. They try to act like they're doing something 'for the people,' like the French Revolution. But it's Communism, plain and simple. And it's dangerous. How thick-headed are you? What do you think we just finished doing over in Korea, for Christ's sake?" His voice is a crescendo of self-righteousness.

"Oh, both of you, stop it!" Alice says, pointing at them with her fork. "It's Thanksgiving, for goodness' sake. And it's been an unspeakable week. Can't we all just be grateful we're here together?"

A temporary silence falls over the table. The only sounds are forks and knives scraping against dishes as everyone pushes their food around on their plates. Moments later, the short-lived truce is broken.

"All I'm saying is that it seems strange. You all have to think it's *strange*, don't you?" Cherie asks her father. He lets out a long exhale and lifts his chin toward the ceiling.

"We all have to think that *what* is strange?" he says, his rage barely contained.

"That Communism is always everyone's reason for anything that's gone wrong in the world," she says.

"Cherie, *let it go*," Alice says. But Cherie doesn't listen. She's too fired up now.

"Take Kennedy's assassination, okay? I'm only saying that on campus, people are talking that it couldn't be just Oswald. How could the President of the United States have been assassinated by just one man?"

"And why the hell not?" her father growls.

"Well," Cherie says, her voice getting louder, "how about the fact the government made him look like a Commie so that everyone would believe it was him? He was set up to take the fall."

Now it's Michael's turn to throw down his napkin. "Interestingly enough, this all sounds like something your friend Henry would think," he says with mock enthusiasm. "Is it, Henry? Do you, in fact, share my daughter's beliefs? Or perhaps planted them in her head to begin with?"

"Michael, please!" Alice cries.

"She wasn't like this until she met you," Michael sneers at Henry.

"Stop blaming him, Daddy!" Cherie shouts, pushing her chair back. "I know it's impossible for you to think this of a woman, but I've got a mind of my own. Henry's just helped open my eyes to a lot of things that I never saw before. And not just him, but lots of other people on campus. Things are changing, times are changing. You can't stop it. None of you can."

Her eyes are lasers scanning the table. Alice's mouth moves but no words come out. Her grandmother gapes, clutches her necklace, and next to her, Jimmy's chin trembles and his eyes fill with tears. Cherie scoffs and runs from the table; moments later the front door slams shut behind her. Henry quickly follows her outside.

She's on the front porch, her face contorted with emotion as she lights a cigarette and takes a rakish draw on it. She looks different, feral. Like a switch has been flipped somewhere deep inside. When she meets his gaze, her green eyes are fluorescent, stinging. And then it hits Henry in a way it's never landed before—he is totally, desperately in love with her.

"Don't say anything," she says, exhaling smoke and pressing her body against his. He feels the warmth coming off her in unbearable waves, like radiation. "I just want to go to the car. Now." She looks at him meaningfully.

So they do.

Chapter Thirteen

MY SKIN'S BURNING as I weave through the makeshift aisles of graves. The sunscreen I slathered on earlier probably wore off two cemeteries ago, likely hastened by my profuse sweating under this blinding nuclear explosion called the August sun in Italy.

I tug on my short sleeves, trying in vain to cover more of my arms. You'd think my darker olive skin could take this, but no. Alessio on the other hand seems unbothered; his brown epidermis must be long impervious to the scorching sun rays. He plods along the southern side of the cemetery, dutifully glancing down at his phone screen at the picture of the mausoleum I shared with him. The guy really is trying. Why, I don't understand, but I don't question it. I have to admit the whole process has indeed moved along efficiently with his help.

But that doesn't change the fact that we've come up with nothing—a truth that fills me with growing dread, although I've managed to suppress it with a Xanax here and there, snuck from the stash in the front pocket of my jeans. We're at Rosanera's sixth mass place of rest already. Only four more to go.

Alessio and I have already established an organized cemetery search system: make a loop around the perimeter first, me in one direction and him in the other. This lets us survey the widest realm of possibilities as well as the first few rows in. Then we work our way into the middle of the cemetery. He takes one half and I the other.

There's been a few false alarms. In the last cemetery, Alessio shouted, "Here!" I ran halfway across the cemetery, leaping over graves like a desperate kid in an obstacle course before coming to a halt when he called, "Ah, sorry."

Twice before, I also thought I'd hit the jackpot. In the tiny pen of tombstones and sculptures nestled next to the five-hundred-year-old *Chiesa Cristo de Eternita*, I could have sworn I was approaching the mausoleum from the side, only to let out a stream of curses when I got around to the front. The other false sighting happened in a particularly somber churchyard where a funeral was in process. The attendees glowered at my irreverent jaunt amongst the tombs.

"Nothing yet?" Alessio calls to me now from the other side of the grassy expanse. *No, I'm standing right here in front of it but I just didn't bother to tell you,* I think irritably.

God, I'm an asshole. He's just trying to help. So I smile and shake my head, shrugging as if I'm unbothered by this fruitless search. He returns my shrug and smile and then keeps going. I wish I had his casual demeanor.

Italians are a strange breed. They seem unbothered by life's most daunting problems, but present them with an unripe tomato and they'll lose their mind for an hour.

A wave of relief washes over me as I come to a shady patch under a giant, gnarled ficus, but the feeling evaporates just as quickly as I look ahead. The remaining part of my section is only headstones—no more mausoleums. Meaning no chance that it's here.

I lean against the tree and close my eyes. My eyelids feel like luggage racks bowing under the weight of a hundred suitcases. I should be optimistic. We have six more cemeteries to search. And even if they all turn up nothing, there's still the library microfiche archives, the medical examiner, and most of all, Giovanni. But I can't help the unease that's soaked into my bones; the worry that this, like everything else in my life, will all come to nothing.

To distract myself, I check my phone. My heart stutters when I see the text notification on the screen—it's from Bastian.

Bonjour chérie, sorry for the delay in writing. Busy week here. You are so close, we must find a chance to see each other before you fly all the way back to America. It has already been 5 years! What is this work trip for? When will you be done? I will wait to hear more. Bises, XO B

The message makes me way happier than it reasonably should. Smiling, I walk over to join Alessio. He sees me coming and returns the smile.

"You look much happier now," he says. "Good news on the phone?"

"Oh," I say, shoving the phone back into my pocket as if it's nothing, "just texting with a friend. They're in Paris."

"In Paris? They are visiting?"

"No, they—he lives there. He's a sommelier, and was hosting this wine tour thing I went on when I was in Paris a long time ago. Just someone I keep in touch with from time to time." Why am I even telling Alessio all this? A sly grin creeps over his face.

"Ah, I see, *a friend*," he nods. "That you meet once, but keep in touch with for many years." He chuckles and starts walking again. I'm annoyed and flustered, though I have no reason to be. Maybe it's because during those two fleeting weeks with Bastian, I had come alive in a way I never had before, or again after. I met Matt a few months after that, and we started dating. Now I wonder if I'd ever loved Matt as much as I thought I did, or if I was trying to Frankenstein a lingering conduit to what I'd experienced with Bastian.

And then there were Bastian's parting words to me, warm and light on my ear, moments before I got into the idling taxi in a daze. And as the car drove away, the unshakable feeling that I'd lost something profound forever.

"Yes, he is a *friend*," I tell Alessio, because it's true. That's all he is. "I was in Paris by myself, doing the whole solo travel thing one summer through Europe. It's fun and all, but it's also nice to meet people and hang out along the way."

"You're fast," he says. I'm ready to jump on him for whatever that means before I realize he's changing the subject. "I still have more to go." He points to his remaining section of the cemetery.

"No, I just had it easier this time," I say. "Less mausoleums in my section, more plain old headstones." He watches me squint up at him and frown at the boiling sun.

"Go back and sit under the tree," he says. "I can finish here alone."

"No, it's fine, I don't mind." I can't possibly be so selfish as to let this guy do my hunting for me while I sit and text men in Paris. Plus, he and I have been powering through the cemeteries with such fierce concentration that we haven't had a chance to talk. I still know nothing about him or his father. Maybe if I at least had an idea of what Giovanni did for a living, or where he went to college, I could begin to piece together where his and Henry's lives might have intersected.

"So tell me about your father," I say. "What does he do? What's he like?"

Alessio plods alongside of me in silence for a few beats. "What does he do?" he repeats.

"Yeah, like, for work."

"He no longer works. He has seventy-four years old."

"Okay, but what did he do when he did work?"

"As long as I live, he works as an auto mechanic."

I can't see how a mechanic would have anything to do with Henry the photographer, activist, or Californian.

"You say 'as long as I was alive.' Did he do something else before you were born?"

Alessio's face darkens, almost imperceptibly, but I see it. He clears his throat. "He was in Vietnam."

Surprised, I stop walking. "He was in the war? I didn't even know Italy sent troops there."

"They didn't. He was a journalist." Alessio also stops and looks over his shoulder at the baked-brown hills in the distance, now partially shrouded in the shadows of the waning day. So how exactly did Giovanni go from journalist to mechanic? It's not exactly a natural transition.

"That must have been incredible," I say. "I mean, terrifying, but incredible. To be part of history like that, watching it unfold, and reporting on it to the rest of the world." A flicker of jealousy passes through me. What I would give for my writing to be so impactful. Or, you know, even existent.

Alessio chews on his bottom lip and looks back at me. "I wouldn't know," he says, and starts walking again. "He does not ever speak about it. My mother told me once he was *una anima tormenta*. Something like 'tortured soul' in English. Those were her words exactly, I will never forget."

It's the first time Alessio has mentioned his mother. I want to ask about her, but I get the sense that it's off-limits, at least for now.

"Well, I'm sure that happened to everyone who was there," I say reassuringly. "It must've been traumatic to be there at all, even if you weren't in a combat role."

Alessio's face is ashen, subdued. "I believe it. No more writing for him. He worked only on cars after that, barely speak to anyone. I know there was more she did not reveal to me, but I did not ask. I was young. Now that she is gone, I deeply regret not doing so, as I will never know. He would never tell me himself, and I dare not bring it up."

Now that she is gone. I must ask. "Alessio, did your mother pass away?"

He glances at me quickly as we walk. "Yes. A long time ago. I had ten years old. Cancer. Of the breast."

"I'm so sorry." If I'd lost Mom at that age, I'd probably have been sent to live with Nana back east. I have no other family. Even though he's still alive (I think), my father might as well be dead too. He cut all ties with Mom and me when I was in kindergarten when he left for greener pastures. Where those may be, I don't know or care. He doesn't need me, so I don't need him. It's that simple.

In a bizarre way, both Alessio and I having lost our mothers feels like an affirmation to me that our lives are in some way linked, and I'm meant to be here on this journey. And though the connection between Henry and Giovanni is still far from clear to me, at least I now know Giovanni once worked in a creative capacity as a writer. Artists associate with other artists—so maybe he and Henry met in Rosanera through those shared interests. I mention this to Alessio.

He cocks his head and squints. "It is possible, I guess," he says. Then his eyes suddenly widen. "But when you meet him, please, you must promise not to mention that I told you anything about his past. He would kill me, honestly. Just ask him about your uncle and nothing more."

I'm taken aback by Alessio's plea. He seems legitimately

terrified of his father. What in God's name must Giovanni be like, then? My confidence about meeting him begins to wane.

"I won't, Alessio, don't worry," I say. He looks mildly relieved.

We come to the end of his section of the cemetery and, shocker, the mausoleum isn't here. We stand for a moment together in shared silence looking out on all the buried loved ones who aren't ours. The sun has started moving lower on the horizon, but its intensity hasn't wavered. Doling out one long, endless burn.

"On to the next one?" Alessio finally asks.

"On to the next," I say.

I have miles to go before I sleep.

Chapter Fourteen

Los Angeles
February 1964

HENRY PAUSES UNDER the colossal palm tree outside Dykstra Hall to light his joint and inhales big. Nothing like morning sex followed by some strong grass to kick start the day. He heads east toward the Fine Arts building to class, nodding to familiar faces here and there. Cherie's scent lingers on his skin, and he feels invincible. At least until he gets to Cartwright's class.

Cartwright is the only nut Henry can't crack in the program, and it drives him crazy. Dean Jacobs hand-picked the man for the Motion Picture program. Cartwright resigned from his twenty-five-year post at Paramount as VP of Production to teach here on campus. But nothing about an academic setting has tempered the guy's industry demeanor. Cartwright shows up to class in those crisp executive suits, hair greased, piercing blue eyes ready to indict any student who claims familiarity with the history, culture, advent, or mechanics of filmmaking.

It is precisely this aloof austerity that drove Henry to take Directing Cameras in the first place. The course catalogue described the class as "an investigation of expressive potential of image within and beyond narrative from directorial perspective. Experiments with working methodologies that stimulate visual creativity and positioning image as fundamental element of cinematic expression."

He wants the challenge. He needs it. The accolades from his fellow students and professors come too willingly and undermine Henry's motivation. He's disturbed that it's becoming easier for him to fall prey to inertia, give in to distraction, get lazy. Is this part of the artist's curse? To be apathetic to praise, and instead crave excoriation? Is this why so many creatives live in a purgatory of gloom? The thought makes him uneasy. He forces it to the back of his mind, where it'll no doubt float up and confront him at two o'clock in the morning, just like all his other fears.

He reaches the Fine Arts building just as its bell tower begins its hourly clanging. Henry takes one last puff of the joint, tosses it, and heads inside to class. He swings into his usual seat in the back of the room, and smiles as he takes out his notebook. Cartwright's going over German Expressionism today, and Henry is certain he's more prepared than anyone else on the subject. His high school fascination with Bertolt Brecht gave him that leg up. Brecht's whole Epic Theatre thing? Henry knows it inside and out—deliberately perform the play so the audience feels alienated and detached from the characters. (All he has to do is imagine his parents). This forces the audience to focus on the cold, hard subject of the play instead of getting tangled up in flighty empathy for the characters—a technique that can cultivate activism. Not entertainment: enlightenment. What Brecht did for the stage Henry would do for film. There's no way Cartwright won't be impressed with that.

At that moment, the door opens and Cartwright walks to the broad desk at the front. He meticulously arranges his materials neatly upon it. He sets down his coffee mug, from which vapors of steam rise, and takes a pack of cigarettes and lighter from the front pocket of his shirt, laying them squarely next to the mug. He shuffles his stack of notes until they're completely flush on all sides.

"Good morning," Cartwright says, his gaze severe as always. "Today we're continuing our work on camera techniques with Fritz Lang and his work on *M*. Specifically, I'd like us to think about how novelist Graham Greene compared the film to," he peers through the wire-rimmed bifocals on the end of his nose at a paper on the desk, "'looking through the eye-piece of a microscope, through which the tangled mind is exposed, laid flat on the slide.'"

Before anyone can answer, the classroom door creaks open. Henry turns. A dark-haired young man is standing with his hand on the doorknob. Although what he's wearing is ordinary—a cream-colored t-shirt and jeans with scuffed black boots—Henry senses that the guy himself is anything but average. Something about the way his grey eyes sweep the classroom. They're wolfish, yet shy.

He parts his full lips to speak. "Sorry to interrupt. Is this Directing Cameras?"

Cartwright straightens. "It is."

The guy looks relieved. "I just enrolled here at the university this morning," he says. "I'm in this class. May I?" He gestures with his brown shoulder bag toward the rows of seats.

Cartwright studies him for a moment, his expression unreadable. "By all means," he finally says.

The few female students can't look away from the guy as he takes the seat diagonally in front of Henry. He's either unaware of the attention or doesn't care. He unzips his bag and takes out a pen and two black-and-white composition notebooks with heavily creased covers. Henry catches a glimpse of Kerouac's *The Dharma Bums* and a book by Baudelaire as the guy closes his bag. He watches the guy curve over his notebook, observing the calm in his eyes, the pensive way he turns his pen around and around in his fingers. Although he can't reasonably explain why, Henry feels like he already knows this person, has known him for some time.

Cartwright continues at the front of the class, outlining the main tenets of German Expressionism and how it relates to film. Henry tries to shift his attention back to the professor and think of a way he can naturally work in Brecht's notion of Epic Theatre in response to the lecture.

"So," Cartwright says, "you can look at Expressionism

as a depiction of what's coming from *within* the artist, not the outside world as it is. Especially fear and anxiety. Lang used a variety of direction techniques in *M* to achieve this, to allow for a state of confusing, altered reality for the audience. Letting the audience sort it out for themselves. Thoughts?"

Henry sits up straighter in his chair and gets ready to roll out his insight on Brecht when the new guy starts talking.

"Well," the guy says in a soft, yet clear voice (and was there just a touch of a Southern accent in there, too?), "this is pretty common for German Modernist thought in general. Nietzsche wrote that 'what is great in man is that he is a bridge and not a goal: what can be loved in man is that he is a going-over and a going-under.' Meaning, artists should offer a bridge to understanding a person's own thoughts and feelings about the world—not just outright tell them how it should be."

Students are turning around in their seats to stare at him. Henry can't help but lean forward on his desk, too, hands tingling. He's never met anyone in the program who talks or thinks like this. Or anyone, for that matter, ever.

"Actually," the guy continues, unfazed by the attention, "there was this group called the Bridge Artists that believed this in the early 1900s, right when Expressionism started. They wrote this whole manifesto called the *Bridge to Utopia*. If I remember right, it said something about how their subversive art could build a 'bridge' to Utopia.

Their idea of utopia being a magical place where the youth smashes the status quo and leads the future."

For the first time Henry has ever witnessed, Cartwright looks astonished. The left side of the professor's mouth curls into a smile.

"Your knowledge of Expressionism is impressive," he says, drawing a cigarette out of the pack on his desk. "Not many people study the Germans anymore. It's no longer in vogue, shall we say." He pauses, tapping the butt of the unlit cigarette on the desk. "What is your name?"

The guy doesn't flinch or flush, just simply closes his tattered notebook and sits back in his chair.

"Jim Morrison," he says.

Chapter Fifteen

My head's throbbing so hard as I walk up to the Rosanera library that I feel like it'll bounce right off my neck. I have no clue how much I actually drank last night, but it must have been colossal, even for me. I lost track after the second bottle of wine. From what little I recall, it was a lovely fruit-forward, medium-bodied Chianti that served as consolation prize for Strike One—failure to locate the mausoleum in the greater Rosanera region. Yesterday, Alessio and I finished checked the remaining cemeteries, and it yielded the same results as the day before: absolutely nothing.

I'm still trying to process it. On some level, I expected this to happen. Even despite Colette telling me the odds were good. Wouldn't it have been way too convenient for the mausoleum to just…be here? Or, what if it *is* here, but Alessio and I missed it? But we both had our eyes peeled the whole time. We looked at every damn grave. There's just no way. I can't even allow myself to linger on that possibility, or I'll go insane. The thought of retracing my steps in each of those ten cemeteries makes me want to give up on the whole endeavor.

There's no point in turning this over in my head anymore. I need to move on to my other leads, which is why I'm at the library. Their website says their microfiche archives go back at least a hundred years. Henry's accident may have been reported in Rosanera's local paper. If it was, any details will help.

I swing open the heavy door and gratefully accept the blast of air conditioning that hits me from head to toe as I enter. Maybe my hangover will ease off in here.

At the front desk sits a woman about my age, who smiles as I approach. The nameplate on the counter in front of her says Gina. I introduce myself and fumble around foolishly in Italian for exactly two seconds before she tells me she speaks English. I thank her profusely.

"Not a problem," she replies. "What do you need?"

I give her the rundown of what I'm looking for and why. She raises her eyebrows, and I get the feeling that this may be the first interesting inquiry she's gotten in months.

"The thing is," I say, a little awkwardly, "I'd need your help going through the archives. As you can tell, my Italian is embarrassingly bad. It shouldn't take too long, though, since I know the date of the accident. I'm guessing we'd just need to look at the newspapers for a few days afterward to see if anything was reported, right?"

"Exactly what I'm thinking," she says, coming out

from behind the counter. "And I'm happy to help. It's a slow day. Our microfiche room is all the way in the back, just follow me."

Relief floods my veins like opium. I follow her back through the rows of bookshelves. The further we go, the stronger that delightful old book smell becomes. You can go to any library in the world and that same universal scent will be waiting. Kind of like a McDonald's, but in a non-shitty way.

Gina's kitten heels click on the wide, worn wood floorboards ahead of me like a metronome. It's so hypnotic and comforting that I'm almost regretful when we come to the green door labeled *Archivi*.

"Here we go," Gina says, flipping through her massive key ring to locate the right key. She slides it into the lock, jiggles the handle and flips on the lights. The overhead fluorescents buzz and flicker.

"Okay, Juliet." She motions me over to the storage cabinets against the back wall. I love how she says my name: *Zhoo-lee-aht*. It's smooth and desirable and unblemished. Everything I am not.

She runs a finger across the labels on the front of the cabinet, all chronicled by subject, document type, and year. "Nineteen-seventy-one, yes?" she says from over her shoulder.

"That's right."

"And the month?"

"July," I say. "It happened on July eighth."

She nods and squats down to access the lower drawers.

"Then we should probably look at all the issues from July ninth through… let us say, the thirteenth, to be safe."

"Great." I look around the little windowless room while Gina roots through the drawer. Three of the four walls are neatly lined with tall metal cabinets. On the other wall there's a long table with two new-looking microfiche projectors, between which is a small printer. I'm surprised by how updated it all looks. Rosanera is such a small town that I assumed the archives room here would look like something out of *Dick Tracy*, complete with a bare interrogation bulb hanging from the ceiling.

"Ah, *voila*." Gina holds up two microfiche cards. "This is all of July."

I stare. "The whole month is on those two things?"

She stands up, laughing. "Hard to believe. But, yes. Just one of these cabinets holds thousands of microfiche cards, which is something like tens of thousands of pages of newspapers."

Not exactly a thumb drive, but still—I have to hand it to the older generations. They were more tech-savvy than anyone gives them credit for.

Gina goes over to a machine, inserts the first card, and powers it on. The screen slowly wakes up, illuminating the front page of a newspaper with paragraphs of Italian reporting. She sits down, and I pull up a chair next to her.

"Okay," she says, "let's start right with July ninth." Her lithe fingers turn the knob to the right and she rolls quickly through the early July dates until she hits it. With fists balled up on my thighs, I watch her soft, deer-like brown eyes scan the decades-old headlines. After a few moments, she shakes her head.

"Mm. Let's try the tenth." She turns the knob a couple inches and she stops again, reading. "Nothing here, either."

Moving on to the eleventh, she pauses again, then moves slowly to the twelfth. I close my eyes and try to tamp down the rising panic in my chest. What if this is a dead end too? The only leads I have left are Giovanni and Dr. Bolla, the medical examiner. The very real possibility that I will return home with my tail between my legs about this ridiculous endeavor in the first place overwhelms me.

"Ah! Here we go!" Gina's voice interrupts my internal laments, and my eyelids fly open.

"What? Are you sure?" I lean over her shoulder, practically attaching myself to her like a cape.

"Yes, yes, I'm sure." She points to the article headline that reads *Uomo Americano Ucciso in Incidente Automobilistico.*

"'American man killed in car crash,'" she interprets for me. "'On Thursday 8 July, a twenty-seven-year-old American male was killed in a car crash on Via Marietta in Rosanera. The incident occurred at approximately 16:45 when the vehicle, a 1961 red Fiat, slammed into the stone wall bordering the ocean overlook. The man was killed on impact. Authorities believe that the American, presumably unfamiliar with the winding road, lost control of the vehicle, which was traveling at nearly seventy-five kilometers per hour around the sharp curve.'" She stops abruptly and falls back in her chair, shoots me a conspiratorial look.

"What? What does it say?" I ask through the grips of tachycardia.

"'However, one reporter spoke to a woman who claimed her six-year-old son witnessed another vehicle driving erratically behind the American's car just prior to the accident,'" Gina continues. "'Mrs. Roberto Sardo of 65 Piazza Spiega reported that her son Maurizio was playing across the street in his grandmother's yard when he allegedly saw another car following closely behind the Fiat, possibly causing it to lose control. Police have since followed up on this lead, but have been unable to find evidence of another car being involved in the fatality. Attempts to locate additional eyewitnesses to corroborate the boy's story have also yielded no results. As such, police have ruled the death accidental.'"

I slide my palms up and down my thighs, digesting what Gina's told me. There was an eyewitness to Henry's car crash. Who saw another car pursuing him. Was it true? Had another driver intentionally run Henry off the road? And if so, why? But how reliable was the account of a six-year-old child, anyway? The local authorities certainly hadn't given it much weight. But that didn't really mean anything, did it? Cops get things wrong all the time. It's practically in their DNA. My head swims, overloaded with deliberations.

"Can you print out this page for me?" I ask Gina.

"Already on it," she tells me, clicking a button. I think

for a moment while she prints it. Does that Sardo family still live at the address listed in this article? What if I could talk to the mother, or better yet to the son, Maurizio? He'd be in his fifties now. It's not so farfetched, is it? After all, Giovanni is still living in the same place after all these years. I decide to head over there after I'm done here. And, of course, I also want to see the site of the crash.

"This stone wall on Via de la Marietta—where the accident happened. Is that still there?" I say.

"Oh, yes. It's been there for centuries. Here, I'll draw you a map. It's very close—only about a kilometer from here." Gina grabs a pencil and pulls the freshly printed article from the printer tray, flipping it over.

I'm finally onto something. I can't believe it. By the end of today, I'll have seen where Henry spent his last moments on Earth. And, maybe I'll even hear a firsthand account of what happened.

Gina finishes writing and hands me the paper. "Here you go."

"I can't thank you enough," I gush. "You're probably the key to me actually figuring all of this out."

"I hope that's true," Gina says, giving my arm a warm squeeze. "Good luck, Juliet."

God knows I need it.

Chapter Sixteen

Los Angeles
October 18, 1964

ABOVE HENRY'S HEAD, two girls in short fringed skirts gyrate in a glass-enclosed booth dangling thirty feet in the air. He's on his fourth scotch already, which makes it all the more hypnotic and alluring. The sprawling dance floor in front of the leather booth where he's sitting is packed with kids from all over Los Angeles—sweaty and feral, bouncing freely to the rock and roll permeating through the discotheque. *Boom, boom, crash. Crash, boom, crash.* It's like he's inside a kaleidoscope; everything a mishmash of glorious colors, delightfully fractured, forever twirling.

A glass tumbler suddenly slams down on the table in front of him, splashing its inebriating contents everywhere. Henry jolts back into his body.

"Drink up, birthday baby," Jim calls to Henry over the

din, through lips clamped around a cigarette. He's back from the bar, expertly balancing two more drinks in his other hand.

Henry grins, holds up the nearly full scotch he's drinking. Jim mock stares.

"That's practically empty," he says. "Go ahead, finish that last sip and we'll keep 'em coming."

Henry guffaws, flecks of spittle dampening the scruff growing in around his mouth. What is it about the guy that makes everything he says seem entirely rational?

"If I didn't know better, I'd think you're trying to take advantage of me, on my *twenty-first,* of all days," Henry drawls, shaking an admonishing finger at his friend.

"Perhaps I am," Jim says. Henry shrugs and downs the rest of his drink. Jim starts roaring. The room tilts and a renewed tidal wave of warmth fills Henry's veins.

"That's what I'm talking about!" Cherie squeals from next to him, planting a sloppy kiss on his cheek. He knows he should slow down, but he doesn't want to. The level he's on right now is where he needs to be, and he wants to go even deeper. Never in his life did he think he'd be on Sunset Boulevard celebrating his birthday in what's come to be one of the hippest places in Hollywood.

"All I know is I'm ready for my next one," Cherie cries, leaning across Henry in the booth to swipe one of ten glasses from Jim's hand. As she sniffs it, her long blonde locks fall forward and draw a momentary curtain around her face. She tosses her head back with a wide grin.

"Yep, 's mine," she proclaims. "G&T. Hell yes. Thank

you." She bats her heavily mascaraed lashes at him, blazing jade eyes peeking up from underneath. Their shared gaze seems to lag just a fraction too long, and Henry's stomach flips. At first, the flirtations between his girlfriend and Jim seemed innocent, playful. The three of them had been hanging out together constantly. They're all attractive. Henry came to accept that there would be some degree of magnetism between Cherie and Jim. And it would be fine if it stayed *only a degree,* he thinks. But isn't it happening more and more now? Isn't he beginning to lose control over the situation?

"Hey, hey! Happy birthday!" A voice calls out over the pulsating beat, thankfully severing Henry from his miserable thoughts. His friend Ray, an MFA student in the film program, is weaving his way over to their table with a group of folks behind him, all with drinks in hand. Henry scoots out of the booth and crooks an arm around Ray.

"You made it!" Henry says. He hugs Ray's girlfriend, Shandra, a tall brunette with a substantial bust, and slaps hands with Lance, a wiry, hyper, carrot-top kid who goes by Father Mobie for reasons Henry can't remember now.

"Happy day of your birth, sir," Father Mobie says, bowing in his eccentric way, then jumps straight back up. A pair of dark sunglasses obscure his eyes, and he flashes his signature lopsided grin, revealing teeth that look like crooked stairs.

Everyone squeezes into the booth that Jim had painstakingly reserved all night, shooting a dead-eyed "no" to any hopeful bystander's gaze that fell on the vacant seats he was saving. That's the thing about Jim. He'll go to the ends of the Earth for Henry. Including single-handedly reserving one of the few booths at the wildly popular Whisky a Go on a Saturday night.

"Man, that line outside was crazy," Ray is saying. "We must've been out there for two hours."

"At *least*," Shandra says, sipping her Manhattan and fanning herself with her manicured hand.

"That's nothing," Cherie says, plucking a cigarette from the pack in Jim's shirt pocket. She's squeezed in between him and Henry, and he gets a front-row seat to witness her fingers brushing his chest. "We got here this afternoon at, like, four o'clock, wasn't it?"

Father Mobie scoffs. "Just shows how much sway the mob still holds around here," he says, real serious. "The cat who owns this place, what's his name?" He snaps his fingers.

"Valentine," Ray answers, lighting a cigarette.

"Valentine!" Mobie says. "Yes! He's this old mobster, gotta be almost seventy now. Anyway, when he opened this place in January, it was *dead*. Couldn't get anyone to come through the doors. So he went down to Hollywood High and paid kids to show up here to make it look legit."

Groans erupt from the table. "No way. I call bullshit," Henry says, throwing back his scotch.

"Can't believe I'm saying this, but Mobie's right," Ray says, eyebrows raised. His grey-blue eyes shine behind his glasses. He's got that matter-of-fact, trustworthy way of speaking. Like a trustworthy salesman. "No joke.

Valentine actually paid high school kids to hang out front here and make it look like something major was up. I kid you not. But would you expect any different? That's how those old Italians are. They always get their way."

A hot poker stabs through Henry's chest at this. Uncle Pietro flashes through his mind. *That's how those old Italians are.* The same thing his mother said to him that day, a thousand years ago. *You have no idea who he is.* The tang of adrenaline springs into his throat as he's transported back to that staircase. Ellen's screaming, his father's palpable rage, his mother's expressionless face, eyes rolling back in her head. Her body like a tiny, broken animal curled in a desperate attempt at protection. Blood, so much blood. Pooling at the base of the stairs, seeping into the floorboards. Henry knows it's still there, forever preserved in the cracks and pores no matter how much it was scrubbed.

No birthday call came for him today. Maybe a card would find its way to him in the post. But a call? No, never. They'd all reached a silent consensus where the simple act of talking is out of bounds. It's too intimate now, as if the mere exchange of words would pull them all back into the nightmare of that day, trapping them there in amber, forever.

And it dawns on Henry here—in this crowded, lively place, thousands of miles from that tainted memory, filled with people who are willing to love him, if he can only manage to not turn it rancid—how dangerously close he is, at any given time, to being totally alone.

"All I know for sure is Jim would've waited a week out there in that roasting sun, as long as it was Hank's birthday," Henry hears Cherie say. It takes him a second to realize she's talking about the queue to get into the Whisky. "He'd do anything for him."

"*Awww*, Jimmy," Father Mobie says, pressing his hands over his heart and pouting. Everyone laughs but Henry. What a surprise that Cherie's comment was more complimentary of Jim than of him.

"My lovely girlfriend, everyone," Henry cheers drily, raising his glass. Cherie's eyes are pinging all over him, faltering, not sure how to respond to his acerbity.

"Huh. Well, it's pretty well known that *he's* your girlfriend, anyway. Not me." She looks away, haughty.

"Oooh, now we're getting somewhere," Father Mobie crows, sliding his shades down his nose and leaning forward on the table. "Do tell!" Mike and Ray are howling, and Shandra tries in vain to get the attention of the one waitress assigned to the roughly two hundred people on the dance floor.

"What the fuck are you talking about?" Henry says.

"Oh, come off it, like you don't know," Cherie says to the table, palms spread. "I can't remember the last time you were apart. The two of you are, like, soulmates." Henry gawks at Jim, eyebrows in his hairline.

"Soulmates," Jim muses, looking pensive. "I'm okay with that."

"You're together so much the fella who owns the shop on Santa Monica thinks the two of you are queers," Cherie says.

"What, you guys just can't get enough of Ah Men?" Ray interjects. Cackling erupts from the table at the mention of the flamboyant menswear store on Santa Monica.

"The film shop next door to it, actually," Jim answers, leisurely blowing a smoke ring. "It's true. Me and Chief, we're in there three times a week at least. Got a lotta term projects going on, what can I say?"

Ray throws him a look. "'Chief?'"

"That's right," Jim says. "Like the Indian in *Cuckoo's Nest*. Don't tell me you haven't read it."

"Haven't got around to it yet," Ray says, tapping his cigarette into the gold pot in the center of the table. "How much time do you think I have? I'm finishing grad school, playing music. I can't just lay up reading fifty books a month like you."

"Philistine," Jim says and shakes his head, lighting another cigarette off the burning butt of the one he's got. "Anyway, Chief—Kesey's Chief—is darker than Hank but reminds me of him nonetheless. Hank doesn't believe me, but I think he's a Native."

Henry's head rolls back and he barks out a laugh.

"Damn lucky to be one, too," Jim continues, unfazed. "One of the rightful owners of this Earth."

Henry tries to focus on Jim. But by now his vision is like a glitching film projector, everything stuttering past his eyes in a series of stitched-together frames rather than one seamless motion picture. Over the summer, Jim's hair had grown out to just below his ears and now falls like soft dove feathers around his chin, accentuating his high cheekbones—those sharp, deep canyons below those glowering eyes.

Then Henry notices Cherie's eyes are on Jim, too, and this time there's no doubt: they're lusty, longing. He gets the deep sense that Jim is struggling not to return the look, and he feels vomit rise in his esophagus. *It's all in your head, all in your head, all in your head.* But it's not, and he knows it.

Over the sound system, The Kinks' "All Day and All of the Night" ends.

"All right, ladies and gents," announces Joanie, the Whisky's alluring blonde house DJ, from her booth suspended to the right side of the main stage. "Everyone give it up for the man you're all here to see. The talented, handsome extravaganza that is *Johnny Rivers*!"

A wild cheer explodes from all corners of the venue as the pompadoured singer and his house band take the stage. Father Mobie leaps up from the table, sweat stains as big as planets under the arms of his grey button-down. "This is what I'm talking about! Who's joining me?"

Jim grabs Mobie's arm. "Before you go, get Hank another couple shots of Johnny Walker, wouldja?" He fishes a five out of his jeans.

"No, no, no," Henry slurs. *I don't want more liquor,* he wants to say. *What I want is for my best friend and my girlfriend not to fuck.*

But Mobie stands erect and salutes Jim. "Right away, your majesty," he says and bounds off to the bar.

"I love this guy," Ray laughs, gesturing at Mobie's back.

"Mobie's a genius," Henry says, fumbling in his front pocket for a cigarette. It takes him nearly a full minute to realize the pack is actually on the table in front of him. "Me and Jim met him in Directing Cameras last semester."

Ray grimaces. "Cartwright, wasn't it? What a hard-ass he is."

"You're not kidding. Hol-eee shit."

"And now he's my camera man," Jim says to Ray. Everyone stares at him, momentarily confused. "Mobie, not Cartwright."

"Wait, what are you doing with a camera man?" Ray asks him. "You know you're in film school, right? Meaning, *you* are supposed to be the camera man?"

Henry laughs, louder and more harshly than he intended. Next to him, Cherie screws her face up at him, but he doesn't care. Ray is a revered MFA student. At least three of his projects have been included at UCLA's prestigious "Night of Student Films" at Royce Hall. Henry is brimming with jealous glee, and tries hard to ignore that touch of shame, that this accomplished filmmaker calls Jim out.

Jim's eyes fall on Henry for a beat, then go back to Ray.

"I'm getting more into directing and writing than cinematography," he says. "So Mobie does the camera work. He's a boss with lighting, too. I give him all the credit for it. He's sublime."

"Oh, I've read your stuff," Cherie gushes. "Who cares if you're not doing the actual camera work? You're a natural writer. You should focus on that, then."

That's it. Henry begins another laugh, a low, rumbling reverberation from his throat. Is he really the only one at this table who sees what's going on? Everyone looks at him benignly, giving him his answer.

"What?" Cherie says. "What did I say?"

Henry wipes his eyes and lets his laugh die out before he continues. "I'm just thinking, it's like Artaud said: 'No one has ever written, painted, sculpted, modeled, built, or invented except literally to get out of hell.'"

A slow smile spreads across Jim's face. He loves Artaud. Introduced Henry to his works, in fact.

Cherie pulls a confused look. "I don't get it." Henry turns to look at her full-on.

"I'm just wondering how many more goddamn films I need to make, then, until it's my fucking turn to get out?"

Chapter Seventeen

Tijuana, Mexico
April 1965

THE COMPACT WAITING room in the anonymous office on Avenue Revolución reeks of bleach and distress. Rickety fans shudder in their metal frames on full blast, trying unsuccessfully to disperse the claustrophobic air. But even if Henry was in an air-conditioned mansion, he wouldn't have been able to breathe.

And after today, he thinks he'll never be able to breathe again.

He shifts in the folding chair and glances at Cherie next to him. She's practically unrecognizable, a supplicant version of herself. Her head is down, free-flowing locks twisted into a low bun at the base of her neck, hands wound together like a vise in her lap. The room around them is packed with women, some Mexican, some

American, all avoiding each other's gaze. The Mexican girl sitting across from Henry looks twelve, her thick black hair woven into childlike plaits. With her is a man who is at least twice her age. Was he her father or her lover? Either way, it makes Henry want to vomit.

    He puts a hot palm over Cherie's hands. "There's still time," he says into her ear. "We can go."

    Cherie shakes her head slowly. Her skin is sallow and wrung out. The wet, dark circles under her eyes look green here, under the buzzing fluorescent lights.

    "We decided," she says. "You cannot imagine what I've been through with this."

    Henry's insides cramp into hot iron. He'll never tell her that she's wrong. That the red stain spreading through his mother's pants like some hideous Rorschach test is burned in his mind, a constant reminder that for some things, there is no way back. He already knows that is true about today.

    "Look," Cherie says, running a shaky hand over her scalp, "just tell me this will all be okay, Henry. All I need from you is to tell me this will all be okay."

    He gently taps under her chin with his finger, and her eyes finally meet his. His throat constricts when he sees the sorrow there, stretching far beyond her years. He tries to imprint this moment in his mind, not because he wants to remember Cherie's grief, but because he imagines it will be the last time they regard each other with any degree of tenderness.

    "It'll be okay," he says, and knows that neither of them believe it.

From down the hall comes the wailing of a woman followed by a man speaking in consoling, rapid Spanish. The waiting room radio's upbeat Norteño music does nothing to shroud the misery of this place.

A dark-skinned woman, barely five feet tall and clad in a crisp, white nursing outfit, walks into the waiting room and stands in the doorway. She glances at her clipboard and calls, "Meesus Jones?" *Yones.*

Cherie raises her hand weakly at the pseudonym she gave, and Henry's heart climbs into his mouth.

"I'm—it's me," Cherie says. She gets to her feet unsteadily with Henry's help. Her face is a pile of wet ash. The nurse offers what she probably thinks is a warm smile, but it just looks like despair.

"We're ready for you," she says, gesturing down the hall with her clipboard.

"Should—can he come back with me?" Cherie asks, looking wildly over her shoulder at Henry. The nurse shakes her head.

"No, I'm sorry," she says. "Only the doctor, and I will be there, too. *No te preocupes, m'ija,* everything fine." Cherie says nothing, only shuffles toward the nurse, who raises her eyebrows at Henry.

"It will be maybe one hour, okay?" she says. "We come get you as soon as it's done."

As soon as it's done. Henry is vaguely aware of nodding as his insides melt into a pool of wax. He tries to say "I love you" before Cherie leaves with the nurse. The words don't come. But it doesn't matter anyway because she's already disappearing down the hall.

He needs air. Henry grabs his bag off the floor and rushes down the stairs, bursting back out onto Revolución. He doubles over, panting, hands on his knees as adrenaline crackles like electricity through his veins. He balls his fists and waits for the vertigo to pass. People saunter by and turn their heads briefly to look at him before moving on. Open-air markets line the avenue today, vendors selling colorful hand-embroidered dresses, ripe produce, piles of discount home goods. Boisterous children a few stalls down from Henry are playing cops and robbers. They weave in and out of the stands screeching and giggling with shiny plastic pistols and donning feathery headdresses, their mothers hollering at them now and again to slow down.

Henry feels his equilibrium return and stands up, takes a deep breath. He spots a phone booth down the block and heads that way. The glass door screeches open and he seals himself inside. Digging into his bag, he fishes out the pouch of pesos he exchanged when they got here this morning.

He lifts the phone receiver. It practically slips right out of his sweaty hand. The operator comes on and asks him the number. He recites it from memory.

"*Cuarenta pesos, por favor*," says the voice. With quivering fingers, he shoves an unknown quantity of pesos into the slot, hoping it's enough. A static-filled pause, then a series of clicks. More silence. He starts to wonder if he should hang up and start over when the ringing finally begins.

"Yeah?" A familiar voice says after seven rings. Henry's shoulders relax.

"Ray, it's Hank. I need to talk to Jim. Is he there?" He raises his voice over the crackling connection and plugs his other ear with his finger. There's a sea of background noise on Ray's end—records playing, voices, sounds of life. His place is never dead.

"Sure, man, I think he's out back," Ray says. "Hold on, lemme find him."

Henry waits. He pictures Jim sprawled out in that turquoise aluminum lounge chair in the yard at Ray's yellow craftsman in Venice Beach, shirt unbuttoned with a notebook and pen at his side. Jim spends more and more of his time there. His passion for filmmaking has waned dramatically over the past six months, replaced by an interest in poetry and music. Even Ray is heavy into playing music now too, with a consignment piano serving as the centerpiece for his minuscule living room, guitars and bass strewn throughout the rest of the little abode. The undertow of this other life tugs at Jim and pulls him further away from Henry every day. Henry feels the expanse between them right now more acutely than ever, alone here in a foreign land.

"Brother," says the deep, familiar voice on the other end. "Been waiting to hear from you. You both okay?"

"She just went in. I—I don't know." Henry is an inch away from breaking. Less.

"It'll be all good, Hank, I promise. This doctor's the best. He's done a bunch of Americans, like I told you guys, remember? She's in good hands. You'll both come home tonight in one piece."

That's the first thing you've ever said that I don't believe, Henry thinks.

"It's a goddamn shame it ever happened," Jim sighs. "But it's for the best, brother. Honestly. Neither of you are ready for this. She always said that if this ever happened, she'd get an abortion. She was prepared."

Henry's body goes limp. Cherie never said anything like that to him. In fact, the two of them had never even broached the subject.

"What did you just say?" Henry asks. A few beats pass. Laughter in the background, and someone practicing scales on the piano.

Jim pauses, clears his throat. "Cherie mentioned to me once that she never wanted to be a mother. It's nothing. Something we talked about forever ago, I don't even remember when, or why."

"No, wait. Stop. You talked to my girlfriend about what her plans were to have *kids*?"

"Chief, it was totally benign—"

"Don't fucking call me that."

"Fine. Hank. Come on, get ahold of yourself, man. I know you're upset right now, but this was just talk. It was probably some time we were all out somewhere, blitzed, and—"

The telephone operator cuts in, presumably asking for more coins to continue the call.

"Shit!" Henry blindly jams more coins into the slot. "Hello? *Hello?*" Nothing. Like he's in outer space. He's floating light years away in another galaxy.

"I can't hear you, Hank," Jim says. "You're cutting out. You there?"

"I'm here! *When* did this happen, Jim?" More sputtering on the phone line. Jim's voice is now just incoherent staccatos. Henry doesn't care, he keeps going.

"You think I don't know?" he seethes. "Shit's not been right with me and her for months. You think I don't know that's got something to do with you?"

On Jim's end, it's a sinister symphony of disembodied voices, plinking piano notes, idiotic laughter. Henry tastes copper in the back of his throat and is suddenly aware of his heart thundering. Finally, the words that he's suppressed for weeks—that he hasn't had the balls to ask Cherie, that he's tried so hard to rationalize away—rise in his throat like magma.

"Am I the father." The words broil his throat on their way out.

"Hen… can't hear a… get back?" Jim says. Henry smashes his fist against the glass of the phone booth, over and over, feeling nothing.

"*Am I the fucking father?*" He screams it into the mouthpiece, holding the phone away from his ear.

The line goes dead. Numbness anesthetizes his exhausted body. He lets the receiver fall from his hand.

It swings back and forth on its tangled cord like a man in a noose.

Henry fumbles a cigarette out of the pack in his pocket, puts it to his lips and lights it, inhaling deeply. He stares unseeing at the world outside the glass pane of the phone booth. It reminds him of *Through the Looking-Glass*. Out there everything is reversed and backwards, including logic. He wants to stay inside the booth forever. Where does he go from here? Where can he possibly go? He has nothing and no one anymore. What was the point of continuing at UCLA after this? What was the point in anything he's been doing in his life so far? All of it, in the end, comes to nothing. Means nothing.

Henry's hands feel for the door handle and slide it open. He goes out onto the street, standing motionless for a moment before walking to a bar a couple doors down. When he enters, the bar's few scattered patrons give him a cursory glance before returning to the sweating brown bottles in front of them.

Henry holds up two fingers to the bartender. "Two cervezas and two whiskeys, *por favor*." The bartender nods and pours the shots first before reaching into the refrigerator for the beers. Henry throws back both shots immediately, then takes his beers over to a cheap Formica dinette set next to the window. Across the street, the kids continue their game of cops and robbers, determined to remain lost in fantasy.

Two hours later, they're in line to cross the border at San Ysidro back into the United States. Cherie shifts gingerly in the passenger seat, pulling the shawl tighter around her shoulders despite the warmth of the day. She presses a warm compress on her lower abdomen. The brown paper bag at her feet bulges with thick maxipads, bandages, ibuprofen, and painkillers. She stares out the window at the cars idling in the other lanes of border traffic.

"We didn't even get to see the beach while we were here," she says softly. "That's why people come to Mexico. Right? The beautiful beaches. Not like California. Prettier, exotic, more private."

Henry says nothing. They finally pull up to the booth where a bored police officer hardly glances up from that week's issue of *Life* before waving them across. On the magazine cover is astronaut Ed White during the spacewalk. He's hovering miles above the Earth, tethered to the Gemini spacecraft by crinkly bronze aluminum tubes. Henry thinks he looks alien and dead, a lonely lifeform condemned to interminable darkness.

They merge onto Interstate 5 headed north through San Diego. Keeping his eyes on the road, Henry finally speaks.

"This is over, isn't it? You and me."

A brief pause. "Yes," she says. It's not unkind, just matter-of-fact. A straight answer to a simple question.

He wants to ask her the same question he demanded of Jim. But whenever he looks at the state of her—deflated and fragile, having just gone through God only knows what physical and emotional pain—he can't. What's the difference now if it's true or not? Instead, he turns his mind to how he and Cherie have, in fact, been over for quite a while now, how his friendship with Jim has moved into territory that can't be repaired, and how he will return to face his final year at UCLA alone.

Chapter Eighteen

THE PRINTOUT GINA gave me turns damp in my grasp as I leave the library. For the first time, I have a real lead. I take out my phone and type in the Sardos' address listed in the article. It's just a couple miles from here, so I power walk back to my car and jump in. Might as well go right now and see if the family still inhabits the place.

As I turn the ignition, my phone pings. It's Alessio. *Ciao. Papa is home early. Do you want to come by?*

My heart is a slingshot inside my ribcage. Giovanni's back two days early. Who knows why, and who cares. First the newspaper article, now him—all within the same hour. I can't believe my luck.

I text back, *Absolutely. Can I come right now?* Not waiting for a response, I throw the car in reverse. I'll follow up with the Sardos later. Giovanni's the priority. I'm about to gun it out of the parking spot when my phone pings again, and I snatch it up, dizzy with glee. Alessio responded. *Yes now is OK. But don't know how much help he will be.*

Hope deflates from my chest like a ruptured balloon. What the hell does that mean? As if already anticipating my question, I see the three bouncing reply dots appear from Alessio. They disappear. Then reappear. Finally: *Just come. He will explain.*

Shit. My knuckles tighten on the steering wheel as I drive, and I try to steady my breath. As much as I wish it weren't true, without Giovanni, I'm not confident I'll ever figure any of this out.

It takes me less than ten minutes to whip through the sinuous streets back to their house on Via della Servi. I coast to a stop in front of the house and yank the e-brake, not caring if my dubious parking spot is completely legal. I hurry to the door and give a courteous rap. Shuffling footsteps from inside, then Alessio swings the door open.

"Hi," I say anxiously, and start to barrel into the house, but he walks out toward me and shuts the door halfway behind him. "Please just remember what I said about Vietnam, eh?" he says in a low voice. "Don't mention I told you that about him."

Vietnam? That was the last thing I'd bring up, as it has nothing to do with why I'm here. But clearly Alessio needs reassurance.

"Yes, I remember. I promise I won't mention it." I crane my neck, trying to see inside behind Alessio, then look back at him. "What did you mean when you said he won't be helpful?"

Alessio fretfully pushes a finger to his lips. I feel like we're standing outside the den of an enraged lion.

"I told him your story," he says. "He said he don't know an American named Henry. It's been a long time for him, you see. He don't remember things so well. I didn't want you to get your hopes up."

Alessio never said anything before about his father being forgetful. Why now?

"Fine," I sigh. "But maybe when I show him the paper from five decades ago, with his name and address written on it, it might jog his memory?"

"Okay, just don't get too hopeful?"

"I won't," I lie. I'll help Giovanni remember, I'm sure of it. Whatever Alessio told him probably got lost in translation. Alessio finally turns and motions for me to follow him in, which I do in great earnest.

"Papa," he calls. "*Juliet e qui.*" I hear another voice grunt, "*Si, entra.*"

Walking into the living room, I see an old man slumped in the thatched reclining chair that days before had stood vacant next to the gaudy crystal lamp. And, just like on that day, Alessio again walks over to the windows and parts the drapes, heavy as theatre curtains, like the opening night of a play no one wants to see.

"*Ciao, piacere di conoscerti,*" I say, extending my hand. I'm impressed with my completely basic Italian, but I seem to be the only one who is. From his seat, Giovanni offers me his hand without expression, and we shake. His palm is a rough cluster of barnacles.

He gestures to the worn sofa with his other hand. "Sit, *per favore*," he says, rumbly as an old lawnmower.

Deep crevices of hard living run through his clean-shaven face, like Keith Richards. His sloping shoulders and concave chest lead down to a bloated stomach that reveals a lifelong drinking habit. He's wearing a white undershirt under a cheap short-sleeved button-down and old khaki pants. He looks like every down-and-out man I've ever seen. It's unfathomable to me that he was once a spry journalist riding the cusp of breaking news during the Vietnam War.

Alessio comes back from the window and sits next to me. He smells good, like warm citrus and sun. It's what I imagine would be the exact opposite of Giovanni's scent.

"So," begins Alessio, "I told Papa your story, how you are here for information on your uncle. But unfortunately, he does not recall, *si?*" He looks at his father for confirmation. The elder household resident nods, and his hard, dark eyes stare at me from under two wrinkled outcrops of brown skin.

"That's right," he says crossly in a heavy, accusatory accent. "I not know any American named Henry. Never did. How you say he know me?" It's a demand, not a question.

"My mother died last month," I begin. His eyes maintain their aggressive surveillance of me without a flicker of emotion. "Going through her things, I found my uncle Henry's personal effects from when he died in a car accident, here in Rosanera, fifty years ago. There wasn't much in there, except a pack of cigarettes and some other stuff. It all seemed pretty routine. But then, tucked down inside the pack of cigarettes, I found a photo of a mausoleum with a very unsettling note on the back of it, along with a piece of paper that had your name and address on it."

He keeps glaring silently at me, and I start to wonder if he doesn't fully understand English. Does he not understand the gravity of what I just said?

"It's as if they were deliberately *hidden* in there," I emphasize. "There was a wallet in with his personal effects, but Henry didn't bother to put them in there. Instead he hid them in with the cigarettes, as if for safekeeping. To keep them out of the wrong hands maybe."

Giovanni crosses his arms and shakes his head. "I don't know him. Sorry." His face is a giant "Wrong Way" road sign, entry forbidden.

That's it? He's not even going to ask to see any of it? His blatant apathy and unwarranted hostility is really starting to piss me off.

I reach into my bag, grab the scrap of paper with his name and address and the mausoleum photo, and thrust them at him.

"Will you at least have a look? Is that your handwriting? Does the photo look familiar? Anything would help. Anything." All politeness has fled from my voice, replaced by a terseness that matches his own.

Reluctantly, he leans forward and says something to Alessio in Italian. Alessio rushes from the room and just as quickly returns with a pair of eyeglasses. Giovanni puts them on and takes the papers from me. I study his frowning face, searching for signs of recognition, of anything, but he's inscrutable. If he did know Henry, why won't he just tell me? Finally, he clears his throat, a John Deere roaring to life.

"No, this is not my writing," he growls. "And this photograph. I never seen this *tombe* before. It could be a thousand places." *No shit!* I want to scream.

"Like I tell you," he continues, "I no remember any American coming here to see me. That's it. What else can I say." He pulls off his eyeglasses and sinks back into the weathered chair.

I stare at him, trying to comprehend how all the build-up in my mind could've led to this crushing reality. It occurs to me that I never gave much thought to what Giovanni would be like as a person, only to the extent of what he knew. I wasn't at all prepared for this stonewalling. But I'm not ready to give up.

"Look, if you didn't know Henry," I demand, leaning my elbows on my knees toward him, "why would he have your name and address? You can't dispute that. This piece of paper didn't just magically appear out of nowhere."

Alessio looks nervously between his father and me. I'm sure it's been forever since Giovanni has been challenged in his own house, especially by a woman. But I couldn't care less.

Two pinpricks of heat appear on each of his cheeks beneath his dark tan. "Like I say," he says, "*I don't know.* Maybe someone give him my name to repair his car while he in town here." He juts out his chin and throws his hands up to his shoulders in a derisive shrug.

For a second, my veins ice over. Oh God, what if he's right? What if this was nothing more than an uncanny coincidence, something as random as a referral for a mechanic? And what if the reason his name and address ended up in Henry's cigarette pack was entirely innocent? Maybe his cigarettes were in the front pocket of his shirt, and it was just an easy place to stash something instead of getting his wallet out. But that doesn't sound right either. I'm starting to doubt everything. Then a thought smacks me in the face.

"Wait," I say, taking out my phone. Why didn't I think of this before? "I have a picture of him. Of Henry. One of his old college friends just emailed it to me. Maybe you'll recognize him."

Something flickers in Giovanni's face, so imperceptible that I'm not even sure I saw it. I open the email attachment from Dave and zoom in on Henry's face at the Formosa dinner.

"Here," I command, shoving the phone at Giovanni. "That's him. That's Henry. Look."

He gazes at me for a few beats, then slowly puts his glasses back on. This time, his hand trembles ever so slightly. Should I be reading into this, or is he maybe just a typical seventy-four-year old man? As he studies it, his expression remains neutral, yet is a touch softer than before. But I guess putting a face to a name could do that.

"No, never seen him," he says, creaking back in his chair once more. Frustration pulls at every hair on my body. But what am I supposed to do? Throw a fit? Accuse him of lying? Even if he is, doing that won't exactly make him more cooperative.

"Well, I guess we're done here," I say ruefully, standing up. Although of course I'm not, and I want to slap him instead of leave. But if I have to stay in this room another minute, I'm going to melt down. I throw my bag over my shoulder and leave.

Alessio's telling me to wait, but I'm already out the door. All I want to do now is head over to the Sardo house and find out if there's anyone in this town who can be of help to me. I stop a few feet outside the house and try to control the angry tears knifing the corners of my eyes. Alessio rushes out to meet me.

"Juliet, I'm sorry he wasn't any help. Really. This is why I didn't want you to get excited."

"It's not your fault, Alessio," I say, closing my eyes. "I just don't get it. Why would my uncle have his info if they didn't even know each other? It makes no sense."

"I understand that it's very strange." Alessio shakes his head, runs his hands through his dark hair. I pause for a minute, wondering how to phrase my next question. Then I just come out with it.

"Do you think he's lying?"

Alessio looks at me with a pained expression. "Honestly, I cannot say. He is like this all the time. So severe, so private. It does not necessarily mean he is lying. It's just the way he is. About everything, every subject. Trust me, I wish he were different."

"Well, at least I have the Sardos," I sigh. "On the off-off-off chance *that* leads to anything."

Alessio screws up his face. "Who?"

I suddenly remember I haven't had a chance yet to tell Alessio the news. I give him a recap of what the newspaper article said about Maurizio, the then-child witness to the accident, and how I'm hoping he might still live here in Rosanera.

"*Merda*, that could be something," Alessio says, raising his eyebrows. I don't know if he really believes that or if it's just apologetic optimism.

"That's what I'm hoping," I say, walking over to my car. "I should get going and see."

He nods. "Let me know how it goes, okay?"

"I will," I say, as I get into my car. The poor guy looks miserable, like he blames himself for his father's unhelpfulness. He shoves his hands in his jeans pockets and watches as I start the engine. I give him a reassuring smile.

Maybe Giovanni's name and address in Henry's wallet really was just a random referral to get his car fixed. Or maybe Henry had been a fleeting acquaintance of Giovanni's. If so, it makes sense that Giovanni wouldn't remember him. After all, I'm the only one who thinks that piece of paper indicates a well-founded connection to my uncle—something for which I have absolutely no evidence.

As I back the car up, a movement in the house catches my eye. I think I saw one of the thick drapes in the living room window pull back.

But when I look again, they're exactly as they were.

Chapter Nineteen

Los Angeles
August 1965

HENRY ARRIVES AT Dean Jacobs' office promptly at eleven o'clock. Rita, Jacobs' secretary, peers over her horn-rimmed glasses at him as he enters.

"Right on time, Mr. Barton," she says, her bright red lips pulled into a professional smile. "He's ready for you now, you can go on in."

"Thank you," Henry says, pushing open the large oak doors to Jacobs' suite.

David Jacobs, clad in a sharp grey suit, sits at his desk in a leather swivel chair observing Henry with the same benevolent gaze as that night at Formosa years ago. Nostalgia paws at his chest as Henry recalls that evening, where the dean had so enthusiastically recognized his work, even though it was second-rate. Jacobs had always been like a father to him. It'll make the news he's come to tell him today that much harder.

"Good to see you, Henry. It's been a long time," Jacobs says. "Please, sit." He motions to the Eames chairs in front of his desk. Henry sinks into the left one, pushes his shaggy hair out of his eyes. They look at each for a moment in polite silence.

"Would you like a coffee, a Coca-Cola? Rita can get you whatever you like."

"No, thank you, sir, I'm fine," Henry says. Jacobs raises his chin slightly and looks at Henry.

"Well, I'll be honest with you Henry, you don't look fine."

"No?"

"No. You look exhausted, like you haven't been sleeping. And you also look distracted. Are you sure you'll be ready to start the semester next week?"

Jacobs swivels gently back and forth in his chair. On the wall behind him hangs a chaotic Cubist painting of what appear to be mourning women among a field of flowers. It could actually be a real Picasso for all Henry knows.

"I've just been busy with my own projects," Henry says, avoiding the question.

"Your own projects."

Over the past sixteen weeks since that horrible day in Tijuana, Henry's focus had evolved. At first, life without Jim or Cherie was debilitating. He feebly wrapped up the spring semester by spending days alone in the darkroom, subsisting on little more than a sandwich a day and whiskey. That morose stretch of time finally bled into summer, when, in an attempt to get him out of his funk, Father Mobie insisted Henry join him on a mushroom-eating tour of Hollywood Hills haunts. Whether he had to thank the drugs themselves, or the subsequent expansion of his mind, Henry still isn't sure. All he knows is that after being lost his whole life, at the end of this summer, he no longer is.

"I wanted to meet with you today to tell you I've decided to move out of film into documentaries," Henry says.

Jacobs' neck jerks. "Oh?"

"Hollywood production doesn't interest me anymore. I came here to create art that changes minds, broadens perspectives. A bunch of contrived, scripted movies isn't going to do that for me."

"I'd argue that's not true," Jacobs responds. "Film absolutely has the power to shift audience perspectives in a wide range of different ways—political, emotional, psychological, what have you. That's one of the reasons we founded this program here at UCLA. No one's saying you need to be Michael Curtiz."

"And what about actual events?"

"Sorry?"

"Reality," Henry says. "Life as it's happening. Like, right now. Outside these golden gates."

Jacobs studies him but stays silent, waits for him to go on.

"Two weeks ago there was a bloodbath just twenty miles away from here," Henry says, pointing out the window. "Thirty-four blacks are dead. Thousands hurt. Why? Because the cops can't admit they brutally twisted and threw an innocent woman across her car for absolutely no reason. And up here, we act like it didn't even happen."

"What happened in Watts is unconscionable, I agree."

"I was there. I filmed it. Everything. I've got ten reels of nightmare footage. Or *evidence*, I should say. Not like anyone would take it seriously for even a minute." He remembers Officer Lockley's contemptuous face when he tried to save Judy Heller. The way everyone in the room, including his mother, had no appetite for truth.

Jacobs clears his throat. "Henry, you realize that we're not here to stifle your creativity, don't you? We're here to foster it. It's entirely acceptable for you to submit a documentary for your senior project. Your Watts footage would be poignant."

"I won't be submitting a senior project, Dr. Jacobs," he says, blood rushing to his head as he prepares his next sentence. "I'm leaving UCLA next week, as I'll be leaving the country."

For the first time, Jacobs' fixed expression morphs into surprise.

"Leaving the country? For where?"

Henry looks out the window and gives a rueful shake of his head. "Did you know that last month we went up to a hundred thousand troops in Vietnam? For something we aren't even calling a war."

Jacobs straightens, cautious and somber. Henry meets his uneasy gaze.

"Yes. I'm going to Vietnam."

"You're…enlisting?"

"No, I'm going as a journalist. No one has the first idea of what's going on over there. Only what the government's telling us, which we can immediately discount. Look at the protest at Berkeley last weekend. At all the protests on campuses across the country. We're in the midst of something huge here. And I'm going to see to it we're not lied to about it."

Jacobs looks pale, and seems to be choosing his words carefully.

"Henry," he says. "While I admire your passion and drive, I can't in good conscience give you my support. This is a bad idea."

"Why?" Henry's voice is icy.

"Because it's incredibly damn dangerous."

"You could say that about downtown L.A."

"Henry, for Christ's sake," Jacobs says, finally roused. "Vietnam is an actual war zone. Hell, if you want to do documentaries, you can stay right here and cover the counter-culture movement that's taking over. God knows there's a tidal wave of something coming. But Vietnam? It's insanity."

Jacobs leans forward in his chair, his crisp blue eyes penetrating Henry's. "I'm telling you as someone who's served. I was in France during the occupation, and…"

His voice trails off, his face crumpling into something

Henry has never seen in Jacobs—resignation and loss. "There's just no describing what you see, Henry."

The air between them feels tangible, three-dimensional.

"You know I'll probably have to go anyway," he says quietly. "They're going to start drafting. At least if I'm a journalist, I get a waiver. I've made my decision."

Other than the distant clicking of Rita's typewriter keys outside Jacobs' sealed doors, the room is silent.

"What station will you be working for?" Jacobs finally asks.

"NBC. I've already signed the contract."

Jacobs lets out an exasperated laugh. "You think there are too many constraints here? At UCLA, in Hollywood? What exactly do you think is going to happen when you work for a network—you're going to have free reign?"

"It's only a six-month contract," Henry says. "After that, I can go independent if I want. It's just something to get me over there. I know they'll cut together whatever BS they want for the nightly news back home. I don't care about that. It's everything I'll be filming every day on my own, keeping in a collection to make into my own documentary at the end. The truth's coming out one way or another, I can promise you that."

"That's a long shot, at best. I've got twenty years in the industry, Henry, and you need to listen to me. I know what I'm talking about."

"Look, Mr. Jacobs, I'm sorry, but I'm going. There's nothing more for me here." Henry lets the full truth of his statement wash over him. Nothing and no one to hold him back.

Jacobs sets his jaw. "Have you told your parents?"

Henry hesitates. "No."

"You don't think you should let them know you're going to *Vietnam*?"

"We're not exactly a tight-knit family," he says. "Trust me, they wouldn't care anyway."

"I seriously doubt that, Henry."

"We'll have to agree to disagree, then," he says.

Jacobs is staring at him, a long and vast sadness in his gaze. Henry tries to ignore the rising guilt in his chest.

"Sir, I want you to know how thankful I am for all you and the faculty have done for me here. I say that with the utmost sincerity and respect. But it's time for me to move on."

Jacobs nods silently and stands as Henry rises from his seat. He extends his hand and the two men shake. Henry turns, walking to the door.

"Henry?" Jacobs' voice is strained. Henry looks over his shoulder and waits. "Take care of yourself."

"You, too, sir. And thanks for everything. Really."

As he leaves the office and heads down the Fine Arts Building's long hallway toward the bright afternoon light, a slow smile spreads across Henry's face.

He has packing to do.

Chapter Twenty

As I DRIVE to the Sardos' house, I try to steel myself for more disappointment. They probably either don't live there anymore or they won't remember a damn thing about a car crash that occurred half a century ago. Both scenarios are equally likely.

I pull up to 65 Piazza Spiega and get out of the car. Straightening my shirt, I walk slowly up to a house that is the complete opposite of Giovanni's. Vibrant yellow begonias smile up at me from wrought-iron plant stands on either side of the polished wooden door. Airy symphony music comes from inside, and I feel an ache in the back of my throat as I remember Mom playing the same in her office.

I knock. After a few beats an attractive, older woman opens the door.

"*Buongiorno*," she says, smiling up at me while drying her hands on a floral linen dish towel. She's teeny, only about four-foot-nine, and she looks to be in her late seventies. I do the math and feel a surge of hope—she's the right age to be Maurizio's mother.

"*Buongiorno,* Signora Sardo?"

"Yes…" she answers, in English. My American accent is pathetically obvious. But thank God people in this town really do put down their roots. Like Giovanni, she's still here in her house, all these years later.

"I'm Juliet Barton," I say quickly, remembering myself. "I'm so sorry to just show up this way, but do you have a son named Maurizio, by any chance?"

She pulls her head back, lifts her delicate eyebrows. "Yes, of course," she says. "He's out at the store, but should be back soon."

Maurizio is in his late fifties. And he's still living with his mother? Damn strange, but it's none of my business.

Her face clouds over. "What is this about?"

"Oh, it's nothing bad," I assure her. "I—don't know how to say this, but I think your son might have witnessed a car accident where someone died. It was my uncle. My uncle Henry who died. A very long time ago. In 1971." My face feels hot and I trail off, waiting to see if anything I've said lands with her.

She lifts the dishtowel to her mouth and her eyes grow wide.

"*Dio mio,*" she whispers. "You are that young man's *nipote*? I cannot believe it. Please, come inside. We can talk."

I float over the threshold into her living room. This

woman actually knows what I'm talking about? She leads me to a comfortable velvet chair and heads to the kitchen. She's back seconds later pushing a glass of cool water into my hand. I thank her, and she takes a seat on the edge of the armchair across from me.

"Call me Daniela, by the way," she says, watching me sip. "It's true. My son witnessed a horrible car accident at his grandfather's that day. He was just outside, playing, and then—" She shakes her head fast. Her sleek silver bob darts left and right. "I'm so sorry to hear that was your uncle."

"Thank you. I never knew him personally, of course, but it is horrible all the same."

"Certainly. And I know this tragedy has stayed with Maurizio. It's one of those things that when you see it as a child, you do not ever forget. Trauma."

As awful as that is, it bodes well for me. I cast an anxious glance toward the front door, willing Maurizio to walk through it right now.

Daniela leans toward me. "But how did you know anything about Maurizio seeing this?"

"Because of this." I reach into my bag and hand her the printout of the newspaper article Gina gave me. I then recite my summary of how and why I came to be here.

"Which is why," I conclude, "I really need to talk to Maurizio to find out what he remembers about this other car he says he saw following my uncle's. The police said they could never confirm there was another car involved, but I think that's bull—er, not true." I catch myself and look around the room for a crucifix. You never know with these old Italians.

Daniela thinks for a minute. "I did not see it for myself, so I cannot say for sure," she admits. "I was inside the house when it happened. But I can still remember the awful sounds—the screeching tires, the crushing metal." She squeezes her eyes shut. "How scared I was when I remembered Maurizio was outside playing, and thinking someone had killed him with their car."

She draws a shaky breath. "When I made it outside, Maurizio was standing so still on the sidewalk, his eyes staring at the man's—" she looks at me apologetically, "your uncle's car, smashed into the cliff. No other people outside, just Maurizio. I ran to him and picked him up, never hugging him so tightly in my life.

"Then I finally start to see the few neighbors open their doors and come outside. There are only a few houses on that part of the road. Someone must have called the police because they show up almost immediately. Maurizio then tell me, *Mama, that other car made that man crash.* I said, *What car, Maurizio? There's no one else here.* But he shake his head and say, very stubborn, *No, Mama. There was a car behind him, but it drive off.*"

I don't speak or move, afraid I might break the spell of her storytelling.

"So, then the police came." She sighs and sits back. "I told them what my son said. Two officers interviewed him and take down his description. But I can tell they don't believe a six-year-old boy. They keep looking at each other the whole time he talks. Later, they said they asked everyone who live on the road. No one else saw the car that Maurizio see. They searched Rosanera to find something that match the description Maurizio gave. But they come up with nothing. So that was it."

"What kind of car was it?"

She purses her lips and inclines her head. "That part I forget," she says. "Maurizio can tell you when he gets here. But, Juliet, I believe my son." Daniela looks me evenly in the eyes. "If he says he saw a car, then he saw one."

Before I can respond, the front door creaks open and a tall, disarmingly attractive man is coming into the room with his arms full of grocery bags. He stops short when he sees me, and looks back and forth between me and his mother.

"*Buongiornio*," he says, an amused smile playing on his mouth. He sets the groceries on the foyer table and takes off his hat to reveal a head of thick, dark locks. As he does, his intense indigo eyes look me up and down. I stand awkwardly to greet him and a hot flush crawls across my cheeks. Maurizio looks absolutely nothing like the man in his fifties I envisioned would still cohabitate with his mother.

"*Amor*, this is Juliet," Daniela says. "She's come to ask you something."

"Oh, yes?" He says, smile growing to show off teeth straight as fence posts. "You've come to see me, *bella*? To what do I owe this honor?"

Before I can start, Daniela tells him in rapid Italian

what I presume is the reason for my visit. As she goes on, the playfulness deserts his eyes. He stares at me.

"He was your uncle?" Maurizio asks. His face is pained, and the trauma of the accident is clear. I've been so wrapped up in finding out what happened to Henry, I haven't even given much thought to what it must've felt like for Maurizio, as a child, to see a man die.

"Yes," I answer, voice cracking. "And I'm so sorry for what you saw."

He walks over to join us and falls heavy into the chair opposite me, eyes never leaving mine. I sit back down.

"I always wondered what his family was like," he says quietly. "In my head, I made up a whole story about him. I've thought about it for years, off and on. About whether he had brothers, or sisters. Who he was. What he was doing here in Italy."

"Funny you should say that," I say, "because that's exactly what I'm here to find out."

"Really?" He reaches for a cigarette from his pack on the table and lights it. He offers me one, but I decline. Daniela opens her mouth and then closes it. I get the feeling that smoking is off limits inside the house, but not today.

"I'm not sure how much your mother told you just now," I say, "but I'm here to find out more about Henry, including how he died." I quickly give him the same background I did with his mother before he came home.

"Wow." He raises his eyebrows and shakes his head. "Honestly, I never thought I'd talk about this again. It was forever ago, but the memory is permanent."

He drags on his cigarette. As he does, beautiful crinkles pop up around his eyes like Richard Gere, like George Clooney, like every man who can look sensual at this age while I'll just look like an old washed-up hag.

He exhales slowly. It's a cross between a sigh and a moan.

"Here is the story," he begins. "I'm outside playing, six years old. All alone. No one else is there. It was beautiful weather, I always remember that. No clouds, not one. Suddenly, there is a roaring engine coming up the *strada*. It scared the hell out of me, that engine, so I turned to look. I see a young guy with dark hair, your uncle, driving a red Fiat. But this is the part I'll never forget: the look on his face. He was terrified."

My spine contorts into barbed wire.

"As he is getting to the curve in the road, there is another car following him. Right on his ass, as Americans say. Almost touching him."

A crisp vision of Henry, horror swept across his face, snaps into focus behind my eyes. There's a sour taste in my mouth.

"I will never forget," he says, "because it was such a strange-looking car following him. A deep blue Alfa Romeo, but with green stripes on the side. I don't remember the driver at all. Maybe because I was so impressed by the car, I wasn't looking at him. *Non lo so.* It makes me crazy that I cannot recall because it is the biggest reason why *la polizia* did not take me seriously. A six-year-old child with no description of the driver. I was outside playing with toy race cars that look almost identical to what I am describing to them. They either thought I was in shock, or just making things up." He stubs out his cigarette into the ashtray on the table.

"The cars were going incredibly fast," he says, "and I can tell by the way the black car starts to swerve that the guy driving doesn't know the road. He doesn't know how sharp the curve is coming up. As soon as he realizes it, I think, it's too late—he can't stop, and the blue car runs him head-on into the rocky wall of the cliff. Then the blue car squeals off and it's silent.

"The man isn't moving, the front of the car destroyed, the windshield shattered and covered in blood. For those few moments, it's so quiet. Me and the wind and the dead man in the car. It occurs to my young mind that for the first time I am seeing death."

I say nothing, spellbound in the worst way imaginable.

"My mother then runs outside, panicked," he says. "'Maurizio, *quello che è successo?*' What happened? The neighbors start making their way outside, too. I burst into tears as soon as my mother grabs me, the horror of the situation settling in. The police came to question me. They must've asked me three million times about this other car. I told them over and over—but nothing. They told my mother they looked into it, but never found this 'supposed' blue and green car. Had never seen it in the town before, and no witnesses had seen it, either. They didn't believe me. It came to nothing."

He looks me straight in the eyes, the gravity of his

story obliterating any sexual desire I'd felt when he walked in the door. I'm positively speechless.

"But I can tell you this, Juliet—the car was real. And what happened was not an accident."

Chapter Twenty-One

Huế, South Vietnam
March 1968

ACROSS FROM THE bombed-out remains of the Jeanne d'Arc church stands the town's last bar with four walls, patched with aluminum siding and thick bamboo slats. The sloping shanty is one of the sole survivors of the Tet Offensive, which decimated the village six weeks before. Inside, Henry stands at a rickety table, the contents of his heavy-duty sea bag spread out in front of him. A group of GIs from the infantry he's traveled with the past couple months lounge throughout the bar on cheap metal folding chairs, exchanging harmless banter. Weapons and sacks lie on the floor next to them within easy reach, but they leisurely roll cigarettes or play cards. It's a rare moment of intermission.

Smoke creeps along the bar's low ceiling. Some of it

wafts up from the GIs' cigarettes and hashish. But most of it is simply the lingering, sour stink of bombs and gunfire. By now Henry knows that in the omnipresent heat and humidity these smells never dissipate, much like the feverish disillusionment that pervades every moment spent in this country.

Henry takes stock of his belongings laid on the table. Almost everything that he'd carried with him in the hulking canvas sack for the last two-and-a-half years was still there. The bound stack of black-and-white composition notebooks, creased pages tattooed with the daily chronology of a surreal existence, and two film cameras—a Polaroid Model 250 instant camera and Canon 35mm SLR, complete with four different lenses.

In the center of the spread sits his documentarian lifeblood: his Portapak video tape recorder with camera. The new technology uses magnetic tape rather than film, meaning the reel doesn't need to be developed, and can also be played back instantly. A game-changer from the Super 8 that's missing from his arsenal right now. *Goddammit,* he thinks. Must've left it back in Da Nang. But such is life here, constantly moving on a whim. He thinks back to right after he first landed in Saigon on New Year's Day two years ago. Those first six months caravanning with infantries seem so extraordinarily innocuous compared to now. They were going around setting up tents and clearing vegetation, slicing down bamboo with machetes, trading stories under star-filled skies. It was more like camping than combat.

Until the bullets had started flying. And they haven't stopped since.

The door to the bar clatters open, and Henry looks up to see two welcome faces—Tyrone, a PFC from Arkansas, and Giovanni, an Italian journalist recently sent by a Roman news network to cover the increasingly contentious war. Ever since Cronkite declared the Tet Offensive a failure for America, although it was factually a success, worldwide support for the war had rapidly declined worldwide. Europe started to send its own reporters to join their American counterparts. And Giovanni was Italy's finest.

"Hank, man, I was wondering where you at!" Tyrone calls, coming over and slapping hands. A brawny, handsome black man with a shaved head and charming smile, Tyrone talked too fast, chewed tobacco incessantly, and held the title of the troop's poker king.

"T, what's good?" Henry says. He slaps at his face, scratching for the millionth time at the mosquito-bitten flesh on his cheeks hidden below three inches of thick, black beard. His itching reopens scabs that never healed—a vicious, hideous cycle.

"Absolutely same shit, different day," Tyrone says, swinging a folding chair over to Henry and plopping down. He pulls a cigarette from his front pocket and lights it. "Keepin' watch for us with all this damn equipment?"

"You know it, man. Always. I left my fuckin Super 8 in Da Nang, though."

"For real? That's some bullshit, man. Sorry to hear."

Tyrone shakes his head, gauging the items on the table and blowing smoke out through his nose like a dragon. "Looks like you got more than enough to keep you going, though. More than that silly-ass Sinatra fool over there!"

From across the bar, Giovanni gives Tyrone the finger and grins at him and Henry, revealing teeth crooked as an ancient staircase. He drops his heavy canvas bag on the floor and wipes his brow, then heads over to play cards with a group of GIs. Over the past few months, Henry has met a torrent of fellow journalists hailing from France, Britain, Holland, Italy, and even Japan, putting the total number to nearly three hundred journalists in Vietnam now—six times the number since Henry arrived in January of '66. Most of these newcomers were talentless and supercilious media whores, jumping on the global news bandwagon ever since Cronkite announced America was losing the war.

Giovanni was different. Tall, lanky, and awkward, he seemed constantly in pursuit of any character attribute that would successfully offset his goofy countenance and make people take him seriously as a journalist. Early on, Giovanni attached himself to Henry, garnering any journalistic knowledge he could from the guy he clearly considered a savant, and Henry was happy to share. Gio was a constant jovial presence in an ocean of misery, as if he misunderstood his mission in Vietnam to be boosting the morale of everyone he met instead of reporting back the day's ghastly events to his media conglomerate employer in Rome. *This guy right here, Hank, he gon' win the Pulitzer!* Gio went around saying to anyone who would listen.

But late into the night, when Gio and Henry stayed awake passing a joint or bottle of cheap bourbon between them, the conversations turned deep. Henry confided in Gio everything he'd never told anyone else. Gio listened. He'd asked about Henry's early days here, before every worldwide network had set up shop.

Henry had told him back then, you could go anywhere you wanted in Vietnam to report. And he personally had. Over the past two years, he had traveled by sampan, foot, car, helicopter, and plane, beginning south of Saigon and moving up north through Pleiku and Da Nang to the Tet Offensive cities including Hué, where he now sat. The whole way, sending his stories and images to the world. There was, of course, no regular transportation, so Henry had learned to run up and down the runways waving at U.S. military pilots, yelling, "Can you give me a lift?", which they did.

On his first plane ride, Henry had sat crouched in a tiny bucket seat, drained and exhausted as the huge C-130 cargo aircraft rattled into the air. In the freight compartment with him, separated from the cockpit, were scores of other Americans. But Henry was the only American alive. All the others were wrapped in green plastic body bags, slain in jungles half a world from home. He found he could only keep his sanity by constantly working on his notes, sifting through and organizing photographs, and planning where he'd go next.

"You get any crazy shit today?" Tyrone asks, jarring Henry back to life. He stares at the GI for a minute, trying to organize his thoughts.

"Nah, man. Just B roll."

"B roll? The fuck is that?"

"Background footage," Henry says. "Just something for them to run on the six o'clock news to remind everyone we're still here."

Tyrone snorts. "I could use some reminding myself. First, what it is we still doing right here in Huế, man. Ain't no VC still hanging about."

Henry tends to agree with him. The infantry was here now because they had been assigned to do recon and clean-up in the aftermath of the Tet massacre. The idea being, there could still be traps, Viet Cong lurking. The North Vietnamese attacked dozens of Southern cities in the Tet Offensive, but Huế fared among the worst. VC armies had stampeded and decimated the city, executing thousands of residents one by one, in addition to lives lost by American troops.

"Hey, man," Tyrone says, ashing his cigarette on the floor. "Can I ask you somethin'?"

"Sure."

Tyrone leans toward Henry. "*Why* you still here? I mean, if I could leave?" He points to his chest and raises his eyebrows to the heavens. "*Shit.*" The word is stretched out over at least five syllables. "I'd've had my ass outta here yesterday."

Henry stops and thinks of how to answer. How

could he describe it? The chance to shape the narrative over here, to make people realize the gravity of what they all experienced every day? The American news stations now clamoring for his footage, as he's become known as one of the most prominent and prolific documentarians in Vietnam? His catalogue of hundreds of hours of GI interviews and thousands of photographs of the people affected by the war? People like Tyrone and other black soldiers, describing their personal accounts that the news stations will never air. Like the prostitutes, barely teenagers, scattered throughout the nation, desperate to be carried away on any aircraft leaving their country in any way possible. Like the soldiers, far younger than he, heads in their hands, M-16s lying in the verdant jungle foliage beside them, beaches like advertisements for paradise if the helicopters and body bags and lines of men, aching to return home alive, were all absent.

"It's just where I'm supposed to be," Henry finally says. "You ever felt like you had a calling? This is mine."

Tyrone shakes his head slowly, eyes large as planets. "Whatever, man. You got some fucked up ideas 'bout your 'calling,' but I respect you."

Henry chuckles and picks up his pack of Marlboros. From the group of GIs behind him, Henry hears Gio exclaim, "A flush! That's a flush! I win, asshole!"

A giant eruption of guffawing and booing erupts from the group as Gio gets up and starts gyrating his hips in triumph.

Suddenly one of the GIs stops laughing, as quickly as

if someone had flipped an off switch. He slumps in slow motion to one side and falls out of his chair, eyes open, his mouth moving but no words coming. At first Henry is stunned. Is the guy having a stroke? An aneurysm? But then he sees the red puddle spreading out on the floor beneath him. The soldier next to him jumps up, and as he does, a hole opens in his throat, unleashing a river of black-cherry liquid. Next comes the sound of rapid, guttural automatic gunfire. Bullets pour through the bar's one cheaply shuttered window.

"Get down!" Henry screams, diving under the table. He knocks his chair on its side and drags it underneath the table as a makeshift shield. As he does, an M-16 that was propped against the wall next to the table clatters to the floor. Henry grabs it and grips it by his side with a white-knuckled hand.

Tyrone hunches down, racing to grab the nearest gun like all the other GIs scrambling for their weapons. Henry looks wildly out from his perch and his stomach drops as he sees Gio standing to one side, completely frozen.

"Gio! Get the fuck over here!" Henry screams. But the slight Italian is paralyzed, rigid with horror and unable to move. Henry's heart assaults his ribcage as he tries to make sense of what's happening. A VC rogue unit? How the fuck did they manage to get past the lookouts?

Seconds later, four VCs smash in the bar's door, instantly killing seven GIs in a torrent of bullets. Tyrone, the only live infantryman remaining, had double-backed to crouch near Henry's table, where he sits now. Their eyes meet. Henry sees what Tyrone is about to do and reaches for him.

"No, no, get under here with me!" His voice sounds like a pleading child, like he did with his mother all those years ago, and he's still begging Tyrone to stay as the man leaps to his feet and manages an animalistic scream, his finger on the trigger of his M-16. Bullets rip through two of the VCs, who collapse lifeless to the ground. Suddenly, though, Tyrone's gun ceases firing.

He pulls repeatedly on the trigger, but the gun only emits a faint click. His drenched, pallid face is awash in horror. One of the two remaining VCs strides over to him and takes enormous pleasure in putting his gun directly to Tyrone's temple, and fires. Henry shoves a fist into his own mouth to suppress a wild scream as he watches Tyrone crumple to the ground. Adrenaline and vomit strangle his windpipe and he's struggling to stay conscious.

The VCs finally turn their fierce gaze on a shell-shocked Giovanni, the crotch of whose plainclothes outfit is wet and dark, his face a bilious green.

"*Nhà báo, nhà báo, no kẻ thù, no Người Mỹ,*" Giovanni stammers. Somehow, he's remembered the script: *I'm a journalist, I'm a journalist, not the enemy, not American.*

The one VC eyes Giovanni up and down, and for a minute Henry crazily thinks that he'll let him go. Instead, he bares his teeth and yanks Gio by his neck, screaming at him, mashing the butt of his rifle into this face over and over. Blood spews from Gio's face with each hit, a sickening dull thump. *He's going to beat his brains in*, Henry thinks. *He's going to fucking kill him.*

As silently as he can Henry changes position from all fours into a crouch. He points the M-16 through the legs of the overturned chair in front of him, trembling fingers confirming that the safety is off and that the gun is loaded. *What if it jams like Tyrone's?* But he has no other choice.

Henry peers through the chair, the stink of sweat, blood, and excrement threatening to make him faint. Stringy, sweaty strands of hair dangle in front of his eyes, partly obscuring his vision. But he dares not move his hand. He tries to ignore Tyrone's empty gaze to his left, which is fixed right on him.

Gio's on the floor whimpering, barely cognizant, the two remaining Viet Cong now arguing with one another. The one, Tyrone's killer, is screaming at the other one, presumably telling him to pull the trigger on Gio. But the other's face just stays a twisted grimace, staring down at beaten and bloody Giovanni, his finger hovering over the trigger.

Henry edges to the front of his makeshift chair-shield and aims up at the VC. For a fraction of a second, they lock eyes. The VC regards Henry with genuine curiosity and surprise, like a child noticing a rat under a table. Henry pulls the machine gun's trigger, blowing away half the VC's face along with his green infantry cap. The VC stays upright, suspended in the air briefly like a puppet, before he falls limply to the ground. Before the other VC can move, Henry turns the gun on him and he too falls to the ground.

The gunfire outside has ceased, and the room is horrifically silent.

Henry pushes the chair aside and clambers the rest of the way out from under the table to Giovanni. "Gio," he says, shaking him urgently. "Giovanni, look at me."

Giovanni had gone into shock, a sickening, vacant look in his eyes. His jaw hangs slack, bruised and bloody from the VC's bashes to his face. As Henry looks around frantically for something warm to cover him with to help with the shock, he hears the pounding of approaching combat boots and yelling in English. He peers out the window to see armed American troops from the other side of the village sprinting toward the bar.

Giovanni looks up at him, confused, his nose already swollen to twice its normal size like a nightmarish clown.

"Hank? What are we doing here in church?" His words are slurred and thick through the blood and saliva filling his mouth. He starts to choke, and Henry props his head up as Giovanni launches into a coughing fit and tries to turn on his side to vomit.

Seconds later, the rest of the Americans stampede into the bar, guns raised, eyes wild. Surveying the damage. Oh Christ, the damage. Those lifeless bodies strewn all over like dolls.

Gio seems for a minute to acknowledge the carnage around him. "*Mi hai salvato la vita*," he stammers between gulps of air and blood. "You save my life."

Henry doesn't respond. He just sits, cradling Gio's head, as a couple GIs rush over to help them. A cacophony of unrest assaults his ears, his soul, his every high-strung nerve. Gio's moans, the wails outside from any remaining anguished villagers, the GIs' commanding shouts flooding the bar. It all blends together with the howling monkeys, and the shrieking birds, and the screeches of the living, breathing jungle suffocating him from all sides until he can't differentiate anymore between those and the ones that are coming from inside his own head.

Chapter Twenty-Two

THE LATE AFTERNOON sky deepens into a violent blue as I approach the stone wall bordering the ocean overlook on Via Marietta. Here, atop these rocky cliffs, sits Rosanera's pinnacle of beauty. Hundreds of feet below me, the mighty Adriatic batters wave after foamy wave against the black rocks, jutting out from the sea sharp as daggers. I pause and squint out at the clear horizon, imagining I can see all the way to Croatia. For a moment, I forget myself and the dreadful reason I'm here.

I've finally reached the very spot Henry died. No, *was killed*. After talking with Maurizio, seeing and hearing for myself his somber conviction, there's not a doubt in my mind that someone deliberately ran Henry off the road. It all makes sense now—why Henry had called Nana earlier that day, wildly upset, telling her he was coming home.

Someone was after him. He had been afraid for his life. But why?

The wind blows ceaselessly around me at this elevation, and I shudder despite the summer sunlight searing my back.

I watch from the sidewalk as cars drive past me, each of them dutifully braking at the apex of the curve, where Henry lost control. On the drive up here from the Sardos' house, I noticed that the wall is only about four feet tall for most of the way up the hill. Presumably, this is because for most of the drive up, there is still a good thirty feet of land between the wall and the cliff's edge.

Not so where the street begins to curve. There, the land recedes completely, and the thick stone wall is the only barrier between the road and the cliff's sharp drop-off. If you were to somehow drive through the wall itself, you'd simply plummet straight down into the sea. It makes sense, then, that the wall at Henry's point of impact is closer to ten feet high, and much more dense.

People navigate around me on the path, chattering families and happy couples on romantic strolls up the hill to enjoy the majestic panorama. But I remain still and silent, chest heaving as I stare at the wall. I don't know what I expected to see: blood, some kind of remains from the crash fifty years ago? Superficial chunks are missing from parts of the wall here and there, and I wonder if Henry's car slamming head-first into it caused any of them.

I fumble in my pocket, find two Xanax, and swallow them dry. After the exhausting events of the day I've had so far, my hangover is returning. A whirlwind that started at the library with Gina, to meeting Giovanni, then over to the Sardos, and now here. Although it's only been the better part of a day, it feels like I've been gone for weeks.

In my bag, my phone vibrates. I reach in, open the text notification and read it, stunned. It's from Bastian: *No, you ruined nothing. You are flawed, I am flawed. We all are. You are perfect the way you are. If you need anything I am here. Bises.*

I frown. What the hell is he talking about? I haven't even responded to his last text from two days ago, when Alessio and I were at the cemetery. Confused, I scroll up in our thread to see what he could possibly be referring to. And then my stomach dives off the cliff next to me.

He was responding to a text I must've sent him last night, when I was dead drunk. Because even though I have zero recollection of doing that, the words stubbornly remain right here in front of my eyes with a timestamp of 2:17 a.m.: *I can't believe I ever left you. This is what I always do. Ruin things. But I'm pretty sure I've always been in [heart emoji] with you.*

No. Oh, no. I stifle a moan and brace myself against the stone wall. A few passersby slow down to stare in my direction. I must look like I'm on the brink of fainting, which isn't far from the truth. What is wrong with me? How could I have actually transmitted that message to him? And how can I have absolutely no memory of doing so? I want to dig a grave for myself right here and crawl in.

Yet the most staggering part of this whole thing is his response. Bastian had nothing to lose by ignoring my drunken text, by never responding at all, and writing me out of his life forever as a mistake he never wants to make again. Instead he chose not only to respond, but to also offer me his unconditional support.

Before I can even consider what to do next, an incoming call from Colette pops up on the screen.

"Juliet, Nana's in a coma," she says as soon as I pick up. Between the benzos kicking in and today's bewildering string of events so far, my mind struggles to make sense of yet another trauma, as if trying to resurface from drowning.

"What?" I rasp.

"She didn't get up at her usual time this morning, so I went in to check on her. She was unresponsive. I called an ambulance, and they just left with her." With the time difference, it's only eight o'clock in the morning back home. I swallow what feels like a boulder and begin walking briskly back to my parked car down the hill.

"Dear God. Is she going to be okay?"

"It's too early to tell," Colette says. "The EMTs said she's stable for now, which is good. I'm heading over to the hospital myself now, but I wanted to call you first."

"Oh, Nana," I whisper, my heart squeezing into a ball. Why is this happening now of all times, when I'm halfway around the world? What do I do? Should I leave and go back home on the first flight out? I ask this aloud to Colette.

She sighs, and I can see her raising those elegant glasses off her nose, rubbing her eyes.

"I don't know, Juliet. I won't know how critical her condition is until I get to the hospital. You might not have to jump on a plane today, but you should probably start making plans to come back in the next day or so."

The next day or so? But I'm finally getting somewhere with Henry. What if I stay a little longer and really find out what happened to him? Then I can share it with Nana, give her the closure she deserves. If she even wakes up, that is. But am I really going to just stay here with my last living relative lying comatose in the hospital? I'm completely torn, a fact I feel like a total asshole about.

"Colette, listen," I say. "Henry was murdered. This was not an accident, and I think I'm onto something here."

There's a long pause before she responds. "*What?* Murdered? What are you talking about? How can you possibly know that?"

I tell her about the newspaper article, about Maurizio and his mother, and then how it all connects to Henry's wildly upset phone call to Nana the day he died.

"It all makes sense now, don't you see?" I say, rushing down the hill past other pedestrians to my car. "The note on the photo, the 'if I don't make it back,' that's not just a random thing anymore, Colette. It's connected. I know it in my bones. There's something in that mausoleum that Henry hid for safekeeping in case something happened to him. I have to find it. I *have* to."

"But in your last text to me, you said it wasn't in any of the Rosanera cemeteries that you searched. So what now?"

Her question hangs over my head like the sword of Damocles. I have no logical response, so I avoid giving an answer.

"Okay, look," I say, finally arriving at my car and fishing out my keys from my bag. "Let me get back to the hotel and figure out flights. Please call me as soon as you know anything from the hospital, okay?"

"Of course. We'll talk soon. Be safe."

I jump into the car and zoom over to the B&B. I leap out and hurry up the steps to my room, put the key in the door and push. It doesn't move. What the hell? I try again, but nothing. The door is hitting against something on the other side and won't open all the way. I put my shoulder against it and shove hard, and it starts to open. Sticking my head through the opening, I see it's my huge, overturned suitcase blocking the door's trajectory—just one of the many strewn-about items that aren't at all where I left them.

The entire room has been ransacked.

⁕

"We called *la polizia,*" Lucca, the proprietress, says in her rustic accent. "Neither me or my husband saw anyone come in here."

She's surveying my room with her hands balled into fists, set firmly into either side of her generous hips. She shakes her head for the hundredth time. "This is incredible. Robbery never happens here on our property, not ever."

My head spins and my stomach roils. This is truly the day from hell. I feel like I'm Jack Bauer.

"You leave a lot of money in here or something like that?" Lucca asks.

"No," I answer. "But, I suppose they may have been

after my Cartier jewels." I pull at the fake gold strands that hang from my neck, bought on sale at Forever 21. Lucca just looks at me and shrugs, not getting the sarcasm.

Even though I've turned my phone's ringer up to the highest volume, I steal another glance at it just to make sure Alessio hasn't returned the frantic voicemail and follow-up text that I left him fifteen minutes ago. I want to update him on everything I learned from Maurizio. This break-in could just be a random coincidence. But my gut screams that of course it has to do with Henry—the biggest indicator being that nothing from my room was actually taken, just rifled through. Whoever did it, it's clear that I'm on to something here in Rosanera, that someone finds my digging for answers threatening.

I can't risk leaving now. I'm so close to finding out what happened to Henry. And what can I really do for Nana at this juncture? Sit idly by her bedside for what could be months while she lies unconscious and completely unaware of my presence anyway? Even if I did do that, and came back here immediately after Nana either regained consciousness or passed away, who knows if the answers will still be waiting? It could very well be that I've disturbed someone in Rosanera enough that in my absence, they'd cover their tracks, or destroy whatever I'm looking for, rendering my entire search hopeless.

Besides, imagine if I do find answers. I can go back and share the truth with Nana about what really happened to her son.

Suddenly my phone jingles with Alessio's number.

"Juliet!" he says, sounding a little out of breath. "I'm sorry, I was outside and didn't hear my phone. I just got your message. What happened?" He sounds genuinely worried.

"Someone broke in, Alessio. I just got home from being out all day."

"Oh, my God. Did they take anything?"

Although I hate myself for doing it, I listen carefully to try to detect any subterfuge in his voice. Does he have something to do with it? He is, after all, one of the only people who knows why I'm here. But he sounds just as stunned as I am, and I erase the thought from my mind.

"No, nothing's missing," I say. "Which is why I know it has to do with Henry. Someone wanted to scare me, wanted me to know that they can get to me if they want to."

I look up and catch Lucca staring at me intently before quickly averting her eyes. Her husband's deep green eyes also flick away from me almost in tandem. A strange feeling tingles my spine, and I turn my back to them and walk to the far side of the room. It dawns on me that on my second day here, I also told Lucca the details of what I'm doing in Rosanera. Come to think of it, she seemed far more interested than I would've expected from a stranger.

"Alessio, listen to me," I say in a low voice. I shoot a glance over my shoulder at the proprietors, but they've moved into the hallway. "Maurizio said Henry was murdered and I believe him. It's creeping me out."

"Okay, okay," he breathes. "We will figure this out together. What is your next step now?"

"It's gotta be talking to the coroner," I say, still talking quietly. "He's the only other person I have left on my list to talk to about this." My heart quickens as I say the words aloud, as I openly admit that after talking to the coroner, I'll fully be in uncharted waters.

"Good," Alessio says. "What's the guy's name? I can look him up."

"I already did, but thanks. He's still alive and living here. I forget his name, let me check." I go over to the desk where the envelope of Henry's final belongings sits exactly where I left it this morning. How bizarre that's the only thing untouched.

I reach in, shuffling around for the death certificate, but can't fish it out. Puckering the long manila envelope and turning it on its side, I let the contents fall out onto the desktop.

"Found it," I say, opening the folded certificate. "Dr. Fabrizio Bolla."

Alessio says something, but I don't hear him. I'm too busy surveying the scant contents on the table before me. Ice water fills my stomach, and my hands tremble as I lay everything out on the table, one by one, until they're all sitting before me. I give the envelope one final peek to make sure it's empty.

"Juliet? Are you there? What's wrong?"

The mausoleum photo is gone.

Chapter Twenty-Three

Paris, France
October 1969

"D'accord, commençons. Jacques Vacher ici. C'est le dix-huit de Octubre, mille neuf cent soixante neuf."

The date, which in French sounds like a calculus equation to Henry, rolls off the young French journalist's tongue like liquid gold. Jacques smiles up at Henry, continuing in English into the microphone on the table between them.

"I have the pleasure of sitting here today with Hank Elysian, renowned Vietnam documentarian and photographer."

Henry smiles, takes one last drag on his Gauloises cigarette before stubbing it out in the red ceramic ashtray. "I don't know about 'renowned,' but *merci beaucoup*."

"Well, here on the indie circuit you most assuredly are."

"Whatever you say, Vacher. Who am I to question a revolutionary like you?"

"*Fraternité, mon frere.*" He laughs it off, but no question he's a legend. Vacher led the French independent broadcasting revolution in May '68 through his unlicensed, illegal radio show *La Vrai Affaire.* It was a big middle finger to the government's state-run radio, and Vacher had literally lived underground for two months during that period of civil unrest reporting from basements and crawlspaces, relocating every couple days to stay ahead of the government and keep broadcasting the real story to the dropouts and freedom riders across France. Henry knows to be interviewed by Vacher now means serious street cred for him.

"So, let's start with your name," Vacher says. "*Hank Elysian.* This is not your given name, *bien sur*?"

"It is not."

"What is it? May I ask?"

Henry pauses. "I'd rather not say." He remembers his early days in L.A. where he craved nothing more than for the world to know his name. Now he couldn't want anything less.

"Respect, man. Can you tell us, then, how you chose your pseudonym?"

Henry clenches and unclenches his right fist, digging his fingernails deep into his calloused palm. One of tics that had followed him back from Vietnam.

"My first name's Henry, so that's where Hank comes from." He doesn't mention that it was none other than Jim Morrison who first gave him the nickname.

"And Elysian?" Vacher says.

Henry pauses. Behind his eyes, he sees jungle foliage strewn with lifeless, mangled corpses; bamboo shoots splintered by incessant bullets. He smells the sulfuric burning of villages; the stink of the winding Ho Chi Minh trail, soaked with blood and mud and boot prints, lacerated into the Earth like the scars on Christ's back. Feels the suffocating heat on his skin even in the comfort of cool, crisp sheets in the middle of the night in his Parisian flat.

"In *The Odyssey*, Homer wrote, 'to the Elysian plain… where life is easiest for men,'" Henry says. "'No snow is there, nor heavy storm, nor ever rain, but ever does Ocean send up blasts of the shrill-blowing West Wind that they may give cooling to men.'" He looks at Vacher. "I needed to believe there was such a place."

"*Merde.* That's heavy, man. You spent almost three years in Vietnam—"

"Three and a half," Henry says, sharper than he means to. Vacher inclines his head in apology.

"*Oui, excusez-moi.* And you left university to document the war, *d'accord?*"

"Right. I was at UCLA with one year to go." Henry pulls a baggie and rolling papers from his shirt pocket. He shrugs. "I left the day after Christmas in 1965. Then I came home—well, to Paris, I mean—on New Year's Day this year. Been here almost a year now." He plucks a rolling paper from its pack, lays it on the table, and sprinkles herb from the baggie onto it.

"You said something very interesting just now—'home.' But obviously, Paris is not home. Do you ever miss it? The U.S., your real home?"

Home. The word has no meaning to Henry anymore. He doesn't even know why he said it just now. His parents, Cherie, Jim, all of UCLA. He's been gone from it so long that he can't remember what any of it felt like. As if it were all a story he'd once read and then packed away.

"No." It's all he can manage to say. He rolls his joint, willing his hands to stop trembling, licks it and lights it. Vacher watches him carefully.

"But you've missed most of the freedom rider movement in *les Etats-Unis*," he says. "San Francisco in '67. All the campus action. The incredible art and music scene. Woodstock. For each of America's imperialistic pigs, there's an idealist that's got balls. But you chose to opt out of it, to be in Vietnam. A courageous act. And then after, to remain abroad and be right here, right now." Vacher points his finger down on the desk, his bushy ginger beard glistening in the dim overhead lights.

Henry shakes his head. "That's not the way I see it."

"How do you mean?"

Henry takes a hit of his joint, welcoming the immediate rush to his head. He wonders what Vacher would say if he told him he'd already intimately known one of the leaders of this incredible American art and music scene, in a way that no journalist ever would. That it was his own ex-girlfriend who appeared next to Jim Morrison in those *Rolling Stone* shoots, and how it was all just one more thing Henry had to accept. But he'd made his choice about how to proceed in spite of it all, and it mattered more than he thought it did.

"I didn't opt out," Henry says. "I opted in. If I hadn't gone to 'Nam, there would be no evidence. No story. We'd forget, in just one generation's time, how the world was burning down, and for who. I won't let it happen."

Vacher nods. "On that note, tell me about your project. You're doing a film and a book, is that right? An incredible undertaking."

Henry runs a trembling hand through his shoulder-length black hair, then down his horseshoe moustache.

"It's a documentary that's focused on the lives of the soldiers instead of the war itself," he says. "Who they were, what they loved, what their story was. Man, I've got thousands of hours of film, and photos. Getting through it's a project in itself. It's brutal work, man. Emotionally and up here, you dig?" He tapped his right temple. Sometimes he'd rise at dawn and work straight through for hours, barely registering that the sun had set. Other times he couldn't move out of a fetal position in bed, the sheets bunched over his eyes to block out the unwelcome light of day.

"As one of the premiere Vietnam reporters of the 'first wave,' your footage, your photography, is some of the most poignant in existence," Vacher says. "It is safe to say that we are all beyond impressed. Your work is alarming, Hank, breathtaking in so many ways. You do not merely report, you are a masterful artist."

This. This is what he has waited to hear his whole life. And yet still, upon hearing it, Henry is numb on so many levels, ironically from the work itself.

"Thank you so much." Henry says, quietly.

"Okay, *Monsieur* Elysian, last question: as a journalist or documentarian, as I myself know, it is incredibly difficult to remain a neutral observer. How, in the face of war, and being in the depths of it for three years as you did, were you able to remain neutral in your documentation?"

"It's impossible," Henry says. "In war, there's no such thing as a neutral observer. You just can't be." He pauses, takes another deep inhale on his joint. "Even if you're not in combat, war gets inside of you. It crawls down your throat. Chokes you. It becomes you, and you it. Inextricable." He exhales and looks at Vacher through half-open eyes. "Forever, I guess."

"And how do you cope?"

"Cope?" he repeats in a hollow voice. "You just open your eyes in the morning. Feel your heart beating. Tell yourself that you're still alive, so you guess you've got no choice—you gotta live another day. You can't think too much. I try to fill the hours with art, my film, this book. It's like any other addiction, really. Telling stories for people who don't have a voice."

※

When Henry arrives at his 11th arrondissement flat after the interview with Vacher, the telephone is screaming from the behind the closed door. He jiggles the keys in the tarnished lock and flings the door open, then hops over the scattered books and records to the titanic desk where the phone is. Hundreds of photos and film reels occupy the desktop real estate. Ghostly images of people who are now deteriorated under either six feet of dirt or the horrors of their own minds.

On the seventh ring, he grabs the phone. "Yeah, hello." Silence, except for a crackling noise that reminds Henry of a flickering fire ready to go out.

"Hello?" he says again. Then, a voice like a phantom floating up behind him, reaching out to touch his spine.

"Brother," it says. That lulling, lyrical voice he's only heard through radio or television for the last three years. Jim. Before he can say anything, the voice continues.

"I opened the paper this morning and saw that Kerouac's dead," the rock star says. "Happened yesterday, it says. Couldn't get you out of my mind."

"How did you find me?" Henry says, finally finding his voice. He falls against the desk, hand gripping the phone like a vise.

"It's funny," Jim says. "When you make a record, turns out people go out of their way to help you, even if you're a shitty drunken imp like me. They'll even go so far as to research old friends and find their phone numbers in foreign countries."

Everything inside him feels jumbled and mixed up and anachronistic. As if the past, present, and future are all welded together, traveling in reverse. Henry had often wondered what he'd feel if he ever spoke to Jim again.

Would he want to hug him? Kill him? Now he knows. It's as if they'd simply picked up where they left off four years ago. He supposes living through a war can put things in perspective.

"So, what do we do now, Hank?" Jim says. "When all our idols are dead? They'll never be another one like him. Or you, for that matter."

"Fuck, man," Henry says. "I don't know." Does he even have any idols? Did he ever? He has no idea what to say, so simply asks, "Did you get what you always wanted?"

"What? This? Fame?"

"Yeah. That. Any of it." Cherie flashes through his mind. He doesn't ask.

Jim pauses. "It's pretty much the same as before, but less important."

"You're on the cover of every magazine. People idolize you. Here you are, talking this noise about idols being dead when you're right here."

Silence. Then, "It's lonely. Desolate. Not thrilling, like it was at first."

Back at UCLA, Henry would've sneered at this poor Icarus tale. But he gets it now. He understands the degree to which life can maim, eviscerate. How it inflicts damage without conscience or prejudice, even if the world adores you.

"I think I'm done with it," Jim says. "The new album's shit." He's referring to *The Soft Parade*. "We phoned it in. I was busy writing poetry. I just want to create something beautiful. A pure expression of joy. A celebration of... existence, you know? Like, uh, the coming of spring or the sun rising or something like that, pure unbounded joy. I feel like I can only do that through writing now. I want to write books, Hank. Novels, anthologies."

In his mind, Henry sees Jim's glassy eyes, hand twirling listlessly in the air as he talks. He wants to tell him that he did create something beautiful, that everything he ever touched always was, but Jim continues: "Tell me about you, about your beautiful soul and what you're doing in gay old Paree."

Henry repeats the rundown he gave Vacher an hour ago while Jim listens intently.

"What did I always tell you, Hank? That you'd do something incredible. And here you are. You went to 'Nam. You lived in that for years, let it under your skin, into your soul, saw and heard and captured shit no one else can begin to understand. You're the one who's doing the real deal, man. You. Not me."

Henry doesn't know how to respond so he says, stupidly: "The Doors didn't play Woodstock, then?"

Jim seems unfazed by the abrupt switch in conversation. "No. We thought it would be this total rip-off of the Monterey Pop Festival. So, no."

"But you didn't play there, either." Henry had never lost track of Jim over the years, as much as he hated to admit it.

"And we weren't fucking asked to, either."

Before he can stop himself, Henry laughs. The sound escapes his throat like a freed slave. Jim joins him and it feels like hours before they settle down.

"Hey, man," Jim says, getting serious again. "You ever get back in touch with your old man and old lady?"

Henry's eyes drift to a sealed, unmailed letter on the desk. He swallows.

"No," he says, an ache spreading through his chest into his extremities. But it was all too late now, too far gone. Looking back now, it seems unbelievable that he never told his family anything—that he was dropping out of school, much less was in Vietnam. What had they thought when his final year's tuition was returned to them? That he'd just disappeared off the face of the Earth? He used to think it wouldn't matter to them. But he's not so sure anymore. When he realized what it was really like when people's children never returned, without a word.

And worse yet, the thought that invades his mind more often nowadays: What if he'd been wrong? About his mother, Pietro, his family? What if everything he'd ever based every decision on was horribly wrong? Maybe we're all broken, he thinks, and we can't love properly, and nothing ever turns out right. He'd poured out these atonements onto paper and stuffed them into the envelope that now lay unmailed on his desk, where it will stay. He's learned to accept a lot of things, but the possibility that he'd receive no letter, no phone call, in response was something he couldn't. He'd survived Vietnam. But he knows he wouldn't survive that, so it's better not to know.

"Yeah, my old man gave up on me for good two years ago," Jim says, jarring Henry out of his thoughts. "He really had it with me after the Miami thing. Too embarrassing for a proper, decorated Naval Officer, you know." Jim's referring to the onstage arrest for exposing himself earlier this year. "'Lewd and lascivious behavior, indecent exposure, profanity, drunkenness.' What the fuck, man."

They both start up laughing again. Henry knows his family may well be gone. But Jim is not. And he needs him now more than he ever thought possible.

"Come visit me, man," Henry says suddenly. "Please."

"I was wondering when you'd ask, brother," Jim says, sounding honestly relieved. "Nothing I'd love more. For sure I will, soon. I'll be in touch."

They say their goodbyes, and as they hang up, Henry closes his eyes and sees Jim that first day back in Cartwright's class—that soft-spoken, idealistic teen. Before the two of them had ended up a pair of grown, parentless children adrift in a collapsing world.

Henry grips the desk, hovering over the stacks of photographs. Here, Tyrone bending down, petting a stray dog in Saigon, his vibrant smile piercing Henry's chest. There, Giovanni in his ridiculous handmade hammock strung between two sagging bamboo branches, poker cards thrown on the ground, his serene eyes searching the sky for God.

Although Henry's shoulders begin to shudder in silent sobs, for the first time in as long as he can remember, he finds his hands are steady.

Chapter Twenty-Four

Paris, France
March 1971

THE FLAT'S HEAVY front door scrapes open and from his seat on the couch next to Jim, Henry hears Cherie's throaty voice say, "Just put it in the fridge. I don't know if he's hungry or not. I know he needs a drink, though, so let's start there."

"*Ouais, d'accord,*" someone says, before launching into a coughing fit. Remy. The cagey Parisian drug lord and fringe music producer who, of course, Cherie befriended straight away when she and Jim got here last month. Over the acid rock music flowing through the room Henry hears bottles clanging and drawers opening and closing, followed by the hiss of carbonation.

Next comes the echoing clunk of thick wedge heels echoing on the centuries-old wooden floorboards, and

Cherie appears holding two beers in one hand and a bottle of cognac in the other.

"Here, my love," she says, smiling sweetly at Jim, keeping her gaze off Henry. She sashays over in a bell-bottomed denim jumpsuit that would've hugged her curves, if there were any left.

"Thanks, baby," Jim says, taking the drinks from her.

"You hungry?"

He shakes his head, removes the cigarette from his mouth and kisses her. She steals a quick glance at Henry before turning away. Jim hands Henry one of the beers, which he starts to drain. *I'm here for him*, he reminds himself, *my brother*. She's just a nasty byproduct. And Jim needs him. Badly, although he'll never admit it. He's deteriorating.

The once slim, leather-clad, godlike performer now looks as common as the middle-aged clerk at the *tabac* store downstairs. His frame is weighed down by an extra twenty pounds and a bushy beard attaches itself to his face like a poorly cut hedge. A tributary of crow's feet bleed from the corners of his eyes.

"I don't read or write much anymore," Jim had told *The Village Voice* a few months ago. "I don't do much of anything. But I will get back in the saddle. I go through cycles of non-productiveness, and then intense periods of creativity."

Henry knew those periods of intense creativity were becoming shorter and shorter. He'd hoped getting Jim out of L.A. would help.

"France is gonna be good for me, Hank, I can feel it," Jim drawls, looking around the half-empty flat, as if reading Henry's thoughts.

"That's great, man," Henry says, kicking a leg up on the marble coffee table in front of them. He's careful to avoid the colossal Warhol-inspired orange ashtray Cherie bought last week, one of the tackiest items Henry could imagine existing. The dope had worn her brain down something fierce. "I'm glad you're feeling it here."

"The vibe here is cerebral," Jim says, then sits up straight looking at Henry. "Did you see all the cameras I brought with me? I'm back to film and writing. That's where my heart is, man. Where it's been this whole time. I've been led astray. You were smart to get out of L.A. when you did."

Regret punctuates his last sentence. He's repeated this sentiment over and over since he got to Paris, and Henry still can't believe that this rock star, this global idol, longs for *his* life.

"You can do whatever you want, man," Henry says. "You got nothing but time." It's something to say, whether it's true or not.

The apartment door bursts open, and a bunch of people spill into the flat. Gavin, Remy's wiry, nervous business partner, leads a gaggle of gorgeous girls in. They're waifish and chic and giggly and French. Their fascinated gazes ping around the room, and upon landing on Jim, they grab each other's hands and giggle.

"Well, well, well," Jim slurs, bleary eyes fixed on the

girls. He picks up an 8mm camera sitting on the worn, crushed velvet sofa beside him. Jim wasn't lying when he said he was back into film. Movie cameras and SLRs haunt every room of the flat. When he went to take a leak, Henry saw there was even a Portapak video camera on top of a Louis XVI-style dresser in the bathroom. When Henry had asked him why he had a camera in the bathroom of all places, Jim had looked at him in surprise, telling him that's where he's most free—standing naked, shaving, making love up against the wall, reciting poetry. Sometimes just starting straight into the camera for minutes on end.

"Ladies, welcome," Jim says, sauntering over to the girls. "The only rule here is that we have to film all of our guests, to document their auras and their place in this mad world."

He raises the camera to his face and starts recording. The tall brunette in the middle titters and bats her eyelashes mockingly. Jim inches closer and all the girls squeal. Remy takes the brunette's purse off her shoulder and comes over next to Henry at the coffee table, where he dumps out a solid brick of white powder. Taking out a pocketknife, he slits open the plastic wrap and intently taps out a pile onto a wooden cutting board. He dips his fingertip in and slides it along his gum line, then smiles up at Henry with crooked, yellow teeth. He reminds Henry of a weasel that slithered out of a trashcan.

"Only the best shit, man. This is how I make my millions."

Fucking bozo. Henry says nothing, pushes himself off the sofa to get another drink when he sees Cherie and stops. Her fawning loyalty has been replaced by shroud of seething darkness, pointed right at Jim. She's standing rigid against the wall, arms sealed across her chest, face contorted into ugly rage. *Isn't she used to this by now?* Henry thinks. Jim's groupies are par for the course. And didn't Cherie have her own side piece, too? Everyone knows Remy wasn't getting paid in cash all the time.

Either way, Jim takes no notice of Cherie, his rapt attention completely on his seductive guests. Cherie catches Henry looking at her and glowers at him, pushes herself off the wall and stalks over to Remy, where she proceeds to hastily cut a line of the powder in front of her. The unexpected pang of pity Henry feels for her is soon forgotten when a gentle, warm palm touches his shoulder. He turns to find one of the alluring Parisiennes smiling up at him with full, bright lips.

"You would like a drink, *oui*?" she asks, to which Henry replies yes, as he does to everything else she offers him into the wee hours of the morning.

⁂

When Henry awakes, it's late morning and the girl is gone. He squints around the room from the mattress on the floor, listening. The flat is deserted. No, nearly deserted. He thinks he hears a raspy, one-sided conversation coming from the living room. Throwing on his jeans, he pauses by the bedroom door and listens to Cherie talking in a low, urgent voice on the other side. He plasters his ear to the crack in the closed door.

"I want to know how much I'm written in for," she says. "If he's changed anything or not. Just fucking figure it out and get back to me."

He opens the door slowly and walks out. "Who are you talking to?"

Cherie jumps, then turns and fixes a narrowed glare on him.

"I gotta go, I'll hit you up later," she says into the receiver, returning the dainty Parisian phone to its cradle. It looks ridiculous in the midst of the ragged, bare-bones apartment riddled with empty bottles and drug paraphernalia.

"What business is it of yours?" she huffs, hunting through the mess on the table, presumably for cigarettes. A paisley scarf is wound around the top of her head, her long blonde locks escaping from the bottom, tangled in her dangling feather earrings. She's got a big purple fur coat on that makes her look like a cat, puffed up to huge proportions with rage.

Henry pulls his smokes from his pocket and offers her one. She stops, looks at him warily, then accepts it. He lights hers, then his.

"Thanks," she mumbles.

"Where's Jim?"

"How should I know?" she snaps, throwing her hand in the air, the smoke circling her head. "He goes where he wants." Dark half-moons are tattooed below her eyes. She looks old, desperate. "You're his best friend. He'll want to see you, not me."

"He doesn't want to see you?"

She snorts. "Seriously? Didn't you see him last night? Eating that shit right up. Knowing he can have anything he wants. I'm just an afterthought."

An uneasy feeling gnaws at Henry's stomach. Who had she been on the phone with?

"He wouldn't be with you if he didn't want to be," he says carefully. "Like you just said, he could have anyone."

Looking at her now, Henry can barely remember who they were together. Life had broken them in different, yet not entirely dissimilar, ways.

"So you were over there in Nam?" she asks, suddenly changing the subject.

"Yeah. Three-and-a-half years."

She looks at him, drags on her cigarette. "You just disappeared. From school. No one knew where you went."

He shrugs. "I didn't think I was breaking anyone's heart."

"You didn't. You weren't. I mean, I'm just saying. It was weird, that's all." For a second, something like sadness flashes across her eyes, but it's gone just as quickly as it came, and Henry can't be sure he saw it at all. "What were you doing the whole time, anyway? Just taking pictures and making movies?" She says it like he's a teenager fumbling around with his first camera.

"Yeah, Cherie. I was taking pictures and making movies. Of people who had no options, no voice. Who woke up every morning not knowing if they'd live or die. And I'm talking about both the Americans and Viets."

"Don't you feel like you missed out?" she says, unfazed. Vacher had asked him the same thing. What is it with these people? They can't imagine a world outside of whatever music festival they went to?

"On what?"

She widens her eyes and cocks her head to one side. "On everything. Back in America. Everything we were doing here, everything going on. You missed it all, man. Over there in that *cesspool*. Was it worth it?"

Henry smashes his cigarette into a nearby ashtray, imagining it's her smirking face.

"It was, actually. And you know why? Because that's already where my head was at. When you and I met. And you told me I was too radical, too passionate. Constantly belittled me for it. Then when you felt like it was finally safe to, you signed right up. Stayed safe in Hollywood, stayed safe fucking Jim, stayed safe in the security of your small, meaningless little life."

Henry grabs his coat from a chair, heads for the door. "So, yeah, Cherie, I guess I do feel like I missed out. On a pathetic existence like yours."

Once down the stairs and outside, he makes the first left into the cafe, where his instincts had correctly told him he'd find Jim. There he sits, hunched over the mirrored, empty bar, a full whiskey glass in front of him. Henry flinches when Jim looks at him. His grey eyes are unfocused, and he looks like he's aged twenty years since last night.

"Hank," Jim says softly. "Walk with me." He slides off the stool and the two leave the bar, heading east.

"Where are we going?" Henry says.

"Over to the 20th." He means the 20th arrondissement, and Henry doesn't ask why. He's just glad to be out of that godforsaken apartment.

As they walk, the sun disappears behind the clouds and the early March chill rushes in. Jim's beard, extra weight, aviator sunglasses, and hat make him virtually unrecognizable. A couple pedestrians slow as they pass by before continuing on their way.

"I gotta talk to you about something, man," Henry says.

"Yeah? What about?"

"Cherie."

Jim looks sidelong at Henry, a smile spreading across his face. He points at him, then shakes his finger.

"Come on, brother," he says, slowing down as they reach a set of towering, ornately carved iron gates. "You said what's done is done."

"Jesus. It's not about that." He's about to go on when he realizes they're standing in front of Père Lachaise Cemetery. It's the oldest and largest in the city limits, wildly popular with tourists and locals alike, including Henry. "Why are we here?"

Jim holds out his hand. "*Apres-vous*. Into Duat, the land of the dead, where Osiris rules."

As they go in, Jim takes off his sunglasses and stands in the center of the main gravel path. Hundreds of beautiful, ancient mausoleums of varying intricacies are packed in beside one another. Some with bronze sculptures, turned green with age, of angels, mourning saints, crosses, or even busts of the deceased. Between the mausoleums are giant stone crypts and tombs, some with just names and dates, others with intricate poems and prayers carved into them. The entirety of the vast cemetery is circumscribed by a smooth stone wall with massive verdant trees arching and bowing over in places.

"The Egyptians believed if you made it through the long, demon-ridden journey through Duat, they'd weigh your heart next to a feather," Jim continues, starting up the path into the sea of mausoleums. "If it was lighter than the feather, you'd be free, granted passage to heaven. And if it outweighed the feather, you'd never leave, walking forever through the darkness."

Henry sighs, anxious to return to the subject at hand. "Seriously, man, about Cherie. I overheard her on the phone this morning."

Jim says nothing, just keeps walking next to him.

"I don't know who she was talking to, man, but she was asking about money," Henry continues. "If she still had access to money, or was 'written in.' It just gave me bad vibes."

Jim laughs, and it's hollow and bizarre sounding.

"The woman manages all my money, Hank," he says. "I hate dealing with that shit, so I gave it over to her. And I'm leaving everything to her. She knows that. We've talked about it. It was probably some accounting thing. Don't worry about it, brother. My old lady's cool."

"Didn't seem like that last night."

"No?"

"*No*, man. You didn't notice? She was fucking pissed when those chicks came over. And she's been in a mood since they showed."

"That's just her." Jim waves his hand. "I've got my girls, and she's got… you know, whoever, I guess. But she knows deep down she's the only one I love."

"You sure about that? She doesn't seem to dig the whole free love thing, man."

"Positive. I appreciate you looking out for me but there's nothing my old lady's gonna do to rob me blind or anything like that. Trust me."

Henry wants to protest but Jim comes to a halt in front of a remarkable mausoleum.

Made of smooth, elegant limestone, it stands about ten feet square and looks about over a century old. There's a wrought-iron double door, speckled with rust in the center. A kaleidoscope of cracked stained glass is embedded in each panel of the door. The left door is shut but the right is open just slightly. Two identical life-sized statues of robed, hooded figures frame the entryway, one anchored on each side of the door.

"Can you imagine this incredible beauty?" Jim says. "This one's the most beautiful of them all. Look at the saints, sobbing for the joy of life and death and no remorse, no regrets." It was terribly sad, but lovely. "This," he points to the mausoleum, "is where I want to be buried."

"I think this one's already taken," Henry says.

Jim doesn't laugh, just tilts his face up to the overcast sky. "Who wouldn't want to spend eternity here in this mecca with the gods, with Osiris looking over you?"

Out of nowhere, a wave of panic grips Henry as he wonders if this is actually a dream. Because suddenly it feels like he and Jim are no longer in Paris, or on Earth, or anywhere at all in the universe, but in fact traversing the underworld of Duat, making their final passage together.

"Brother, don't worry," Jim says. "About anything. From now on, there's going to be nothing but beauty and salvation and peace."

He turns his soft grey, haunted eyes on Henry. "And you and I, we're in this together."

Chapter Twenty-Five

Paris, France
July 3, 1971
6:33 a.m.

HENRY WIPES HIS mouth, still tasting vomit. He's reeling in the dark hallway in front of the apartment door. The phone call came fifteen minutes ago, and he'd made it here in ten, leaving his car parked at a crazy angle outside.

He raises his hand to knock, but falters. Because once he does, once he goes in and sees and verifies, the horror will be real and nothing will ever be the same again. Like so many times before, he's staring down another sickening revelation.

Jim is dead.

He doesn't know how yet. He hung up on Cherie as soon as she choked out the words, then rushed to the sink where he heaved up the contents of his stomach. *Man up*, he thinks. *You need to man up. For Jim.*

He finally knocks and jumps at the sound, hollow and deep like a bottomless well. Scampering footsteps from the other side, then Cherie flings it open. She's still dressed up from the night before, mascara raked down her cheeks. Her puffy, raw eyes search Henry's clammy face and before he says anything she pulls him inside, convulsing into guttural sobs.

"He's dead. He's fucking dead, Henry." She falls against the wall, crying so hard she's nearly folded in half. "I got up and he was in the—the tub, wasn't breathing—and he—he—oh my god."

The sour afterburn of vomit creeps up Henry's throat and his ears start to ring. He walks in and shuts the door behind him, trying to maintain his balance.

"Did you call the ambulance like I said?"

Silence. She peers up at him with fearful, owlish eyes. "No," she whispers.

He stares at her, imagines what it would be like to wrap his hands around her neck and squeeze. "Why the fuck not?"

"Because, like I told you, there's no point! He doesn't need an *ambulance*. His body's cold. I can't deal with cops yet, I can't. I just found him twenty minutes ago, Henry! And there's drugs all over the fucking place. We gotta clean up first."

She rushes past him into the living room and grabs a trash bag, presumably to pick up where she'd left off seconds ago before Henry arrived. She goes around the room, sweeping in strewn-about needles and baggies, dumping ashtrays.

Henry starts for the bathroom, but stops as he passes the kitchen and does a double-take. Remy is at the sink, quietly cleaning up. He looks up at Henry, his face blanched and somber. What is he doing here? On the phone, didn't Cherie say she was alone?

Henry ignores him and heads to the bathroom, moving in slow-motion, like he's underwater. *This isn't real, this can't be real, dear God please let this be a twisted joke.* By the time he gets to the half-open door, he's struggling to contain his growing hysteria. He can't see the tub from this angle, only the sink and part of the dresser, its surface heaped with random bottles, toiletries, and the Portapak camera. *Go on. You have to do it.*

He pushes open the door to reveal a half-submerged body in the bathtub. Reflexively, Henry stumbles to the sink, gripping the cold ceramic on either side as he empties his stomach of its remaining bile, for what feels like ages. When he's finished he slumps against the wall, trembling, forcing himself to face his friend.

Cherie is right. Jim's been dead a while, at least a couple hours. His face has already taken on that telltale bloated sheen Henry has seen too many times in Vietnam, the skin white and stiff as a marble slab. Jim's eyes are closed and his mouth hangs open slightly, his full bottom lip now the color of frozen fish. Strands of hair below his ears float like delicate tendrils in the water. Stillness and loss pervade every inch of the room. Yet Jim's body still holds a sense of quiet power, even now, in the cruel absence of dignity that death demands.

Henry inches closer. There is no visible bruising or blood. A balled-up washcloth lies on the floor next to the tub along with a near-empty whiskey bottle and pack of cigarettes. An ashtray and two burned-down, squat red candles sit a couple feet away. The wax had dripped onto the black-and-white tile floor and dried like congealed blood. Henry turns, and through blurred vision, feels his way out of the room.

He staggers back into the living room where Cherie is sunken into the emerald velvet sofa. Remy sits perched on the arm next to her like a vulture. He stares at Henry, expressionless.

"We're done," she says mechanically. "Everything's thrown out, and I called the cops."

Henry collapses into the chair opposite Cherie and Remy and scrubs his face with his sweaty hands.

"Tell me again what happened," he says through his fingers.

Cherie exhales, low and long. "It's like I told you. Me and him went out last night to dinner, then saw a movie. Then we met up with Remy and Gavin in Bastille for drinks. Remy came back with us."

"And what time was that?"

"I don't know. Two or three?" she says, looking at Remy for confirmation. He nods.

"Then what?"

"We had more drinks here. Remy had some good coke, so Jim did a few lines with us. Then he said he wanted to go take a bath," she says, her voice breaking. Remy shifts and looks intently at Cherie. Is he trying to catch her eye?

"In eighty-five degree weather, he wanted to take a bath?" Henry says.

"I didn't say it was a *warm* bath. You know the crazy shit that gets into his head."

Henry glares at Remy. "That how you remember it, too?"

"Yes. Exactly as she said."

The whole thing feels off. He can't shake the image of Cherie on the phone a few months back, demanding to know where she stood in Jim's will. When Henry mentioned it, Jim couldn't have cared less. He assured him it was nothing. Was it really? Henry doesn't know to think, and his mind swirls.

"Then what?" Henry asks again.

"I heard him in there coughing again," Cherie says. "He'd been coughing the whole goddamn night. I told him to quit it with the cigarettes, go to the doctor again in the morning. He kept saying there was no point, the doctors didn't know anything."

It's true Jim's cough had gotten much worse. What started as a dry hack over the winter turned into alarming, ceaseless fits where Jim's hand would come away from his mouth covered in blood. The doctors had done myriad x-rays and tests, all of them inconclusive.

"Then he got in the tub, and I heard him hacking up a lung in there too," she continues. "Then he starts singing and talking to himself. Like he always did in there."

A sudden thought clamps down on Henry. The

Portapak video camera on the bathroom dresser. Had Jim been recording himself last night?

"I went in one more time to check on him," Cherie says, voice wavering. "He was out of his mind, drunk and high. 'Come on, get out of the tub and come to bed,' I said. He wouldn't, so I gave up and went to sleep.

"I got up around six to pee and I found him in there, like *that*," she finishes hoarsely.

Henry stands up and paces the room. He's got to check the Portapak, and he's got to do it now. Before the cops get here and the whole flat becomes off-limits. He pretends to choke up, and heads in the direction of the bathroom. Cherie's eyes follow him.

"Where are you going?"

"I just need another minute with him before they take him away," he says, covering his face as though he can't bear to look at them anymore. Before anyone can protest, he hurries into the bathroom and shuts the door quietly. He struggles to focus on the Portapak instead of Jim's body. The two-piece unit, a video camera plugged into a square, battery-driven, reel-to-reel video tape recorder, sits as still and lifeless as its owner. But the camera's eye is pointed right at the bathtub. Could it be that Jim unwittingly recorded his last moments on Earth? Adrenaline roars through Henry's head like a freight train.

He lifts the recorder's plastic case, revealing the two video tape reels inside. The left one is empty, the right one full. A completed recording. Of exactly what, he doesn't know, but he's going to find out. He removes the full reel from its cradle, slips it into the front of his jeans, then closes the lid. In front of the mirror, Henry adjusts his clothes, tightening his belt and billowing out his shirt to look as natural as possible. Thank God the reel isn't big—only six inches long and half an inch thick. If he can slouch a little and keep his hands in his pockets, no one will notice.

Before he goes, he takes one final look at Jim in the mirror. The early morning sun begins to trickle in through the transparent curtains, casting prisms of soft light across his friend's cold, pallid face. He thinks of everything he's left unsaid, of all the things he wants to tell Jim right now, before they must part ways forever. Before Jim is no longer just his, and becomes the world's loss to mourn. *There will be time, there will be time,* T.S. Eliot wrote.

But when the end comes, there never is.

"So long, brother," Henry whispers. "If you left me something, I promise you I'll find it."

~

Back at his flat, Henry moves from window to window yanking the curtains closed, then turns on the projector. The familiar kick of its motor whirs to life, and as the lightbulb warms up, a white square gradually appears on the wall across from him. He unscrews a whiskey bottle and gulps from it without any sense of taste. His ravaged stomach lurches in protest but he forces the alcohol down anyway.

The lighted square on the wall now glows with full

luminosity. Each Portapak reel can record about half an hour of footage. Would this one contain the thirty precious minutes before Jim died? Or would it be a naked rambling from weeks ago? *Only one way to find out.*

Henry hits play and the rat-tat-tat of the tape reel assaults the room. A black-and-white image of a shirtless Jim Morrison snaps into focus on the wall across from the projector. He's in front of the bathtub with both faucets running, exactly where the camera's eye was pointed this morning when Henry found it.

Jim peers into the camera, eyes unfocused, and sways while humming a tune Henry doesn't recognize. He leans over to pull off his underwear, and the two burned-down red candles are right there behind him, burning bright.

Henry's stomach turns to slush. The footage *is* from last night.

Jim stands back up, murmuring. Henry pushes his ear to the projector's speaker, but can't make out what he's saying. Then, the rock star starts coughing, at first like a tickle in his throat. But it soon transforms into a debilitating fit. Henry grimaces as he watches his friend gasp and gag, spitting into the sink for almost a full minute. When he faces the camera again, traces of dark-colored spittle decorate his lower lip. Henry hadn't realized it had gotten this bad.

Jim wipes his mouth, closes his eyes and seems to reclaim his breath. Then the bathroom door creaks open and Cherie comes in.

"Jesus Christ, will you stop with these fucking things

already?" she snaps, grabbing the ashtray next to him and stamping out his cigarette. Jim tries to focus his drunken stare on her.

"Why do you have to take it all from me, huh? Why, Cherie?"

She sighs and looks away, disgusted. But Jim grabs her, turns her to face him. She tries to pull away but he holds her steady.

"Go out there and fuck your boyfriend," he sneers, pointing over his shoulder. "Go ahead. You think I haven't had my share of women? Right here, exactly where you stand?" He's smirking like a child who let a secret fly.

"Fuck you, Jim. What do you even think you're doing anymore with your life?" She surveys him and barks out a bitter laugh. "Look at you. Pathetic. You're just getting old and irrelevant, man." Then she stamps out.

"Hey, bring me back some whiskey!" he shouts after her. She yells something back, but Henry can't make it out.

Jim looks into the camera. "The love of my fuckin' life, ladies and gentlemen," he says, bowing, then starts cackling. Staggering back from the camera, he turns and his bare ass gets into the tub. He sinks into the water and starts singing Jimmy Reed's "Baby What You Want Me to Do."

"I'm goin' down… I'm goin' up, down, down, up… Anyway ya wanna let it roll," he sings, beautifully on key for how astonishingly high and drunk he clearly is. Henry glances at the projector reel. It's over halfway gone now, and he knows there's less than fifteen minutes of footage left. *Please,* he prays. *Show me what happened.*

Jim takes a washcloth hanging on the side of the tub, soaks it, then wrings it out and makes it into a pillow behind his head. He leans over to grab a half-full bottle of whiskey from the floor next to him.

"I got my drink right here! I don't need you to bring me shit!" he hollers. Then he guzzles from it and goes back to singing. "Yeah, yeah, yeah…You've got me doin' what you want me…A-baby why'd you wanna let go…"

But he's stopped short by another coughing fit, this one like a volcanic eruption. Jim drops the whiskey and the bottle clatters to the floor as he leans forward, hacking straight into the bathtub. Bloody saliva drips from his mouth into the water.

Henry frowns. When he looked this morning, the bathtub water was clear. Where was the blood?

Jim keeps coughing, and it sounds like he's actually dying. Half a minute later, Cherie comes back in.

She moves toward Jim, then stops. She's standing just inches away from him with her arms crossed, glowering at him as he grunts and gasps for air. Jim reaches for her, eyes pleading. But she doesn't move. Her shoulders rise and fall quickly. Remy comes in behind her, and Cherie whips around. She's crying bitterly. Remy looks between her and Jim, and a savage darkness washes over his features.

"Do it!" Remy shouts. "Now's the time. Just end it!"

Henry sinks his fingernails into his cheeks until he can't feel his face. It's like watching someone skin a live cat.

Cherie bawls, "I can't! Remy, I can't."

Jim's coughing has started to wind down, but by now, the intensity of the fit plus the drugs and alcohol have left him barely cognizant. His head falls against the tub, eyes closed as tiny moans escape his lips.

Remy lurches forward, grabs the washcloth out of the water.

"You're always telling me you want it over with, here's your chance! Do you want to be free or not?" He shakes the sopping washcloth at her, and motions toward Jim's mouth.

"Do you know what you're asking me to do?" she yells.

"Of course I do! It's what you talk to me about every fucking night! What you say you wish would happen!"

Cherie screams, smashes her fists all over Remy, and the two of them struggle with each other, clawing and fighting until she grabs the washcloth from him.

"Is this what you want? To see me do this?" Her eyes are inhuman lenses as she bends down and shoves the washrag over Jim's mouth.

He immediately starts coughing again, the fit going deep down into his lungs with a sickening gurgle. In horror, Cherie tries to jerk her hand away before Remy clamps his down on top of hers, sealing Jim's nose and mouth. A dark stain spreads through the cloth.

Henry watches paralyzed in the dark, an impotent witness to the life draining out of his friend on the projected image before him.

Jim's coughing wanes. He's flailing, but weakly now.

Cherie turns away from him, unwittingly facing the camera head-on, sobbing. Remy keeps his hand fused over Cherie's. Henry is vaguely aware of noises escaping Jim's throat, but couldn't say what they are. Jim's body spasms violently. Then he goes still.

His right arms splashes down into the water, his left over the side of the bathtub, hitting Cherie. She shrieks and crab-walks back from him. The washcloth stays glued over Jim's mouth like a piece of wallpaper. It's utterly motionless.

Cherie's wailing as Remy grabs the washcloth off of Jim's face and shoves it over hers, which makes her scream even more violently.

"Shut *the fuck* up!" he hisses. "We have to be silent. Everyone will hear!"

Her howling diminishes into soft whimpers. Remy drops the rag from her mouth. He holds and rocks her on the floor in front of Jim's body.

"It had to be done, it had to be done," Remy repeats, smoothing Cherie's sweaty, tangled hair. "He would've killed himself soon enough anyway. You know it's true."

Henry thinks Cherie says something then, but he can't be sure, because right then the whole room, the projector, and the image of his murdered friend tunnels smaller and smaller before his eyes, as if he's being yanked away from it all at the speed of light until there's nothing.

Chapter Twenty-Six

Dr. Bolla's gnarled hands open and close around the top of his smooth oak cane as we sit across from each other in his darkening living room. Thunder crashes in the distance from somewhere in the hills beyond his stone farmhouse, churning up a cool breeze through the open windows. I stifle a shiver. Purple shadows the color of bruises spring up from the corners of the room like ghosts revealing themselves.

"Thank you for meeting with me, Doctor," I say. I called Bolla the moment I'd hung up with Alessio back at the B&B. Not only did Bolla answer his phone, but even after my erratic explanation of why I was calling, he agreed to see me right away.

Despite the chaos of today, I can't help but feel a swell of satisfaction. For once, in as long as I can remember, I was right. The mausoleum photo is clearly connected to

Henry's death. It had to be, or else whoever broke into my room wouldn't have been looking for it.

But my self-gratification is fleeting. I now have to figure out *who* took it, and to what end. Was it Henry's killer? Someone covering for his killer? Do they know where the mausoleum is, and what's hidden there?

And worst of all, are they going to get to it before I can?

"It is no trouble," Bolla says, but his face looks strained. "As I told you on the phone, I remember your uncle's accident. Tragic."

"Yes, it was," I say. "But more than that, it was criminal."

Bolla's expression doesn't change, which throws me. Shouldn't he be taken aback like everyone else?

"Look, Dr. Bolla, I'll get right to the point," I continue. "This afternoon, I spoke to Maurizio Sardo. My uncle's crash wasn't an accident. He swears he saw a car purposely run him into the cliff wall. I absolutely believe him. Especially since something crucial to all this was stolen from my room today."

That piques his interest. Bolla sits up straighter and his eyes get wide.

"What did they take?" he asks hoarsely. I start to answer, then stop, suddenly wary. Why am I the one sitting here, giving him information when he's the one who examined my uncle's dead body? Isn't he the one who owes me an explanation? And as crazy as it sounds, how do I know that Bolla isn't involved in the cover-up?

"You examined Henry's body, Dr. Bolla," I say, ignoring his question. "Did you find anything that looked suspicious?"

"His death was the result of a car accident. It is up to the police to investigate the death."

"But you're the medical examiner. *You* determine the cause of death."

He hesitates. When he speaks again, his voice is as shaky as a child's crayon drawing.

"That is true. But in this case, the cause of death was the head-on impact of the collision. Whether or not that was caused intentionally is a matter for the police, not the Coroner's Office."

That's it. My patience evaporates. I'm done with pleasantries, half-truths, and most of all, interviewing reticent old men.

"Dr. Bolla, I'm sick to death of running into dead ends in this town," I say flatly. "What aren't you telling me? My family and I deserve to know what happened to my uncle, and why, after *fifty* years, no one wants to—"

Bolla holds up his hand, and I pause. He takes off his glasses, and the wrinkled skin under his eyes glistens. Earsplitting thunder explodes over the house and rattles the untouched espresso cups and biscotti on the small table between us.

"It was horrible," he says. "I—I didn't know what to do."

"What are you talking about?"

When he looks at me, he's utterly devastated.

"Everything was different back then, the times were crazy. You must believe me. I wanted to say something, but I couldn't."

I stare at Bolla, my breath shallow in my lungs.

"The day before we released your uncle's body, someone came to talk to me about him," he says. I sit up ramrod straight.

"Before I tell you, I must explain." His weary eyes search mine. "I never told anyone about this, and I'm deeply sorry for it. But you have to remember, those times…those were not normal times."

I want to ask him when exactly he believes the times have ever been "normal," but I'm terrified to break the spell of his confession.

"In 1971, it felt like the world was collapsing," he says. "I was so young. I had only thirty years. Everything had changed drastically, everyone felt in danger of the future. Even here, in the tiny village of Rosanera, there was uprisings and violence. Political unrest. Extremist riots in those years, bombings and killings throughout Italy. No trust. Families torn apart. And so many drugs—overdoses, robberies. It all seemed to come out of nowhere."

He looks absolutely petrified, as if merely recounting the past would will it into existence once more. It's common knowledge that the '60s and '70s were wild, unstable, chaotic. But Bolla's personal experience seems to have crossed the line into acute trauma. What could have possibly happened?

"You must believe me," he pleads. "I told no one

about this because at the time, I genuinely feared for my life. And for some time after that."

"Please just tell me," I say hoarsely. He falls back in his chair and closes his eyes.

"*Dio aiutami,*" he murmurs. "The morning after your uncle died, a woman and man came to see me in my office. Very early in the day. They were already waiting for me outside when I arrived to work. He was French and she was American, both around my age."

A French guy and an American lady? I don't know what I expected to hear, but it wasn't this.

"She said she was your uncle's sister, come to claim the body," he says. "But I had just contacted your family the night before, and they had authorized us to prepare the body for shipment back to America. I asked her about this, but she said plans had changed. That she had booked a flight right after the phone call, and wanted to see the body first.

"I immediately knew it was a lie. For one thing, both she and the man looked restless and impatient, not sad. And I could see that desperate look of drug addiction in her eyes. She said she just wanted to see the body and collect the final belongings right away. I knew something was very wrong."

An invisible noose tightens around my neck as he speaks.

"After a few minutes of back and forth, the Frenchman take a pistol out of his pants and tell me to get in my office. He shoved me inside and the girl followed. He hold the gun to my head the whole time. 'Where are his things?' she says. 'Whatever he had on him and in the car. Give them to me now.'

"I tell her, 'I don't know what you're looking for. He had nothing of value. He had no money, *I* have no money. You come to the wrong place if you want money.' She laughs, and then says to me—this I will never forget—'You think I need money? Don't you know who I am? Don't you read the magazines?' I just stare at her and shake my head. She says, 'I'm Jim Morrison's wife. I don't need your *merda* money.'"

I blink at Bolla's pained face, trying to comprehend what he just said. He might as well have just told me that we were actually living on Mars.

"Jim Morrison? As in, The Doors?" I say. Bolla nods.

It's so absurd, I almost want to laugh. What in God's name could Jim Morrison possibly have to do with anything? And his *wife*, of all people? Was Jim Morrison ever even married? Although I'm not a huge Doors fan, I know enough to remember the guy getting blowjobs in elevators and drinking himself into oblivion alone. Not like marriage precludes these actions, mind you, but it still seemed unlikely.

But beyond that, what could this possibly have to do with Henry? Bolla can't be right. He must be senile, or delusional.

"I was so shocked that I said nothing, wondering if it was true," Bolla says. "And if so, what does she have to do with this regular American guy?" He echoes my exact thoughts. "All I knew for certain is this French guy has a gun to my head. He cock the pistol and she says, 'Is this really worth dying over?' I see in her eyes she means it—both of them do. So I finally go to my filing cabinet and hand the envelope to her.

"She dump everything out on my desk, and I can tell right away she's furious, can't find what she was looking for. 'You see?' I tell her, trying to calm her down. 'I wasn't hiding anything from you.' She looks at me a moment and then in great anger, shoves the envelope and everything off my desk onto the floor. In that moment I honestly thought they would kill me. Then she says, 'If you ever tell anyone I was here, I will kill you. I have nothing but time on my hands. Do you understand?' I promise them, and they leave. I stay on the floor, crying for I don't remember how long.

"It was only two days before that, everyone found out Jim Morrison was dead. So I go and look through the magazines about Morrison, and sure enough, this girl, she is in some pictures with him. I couldn't believe it was true. But it gave me enough fear that I never said a word to anyone. Not to your family, and certainly not to *la polizia*. I couldn't bring myself to do it. Please forgive me."

I feel like I'm outside myself, floating high above, watching Bolla talk. How can this be true?

"Just so I understand," I say slowly. "Jim Morrison's wife and some French guy demanded to see Henry's stuff, didn't find what they were looking for, threatened to kill you if you ever told anyone about it, and then left?"

Bolla nods miserably.

"So, what does that mean? *They* killed him? Jim Morrison's wife and some French guy murdered Henry by running him off the road?"

Just saying the words aloud sounded insane. But really, was it? Henry could've become involved in all kinds of stuff, with all kinds of people. Like Bolla said, those were not normal times.

"That, I cannot say," Bolla answers. "I have no idea of the connection, but there certainly is one. To me, it is too much of a coincidence that he died in an 'accident' with people like that after him."

All of a sudden, I start laughing. It's an unfamiliar, hysterical sound. I want so badly to call my mother. *Mom, did you know? Jim Morrison's wife and a random Frenchman killed your brother.* But Mom's dead, and she'll never know that this happened. Disturbingly, this fact makes me laugh even harder.

Bolla stares at me, unsure of what to do. Part of me wants to leap over and shake his old, ratty frame, demanding to know how he could've have been so weak. How he refused, even fifty years later, to tell anyone about it. To think of everything Nana, Pop-Pop, and Mom could've learned about Henry and his life if an official investigation had ever happened.

But, no. Instead, these buried enigmas continued to fester until half a century later when I dug out Henry's envelope from the back of my dead mother's closet. And now everything's too deteriorated to make any sense out of. I stop laughing and wipe my eyes, start to regather my wits. And as I look at Bolla, my anger fades. This shrunken, small man has been tortured enough by his own conscience.

My head throbs as I try to piece together what I've learned here. Henry was murdered. Likely by Jim Morrison's wife and her friend. The obvious question is why? Did he steal something from them? Or was it something of *his* that they wanted, like the mausoleum photo? Did Henry hide it in his cigarette pack specifically to keep it away from the two of them?

And maybe whoever stole the photo from my room knows what's there—whatever Morrison's wife and friend were desperate to find all those years ago. I think about the cocked gun pressed to Bolla's temple and flinch, instinctively swiping away an invisible metallic coldness at my own temple. Whatever is or was in the mausoleum, I have to find it, and fast.

I can feel it in my gut—time is running out.

Chapter Twenty-Seven

Paris, France
July 4, 1971

THE SCREAM OF the telephone slashes through Henry's tormented sleep. He shoots up in the tangled mess of sweaty bedsheets, his mind still held hostage by nightmarish hallucinations. He stumbles over empty bottles on the floor to the phone.

"Yeah," he rasps.

"It's me," Cherie says.

Her voice makes his scalp freeze, and he suppresses a gag reflex. There's nothing left in his mind now except the footage of Jim's murder.

"Yeah," he says again, struggling to sound normal. As much as he wants to, he can't let on that he knows. Not yet.

"Just wanted to let you know there's no funeral plans yet," she says. "But we're trying to get him a plot at Père

Lachaise. It's where he was always talking about being buried."

Henry's heart shrivels as he thinks back to the day Jim pointed out the mausoleum where he wanted to spend eternity.

"But of course the French are snotty assholes. They'll never approve a plot there for someone like Jim," she sighs. "It's gotta be done under the radar, so Remy's figuring it out. He's got hook-ups." *No question about that*, Henry thinks.

"There's already rumors all over the city that he's dead," she continues.

"Yeah?"

"The press has been calling here nonstop. It's awful. I don't know what to say. I'm trying to buy us some time by telling them he's in the hospital with exhaustion. Once we get the plot secured, we can bury him. Then announce it. So it goes without saying, but don't say anything to anyone. Okay?"

Henry closes his eyes and dry swallows. His head feels like a shipwreck. He hadn't even thought about how or when it would be reported to the world that Jim Morrison was dead. All he's focused on is what he needs to do next.

"Fine. Let me know when you get it figured out," he says. It doesn't matter when the funeral is, though. Henry knows he'll be gone long before then.

Then, trying to keep his voice neutral, he says, "What was the cause of death?"

Only the sound of the line crackling on the other end. "Heart failure," she finally says.

"Heart failure," he repeats. "Due to what?"

"They aren't sure. Could be the horrible cough he had, all the booze, the coke. It's hard to say. His heart just stopped." *Funny how asphyxiation does that*, he thinks.

"You'd think the autopsy would've showed something," he counters. He knows he's pushing it, but can't help himself. There's nothing more he wants right now than to tell her he has the evidence. The time is coming, but he's not there yet.

"They're not doing one," she says.

His eyes fly open. "Why not?" This heinous bitch.

"Why would they, Henry?" she says edgily.

Careful, he tells himself. "Isn't it pretty fucking rare for a twenty-seven-year-old to die of heart failure? You'd just think they'd do one, that's all."

There's the flick of a lighter, then Cherie inhales. "He partied hard and he didn't take care of himself," she says flatly. "You heard his miserable cough. It is what it is. The M.E. ruled it heart failure. No use in dragging everything out, cutting him up. For what? We just want this behind us." *Oh, I bet you do*, Henry thinks. *Too bad it ain't gonna end up that way.*

"Listen, I'll call you when we've got the burial figured out," she says, and they hang up.

Henry shakes a cigarette out of his pack, lights it, and starts walking the creaky floorboards of his flat.

What the hell was he going to do about the tape? He's thought about nothing else since he saw it. Clearly, Cherie doesn't know he has it. But isn't it only a matter of time until she does?

Going to the cops with the tape was out, at least for now. If it were just Cherie on the tape, Henry would've been on his fifth cup of coffee with Parisian detectives right now.

But it's not just her. It's Remy too. He heads up the largest heroin ring in France and Amsterdam, and is expanding fast into the UK. And as much of a tool Remy is, he doesn't fuck around. Diming on him would be like doing the same to Lucky Luciano. Henry knows he'd find himself dead within days.

I gotta get outta here and think, he decides. It's not going to be long before either Cherie or Remy realizes the tape is missing. He'll just pack up, take the tape, and get out of town.

Wait, no. What if they follow him? If they do, and they find him, he can't actually have the tape *on* him. Better to stash it somewhere safe and come back for it later. In a few weeks, a month. After the heat dies down a little. After he has a minute to *just think clearly*.

Henry's fingers shake as he takes another cigarette out of the pack and chain-smokes it.

Fine. Where can he go? L.A. is too risky; they'd find him easily there. And Cherie knows his family is in Philly. Not like he can even imagine going back there, even now in the depths of desperation. He imagines what it would be like if he'd just dropped them a goddamn word somewhere along the way. *But you didn't,* he thinks. *So, don't make the situation worse by thinking about what will never be.*

Once he fled Paris, Cherie and Remy would for sure know something was up. And who knows how far Remy's reach extended? Maybe Henry could fly to Shanghai and he'd still end up dead in a week by Remy's orchestration. One of the most famous rock stars ever was just murdered. If Henry broke the news, the story would be earth-shattering. Like JFK. Maybe bigger.

Then it comes to him. The safest place he can think of, where Cherie wouldn't have an idea. Henry rushes to his desk, opening and closing drawers, tearing through the contents until he finds it: the tattered notebook he'd kept with him every day through Vietnam. He flips through it until, there—Giovanni's phone number. He seizes the phone and dials.

It rings seven times before someone picks up. "*Pronto,*" says a drowsy, distant voice.

"Gio? Giovanni? Is that you?" The guy on the other end sounds like a tired, seventy-year-old man.

A pause. "*Si,*" the heavily accented response comes slowly. "Who is this?"

"It's Hank, man. Hank Elysian. Damn, it's so good to hear your voice. I can't even tell you."

The silence on Gio's side drags on and Henry goes cold. *Doesn't he remember me? The guy who saved his life?*

"Hank! What you doin', man? Holy shit! We not talk for almost, what, two year?" Gio's voice wakes up, returns to a semblance of what Henry remembers, though it's still soaked in a strange, hazy slowness.

"Look, man, I can't explain right now, but I gotta get

outta here. I need a place to stay, can I come crash with you for a while?"

"A-course, a-course, you always welcome wi' me. You in trouble? Where you at now?"

"Gio, I really can't go into it, but I gotta leave like *right now*. What's the closest airport to you?"

"*Firenze*. About a hour, maybe little more drive."

"Solid, man," Henry says. "Give me your address. I'll figure out how to get there." He looks around wildly for something to write with, finally digs a pencil out from under a stack of black-and-white prints. He scrawls on the pad next to the phone: *Giovanni, 57 Via della Servi, Rosanera.*

Henry hangs up, tears the paper off the notepad and shoves it in his pocket. He snatches a padded envelope from one of the gaping desk drawers. Gingerly, heart hammering, he slips the odious Portapak reel inside and seals it. Then he stands up and scans his flat. *If I'm really leaving, I'm* really *leaving.* Once he splits, he may not be able to come back here. Ever.

His gaze falls on the two titanium padded storage cases, one small and one large, that he'd used to safeguard all his expensive equipment while slugging through Vietnam. Henry starts emptying his bookcase and desk drawers, filling the large case with his most precious belongings: several beloved cameras, portfolio books inflated with film negatives and prints, journals, everything he could fit that meant something.

Into the small case, he tucks the padded envelope and a folder of his most recent papers, prints, and journal. He moves to the closet and yanks out a wadded-up duffel bag, stuffing it with clothes and other basics. Once he's done, he looks around in dismay. Still so much that will be left behind. Who will find it all? And when? But there's no time to think about it, so he takes one last glance behind him, shoulders the duffle, and heaves the titanium cases down to the street to catch a taxi.

Downstairs, he doesn't have to wait long before a black Peugeot with a lighted taxi sign pulls over. Henry jumps in the backseat, shoving the bag and cases in next to him. The dour chauffeur just looks at him and says, "*Aéroport?*"

"*Oui*, but I need to stop somewhere first," Henry says, and tells the driver where to go. The man furrows his brow at him in the rearview mirror, but then shrugs and puts the car in drive. As they pull away, Henry twists around in his seat, his eyes crawling every inch of his surroundings for signs of being watched or followed, but he finds none. He prays that his plan to secure the tape, until he can come back and get it, will work.

Ten minutes later, the taxi slows in front of their destination. Henry looks up at the familiar stone archway flanked by the two enormous iron gates. He opens the large titanium case next to him, takes out his Polaroid. Then he grabs the small case and says, "I'll be back in less than five minutes."

The chauffeur nods noncommittally and points at the meter. "I still run it," he warns.

Henry leaps from the cab, small case in one hand and Polaroid in the other, trying not to run into Père Lachaise cemetery. The place is virtually deserted. It's still early morning, and the cemetery has just opened for the day. Pure adrenaline propels him to the mausoleum that Jim had singled out that day. Henry winds up the walk and at the first sharp turn comes face-to-face with it. It stands as it has for over a century, those delicately carved, weeping saints on either side of the rusted, open doors. It's achingly gorgeous in its deterioration.

Henry glances around, but there's no one. Only the silent, warm shafts of summer sun bleeding through the vast oaks that shelter these acres of interred. He creeps in through the opening, lets his eyes adjust to the darkness. Inside, piles of dead leaves huddle at the base of three stately tombs. Inches of dirt cover the cement floor. A collection of prayer candles, caked thick with dust, sits on the ledge in front of the tiny, cracked stained-glass window at the back of the structure. Henry exhales. *No one's been here in forever, and probably won't be again.*

He peers behind the third tomb. There's enough space between it and the wall for the small case containing the Portapak reel. He crouches down, carefully wedging the titanium box into the space. Then he walks a few paces back toward the door, turns, and smiles. The case is completely hidden. In the extraordinary event that anyone besides himself ever stepped into this mausoleum again, they'd never have any reason to look behind the tomb in that dark corner. But just for good measure, he scoops some of the dead leaves and dirt on top of the case.

At the mausoleum's doors, Henry scans the landscape

before exiting. Certain he's not been seen, he comes out and raises the Polaroid to his face. When he has the mausoleum in full view, he clicks the shutter. The camera whirs and whines before it deposits a blanched-white piece of photographic paper into his hand. He watches as a copy of the mausoleum appears on the page before him like an apparition.

By the time he's back in the cab and on the way to the airport, the image on the photo is in full bloom. Those weeping statues and rusted doors, revealing that slit of darkness leading to a secret only he knows. The tape is entirely safe. Cherie, Remy, or any other godforsaken person would have absolutely no idea to look here. It will slumber there, quiet and undisturbed as the tombs' inhabitants around it, until Henry returns.

If he returns. His stomach drops into his shoes.

It's not something he wants to dwell on, but he needs to admit it's possible. He thinks for a minute, then flips over the photo and writes, *If I don't make it back, third tomb, lower left.* Someone will put it together. *They'll have to*, he thinks, and he goes to put the photo in his wallet. He hesitates. Too easy; anyone could find it there. He sticks it in his cigarette pack instead. Was that really any better? He doesn't know, but he's too exhausted to think any more about it right now. As the city he's come to know as home whizzes by him, he prays that his instructions—however ambiguous—will never need to be pursued by anyone other than him.

Chapter Twenty-Eight

Rain hammers the roof of my car like Gatling gunfire. Inside, I sit in the dark with the windows fogged up, staring into my phone's phosphorescent glare. I'm still parked outside Bolla's house. My trembling fingers type "Jim Morrison" into the browser. I click on the first result, which is the quintessential black-and-white shirtless photo that's on the wall of every college dorm room. In fact, I tacked a poster of it to my own bedroom wall in ninth grade, when I started getting into music. The image is so familiar to me that I'm completely unnerved by how his soulful grey eyes seem to bore into mine so intensely right now, it's like he's sitting right across from me.

Morrison embodies the liminal space between shadow and light, presence and absence. The soft angles around his temples and jaw are brushed with layers of wavy, dark hair that fall just shy of his shoulders. His chin points up, maybe in defiance, maybe just in the assertion that he exists. *Here is proof that I was once here, like you,* he seems to say. *Once young and vibrant and beautiful and mystifying. But it's all ephemeral.*

No one here gets out alive.

To think Henry's life was in some way entwined with that of this global music icon—closely enough for him to have known the guy's wife, mind you—leaves me dumbstruck. Speaking of her, I come out of my daze and hastily scroll through Morrison's Wiki bio.

I'm desperate to know who she is. The woman who murdered my uncle.

I get to the Personal Wiki section and scan the text. I was right—Jim Morrison was never married. But he did have a longtime girlfriend, Cherie Atkins. This must have been the woman Bolla was talking about. I hunch so close to my phone I could crawl into the screen.

She reminds me of Jenny in *Forrest Gump,* but prettier. Less of Robin Wright's squared-off features. Softer, like Sharon Tate. Heart-shaped face, long blonde hair, wide-set, almond-shaped turquoise eyes. A nose that comes to a delicate point, situated the perfect distance above a set of lips like a painted china doll's.

But something underneath all that beauty seems terribly wrong. Is it her vacant stare? Or that her barely-there smile looks like it could flip into a sneer at any given second? I get the sense that if I look at the photo too long, her face will contort into a demon's. Or maybe I've just seen way too many bad horror movies.

Could Cherie be the one who's dogging me here in

Rosanera, all these decades later? The person who broke into my room and stole the mausoleum photo? It seems insane, but you know what they say about truth and fiction. I read on in the Wiki page, and then my hopes crash as quickly as they soared. No, apparently Ms. Atkins died in 1980 of a drug overdose. In Denver, of all places.

I put my phone down, take a deep breath, and let my tired eyes close. I need to reset, come at this from a different angle. How would Henry have known Cherie? Was it through Jim? But how would Henry have ever met Jim, though? If he did, it had to have been before Morrison was famous. Once you're famous, you only hang with other celebrities. And my uncle was definitely not well-known in any way. I've already established that through my Google searches that rendered zero results.

Wait. My eyes fly open. Didn't Jim Morrison go to film school in L.A.? I scroll up the phone screen, text whizzing past my eyes until I stop at the Education section. There it is: UCLA film school graduate, 1965. My diaphragm hitches. Was Henry still at UCLA then? Dave Sherman told me Henry was supposed to graduate with him, in 1966. Assuming Henry *was* still there in 1965, all three of those guys would have been in film school together.

But Dave didn't say a word about Jim Morrison to me. Wouldn't he have mentioned that? It's kind of a big deal that he was in the same program with a dude who became one of the most famous singers ever. Then again, Dave also said he lost touch with Henry sophomore year. If Henry had become friends with Jim, maybe Dave didn't even know about it. After all, Jim was a nobody then. If Jim wasn't a friend of Dave's, what reason would Dave have had to pay attention to Jim and who he was friends with? Adrenaline jets into my fingers and toes. Who knows for sure, but the connection between Jim Morrison, Cherie, and Henry is certainly possible. And that gives Bolla's story teeth.

Still, it brings me no closer to answering the most crucial question at hand: Why would Cherie kill Henry? I go back to what Bolla had told me just moments earlier inside his house—that Cherie showed up in his office the day after Henry's car crash. That would have been July 11, 1971. On the Wiki page, I double-check Morrison's date of death—July 3, 1971, in Paris. Then she would have been coming to Rosanera straight from France.

I bolt upright so fast that my knee smashes into the steering wheel.

Maybe Henry hadn't been living here in Rosanera at all.

Maybe he'd come here *after* Jim died. What if he had also been living in Paris? Cherie was clearly looking for something of extreme importance when she came to Bolla's office that day. Something so precious that she was evidently willing to commit murder over it. Did Henry rob her after Jim died, and then bounce? Maybe he took something that belonged to Jim? Something personal and intimate that Cherie desperately wanted back? At least that provides a motive to kill him.

But I still don't understand why Henry would have

chosen to come to this little, strange, remote town of Rosanera. It has to come back to Giovanni. I suppose it's *possible* that Giovanni is telling the truth. That he truly doesn't remember Henry. Maybe Henry was, in fact, given Giovanni's name and address by someone else, for God only knows what reason, and Henry had intended to see Giovanni, but never made it over to his house.

My head pounds with these unanswerable what-ifs, and I scroll absently through Morrison's Wiki page as I try to make sense of it all.

Then I stop, my gut swimming in lava.

On my phone screen is a photo of Morrison's grave. The plot itself is surprisingly simple. A section of ground cordoned off by a short, rectangular stone border roughly the size of a standard coffin. The unembellished marble headstone, littered with flowers and melted wax from countless candles, features an oxidized brass plaque in the center that reads *James Douglas Morrison, 1943-1971,* KATA TON ΔAIMONA EAYTOY.

But that's not what's captured me. Surrounding Morrison's modest gravesite are stately mausoleums that go on as far as the eye can see. Gorgeous, ancient, marble, eloquently carved mausoleums. Their architecture, the trees and flora in between each one, the overall vibe of the place—and I just know it. I know it in my heart, with more conviction than I've known anything in my life.

Henry's mausoleum is there. Without a doubt. In Père Lachaise Cemetery.

I close the browser and feverishly dial Alessio. To my surprise, he picks up on the second ring.

"Alessio, I just got done talking with Bolla, and you will never guess what I found out." It all comes out of me in one breath with no punctuation.

"Juliet! What incredible timing. I was just going to phone you." His elation seems to match my own. "I also have news. I was going—"

But I cut him off, feeling like I'll explode if I have to stay mum another second.

"Alessio, please! What I'm going to tell you is huge, trust me. I know where the mausoleum is. I know where it is! It's in Paris!" I let out a hysterical, shrill laugh.

And as I say the last word aloud, another realization hammers me. Bastian! Oh, dear, sweet, amazing Bastian, in Paris. I still haven't returned his last text. This revelation gives me a damn good reason to, and I make a mental note to do that next.

"Wait, Juliet, *aspetta, per favore*," Alessio commands. "For God's sake, I'm trying to tell you something that may be even more important than that."

Stunned, I fall quiet. What could possibly be more mission-critical than finally figuring out where the mausoleum is?

"You won't believe this," he says. "Even I can't believe it. But I'm standing here looking at a box that belonged to your uncle."

Chapter Twenty-Nine

Paris, France
July 7, 1971

CHERIE DRAGS THE charcoal eyeliner across her right lid in front of the bathroom mirror. She tries to keep her focus locked on her own reflection, but like a magnet, her eyes always stray to the bathtub. It happens again now. She swallows sandpaper and snaps her gaze back to herself, then frowns. Like always, she's been too heavy handed with the make-up pencil the first time around. Cherie snatches up a tissue, wraps it around her index finger and dabs at her eyelid, trying to smooth out the shaky onyx line.

She still has time, but not much. Jim's burial starts in an hour. And it would be exactly that—a burial, not a funeral. A funeral implies a service, a celebration of life, a gathering. But no one would be there today except

Cherie, Remy, and a few others. She did call Jim's parents. But they couldn't, or wouldn't, come on such short notice. Of course, the first person she had notified was the lawyer, who after a long silence and fumbling for words repeated what he had already confirmed to Cherie on that phone call back in March—that she's the sole heir and executor of Jim's will.

Cherie drops the tissue, straightens up and stares at herself. Her eyeliner is more or less even. The under-eye concealer hides some of the green hue that has overtaken the area since the night Jim died. *Was murdered. By you*, the voice in her head counters. "Shut up," she hisses at her reflection. She picks up a cigarette, lights it and throws the matches down. She looks sideways at the swirling blue smoke aching to escape through the open window behind her.

The rest of the world is blissfully unaware that Jim Morrison is dead. Cherie will make sure that news comes tomorrow, after today is all said and done. A quick, private, and uneventful burial. No press, no interviews, no commotion at the cemetery.

And no inquiries.

But one notable person is apparently going to be absent: Henry.

An ugly, deep frown cuts across her face now, as it always does when that name comes up. Where in the hell is he? She draws on her cigarette, lets it linger against her lower lip as she exhales.

It just doesn't make sense. Cherie replays the past three

days since she last spoke with him. She'd called Henry to let him know about the funeral. That was on the fourth—the day after Jim died. She'd rung him again on the fifth and again yesterday, with no answer. Finally, last night, she'd gone to Henry's flat and beat on the door. Only an unsettling, empty echo on the other side. She'd pressed her against the door before she left. It was like listening to the conch shells her father picked up on their walks at Manhattan Beach when she was little. That rushing, eternal silence.

She'd stood outside his door for a moment, thinking. Henry's non-response left three possibilities. First, he was in his flat, but dead; he was in his flat, avoiding her; or he wasn't in there at all. It's the last two that worry her. Because there's only one reason for either: he knows what she did. Which makes her fear very real and palpable.

Cherie had returned to her flat and told Remy of her worry, but he waved it off.

"How could he possibly know?" the drug lord had said, cigarette pinched between his thumb and forefinger. "At most, he could only have suspicion. And even if he does suspect, who cares? Who is he? Just a guy. With no evidence. Who hates you, by the way. The police wouldn't give it one moment's thought."

But Remy's unfazed rationale hadn't helped much. Cherie knows that if there's one thing in his life that Henry loved to his core, it was Jim. He wouldn't miss his funeral. It's out of the question. She crushes her cigarette in the ashtray on the sink, then crosses her arms tightly around her, chilled despite the summer breeze writhing into the bathroom. Something is very wrong.

But there's nothing she can do about it right now. After the burial, she's going to Henry's flat again. And if he doesn't answer this time, Cherie is going in no matter what. These old Parisian front doors aren't exactly iron mountains.

She inhales deeply, takes one last look at herself. "It'll all be over soon," she whispers to the empty room.

Cherie turns to leave, but something catches her eye and she stops. Her veins fill with glacial water.

The video camera and recorder.

It's as if she's just noticing them for the first time. They've been here so long, from the very first night they'd moved in back in March, that the device had simply become another of the room's fixtures to her.

No. No, this is madness. It isn't possible. Could Jim have been recording that night? Before she and Remy had come in? No, it can't be. *Just look,* she thinks. *Just look, and the tape will be in there, and it'll be from weeks ago, from some drunken random night weeks ago.*

Her clammy fingers lift the tinted plastic cover on the tape recorder. She gapes, not comprehending, her mouth a chasm of horror.

"Remy!" Cherie screams.

※

"*Plus rapide! Merde!*" Remy shouts at the driver as they roar away from Père Lachaise in a taxi headed north toward Henry's flat. The driver gives Remy a saturnine glare in the rearview mirror, but does as he's told. As the car swerves through the streets, Cherie quivers in the back next to Remy like a weak flame in the wind.

She can only imagine what she and Remy had looked like just now to the handful of other mourners at Jim's grave. Bill Siddons, The Doors' manager, and Agnès Varda, the Belgian avant garde filmmaker who Jim worshipped. She hopes everyone had chalked up her stark-white face and blank stare to grief rather than the extraordinary terror coursing through her and mounting with every pulse of her heart.

At the end of Jim's fifteen-minute service, Cherie had passed around mechanical hugs and promises to talk at length soon, when in her mind she was already with Remy at Henry's flat, kicking down his front door.

What a fool she's been. Or, rather, a foolish fucking junkie. If she wasn't always tripping or spaced-out, she would've seen exactly what Henry did.

There's no question in her mind what happened. That goddamn machine recorded Jim's murder and Henry had the tape. Cherie remembers how Henry split right after he'd gone back into the bathroom to see Jim one final time. Then there were all the questions when she'd called him the next day. Henry went on at her about the autopsy, how a young guy couldn't have died of heart failure.

And then, suddenly, Henry disappears. It doesn't take Einstein to figure it out.

The taxi driver punches the brakes hard in front of

Henry's building. Remy tosses a fistful of francs to the driver, then bolts out of the seat with Cherie behind him. They sprint into the building up the narrow, dark stairway to Henry's third-floor flat. Remy hammers on the door.

"Henry! Open up, now!" he bellows, sweaty brown curls falling into his eyes. His hairstyle, along with his Roman nose and beard, make him look like an angry bust of Nero.

There is no answer.

Remy backs up a few paces and readies himself, rolling his shoulders and cocking his neck.

"Watch out," he mutters, and Cherie moves aside as he runs forward and kicks the door with all his might. It flings open right away, splintered wood bursting out around the ancient hinges like a crown of thorns. With eyes large as planets, Remy motions at her to stay still. They pause, waiting to see if their illegal entry has alarmed anyone.

Silence. By some stroke of good fortune, everyone must be out. They go inside.

Cherie surveys the mess in front of her while Remy storms through the flat. It smells musky and old. The shades are drawn. Ashtrays and bottles scatter the floor, coffee table, and desk. The desk drawers all hang open, as does the tiny closet behind it. Although the place is brimming with photographs, film negatives, books, and magazines, it has a distinctly empty feel. The room looks like a Hollywood set. A jumble of random props, the important stuff missing. Cherie knows there's no point looking for the tape here. It's long gone, along with Henry.

Remy comes back into the living room, looking aggrieved. He stares at Cherie for a moment. Then he slams his fist on the desk so hard that the bell inside the telephone clangs.

"Who knows where the fuck he's gone! How are we going to find him? You have to think, Cherie. Think where he would go! Back to America, maybe? To L.A.?"

He gestures wildly as he talks, but Cherie is totally still with her eyes on the telephone.

"Shut up a minute," Cherie says. Remy stops and glares at her. She goes over to the phone. Next to it is a blank notepad. She traces her fingertip over the top sheet and feels slight depressions running across the page.

"Quick, find me a pencil," she says, snapping her fingers. He stares dumbly for a second before understanding. Rummaging loudly through the open desk drawers, he finds a ground-down Ticonderoga and hands it to her.

Cherie uses the trick her mother taught her when she was a little girl, scratching the pencil lightly across the notepad. *Ghost messages,* her mom called them. And the ghosts hadn't failed Cherie this time, either. *Oh, Henry,* she thinks. *As brilliant as you are, you can be so pitifully stupid.*

She tears the page off the pad and waves it at Remy, a smile spreading across her face.

"Let's go," she says.

Chapter Thirty

"Where is it?" I breathe, stumbling into Alessio's house. "What did your dad say when you found it? *Where* did you even find it? How do you know it's Henry's stuff? Oh my god, I have so many questions!"

I can barely keep still, then I look into his red-rimmed, deep brown eyes and go still. It's like he's utterly destroyed. There are lines on his face that weren't there before, along with a new five o'clock shadow. Suddenly, I'm afraid. Did he find something awful in with Henry's things? I can't imagine another reason for his grim appearance.

"It's in here," he says, walking into the kitchen. I follow him slowly. There on the table is a weathered cardboard box, maybe about a foot and a half square. I pause in the doorway, unsure of coming any closer.

"To answer your question, I found it in my father's closet. Way in the back." He folds his arms and shakes his head ruefully, chin pointed at the ceiling. "I don't know why I searched in there. I am not proud of it."

My shoulders come down a notch. Is that why he's so upset, because he's ashamed he went through Giovanni's things? While I get that it might've been snooping, it's not like Alessio set his dad's stuff on fire. I wonder again at just how tenuous his and his father's relationship must truly be.

"We have always respected one another's personal areas," Alessio says. "But this whole experience with you, Juliet, it's made me so curious about my own father and his past. He and I, we have, how you say," Alessio twirls his hand in the air, searching for the right phrase in English, "unsaid agreement. We live together under one roof, but very separate lives. We are father and son by blood. Nothing more. Not friends."

I open my mouth to let him know he doesn't owe me an explanation, that I'm the last one to judge. But he holds up his hand, and I stay silent.

"There is not any hate with us, please don't misunderstand me," Alessio continues. "But there is also no love. I know nothing about this man who helped create me. Nothing beyond his preferences for fishing and the *scemo* TV he watches before going to sleep. And I will never know more. I think I was hoping to find in his room something that explained who he is. *Why* he is. Instead, I found that." He gestures at the box with dismay.

"It makes me sick, Juliet. Why does my father have your uncle's things? After saying to us he never met him? What are they *doing* here?"

He has saved me the time of asking those same questions aloud.

"Alessio, I have no idea. I am just as puzzled as you." I'm also itching to plunge into the box, but Alessio looks absolutely destroyed. I feel for him. It can't feel good to know your own father has never taken you into his confidence, not even once.

"I assume, then, that you haven't asked your father about Henry's stuff?" As I say this, I look around nervously, wondering if Giovanni will stalk in here at any moment and go berserk on the two of us.

Alessio sniffs. "No. I don't even know where he is. He went out right after you came over earlier today, and he hasn't been back."

"Then we should make quick work of this before he returns. May I have a look inside?"

"Go ahead. Technically, they are yours. Next of kin, aren't you?"

When I think of how that title officially belongs to Nana, a tidal wave of guilt crashes over me. I told Colette I'd get back to her about me getting a flight home, but that was hours ago. Everything's moving at warp speed, and I've hardly had a second to process the fact Nana is in a coma. I turn clammy as I think of my grandmother, so tiny and frail, her tissue-paper skin punctured with IVs and tubes.

Will she ever wake up? Will I even get to see her again?

I lock these thoughts down and try to focus on the golden goose in front of me: Henry's box. Wouldn't Nana want me to be here right now, solving her son's murder, rather than sitting helplessly at her bedside while she's unconscious? And I know for damn sure it's what Mom would've wanted.

Peeling back the flaps on the cardboard box one at a time, I peer inside. A few crumpled t-shirts, a pair of sneakers, and a small collection of documents stare back at me. I shake out one of the tees. It's only one size larger than me, and I'm fairly small. I bring it to my face and breathe in, craving any trace of him. But it just reeks of cigarettes. Probably from Giovanni's decades of heavy smoking inside the house.

I lay it back down and move on to the documents. My heart thunders as I pick up what I realize is his passport. Inside the cover is a black-and-white of a handsome man in his early twenties with a beard and mustache. He's got very dark olive-brown skin and longish brown hair. There was no need for me to see the name, but there it is all the same:

Name: Barton, Henry Anthony.

Date of Issue: 08-08-1965

I move to the next card. Another black-and-white photo of Henry stares out at me, this time from a press ID card. *Serial No. 015872. United States of America, Department of Defense—Noncombatant's Certificate of Identity.*

Name: Barton, Henry Anthony
Position: News Correspondent
Date Issued: 15-09-1965

It takes me a couple minutes, then it clicks. News correspondent, noncombatant, 1965.

"Henry was a journalist in Vietnam. So that's how he knows your dad." My gaze meets Alessio's. "That's the connection right there."

He nods. "Seems so."

"But why would your dad try to hide that? So they were both journalists in Vietnam. So what? It's not a huge deal."

Alessio's face darkens. "I told you, he will never mention Vietnam to no one. Never."

My gaze drops and falls on another piece of paper. This time, it's a boarding pass. The carbon-copy typeface is barely visible, but it's there. I take it out and hold it up overhead to the light.

Airlec Air Espace—Carte d'Embarquement
DEP Orly Aeroport 17:57
ARR Aeroporto di Firenze-Peretola 19:42
04 July 1971

Orly Airport. "I was right, Alessio! Henry was living in Paris, not Rosanera. He came here from Paris, and here's proof!" I shove the boarding pass at Alessio and his face creases into confusion. "I knew the mausoleum was there! After I saw Jim Morrison's grave, I just knew it."

I cackle like someone unhinged as I take out my phone and start to photograph everything in the box.

Alessio puts his hand over mine. "What are you talking about, Jim Morrison's grave? What does he have to do with anything?"

I stare. "Oh, my God, Alessio. That's what I was trying to tell you on the phone! You'll never believe what Bolla told me."

I regurgitate the story Bolla relayed to me. How *Jim Morrison's girlfriend*, along with some French guy, held Bolla at gunpoint, demanded to go through Henry's things, didn't find what they were looking for, and took off. I add in how Morrison went to UCLA, and that's likely how Henry knew him. As unbelievable as the story sounds, it's plausible.

Alessio is fumbling for words, his mouth half-open in a grimace. I'm laughing again.

"I know, I know! You can't even imagine it, right? But, look. Whatever those two were looking for in Henry's things at Bolla's office, it couldn't have been here, either. I mean, a press ID card? Passport? His boarding pass? No way."

"It's the mausoleum, Alessio. 'If I don't make it back, third tomb, lower left.' Henry left a message, plain and simple. The answer is somewhere in Père Lachaise. The same place Morrison is buried."

"You are certain, Juliet? Père Lachaise? Really?"

I pick up my phone and turn the screen to face him, scrolling through the Google images of Père Lachaise. I swipe through photo after photo of mausoleum, crypt, and gravesite.

"Sure, it does look a lot like your photo," he says, running a restless hand through his uncombed hair. He exhales and puts his arms in the air. "But, Juliet, what if it's not?"

I drop my phone, exasperated. "Then I'll have to take that chance. What else am I going to do, stay here? We've already been to every cemetery in Rosanera. It's not here. So that leaves the entire rest of the world, or me going to Père Lachaise on a gut feeling. I don't think me asking your dad about it again is going to help."

Alessio nearly rockets through the ceiling. "No, please, he cannot know we found this!"

I sigh. "I know, Alessio. That's what I'm saying. He's not going to admit to knowing anything, anyway. He obviously wants to keep this private. I don't know why, but he does. It'd ruin your life with him if I ever brought it up. I wouldn't do that to you."

Alessio looks simultaneously relieved and pained.

"Look," I continue. "I'm dying to know the connection between your dad and Henry. Beyond the journalism thing—why Henry came here to see him in his last days. But your dad won't tell me, and Bolla was my last lead. There's nothing more for me to learn here in Rosanera."

Alessio's jaw twitches. "Do you think he had something to do with it." It's a statement, not a question. And it was only a matter of time before the elephant in the room bellowed.

"I—don't know, Alessio," I say. "Honestly? I think it's extremely strange your father said he didn't know Henry, and here he has a box of his things. It doesn't look good. But maybe he has his reasons. Maybe he and Henry were close, and it's painful for your dad to talk about death." Alessio nods slowly, but I wonder if it's just perfunctory.

In the end, it doesn't matter what I think, does it? It's Alessio who has to grapple with Giovanni, with that endless gulf between himself and his own father.

"You already said he won't utter a word about Vietnam," I say. "He's clearly suffering from PTSD. And who knows what else. Maybe it's just too much for him to talk about my uncle, to recall those times. And I'm not even sure it matters, Alessio. What Bolla told me about Cherie Atkins and the French guy makes it pretty obvious that they killed Henry."

Instead of Alessio looking relieved, as my words had intended, a darkness spreads over his face, malicious as a fast-moving storm.

"I'm going to the garage," he says, stomping over to the drawer behind me with a sudden rage that astounds me.

"The garage? What garage?"

He yanks the drawer out from its tracks and attacks the contents, finally producing an old key on a red tomato keychain. He holds it in the air, his mouth a resentful line.

"It's where my father spends so much of his time," he says bitterly. "I've never once gone into it, on his wishes. It's up the hill in the back, where he used to work on all his cars."

I'm stunned. I don't understand how we got from leaving for France to Giovanni's garage. Then Alessio clarifies.

"If my father has more to hide, it's up there. I was never allowed in. And now—I can't get it out of my mind."

"What do you think he really has in there?"

"I don't know!" he explodes. "But he's hidden

everything from me my whole life, and it is obvious that I don't even know who I'm living with."

His eyes are filling as I fidget at the table. Dammit. I feel for him, I really do. But I just want to get back to the B&B, pack my shit, and book the next flight to Paris. He can see the longing to leave in my eyes and turns on me.

"You know, Juliet," he snarls, "you're not the only person tortured by a broken family. You're not the only one with problems, with secrets, with unanswered questions. I agreed to help you with your exploration here because I genuinely cared about your search. And I know what it means to have no mother. To be totally alone in this *cazzo di mondo*! It isn't always just about you."

Blood rushes to my face as I remember the voice of my ex-husband, just a few weeks ago at our house. *You think you're the only one who's had it bad?* Matt is right. This whole time, I've been treating Alessio like some disposable tagalong, blind to how it's making him feel.

I stand up and Alessio's angry expression falters. It's like he's wondering if he's gone too far with those bitter words I so deserved, and needed to hear. He opens his mouth, but I stop him from talking by wrapping my arms around him. I rest my head on his chest. His arms hang at his sides a moment before he returns the embrace. He feels like family. The brother I never had. I pull back and look up at him.

"Lead the way," I say.

Chapter Thirty-One

Rosanera
July 8, 1971
Morning

ALTHOUGH HE'S BEEN lying the sofa for over seven hours, Henry hasn't slept. Like the previous three nights since arriving at Gio's, he passes the nocturnal expanse drowning in his own thoughts. About where he's been, how far he's come.

And where to go from here.

Until coming to Giovanni's, Henry hadn't been aware of the extent to which he's become numb. For so long, he's felt nothing at all.

Since Vietnam, to be sure. But it started long before that. The infection began with the staircase incident. His own mother, her lower half drenched in blood—blood he caused, a life extinguished. The blood on his hands of things that cannot be repaired. It's as if he's been trapped in some Shakespearian drama, all his misery and ill-fate stemming from that one day almost ten years ago now.

The wrong he never righted.

Staring up at the cracked ceiling, Henry thinks about his sister, Ellen, who is eighteen now, well on her way to adulthood. Is she in college? Who is she?

And his parents. Does his mother still sit at that same Victorian vanity each night and spend her days methodically keeping the house? Is his father retired now, busying himself with his projects in the basement? Henry's chest balloons as he remembers the darkroom his father built with fierce dedication for him all those years ago. Is it just a useless storage receptacle now?

Have you heard of Hank Elysian? Henry thinks. *And do you still love me?*

Henry tosses onto his side. His tattered copy of *On the Road* lies on the floor. He'd found it at the bottom of his bag the night he got here to Gio's. It must've been in there for years, and Henry took no notice of it while frantically packing to leave Paris. Kerouac's testament to the raggedy madness and the senseless emptiness of our lives was the one dog-eared page he'd always returned to throughout his life. More times than he'd like to admit.

Now I know that raggedy madness, Henry thinks. *Now I am that senseless emptiness.* But maybe life isn't supposed to be anything more than that. Maybe in the end, our time here isn't supposed to amount to anything at all.

The resolution is, there is no resolution.

Henry pushes himself upright and squints at the pale

morning light fighting to enter through the living room's heavily curtained windows. Reality attaches itself to him once again like a villain's cape.

What he should do about Jim's tape.

Henry gets up and pulls on his t-shirt and jeans from their fabric puddle on the floor. As he pads to the front door, he steps on something sharp and stifles a loud expletive. He examines the bottom of his foot and frowns. There's a tiny orange cap stuck to his arch.

He mutters under his breath, picking it off and pocketing it. They're scattered all over Gio's house, especially in the bathroom, right near the cigar box playing host to spoons, lighters, and needles.

Henry turns the doorknob silently, though it wouldn't matter if he ripped it off its hinges, the state Gio's in. He wouldn't hear a thing.

Stepping outside, Henry grabs the morning paper and hurries back inside, already shuffling through the pages before he gets back to the living room. Pointless, he knows. When the news comes, it will be page one. He tosses the newspaper aside and drops onto the sofa, hanging his head in his hands.

Why hasn't Jim's death been announced yet? The man has been dead for five days now. Has Cherie even buried him yet? Did he end up in Père Lachaise? If so, his grave could be just yards away from the mausoleum where the tape is stashed. The thought makes Henry's palms slick.

He gets up, starts pacing the room. By now, Cherie and Remy definitely know he's left town. They may be sociopaths, but they aren't stupid. They must've figured out the tape is missing by now. And that means there is a death warrant out for him. They're probably on their way right now to hunt him down and kill him. *Jesus, stop it already!* he commands himself. *There's no way they can find you. No one knows about Gio. Not even Jim did.*

Henry goes still and forces himself to take a slow, deep breath. *Get ahold of yourself. You've got a plan.*

He does, and it is this: when the news of Jim's death breaks—and when Henry knows for sure he's been buried—he'll go back to Paris, get the tape, fly home to Philadelphia, and, from the relative safety of three-thousand miles' distance and U.S. citizenship, turn it over to the cops there.

He knows he is taking an enormous gamble by going back to Philly. His parents could reject him out of hand. Then he'd know for sure he is utterly alone in the world.

But what better option is there? Where else could he go? Henry doesn't doubt for a second that Cherie already has people on the lookout for him in L.A. That means Philly is the safest, most familiar choice. And he has a duty to get the tape into the hands of authorities who would actually *do* something about it; not these incompetent Europeans who don't even have the brains to order an autopsy on a twenty-seven-year-old rock star.

A sudden fit of sniffling and coughing comes from the kitchen behind Henry. Gio, drowsy and lethargic, emerges from the depths of the darkened bedroom, his pinpoint pupils trying to focus on Henry inside their puffy sockets.

Despite the July heat, a rumpled long-sleeved shirt hangs from Gio's pale, emaciated frame. The same one, in fact, he's been wearing since he opened the door to greet Henry three days ago. Gio clutches at his right forearm with a hand curled into a nervous claw.

"'Mornin', Hank," he says in a slurred voice, a mirthless smile spreading across his face. "I was uhhhh, gonna make some *café*, you wanna?"

All former traces of the levity and innocence Henry remembered so well, which were so quintessentially Gio, have completely evacuated his friend's being. He'd expected some of that as a natural response to what had gone down in Huế. But he hadn't expected the junk use to be this bad.

"Yeah, man, if you want to make it," he says. Gio nods, his eyes blinking long and sleepy as he turns back into the kitchen. Henry follows him.

The place is a disaster. Dirty dishes congregate in groups all over the counter and stove top. Ashtrays and crumpled, used foil packets litter the kitchen table. The trashcan overflows with old food, bottles, TV dinner boxes, and random waste, including a syringe that peeks out from a bevy of crushed beer cans.

Giovanni lifts the aluminum coffee carafe from the front stove burner, opens the lid and dumps a heap of coffee grounds onto the already festering pile of trash. Henry's stomach lurches. Gio finally manages to get the coffee pot put together, turns on the burner and slinks into a chair at the table across from Henry.

"So, you still not gon' tell me what wen' down in France, eh?" Gio finally says, his eyes straining to focus.

Henry sighs. "Gio, look, I told you. It's better if I don't involve you, or anyone for that matter."

Gio shrugs. "Some heavy *merda*, though."

Henry looks at him, at his sad eyes. The two of them know all about that.

"Yeah," Henry says softly. "Some real heavy shit. But like I told you, I'll be outta here in a week or so, tops. I really appreciate you doing this for me, man. I didn't have anywhere else to go."

Gio waves a sleepy hand in the air.

"I tol' you, Hank, iss fine. I don't have much goin' on here, you know. My life here is juss working on cars. I love cars, man. You know, the writing… iss not so much for me no more. Too, how you say, tedious. You know? Like uhh, too much thinking, and iss all useless, really. Why to focus on the past?

"To try to dig these levels of the mind," he points at his head, "ann of the soul," he pokes at his chest, "where we're not supposed to be. Nothing good can come of it, man. Nothing."

He isn't totally wrong, Henry thinks.

"My father, you know, he work on cars, he teach me," Gio goes on. "I always use'a tell him, 'Cam' on, Papa… why with the cars alla time, you know I like books an' the pen an' paper.'" Gio shakes his head. "But you know Hank, now? I like it. Really. I got my garage, I do the engine repair, change oil, replace this or that tube, you know. What can I say, it lets me be to myself, alone."

Now's the time for Henry to bring it up. Since he got here, they've both been dancing around the subject, but no more.

"I get it man, I do," Henry says. "It's good to be alone sometimes. To think. I mean, not many people can say they went through what we did. To most of the world, Huế is just part of a headline. But not you and me, brother." Henry raises an eyebrow and inclines his head.

Gio stares blankly at Henry. He looks as unfazed as if someone had told him the weather report.

"Huế?" Gio says. "What about Huế?"

Henry stares back, their gazes suspended by an invisible string. The room is silent besides the old metal clock on the kitchen wall, counting down the seconds.

"What about it? Gio, I'm talking about fuckin' *Huế*, man." He leans forward on the rickety kitchen table, his brows knotted in incredulity. *This can't actually be happening.*

After a few beats, Giovanni laughs. "Ahh, you muss mean th' monkeys, eh? Th' monkeys, Hank, yessss. They were ever'where in Huế, man—every tree, each'a bush. Screeching the whole night! Yeah, you an' me, we use to sit up an try ahh coun'em, eh?"

He trails off into a nonsensical stream of consciousness under his breath, punctuated with childish giggles.

Henry gapes at him. *He doesn't remember. He doesn't remember anything at all.*

Whether it's shell shock, the junk in his veins, or something else completely, Henry isn't sure. But what he's certain of is that his friend is clearly gone. Like the rest of their entire generation, it seemed. Even Henry feels like he is on the brink of madness, just waiting for God to reach his arm through the sky and give him that final push off the ledge. The room starts to shrink around him.

"Look, man, there's something I really gotta go do," Henry says, standing up. He's going to suffocate if he stays here a minute longer. "Can I use the car?"

Gio peers up at Henry, flipping his long hair to one side. His eyes seem to focus on Henry for just a split second, as if for one fleeting moment he is lucid again. For that fraction of time, Henry catches a glimpse of his old friend.

"*Sicuro,* man, take it. Keys are there." Gio points to the hallway table.

"Thanks. See you later on."

Everything feels so far out of Henry's reach. Even the very steps he takes toward the front door feel like a dream—as if he's looking at some mimeograph of reality. It's like he is an actor in one of those hideous German Expressionism films, the nature of which Jim explained so eloquently all those years ago in Cartwright's class, before the world had unraveled, and when Henry still believed there was a future.

He scoops up the car keys and goes out into the light.

Chapter Thirty-Two

Alessio jams the key into the padlock hanging from the sliding wood door on his father's garage. It clicks right open, as if it's been waiting for him all along. Our eyes meet, then he rolls back the heavy door. It rumbles like a budding earthquake, the epicenter of which we're standing on. We stare into the darkness.

"Wait here," Alessio says. "Let me find the light."

I hear his footsteps pad around then stop. A series of three overhead lightbulbs flick on and buzz above us. Alessio moves from the corner with the light switch, and I follow him in, looking around doubtfully.

It's about six hundred square feet, containing the usual garage fare—metal tool chests with dozens of drawers, a couple sawhorses, empty coffee cans and mason jars packed with paint brushes and random nails and screws, and a stack of boxes in one corner. In the middle are three vehicles draped in dusty green vinyl covers. It hardly looks like a place that I'd forbid my son entry, as Alessio claims Giovanni did.

I wonder if that's really the case or if Alessio misinterpreted his father's admonishments about this place. Maybe this was simply Giovanni's place of refuge, where he liked to be alone and work. Perhaps Alessio wasn't actually forbidden from coming here, but instead discouraged. Either way, I felt bad for him. It couldn't feel great to have your own father exclude you from a major part of his life.

"What are you looking for, Alessio?" I ask gently. His face is sullen and defeated as he surveys the space.

"I don't know," he says, shrugging irritably. Then his eyes fall on the stack of boxes in the corner. He walks over and grabs the top one, plopping it down on the ground. "I'll start with these. There must be some reason he kept me out of this place."

I bite my lip and watch Alessio dig in. I seriously doubt Giovanni has any secrets in here. But I can humor Alessio and hang out here with him for a half hour or so, can't I? It's a small price to pay for all the support he's given me. I check my phone. It's seven o'clock. Even if I'm able to book a flight to Paris tonight, Père Lachaise will be long closed by the time I land. I'll have to wait until tomorrow morning to go there, anyway.

I wander around the garage, the massive fatigue of the day starting to set in. It feels impossible that in the span of ten hours, I went to the Rosanera library, talked to Giovanni, met with Maurizio, found my room ransacked and the mausoleum photo gone, learned Nana is in a coma, spoke to Bolla and discovered Jim Morrison's girlfriend probably murdered my uncle, *and* sifted through a box of Henry's things.

They're not kidding when they say everything happens at once.

Absently, I lift one of the dusty vinyl car covers to reveal the back of an old red Fiat Moretti Coupe. It looks sporty, kind of like an MG Midget.

"Wow. Are all these cars your dad's?"

"Probably," he says, still focused on the boxes in front of him. "He fixed and restored many cars over the years. Not surprising he kept his favorites."

I move on to the next one, peeking under the cover to find a cream-colored Mercedes 450 SL. Also in decent condition, but looks at least forty years old. Could be worth a small fortune, for all I know. I stifle a yawn and lift the third cover to reveal a car painted a stunning shade of deep Pacific blue. It's a gorgeous color, unlike any blue you see on the road. Must be a custom paint job. I peel the cover back further to admire the car. Then I stop dead, my stomach flooded with ice.

Two neatly painted green stripes begin on the driver's side door and run the length of the car. Maurizio's words thrum in my ears: *I will never forget, because it was such a strange-looking car. A deep blue Alfa Romeo with green stripes down the side.* Not breathing, I move slowly to the back of the car.

The Alfa Romeo medallion stares blindly at me from the center of the trunk.

❦

"Sip on this," Alessio says, returning from the kitchen with a glass of water. I'm sprawled on the scratchy sofa in his uncongenial living room. From the blanched look of him, Alessio needs to lie down too. After I'd feebly managed to explain the reason for my horror in the garage, he and I had trudged back down the road to his house like zombies.

I take the glass from him and give a silent nod of thanks. He sits down heavily next to me.

"He's still not answering the phone," he murmurs. We both avoid speaking aloud the ghastly truth that hangs in the air like the pungent stink of old cigarette smoke: that Giovanni, Alessio's own father, had in his possession the car that killed Henry.

"Are you okay?" I ask, trying to hold the glass steady.

"Far from it."

"I know. I'm sorry, I don't know why I even asked." Henry's death is just as wretched for him as it is for me, for perhaps even more tragic reasons.

"What do I do now?" Alessio chokes out. "How can I possibly look at him ever again, knowing what he did? That he killed someone. That my own father, my flesh and blood, is a murderer. He disgusts me. When I find him I don't know what I'll do to him. I want to kill him myself. How could this *ever* have happened?"

I desperately wish, for Alessio's sake, that it somehow wasn't Giovanni who killed Henry. That the car was stolen;

that someone else was driving it that day; that Giovanni didn't even know about it. If that was all there is to consider, then maybe I could convince myself.

But compounded with my ransacked room, and the stolen photo? Who else but Giovanni? The man who's been gone for almost eight hours now and won't pick up his phone when his own son is calling him repeatedly?

"We don't know anything yet, Alessio," I say, putting my hand on his arm. "It could be that your dad didn't do it at all. Maybe he's scared and has been covering for someone else all these years. We won't know until we talk to him."

"And that makes it better? That he'd cover for a murderer? *Fotutto codardo*," Alessio glowers.

He's right. Covering for a murder isn't much better. But still, I wish it were true. Everything points to Giovanni himself.

He must've put all the pieces together after I met with him this morning. He knew Henry had come from Paris to Rosanera all those years ago. And then I, like an idiot, showed him the mausoleum photo. Pointed out the urgent message Henry wrote on the back, mentioned something of significance being there.

A little research, and Giovanni soon would've figured out the mausoleum was likely in Père Lachaise, the biggest cemetery in Paris. Hell, he probably already knew about Henry's connection to Jim Morrison and figured it out that way. I might as well have drawn the guy a map. A map that he is, no doubt, following right this minute as I sit here miserably.

"We have to figure out how far he's gotten already," I say, my urgency returning. "I can't have him getting to the mausoleum before me and taking whatever Henry put there." Saying the words aloud trigger a new flood of anxiety, and I stand up unsteadily.

"He probably already got it," I say. "He probably deboarded the plane hours ago, found it, and did God knows what with whatever's there!"

"I told you, Juliet. If we're right, and he did go to Paris, there's no way he took a plane. He's terrified of flying."

"But in this case, he might have!"

"Believe me." Alessio stands up and takes my hands firmly, forces me to look at him. "Clearly, I don't know much about my father, but there is one thing I am certain of. He will never set foot on a plane. If he is in fact en route to Paris as you suspect, it's in his *auto*."

I pull my hands away and run my fingers through my tangled hair. I don't know what to believe anymore. Everything is falling apart around me, just as I knew it always would.

"He left the house around twelve o'clock this afternoon," Alessio says. "It's seven-thirty now. That's almost eight hours. The map online said nearly twelve hours total driving from Rosanera to Paris. So, there is no possible way he has arrived there yet."

I rub my cheeks and stare at him. I can't argue with him there.

"That means when he does arrive tonight, the cemetery will be closed. *And* he still needs to find where the mausoleum is. Père Lachaise is enormous; one hundred acres big. Do not worry, Juliet. He won't get to it before you. Before *us*."

He offers me a sad smile, and my heart lurches. Despite my current intense hatred for Giovanni, I know there's no way I could ever project that onto Alessio.

Suddenly, Alessio shoots up from the couch, grabbing his phone from his back pocket.

"What's happening?" I say. "Is he calling you?"

"No, I just remembered there's a way we can tell for sure if he is on his way to Paris." His thumbs punch at his phone screen.

"Oh! A GPS tracker on his phone?" I ask excitedly.

"Not quite. But I take care of paying all his bills. He hates to do it, and passed it on to me. I'm logging into his credit card account now. Maybe, hopefully, he stopped to get petrol, something to eat. And not thinking about it, charged it to his card."

I hold my breath and wait for Alessio to say something. His face changes.

"A pending charge," he rasps, looking at me. "Mâcon, France. Petrol station."

"What time?" I'm already whipping out my phone and mapping Mâcon.

"No time. It just says it was today."

I'm too filled with anticipation to be simultaneously horrified that I was right. Giovanni is headed to Père Lachaise. And Alessio was right, too, about his father driving the ridiculous distance there instead of simply getting on a plane.

"Okay, this says Mâcon is about four hours outside Paris," I say. "So he's definitely getting close." I look up and our eyes meet. Time is running out.

"What now?" Alessio says.

"We book flights to Paris, pack my stuff, and hurry to the Florence airport like we're on the goddamn bullet train," I say, going back to the kitchen and picking up Henry's box from the table. But there's one thing I need to do before all of that.

I get out my phone, dial Bastian's number, and pray that he answers.

Chapter Thirty-Three

Rosanera
July 8, 1971
Evening

From the top of the rocky cliffs where Henry gazes out at the sea, the curvature of the Earth seems limitless. The sun has moved behind him now, the day waning toward darkness. Still, the rich golden rays illuminate the Adriatic's vast expanse, painting it the purest shade of blue. Above, cotton ball clouds float weightlessly in their celestial abode. Like the ceiling of the Sistine Chapel, he imagines. He lets his eyelids fall and lift his arms, letting the wind rock him gently from side to side.

A shriek pierces the air, and Henry's eyes fly open to watch a group of children giggling and squealing in a flat, sandy area of the cliffs. A trim, bathing-suit clad woman his age scolds the kids in Italian, every other word punctuated by her index and middle fingers, between which a burning cigarette is firmly clasped. Her blonde hair, tied back in a checkered scarf, whips around her face in the breeze. The kids scamper off, laughing, impervious to her reproaches.

One boy sits off to the side alone. He is silent, unmoving, eyes glued to the panoramic view before him. He reminds Henry of someone he can't place. As if sensing this, the boy turns his head and locks eyes with Henry, who offers him a small smile. The boy returns it, gives a tiny salute, then looks away.

That's Henry's cue to get moving. *I've killed enough time*, he thinks. He'd spent the whole afternoon walking what seemed like the entire town of Rosanera three times over to get up the nerve to do what he must. He had traipsed through gardens in full bloom, circled both crowded and deserted piazzas, and wound through centuries-old avenues, passing endless, nameless faces before returning to the cliffs where he had parked Gio's car hours ago, and where he stands now.

Henry inhales deeply, turns his back to the sea, and crosses the road. He goes into the phone booth and draws the door closed behind him. The operator asks where to direct his call.

"*Internazionale, Stati Uniti.* Collect call, *per favore.*" Thankfully, the woman understands the English term, and he proceeds to give her the number.

"And your name, sir?" asks the polite disembodied voice. He gives it. "*Grazie,* please hold."

Henry shifts, damp stains growing underneath his arms

as a series of clicks rattle off on the line. He only has seconds before—if—there is an answer, and he fights the fearful urge to hang up. Then, a distant but familiar *hello?* graces his ear. His muscles constrict into coiled rope. The operator cheerfully explains to the recipient she has a collect call from Henry in Italy, and will she accept the charges?

A pause a thousand years wide.

Henry crumples at the silence. *What the hell was I thinking?* He grips the receiver hard, wishing he could crush it into a fine powder that the wind would carry away like ash.

Then he hears his mother say breathlessly, "Yes. Yes, of course." The operator thanks them both and clicks off.

He and she are alone together, thousands of miles apart. His voice breaks as he says the word aloud for the first time in almost a decade. "Mom?"

"Henry?" It's a cross between faint, distant, echoing. The line crackles, and he plugs his ear with this finger.

"Yes! It's me, Mom."

"Oh my God, Henry? It is really you? Where are you? Are you alright?" Her voice rises an octave and holds a tremulous key.

He can't answer yet, not through his sobs. Enormous, wailing surges of relief escape from his throat. She is *glad* to hear from him! She has missed him, worried about him, wondered where he's been. Henry tries to speak but cannot, so he just falls against the glass wall of the booth, weeping. She cries in tandem. After a few more beats, Henry wipes his face and forces himself to composure.

"It's so good to hear your voice, Mom," he says, his voice nasal and thick. It echoes in his ear, like he's standing in a cavern.

"Mom?" He raises his voice as the line begins to crack and sputter. "Look, I wanted to tell you. I'm coming home soon. Very soon. As soon as I can get a flight."

He waits for a response, but the phone just hisses in his ear like a poised cobra. He can hear her talking behind the wall of static.

"Are you there?" He pleads with the universe to let him hear what she's saying, but the only sound that greets him is like a sizzling steak on a grill.

"Listen, Mom, I can't hear you! I'm gonna hang up and call you back, okay?" The buzzing in the phone receiver grows thunderous, completing obscuring her voice.

He yanks his head away and slams the receiver down only to seize it from its cradle again a second later. He repeats the process with the operator and twists the phone cord around his fist until it's numb as he waits for his mother to pick up again.

"Henry?" she says, frantic. "Did you say you were coming *home*?"

"Yes! I'll be back as soon as I can. How are you? How is Dad and Ellen? Mom, there's so much I want to ask—"

The roaring static starts again. He presses the receiver so close to his head he feels like it'll go into his brain. "Can you hear me?" he yells. Nothing but noise. He bangs the receiver down again and runs his hands over his face, eyes acidic with tears. The relief; oh, sweet Jesus, the sheer relief! She loves him. She hasn't quit on him. Even after all the pain, all the years of estrangement, he still has somewhere for refuge.

When the moment finally passes, he slides open the phone booth door. He fishes in his pocket for keys, makes his way to Gio's parked car and gets in, turning the ignition. He gazes out at the shining sea, at the microscopic boats skimming the horizon, and smiles.

Nothing else matters now. He isn't alone.

He pulls away from the curb and heads back down the hill toward Gio's house. Poor, disgraced Gio. Another casualty of this heavy life. Part of Henry feels like shit when he thinks about how he'll be safe and stateside in a day or two, while Gio will still be wasting away here, alone, expeditiously making his way toward death.

Then Henry catches sight of a man walking up the side of the road toward him. Shock zings through his body, and he stamps his foot down on the brake. The guy looks positively identical to his Uncle Pietro.

It is *him*, he thinks wildly. *Pietro!* But how can it be? Pietro is long dead, and buried in America. Still…

Pietro's doppelgänger continues up the road toward Henry. For a minute, his eyes play a trick on him—the man looks like he's *floating,* not walking, each footfall hovering an inch above the ground. Their eyes meet, and the man gives Henry a small salute, just like the boy on the cliffs did before. *What's with the salute? Is it an Italian thing?*

Henry passes him slowly, peering intently out the passenger window, and, having no better idea of what he should do, returns the salute. The man smiles and lowers his gaze. In the rearview mirror, Henry watches him recede from view until he is around the corner and gone.

He returns to a normal driving speed, trying to calm his racing pulse and process the uncanny image he just saw. In a daze, Henry follows the narrow, winding road, the majestic bluffs with the sea on one side, fifteen feet of sheer rocky wall on the other. As he drives, his mind wanders to Jim. Will tomorrow be the day? The day he unrolls the paper to find Jim's face on the front page? The day he can finally go home?

A deafening roar suddenly fills the air, and Henry bolts up in his seat. It sounds like an airplane hurtling down a runway. His eyes lock onto a hulking blue car in his rearview, which appeared from nowhere. The car rides him close, so close its front bumper is practically attached to his rear.

"What's this dude's problem?" he demands aloud to no one.

The blue car growls up and to the left of Henry's car, as if to pass him. As it advances closer, he can see it has flashy green stripes painted down the side of it. Was it some psycho trying to race him? Henry brakes instinctively and scans the road for somewhere to pull over, but there isn't any. The narrow two-lane thoroughfare has no shoulder, firmly hemmed in by land one side and rocky wall on the other.

Henry rolls down his window at high speed and sticks his hand out, motioning the guy to go around.

"The hell's your problem, man? Go around if you're in such a goddamn hurry!"

But instead of passing him, the car drops back to ride his ass again, braking and accelerating in near-perfect time with Henry, inches from his rear bumper.

Frantic, Henry speeds up. The town center can't be far now. Houses were now starting to appear on the other side of the road where empty land has been. The blue monster guns its engine again behind him, and fear drives a spike through Henry's chest. Whoever this guy is, it's clear he isn't just pissed. He wants to seriously hurt him. Maybe even kill him. And he's completely trapped.

In his desperation, Henry floors the gas and races faster than he can control down the hill —skidding around corners, some far sharper than others. He chances another look into his rearview, and this time he finally gets a clear look at the driver.

What he sees nearly paralyzes him.

The mirror reflects an agonized, pale face, splotched red, and shining wet with tears, the mouth contorted into a tortured grimace. It's not an expression of rage, but one of horror and deep regret. The person is weeping, screaming.

"Gio?" Henry hears himself say.

His eyes flit back to the windshield, and he sees the rock wall rushing straight at him. Too fast, unstoppable. The moment takes hours, but also only seconds, to unfold. Behind his eyes appear those streaks of his life, his mind relinquishing the best ones, the ones he's forgotten, or never even knew he had; recollections of love, acceptance, calm. All those bright seconds he has buried—always choosing the dark in favor of the light, consciously or not.

Gravity is lost and Henry spins out, both tethered and free, like the Earth turning at its one-thousand-miles-an-hour pace on a predetermined trajectory, forever.

His last thought is of salvation.

Chapter Thirty-Four

"Yes, I'm looking at the picture right now," Bastian's voice says from my speaker phone. He lets out a long exhale. I feel the vibration of it in my palm. I've just texted him the photo of the mausoleum while trying to catch him up on the super-truncated whole story of everything. And I have to admit, he's doing pretty well with processing it all. Alessio is driving my rental car back to my B&B, zipping through the streets as I sit in the passenger seat coordinating with Bastian.

"It definitely looks like Père Lachaise, *chérie*," Bastian continues. Alessio shoots me an amused look at the term of endearment, and blood rushes to my face. The word "cherie" doesn't sound so lovely to me anymore.

"Again, I am so sorry to ask this of you, but this is probably the most urgent request I will ever have in my life. No joke. Can you please, *please* be at Père Lachaise right when it opens tomorrow and start looking for the mausoleum? We have to get there before Giovanni does. It's too late for Alessio and me to make the last flight to Paris tonight. The soonest one we could get leaves tomorrow morning at seven forty-five."

"I assure you, Juliet, I will be at the cemetery when it opens, and I'll begin searching."

"At eight o'clock. Remember it opens at eight." Why don't I just ask him if he also did his homework and made his bed?

"Yes, eight o'clock," he replies patiently.

"Oh, Bastian, I can't thank you enough. You have no idea what this means to me."

"Don't thank me yet. I still have to find it."

"You will. I have faith." I don't know that I do, but this sounds like the right thing to say. "Giovanni will probably be there right when it opens, too. I should tell you what he looks like; you might see him waiting at the entrance when you get there."

"Père Lachaise is enormous," Bastian says. "There are five different gates located on different streets. And even if I do see him, then what? I make a citizen's arrest?"

He is joking, but he has a point. "God, I don't know!" I say. "But what if he gets to the mausoleum first?"

"Then he gets there first," Bastian says gently. "There is nothing else we can do."

That is what I lack: the ability to accept what is out of my control. My entire life has been built upon orchestrating things that were never mine, then searing with resentment when they are lost to me. But this particular situation demands the full illusion of my control. Otherwise, I will go insane.

"We land at nine-thirty," I continue, "so we should be able to meet you there by ten-thirty tops. But that gives you over two hours to search. That's a lot of time. You'll find it, Bastian, I know you will."

"This is an incredible amount of pressure, Juliet. You must know that. I cannot promise you a thing."

There is a long pause.

"I know," I say finally. "I'm sorry, and I know." What else can I say?

We end the call as Alessio takes a hard right into the B&B's driveway and jerks to a halt in front of the entrance. My eyes dart to the dashboard clock. Eight-thirty. Giovanni must be just a couple hours outside Paris by now. Alessio turns to me.

"Do you need help packing?" he asks.

"Thanks, but no. I'll be down in ten minutes tops." I start to open the car door when Alessio grabs my arm.

"Are you sure you don't want to drive there instead? We can start now, drive straight through the night."

My sense of urgency is so intense that, yes, on one hand, I want nothing more than to put the pedal to the floor and get moving. But I need to be realistic.

"It's twelve hours' drive. Even if we left now, we'd be getting there at almost the same time our flight lands tomorrow morning. And that's driving straight through, no traffic, no unexpected stuff. Better to just get to the airport tonight, crash there, and be ready to go first thing in the morning."

"Okay," he nods. "Whatever you want." I smile and thank him.

Over the horizon, twilight sets in, and with it the uncanny sense that this is my last night on Earth.

⁂

When we touch ground at Charles de Gaulle the next morning, I immediately turn on my phone. The satellite searches for a signal, and I brace for any texts or missed calls. But there are none. Bastian has presumably been at the cemetery for an hour and a half now. I try to settle my roiling stomach.

Alessio and I de-board and make our way hastily down the long airport corridor. All around us, people are entangled in excited greetings and emotional good-byes, but we're stampeding down the hall like soldiers in the Blitz. In a way, it's not an altogether outrageous comparison.

Once outside, we get a taxi in the long queue and begin our trek into central Paris. The two of us stay mostly silent with tension, exchanging hopeful looks here and there. I check my phone every other minute for a possible missed text or call, but none come. After nearly forty-five minutes, my phone finally pings. I look down and my mouth goes dry. A text from Bastian.

Found it. Call me as soon as you get here. Enter at Rue de la Roquette.

I open the message and view the photo that he

attached. It's the image that's now tattooed on the back of my eyelids.

The mausoleum. In all its hi-res, colorful, modern-day glory. I gulp for air and cover my mouth. Can this actually be real? Alessio turns to me and I show him the screen. His expression softens into a wistful smile.

"*Congratulazioni*," he says. I squeeze his hand.

Out the window, I see a sign: *Père Lachaise Cemetery 1 km*. I lean forward in my seat. "*L'entrée dans Rue de la Roquette, s'il vous plaît*," I say to the driver, and he nods.

Five minutes later, we pull up to an enormous wrought-iron gate, green with decades of oxidation, set inside a ten-foot-high stone wall that goes on for blocks. The gate's doors are pinned open with huge iron stakes in the ground, like two massive, restrained arms. I catch a glimpse of the sea of mausoleums, tombstones, and statues inside. I quickly pay the driver and jump out, dialing Bastian as Alessio and I grab my bags from the trunk.

"Juliet? You are here?" Bastian says.

"I told you you'd find it!" I shriek into the phone. "Bastian, you're incredible! You're beyond amazing. Yes, we're here at the gate! Where do we go?"

I shove my arms through my backpack straps and drag my suitcase up the stone path into the cemetery, throwing a glance over my shoulder to make sure Alessio's following. He's a few steps behind me, shooting a sharp, solemn gaze all around as he walks.

"Okay, once you are inside, walk up the path for about five minutes until you get to the big Napoleon statue.

Turn left, and follow the curve. Stay on this walk until you get to the—"

Then I hear what sounds like a grunt followed by silence.

"Bastian. Bastian, are you there?" Nothing but rapid beeping, indicating that the call has ended.

I hit redial, turning to Alessio. He sees my expression, and his face grows concerned.

"What is it? What's wrong?" he says.

"I—don't know. We got disconnected. He said follow this straight ahead to the Napoleon statue, then turn left. That's really all I heard. I'm calling him back."

I plow ahead with the phone up to my ear, already out of breath from hoofing it this far with my suitcase bouncing and twisting behind me on the uneven path. Some passersby look curiously at me as I race on, determined.

Bastian's phone rings and rings. *Dammit!* I hang up and try again, but it's the same thing. A growing sickness spreads through my gut. Was that really a grunt I heard? I try once more, and this time the call goes directly to voicemail without ringing. Exasperated, I shove the phone in my pocket. Alessio strides quickly next to me.

"He's not answering, Alessio. Something's wrong."

"We must hurry."

To my potent relief, the Napoleon statue comes into view ahead of us. The general stares blindly into the distance upon his stone horse.

"There's the statue," Alessio says. "Now, left?"

"Yes. Left, then follow the curve. After that, I don't know. We didn't get that far."

I try to quell the rising panic in my voice, but I know Alessio can see right through me. We understand each other perfectly. He grabs my suitcase from me, holding it in the air. His eyes, like mine, are wild and fraught.

"Run," he says.

Chapter Thirty-Five

I RUN. I run past weeping statues, frozen cherubs, mausoleums of all shapes and sizes. *Turn left, follow the curve until you get to the*—the what, the *what*? My eyes dart all around, hoping for landmarks that Bastian could have meant, but they're everywhere; anything could be one.

"You look on the right, I'll take the left!" I shout over my shoulder to Alessio. He's still keeping pace right behind me, even while clutching my suitcase to his chest. Like me, he must be fueled purely by adrenaline.

My mind reels as I scour the landscape. What the hell happened to Bastian? Is he really in danger, or is it just terrible cell phone service? I'm so paranoid and exhausted I can't tell what's real or not anymore.

But how could I have sent him here, knowing Giovanni is a killer? Did I really think some tourist destination in the brightness of morning would stop Giovanni from doing something to him? Violent acts happen all the time in broad daylight, with dozens of people around. I'm horrified by what I've done.

An enormous dogwood tree in full bloom appears in the middle of the path ahead of me. Breathless, I stop, and Alessio nearly slams into me.

"Sorry," I gasp at him. Bastian's words ring in my mind—*follow the curve, until you get to…* Could it be this huge, looming tree? It is certainly a major landmark. I walk a few paces down past the tree, desperately scanning the sea of mausoleums. I'm about to give up and return to Alessio when my breath seizes in my throat.

There it is.

About twenty feet down the path on the right. The two weeping statues on either side of those closed, oxidized iron doors. *Closed?* But in the photo Bastian texted me minutes ago, the right door had been open. Sickness floods my veins.

"It's over there!" I yell, whipping my head around to Alessio, pointing ahead. I break into a run again and pound down the stone path, turning onto the grass and scrambling between graves. The mausoleum sits a few rows back from the main path, and it's quieter and more secluded here than I thought.

Than I'd like.

When I reach it, I put my palm against the cold door. The air behind it feels freezing, as if it's blowing up from a cavernous, open grave. Shuddering, I push the door open, my head flooded with the white noise of pumping blood. I'm vaguely aware that Alessio is now behind me, saying something. But I've already stepped inside and am peering into the blackness.

The silent chamber is faintly lit thanks to a small, broken window high up in the back wall. It illuminates three evenly spaced tombs atop a stone floor caked with dirt and dust. I can't fully tell since my eyes are still adjusting, but the place seems to be deserted.

Alessio steps in behind me. "Careful," he whispers harshly in my ear, hand on my back. As my vision acclimates, a figure slumped on the floor next to the left-hand tomb begins to appear. It's like an old Polaroid developing right in front of me. The person stares at me imploringly, and he gives a barely perceptible shake of his head.

"Oh, my God. Bastian." I rush toward him.

"No," comes the groggy response, "Juliet, don't—"

Suddenly, a hand leaps out of the darkness and clamps down on my right arm. Before I can react, it's followed by the pressure of cold steel sinking against my neck. My body turns to ice.

"Get over here, and keep your mouth shut," says the gruff voice with the thick Italian accent.

Behind me, I hear Alessio's breath quicken and start to heave and rattle.

"Papa." He chokes out the word, drops my suitcase to the ground. "*Che diavolo stai facendo?*"

"*Stai indietro,*" Giovanni growls, grabbing me tighter and pushing the gun's muzzle deeper into my neck. A thin whine begins ringing in my ears, and it takes me a minute to realize the sound is coming from my own throat.

Alessio's face exudes a horrifying mix of hatred and betrayal, the intensity of which has altered his features. He actually looks like a different person as he comes toward us.

"*Stai indietro!*" Giovanni shouts at him. Alessio doesn't take his eyes away from his father's as he slowly closes the mausoleum door behind him, sealing the four of us inside. Giovanni suddenly lets me go and pushes me across the room.

"Over there," he barks. I stumble over to Bastian and fall to the floor next to him. He wraps his arms around me, and I whisper apologies to him. I'm horrified by my stupidity and selfishness, getting him mixed up in this.

"Shhh," Bastian murmurs. "It will be okay."

I fearfully take in my surroundings. The damp, cold chamber around us is about twenty-by-twelve feet in size. There's a shelf carved into the wall underneath the tiny window upon which several red glass candles sit under a thick cover of dust. Besides them and the three tombs, the room is devoid of anything else.

Wait. That's not entirely right.

As my eyes fully adjust, I notice what looks like a square briefcase on the ground next to where Giovanni stands. It was nearly impossible to see it at first because like everything else in here, it is buried under a quilt of dust. My pulse surges. Is that *it*? The thing Henry left behind?

Giovanni's wild eyes glare at me from his leathery, aged face. His expression, possessive and desperate, says it all. I suppress the urge to jump up and grab the briefcase, tear the lid open.

"*Laggiù con i tuoi amici, figlio*," Giovanni demands of Alessio, gesturing with his gun for Alessio to move over to us. But Alessio doesn't move. He straightens up and sets his jaw.

"Or what? You will kill me?" Has he switched over to English for my benefit? Giovanni's expression falters, a crack in his rage where shame leaks out. Alessio steps closer to him and opens his arms wide.

"Then do it, Papa," he says, the words drenched in poison. "Do it. What does it matter anymore, eh?"

The gun trembles in Giovanni's knotted, old hand. His jowls quiver.

"You know who you really are. A murderer. *Un fottuto assassino!*" Alessio slams his fist down on the tomb in front of him and it echoes throughout the chamber.

Can anyone outside hear us? I hold fast to the vain hope that some passerby will catch the commotion and come investigate. But deep down I know better. We're too far from the main path, and the heavy iron doors are closed.

Giovanni's mouth turns into a shaking frown. He looks like he is on the brink of falling apart completely.

"You make me sick," Alessio spits. "All these years, you keeping me at arm's length. Making me feel like I was the one who wasn't good enough. Never good enough to earn your trust, to get close to you, to do anything, even after Mama died. I just had to respect you. Respect your space, respect your silence, respect how you make me feel like nothing. Only for this? To find out you murdered this girl's uncle? You are nothing!"

"No!" Giovanni shouts, but it's more of a plea than rage. "It isn't what you think. You don' understand, *figlio*, you don' understand me." Giovanni shakes his head fiercely, tears surging from his sunken eyes. "You don' know what happened, it was a mistake. They make me do it."

"What? *Who?* Who made you do it?"

Giovanni falters, and the gun starts to fall. Alessio moves toward him but Giovanni perks right up, raising it at Bastian and me again. Sobs rise up from somewhere deep inside his afflicted being, but Alessio is unmoved. He regards his father as impassively as if he were watching a fly drown in a swimming pool.

"Tell me what you did."

Giovanni mumbles, his words falling all over each other before evaporating like the souls that had once inhabited the bodies in the tombs between us.

"*Che cosa?*" Alessio says.

Giovanni repeats the blubbering speech.

"Speak up!"

"I said I had no choice!" Giovanni's proclamation bounces off the walls. "*Non avevo scelta fottuta*, Alessio. *Per favore, credimi.* Believe me, please."

"Tell me what you did."

"Alessio, *per favore*, no—"

"You tell me what you did, *figlio di puttana*!" He steps toward him and draws his fist back.

Giovanni scrambles away from his son, back against the wall, and, with a ghastly wail, raises the gun to his own head.

Chapter Thirty-Six

Rosanera
July 8, 1971
Afternoon

THE BANGING ON the door startles Giovanni awake. He looks around the kitchen, puzzled, and wonders where Hank is. Hadn't they just been talking? Then the memory slowly descends on Giovanni. That's right. Hank said he was going out somewhere, he had something to do. Giovanni drags his shirtsleeve across his mouth to remove the dried, putrid saliva. The pounding on the door resumes, even more insistent now. He shuffles to the front door. Hardly anyone ever visits besides his mother. She comes a few times a week to hand him a home-cooked meal, her doleful eyes scrutinizing the wretched state of her only child.

Giovanni opens the door, and squints into the bright summer sun. It is most definitely not his mother. A tall man with wild, dark curls leans in and smirks at Giovanni, his elbow propped on the doorframe. Behind him stands an attractive, petite blond, her long hair tied back in a scarf that emphasizes her well-proportioned facial features. She might've been even prettier, Giovanni thinks, if it weren't for her scowl. He struggles to keep his eyes open as he surveys the two strangers. Everything floats a few beats behind real time, as is typical after his late-morning dose. All the pain, the grim memories temporarily frozen like ice.

Who are these people, and what are they doing here?

"*Buongiorno,*" the man at the door says, but with a French accent. "You Giovanni?"

Giovanni nods, shifting on his feet. The man studies Giovanni's face for a second, then sniffs and turns to the woman.

"This is gonna be easier than we thought," he laughs. She just looks at the man and then back at Giovanni, her expression unchanged.

"Wha' you wan', man? How you know me?" Giovanni says. Even in his hazy state, he senses something is very off. The Frenchman cranes his neck, peering into the house behind Giovanni.

"We're just looking for our friend," he says, flashing a cold smile. "And we hear he's crashing here. With you." A long, crooked finger points at Giovanni.

Giovanni's blood drops into his feet, and he feels his neck get clammy. These people are clearly involved in whatever heavy shit happened to Hank in France.

"Who? No, man, no, sorry. No one stayin' here man, jus' me. You gotta wron' place," Giovanni says and starts to close the door.

The man shoves his foot into the doorway. Keeping his malicious gaze fixed on Giovanni's, he lifts the hem of his shirt to reveal the butt of a gun tucked into his waistband. Giovanni's breath hitches.

"I think you're wrong about that, *amico*," the Frenchman says. He beckons to the woman, and they both barge past Giovanni into the house.

"Henry? Hank! Come on out, *mon frere*! You knew we'd find you sooner or later!" The man yells. He and the woman begin storming through the house. With a trembling hand, Giovanni closes the front door and goes into the living room, where the woman tears through Hank's sparse luggage.

"I found his stuff, Remy!" she yells. Remy? Giovanni racks his boggled brain. Didn't sound familiar. What could Hank have possibly gotten himself into? To Giovanni, Hank always seemed like the one who had his shit together.

The woman turns Hank's canvas bag upside down and rummages through his titanium suitcase. Photographs and papers flutter around her.

"Hey, don' touch that," Giovanni protests, trying to snatch the bag from the woman's grasp. But she yanks it out of his reach.

"Wha' you lookin' for? He don' have no money or anything like that!" Giovanni's face flushes as the words leave his mouth. He'd already gone through Hank's things to make sure of that.

Remy thunders back into the living room. "He's not here. You find anything?"

"No," she says shortly, holding up the empty bag. "Just a bunch of bullshit." They both turn to Giovanni.

The woman gets to her feet, and Remy pulls the gun out of his pants, lets it hang at his side. Breathing rapidly, the woman walks over to Giovanni and stands with her face inches from him.

"Where is it?" she demands. "Where did he hide it?"

"Lady, I don' know what you talkin' bout—"

"Cut the shit! Where the fuck is my video reel?"

Video reel? What in God's name is she talking about? All of this, over some *film*? He can't imagine what kind of film warrants the threat of murder. Pornography, maybe? Even still…

"I—I—there's no—"

Remy steps forward and looks straight into Giovanni's eyes for a few beats. To Giovanni's extraordinary relief, his genuine bewilderment must appear as such, because Remy shakes his head in disgust and turns to the girl.

"This is a fuckin' waste of time," he says. "Look at him. He's just a pathetic fuckin' junkie, he doesn't know shit. We gotta go through the rest of the house. Closets, drawers, whatever. Dump it all. And do it fast."

"You better fuckin' hope, for your sake, we find what we're looking for," the girl seethes at Giovanni, then leaves the room.

Giovanni sinks onto the sofa as drawers are ripped open, silverware, pots, and pans crash to the floor. He can feel his dose wearing off, the temporary armor it provides beginning to crack. He knows he is now entering dangerous territory. Where all the ruin, the nightmares, the torrent of recollection can flow freely. His forehead grows slick.

"Where's Hank?" Remy says.

"I don' know," Giovanni answers. "I honestly don'. He left this morning, took the car. Said he had to go take care ah somethin'."

The woman stamps out of the kitchen and blows past Remy and Giovanni into the bedroom, where she begins to attack the dresser.

"Then when is he coming back?" Remy says.

"I don' know."

"*'I don' know, I don' know.'* Well, that's too fuckin' bad, man. For both him and you."

"Look, I'm tellin' you, he has *no video reel*, okay? I wen' through his shit when he get here, and I never saw it. I swear. Maybe is a mistake. Maybe someone else has it."

A frustrated scream erupts from the bedroom. The woman flies of the room and moves on to the bathroom. Giovanni's heart stutters with fear. *My stash*!

"*Aspetta*! Please, be careful!" he begs. He winces as he hears the cigar box, with all his goods inside, smash on the floor, followed by the tinkling of needles rolling on the cold tiles.

"Fucking dopehead. They're all the same. Useless!"

She storms back into the living room, her breathing as thick as mud. Her scarf has come undone. Pieces of her blonde hair stick to her sweaty, red cheeks.

"Fuck this," Remy says. He strides over to Giovanni, jamming the weapon against his temple.

Giovanni feels his bladder loosen. All of a sudden, he is in Huế again. In that hideous hut that doubled as a bar. He can see Hank sitting at the long table near the back, all his cameras and microphones and photos spread out before him. When Giovanni looks back at Remy holding the gun to his head, he has transformed into a VC—narrowed eyes blazing with hatred.

"Remy!" The woman says, but he ignores her.

"Tell me where Henry is." He cocks the gun against Giovanni's temple.

"I tol' you, I don' know, I don' know," Giovanni croaks. In front of his eyes, the man flickers between himself and the VC in Huế, like someone rapidly snapping the lever on a View-Master.

"*Remy!*"

"What?" He snaps, looking at Cherie. She walks toward him, chin tilted up to look into his eyes.

"We should wait until he comes back, and try to get it out of him."

"The reel's not here, Cherie. Which means it's stashed somewhere."

"And you don't want to know where that is?"

Remy growls, dropping the gun from Giovanni's temple and tearing his free hand through his hair.

"Henry's not going to tell us shit. He'd rather have us kill him first! You know it's true. And then what? We have to do him right here, in this house? Leave bodies and evidence all over the place?" Giovanni shudders at the plural use of the word. "We might as well just skip the middle step and get straight to it."

Now the woman is breathing hard, saying nothing.

"The news is gonna hit soon, and we can't have this shit still hanging over our heads!" Remy shouts.

What news? Giovanni thinks. Did they tell him about something that he's already forgotten? He can't think straight. Never can. He hates himself, hates how his thoughts are always an anachronistic pile of worthless pieces.

"So, what, we're gonna take him out?" says the girl (Cherie? Was that her name, or just the Frenchman's term of endearment?).

"No," Remy says slowly, looking at Giovanni. "*We're* not gonna do anything."

Giovanni stops breathing. He shoots a pleading glance at Remy, but the man is looking at Cherie. *No, no, I won't do it,* he thinks. *There is no way they can force me to.*

"So here's the deal, Giovanni," Remy says, his voice turning calm. He shoves the gun back into his waistband and backs up a few paces, running a weary palm over his stubbly jaw. "I'm out of time and patience. This whole Hank thing? Needs to be wrapped up, now. Today.

"But I'm not totally without heart," he goes on. "I know we'd be asking you a big favor. What do you think about, say…" He scrunches up his face in thought, surveying the wreck of a house around him. "Two large? U.S., of course."

Giovanni can't move. *Two thousand* American dollars? His hand instinctively leaps to his opposite arm, itching the punctures that lie beneath his long sleeve. Cherie notices and a sly smile spreads across her face.

"And you won't believe your luck, man," she says, sauntering toward him. "My friend here? He runs the biggest horse ring in France. No shit. He can get you a quarter-kilo of H by the end of today. Isn't that right?" She peers coquettishly at Remy, who returns a placid smile.

"It's true," he says. "I don't have the dope on me, but she's right. I can get it from my guy in Firenze. Like the lady said. End of today."

Giovanni goes faint at the suggestion. A quarter-kilo of heroin will last him years. That, plus two thousand dollars? He'd never have to worry about sourcing his habit again, about getting caught. Just sweet, perpetual oblivion for as long as he needed it. The night terrors, the endless torment that plagued each waking moment. The agony nothing can absolve or allay except for that soft, brown talc.

"*Merda*," Giovanni manages. "I don't believe you."

Cherie motions to Remy. He digs into his pocket and draws out a huge wad of cash. He fans out the thick stack of United States one-hundred-dollar bills as casually as if he'd taken out a handkerchief.

Giovanni trembles, sits down heavily on the couch.

Everything could be so, so easy from now on. All he would have to do is—

Then the excruciating image that he's tried to keep at bay for so long, tried to bury with all his might, bubbles to the surface of his mind. He sees Hank leaning over him in the sweltering hut, the air permeated with the tang of iron and blood and sulfur and death. Hank sheltering him, keeping him warm. Screaming for help.

Sustaining his life.

He can't. *He won't.*

"No, no, no, I can', I can'," he moans, shoulders crumpling. "Hank, he save my life. You don' know, you have no idea. He save my life."

Cherie raises her eyebrows in mock surprise. "And look what you've done with it," she says, gesturing all around her and back at him. "Impressive."

Remy's face hardens. He comes over to Giovanni, leans down with his hands on his knees and puts his own face just inches from his.

"Let me put it to you this way: you do it or I kill the both of you," he says. "And I won't stop there. No, Giovanni, that's only the start. After I'm done with you, I'll kill your parents. Who I know live just around the corner, by the way."

Giovanni's heart somersaults in his throat. How in God's name does he know that?

"Then I'll go to Philly, and do Henry's parents, too. You think I'm messing around? Try me."

Giovanni, now coldly sober, stares into the man's eyes.

He tastes vomit in the back of his throat. *These people, they're demons.*

"You see, Giovanni," Cherie says, coming up to them, "what Henry took from me is extremely precious. Like, we're talking the Crown-fuckin'-Jewels. It wasn't his to take. It was *mine*, and he stole it from me.

"So listen. You do this for us, and keep your mouth shut about it forever? Everybody wins. You get the money and the dope, and you stay on cloud nine forever. If you don't?" She smiles mirthlessly. "Well. Remy's already explained what'll happen. And if you think I'm bullshitting—that Remy and I don't have the power to do whatever we want—try us. You want to try us, Giovanni?"

Giovanni can no longer see them through his tears. He knows she is telling the truth. They'd both scared Hank enough for him to flee Paris in an absolute panic and hide out here. And Remy casually whipping out over one thousand dollars only reinforced that they have resources, which also means heavy sway.

But how can he possibly do this to Hank?

Giovanni remembers a conversation with his father right after he returned home from Hué. A devout Catholic, his father had tried to help assuage his son's agony, reminding him that all events in life—past, present, and future—have already been decided by God. And that try as one may, human actions can't interfere with the outcomes of this pre-established chain. All Giovanni could do to heal from his trauma was to accept that whatever horror he'd undergone was God's will. "We don't have a choice," he'd told Giovanni. "Even when we think we do."

Maybe I don't have a choice, Giovanni thinks. *Either way, Hank will die. But in the other option, so do our families.*

Cherie seems to sense his resignation. "There. Now stop crying and think," she says. "If you were Hank, where would you be right now?"

Giovanni's soul feels like an eviscerated animal left to rot in the baking sun.

"He—he like to go to the… the *scogliere*," he waves his hand vaguely, forgetting the English word.

"Cliffs," Remy says, arms folded in satisfaction. Giovanni nods weakly.

"Well, Giovanni, it sounds like you're in luck again," Cherie says. "Seems like enough dangerous *scogliere* in this town that an eager, doped-up, hippie American tourist could easily meet his unfortunate end. By accident, of course."

Giovanni's eyes met hers. She makes sure he understands.

"Your town's small enough," she says, sinking down into the chair behind her and crossing her legs demurely. "I'm sure you can find him. But I suggest you get going soon."

Remy nods. "Better figure it out. Because we ain't leaving 'til it's done."

Chapter Thirty-Seven

I FALL AGAINST the cold sarcophagus next to me, dry heaving. Bastian tries to steady me in an awkward embrace, but I push away from him weakly, desperate for air. Did Alessio's father just admit he murdered Henry? I bite down on my fist through feverish, choking cries, watching Giovanni. He's crouched on the floor, sniveling, with the gun still jammed hard to his temple. Even though it's dim, I can see his white knuckle wrapped around the trigger. His wailing sounds like a savage animal raging in a trap.

My mind tries to make sense of what I just heard. Henry was a photojournalist in Vietnam. Henry saved Giovanni's life in Vietnam. Henry stole a video tape from Jim Morrison's girlfriend and her French drug lord boyfriend, a crime for which Giovanni murdered Henry on their behalf.

I want to scream at Giovanni. Shout the kind of words that permanently maim; the kinds that still haunt you on your deathbed. I want to kick him until he spits up blood. Wrap my hands around his wrinkled neck and choke the remaining miserable life out of him. The only thing that stops me is seeing Alessio. He's shivering and barely standing up, hand clamped over his mouth, his shoulders hitching and shaking in time with his muted sobs. He looks on at his father with pure agony.

"So I do it," Giovanni moans from the floor, "I do as they tell me. I cause the car accident. I kill Hank. I'm sorry. I'm so sorry." He devolves into a new guttural howl. After several failed attempts, he catches his breath and continues. "But, please, I only do it to save everyone else. They were gon'a kill everyone. Hank's family, my family. Please believe me. I did it to save my mother, to save Hank's mother!"

"And *yourself!*" I shout, stepping forward. "Don't forget about that, or the money or drugs you were given to do it!"

As soon the acerbic words leave my mouth, I feel sick. Will that make him pull the trigger? Right here, in front of his son? If Alessio has to see that on account of me, I'll never forgive myself.

Giovanni's liquidy eyes flash to me briefly before he squeezes them shut. He shakes his head slowly from side to side, still weeping. Then he cocks the gun and pushes it impossibly harder against his temple.

"Papa!" Alessio shrieks, moving toward Giovanni. "Papa, no, no, please, just look at me." He extends a trembling hand to his father, but Giovanni refuses, shrinking away from him.

"I know I worthless," Giovanni says. "I don' deserve to be here when Hank—when he—isn't. I never shoulda' been here at all."

"Papa, *per favore*, put the gun down," Alessio begs. "We can fix this."

"But you have to understand, thas why I come here," Giovanni says, ignoring Alessio's pleas. He looks right at me.

"When you show up my door—*Dio santo*." A sadness that knows no depth spreads through his gaze. "You look juss like him. You could be his daughter, no niece. It kills me to see you.

"Then you tell me about this *fotografia*, and the *messaggio* on the back. How you are sure Hank hid somethin' here in this *tomba*. Somethin' *molto importante*, like a secret—*a secret;* I remember you say it just like that.

"And then it come to me. This must be where Hank stash it. All those years ago. The video those…*fottute persone* wanted from him."

My breath comes in rapid, shallow spurts. I feel like I'm going to faint. If it weren't for Bastian holding me up, I might well have already. My eyes never leave Giovanni's, despite the spots creeping in around the edges of my vision.

"I remember Hank come to me from Paris. And so after you visit me, I think to myself, what is the biggest *cimitero* there?" Giovanni spreads out his free hand. "Père

Lachaise. On this chance, I take the photo from your room. And I drive here, hundreds of kilometers, to find it.

"I *had* to come here, you understand?" His voice scales up an octave as his eyes rivet into mine. "I had to know what I did this for. What I was force to kill my friend for! What was so precious, this *pezzo di merda*, for me to take him from this world! I had to know, I had to know…" He breaks off into sobs.

Magma pumps in my veins at a thousand miles an hour. I can't hold back.

"*You* had to know?" I sputter. "What about *me*? My mother? Or *Henry's* mother? Who is still alive, by the way, but just barely. Right this minute, she's in a coma back in California. You don't think *she* has a right to whatever her murdered son left behind?"

Giovanni flinches and blinks, the gun still stubbornly pushed into the side of his head.

I stab a finger at the dusty black case Henry hid here half a century ago, now sitting benignly at Giovanni's feet.

"Whatever's in there doesn't belong to you," I growl. "This isn't about you getting the privilege to 'understand' why you did it. You don't *get* to know that comfort. Why is that so difficult for you to comprehend?"

At that, Giovanni's face abruptly turns catatonic. I don't know what I expected, but it wasn't this.

"You are right," he says, his voice vacant. "I don' deserve any answers."

Then he pulls the trigger.

In that paralyzing split-second, which seems to last

hours, all I hear is a dull click. Then Alessio leaps on his father and the pistol goes skidding past me across the dirty floor to the entryway.

It didn't fire.

Bastian springs to life behind me, runs to the doorway and picks it up. He points the muzzle at the floor and away from all of us, examining the hammer. I get a clearer look at it from this angle. I don't know much about guns, but the weapon looks ancient. Did Giovanni bring it home with him from Vietnam? If so, no wonder it misfired. The thing is probably filthy inside, likely still loaded with the original ammo from fifty years ago. Bastian opens the gun and takes out the cartridge. He runs his thumb up the side and pushes out the bullets. I shudder as they clink onto the cold mausoleum floor, worthless as pennies.

He lays the empty pistol on the sarcophagus closest to him, then strides over to me and folds me into his chest. The five-year expanse between us evaporates right away, and it's like we haven't been apart for more than a few weeks.

Against the wall opposite us, Alessio also has his arms wrapped around his father. He rocks him back and forth, runs his hand over and over Giovanni's head as if he's comforting a child. Through his tears, he murmurs to him in reassuring tones.

Giovanni is silent. He must be in shock. But in their embrace, I see his hands are gripping Alessio's back like desperate talons.

"It's okay, Papa," Alessio breathes into his father's neck. "I didn't know. I didn't know what you went through."

Giovanni pulls away from him, and his eyes dart all around the chamber. They land on me and Bastian, fearfully. It appears to finally dawn on him that he almost committed suicide right in front of his son, and that he has also confessed to murder.

He takes Alessio's hands in his own.

"*Figlio*," he begins. "*Ti ho deluso*. Your whole life I failed you. Do you know when I met your mother, years after this horror, I try. I try so badly to make a new start with her. To be good. To be a man. I quit the drugs. Oh, I go through hell, meeting the devil himself. But I do it somehow. And when she get pregnant with you, Alessio—it happened. You were my new start. Something to live for. But even in that, I failed. Even my second chance."

Alessio's weeping nearly drowns out his father's monologue. He is squeezing the elderly man's hands so tightly I think he'll crush them into dust.

"I have been *un padre orribile* to you, Alessio. *Ti amo molto*. More than you know. But I am too far gone, *figlio*. My mind is collapse. In Huế, even though my body survive that day, I died. When I return Rosanera, *mio corpo* breathe and move, but I was dead. *Capisce*? I been dead fifty years. There is no forgiving what I done. God will no' forgive me, and neither should you."

"Papa," Alessio manages through his crying. He can't, or won't, say any more.

When I catch a glimpse of Alessio's face, it is unlike

any emotional transformation I've ever seen. A powerful light emerging from within a deep, uninhabited cave.

I see it now. This is all Alessio ever needed. To know he is wanted, loved. Seeing the two of them together erodes my vengeance.

All I feel is pity.

Not enough to change the fact Giovanni is a killer, though. Doesn't he deserve to be held accountable for what he did to my uncle? I should turn him over to the Italian authorities, let them all sort it the hell out.

Or has he suffered enough already? Clearly, the man has lived an isolated existence tortured by a crippling heroin addiction and acute post-traumatic stress disorder. He has had no relationship with his own son. Not to mention, his guilt over Henry's death is so colossal that he was willing to end his life over it just moments ago.

What good would it really do now to send this wretched old man to prison? More importantly, how can I deprive Alessio of his only living parent, just when that person has finally made it clear to him that he is loved and needed?

Maybe it should be enough that I now know the truth about what happened to Henry. And maybe someday it will be. I really don't know. But I have more pressing matters in front of me right now.

Moving as if in a dream, I walk over to the dust-covered black briefcase and kneel beside it. Ironically, it's still sitting next to the third tomb, bottom right, exactly in line with the instructions Henry jotted on the back of the photo fifty years ago. This long overdue cry for remembrance; a fervent wish to not be forgotten. Bastian comes up behind me and slips his warm hand onto my back, letting me know that I'm not forgotten, either.

With trembling hands, I flip the latches and open the lid.

Chapter Thirty-Eight

Paris, France
One week after

"Still nothing? No signs of change at all?" I say into the speaker phone as I sink onto Bastian's couch. I search for a free spot on the coffee table in front of me to set my fifth steaming mug of the day, before giving up and resting it on the sofa arm instead. The work surface is dominated by my laptop, its screen glowing with fifteen open browser tabs for "Hank Elysian," and all of the carefully organized contents I found inside Henry's case. They are more precious than I could have ever imagined: rubber-band-wrapped stacks of his photographs, a couple notebooks, and a gorgeous Minolta SLR. I've spent almost every waking hour since the horror at Père Lachaise at this table, attending it like a prayer altar.

"Nothing yet," Colette says, stifling a yawn. I don't

blame her. It's only six o'clock in the morning in California. "For now, all her vitals and brain activity are stable. Pretty surprising for someone her age. Your Nana's a tough one."

That she is. I wonder what it must be like to be her: in your nineties, having outlived your husband and both your children. Yeah, you would have to be pretty goddamn resilient. I can only hope she is dogged enough to hang on until I get back there.

As if reading my mind, Colette says, "Any idea yet when you're coming back? She's maintaining now, but that could change at any time. You should get here as soon as you possibly can, Jules."

Urgency rises in my throat like battery acid. I am keenly aware that my grandmother's life hangs in a liminal space that could take a hard turn for the worst at any moment. But I would be doing her a grave disservice if I left Paris without a final consensus on Henry's tape—is it salvageable or not?

"Believe me, Colette, I'm trying to get out of here as fast as I can." Not a statement one often makes in reference to Paris, but under the circumstances it couldn't be more genuine. "We're still waiting to hear back from the video restoration guy."

She sighs. "Are you sure he knows what he's doing?"

I blow on my hot coffee, then venture a sip. The strong taste of chicory is sublime. I've masked it for so long with adding in Bailey's that I've forgotten about the seed's pungent delight.

"Bastian says he's the best," I tell her. "He and Matthieu

have been friends for, like, twenty years. I'm certain that Bastian would not trust this process to anyone less than an expert. He knows the stakes."

The irony that I hail from a region known as the film capital of the world is not lost on me. Once home, I would have no trouble accessing video restoration experts just as talented as Matthieu, if not more so.

But I am not about to subject the invaluable relic to airport security's graceless scrutiny or the assault of countless x-rays on a six-thousand-mile journey back to California. No, if the tape is to be restored at all, it needs to be done here in Paris first.

"It should only be a couple more days at the most," I say. "Matthieu said about a week, and we've just passed that mark."

"I trust your judgment," Colette says, which throws me. I can't recall the last time anyone has told me that, or the last time I've said it to myself. "How confident is Matthieu that he'll be able to recover anything?"

The odds are that the tape's contents are lost forever. I have to continuously put the thought out of my mind to keep from going insane, and I don't even want to say it aloud right now for fear of manifesting it into existence.

"He thinks there's a chance," I say instead. "He says the problem is, video tape deteriorates way faster than regular film because of the magnetic encoding. Video usually only survives something like twenty-five years max because of this thing that happens called sticky tape syndrome."

"Never heard of that. What is it?"

I lean forward and click through my laptop's open tabs to find the exact explanation that I've already read a hundred times but can't seem to memorize.

"It's when the binding that holds the magnetizable coating to the tape starts lifting," I read off the webpage. "Once it peels away, the tape definitely can't be played, and whatever's recorded is at high risk of being completely erased. But Matthieu told us he could maybe 'bake' the tape." I scroll down the page to find the section on that. "Ah, here. It's this crazy process where they literally bake the video tape in low temperatures in an effort to reattach the magnetic binders. If it works, it should preserve tape's contents while also making it firm enough to transfer over to a brand-new tape. From there, Matthieu said he could then pretty easily convert it to a digital file. Not a guaranteed fix, but it's our only shot."

Colette is silent for a few beats, seems to be taking it all in. "I sincerely hope Matthieu can make it happen. But if not, Juliet—your discovery itself is astonishing. The case was there, right where you knew in your gut Henry left something. Even without the tape, you still found him. You found Henry. His photos, his notebooks, the essence of who he was and where he went; it's all yours to unpack now. That is an unbelievable gift. I hope you'll remember that."

As her message washes over me, I hear Mom speak the words instead of Colette. There's an ache at the back of my throat as we say our I love yous and hang up. I prop my chin in my hands, elbows on my knees, and stare at the tabletop before me.

This is what I now know: Henry Barton, or Hank Elysian, was an artist, a documentarian, a humanitarian. He was brave and afraid; shy and arrogant; unapologetic and forgiving. He and Cherie Atkins were once in love. He had a deep friendship with one of history's greatest rock legends. He quit UCLA's preeminent film school a year before he was supposed to graduate so he could chronicle—with remarkable passion—one of the most controversial wars in modern history. He wanted to believe the world could be better than it is, and took personal offense when it was not.

Over the past seven days, I've devoured what he left me over and over again, slowly rendering a three-dimensional persona of the uncle I never knew, the young man that his own parents and sister never knew.

Except for the bouts of intense intimacy with Bastian, just as soul-stirring as they were five years ago, and my broken attempts at sleep afterward, I stay up alone well into the dead hours of the night arranging Henry's hundreds of photographs into chronological order. Fortunately, the task is pretty straightforward thanks to his meticulous labeling on the back of each one.

The handsome, grinning Black GI is *Tyrone, Saigon, Mar. 1967*. The barely eighteen-year-old, coquettish blonde posing in front of Grauman's Chinese Theatre is *Cherie, Hollywood Bl, Apr. 1963*. The Doors' budding frontman standing in a backyard, squinting into the sun with a half-smile, with two other guys lounging on the grass is *Jim, Ray, Mike, May 1965, Venice*. And the impossibly young, dark-haired, laughing pair of friends, arms draped over each other's shoulders, is *Me & Gio, Da Nang. Oct. 1967.* Stitching together these discrete moments breaks my heart and offers me comfort.

I stand up to stretch my aching back when my phone pings. Alessio emailed me back. I swipe my screen and open his message:

"All going as well as can be, thanks for asking. Papa is resting a lot, not eating much. We are both still very tired. But we have talked so much ever since returning home. About everything. His life in Vietnam, afterwards coming home, and the details of my mother. It is as if I'm discovering an entirely new life. A new existence." I smile, knowing exactly how he feels. "To my knowledge, he is being completely honest with me, and is unafraid to tell me anything I wish to know now. I am still hesitant to leave him in the house alone, so I will not go back to work until we feel it is okay. I think of you every day. Let me know as soon as you hear anything about the tape. Praying for good news. *Baci.*"

I'd be lying if I said there isn't a tiny part of me that still wonders if I should have turned Giovanni in. My eternal need for justice, fairness, for people to get what they deserve. An attempt to restore order and square wrongs with rights. It's the false sense of control that has held me hostage in every venture in life, that I always cling to, no matter how damaging it's been to myself and everyone I love.

I start to reach into my front pocket for a Xanax, but my hand halts in mid-air. It occurs to me that I haven't popped one since the night in Giovanni's garage more than a week ago, nor have I opened more than a couple bottles of wine. Am I getting better or just distracted?

The front door clicks open, interrupting my thoughts, and Bastian walks in. "*Bonjour, ma poulette,*" he calls from the hallway, and I hear him kicking off his shoes. He comes into the living room wearing a warm smile and holding a bouquet of stunningly simple flowers, wrapped in a sheet of plain brown paper and tied in a twine bow.

"Thank you, I love them." We kiss and I breathe in the bouquet's earthy, sweet fragrance. What I used to dismiss as a cliched attempt to please a woman reads as painfully genuine coming from Bastian.

"You are most welcome," he says. But he keeps standing there, just smiling at me.

"What?" I laugh. "Why are you looking at me like that?"

"Because I have something else for you. A gift."

"A gift? Where?" His hands are empty.

"Come with me." He takes my hand and leads me over to the sofa where we sit. He reaches into his pocket and pulls out a thumb drive. After a couple confused seconds, my chest swells.

"Is that—" I say, my hands plastered to my face. He nods, still smiling, but softer now.

"Matthieu called me this morning, so I left work early to pick it up on my way home," he says. "He tells me there was some irreversible damage to the quality of the film. Both audio and visual. I am afraid it is far from perfect, but he maintains there is enough to clearly understand the contents."

I wipe at the tears on my face, which I'd barely registered had begun.

"One more thing, Juliet," he says, taking my icy hands from my face and folding them into the warmth of his. "I want to prepare you. He told me that what's on here is very upsetting. So much so, that he couldn't believe what he was seeing. And that it's indeed incredibly significant."

I just nod dumbly.

"When I asked if this was the only copy, as he promised us in the very beginning it would be, he assured me it was," Bastian continues. "I have known Matthieu a long time. I trust him and will take him at his word. But you and I really have no choice anyway, Juliet. We needed someone's help with this; we couldn't restore it ourselves."

Again, I nod mechanically, taking the thumb drive from Bastian. Copies of the tape are the furthest thing from my mind right now. I can only think about how I'm holding my own personal equivalent of the Holy Grail.

"Are you ready?" I say.

"Are *you*?"

"I have to be."

I snap the thumb drive into my laptop, and an MP4 file pops up. The thumbnail is a fuzzy black-and-white still frame of what appears to be Jim Morrison looking directly into the camera. Gripping Bastian's hand, and summoning whatever residual strength lives within me, I press play.

Chapter Thirty-Nine

San Diego, California
Three weeks after

THE VENTILATOR NEXT to Nana's hospital bed thrums in time with my pulsing headache. By now I am so used to the dull pain that I almost can't remember a time when it was absent. It started as soon as I deboarded the plane from Paris two weeks ago and has remained my constant companion ever since.

For what it's worth, I made it. Here I am at Nana's bedside, where I've been every day since I returned, like a good granddaughter. But the relief I expected to come, hasn't. Instead I'm empty, restless. Consumed by the feeling that it's too late. Nana's condition remains unchanged.

I rub my temples and curl my feet underneath me in the vinyl easy chair stationed next to her bed. A vibration tickles the underside of my thigh. Like Pavlov's dog, I reach for my phone, but stop short.

Do I really need to go down that rabbit hole right now? To get confirmation that I've reached 500k followers on Twitter? Scroll through the torrent of new #justiceforjim posts and read my mentions, piling up by the second? Learn that network X wants an interview? Or respond to the swath of emails and texts from acquaintances and old friends about what the actual fuck happened that day in Père Lachaise?

I won't lie. At first it was thrilling, interviewing with the famed journalist at *The New York Times* and their authentication of the video. Exhuming Hank Elysian from history and gifting him his overdue recognition.

Once I gave up my power as the sole keeper of this colossal secret, the law of diminishing returns rushed in. For me, Henry is the center of this whole heinous event. Without his ceaseless loyalty to Jim, this whole mess wouldn't have ever been discovered.

Morrison's death is sickening and tragic. But so is Henry's.

But to the rest of the world, Hank Elysian is a mildly interesting background character, a means to an end. I'm gutted that any initial curiosity about Hank Elysian was immediately dwarfed by the online quests and vociferous demands for the unreleased footage of Jim Morrison being suffocated to death in a bathtub. The flashback sets my guts churning. That raw footage, with the boom mics and actors and camera crew stripped away, burrowed into my soul in a way I never imagined possible.

But our "pictures, or it didn't happen," fake-news-wearied culture won't settle for the word of authorities any more than a famished lion would settle for a salad.

I sigh and turn my gaze back to Nana. She seems so tiny underneath the heaps of bed linens, more like a cat burrowed under the blankets than a person. Still, a stubborn swipe of color highlights her cheekbones despite whatever functions her body is otherwise insistent to shut down. *Wake up,* I will her. *You have to wake up.* What if she can never hear her son's story?

There's a courteous rap on the door and a young nurse I haven't seen before comes in. She gives me a bright smile, too bright for any hospital on the planet. Her name tag says Amanda.

"Just popping in for Livia's bed check," Amanda says, coming around to the foot of the bed and picking up Nana's chart. "How are we doing today?"

"No change yet," I say. The nurse gives me a sympathetic twist of her mouth, and her gaze lingers on me for a few beats. I imagine the curious questions that run through her mind about me, probably the same ones everyone wants to know.

Amanda leans over Nana, carefully adjusting the network of wires and tubes rising from her chest. She tucks red and black EKG wires into place, secures the feeding tube and ventilator hose, then straightens up again. She crosses her arms tight on her chest and looks sheepishly at me.

"I'm sorry, this is so weird," she says. "I'm sure you know, Livia's become kind of a celebrity around here. And, well, of course *you*."

I give a tight smile. "Yeah. It feels completely unreal. Sometimes I'm not sure that any of it even happened."

Amanda bites her lip. "I still cannot believe what you found over there. Actual footage of Jim Morrison being killed." Her eyes are like two emblazoned pieces of coal burning into mine.

"It was awful," I say quietly. "Nothing could have prepared me for that."

I think about the recent photos I've scrolled through online of Jim's gravesite, the entire plot obfuscated by heaps of flowers rising a couple feet in the air. The newly appointed guards at Père Lachaise, hired to manage the exponential influx of tourists, probably curse me to hell. What none of those people know, however, is which mausoleum in the cemetery housed the revelatory murder footage for nearly fifty years. After all, something should remain mine. I look at Nana. *Ours.*

"You really had no clue what might be on the tape when you found it?" Amanda says.

"None. I assumed it was something vital, or else my uncle wouldn't have stowed it in the first place. But certainly not that, of all things."

Amanda pauses. "I get it, you know. Your uncle being estranged. My brother doesn't speak to our parents. Ever. Hasn't for years. They had a huge thing, and, well." She shrugs. "All of this just made me think."

The things we do to each other. These wounds, withholdings, withering words we inflict on one another and ourselves. And in the end, for what?

"What did the FBI say when you turned the tape over to them?" Amanda says.

"I gave the tape to the *Times*, not the FBI." I would never have gone to the authorities first and risked them sealing the tape away along with whatever the hell happened to JFK. The world needed to know what Henry died for, just as much as everything he lived for.

She frowns. "But your Twitter said you talked to the FBI."

"That was after the *Times* story broke. Three different agents interviewed me about the whole thing, for hours. They wanted to know how in the hell I'd gotten my hands on this kind of evidence. Understandable. I told them everything I could."

Okay, not everything. In the end, as I did with the *Times* interview, I decided to completely omit Giovanni's involvement to protect Alessio. The story went, I managed to figure out the mausoleum's location by talking to Bastian, who, after studying it in detail, had a strong suspicion that it was in Père Lachaise.

I did, however, tell both the paper and the FBI about Henry's murder. I talked about Maurizio, who witnessed the car run Henry off the road. About how Cherie and the French guy—who has now been identified as Remy Villier, a Parisian drug lord who died of brain cancer ten years ago in Marseilles—threatened to kill Dr. Bolla, demanding he turn over Henry's personal effects. I explained that I believe Cherie and Remy killed Henry by running him off the road, a claim that was met with nods and quick jotting in notebooks by the bureau agents.

Nothing will be done, of course. Both Cherie and Remy are dead, and it was all so terribly long ago. Justice won't be served for Jim or for Henry, at least not in the conventional sense.

I'm about to say something else to Amanda when the air fills with noise. Screeching alarms sound from virtually every electronic device in the room, and I leap up, scooting the chair back as medical staff and their equipment crowd into the room around me.

"Ma'am, we're going to need you to step out, right now," a terse female voice tells me. As I'm ushered from the room by a stocky nurse's assistant, I catch sight of the screens above Nana's head and my armpits turn slick.

The heart monitor is flat.

Chapter Forty

San Diego, California
Eight weeks after

WHEN I WAS about five or six, my mother told me that I was born under a lucky star.

"It's true, Jules," she'd said, brushing my soft bangs out of my eyes and tucking my stuffed Calico cat in next to me under the covers. "The day you were born, there was a huge shooting star that traveled over California. Almost like a comet. People came out of their houses, stood out in their yards, looking up at the sky, waiting for it. It was all over the news. Some folks swore it had a rainbow tail." She punctuated the last word with a light boop on my nose.

I looked up at her from my warm cocoon and smiled.

"Nuh-uh," I said. Her eyebrows shot up to her hairline and she cocked her head, wavy blonde hair falling over her shoulder.

"You don't believe your mama?"

"No, I do."

"Then what?" she said.

"How do you know it was lucky?"

"Well, why wouldn't it be? It's very, very rare that a shooting star like that happens," she said.

I thought for a moment. "But if it's shooting through the sky, traveling very fast, that means it crashed somewhere. Then it's not lucky at all. It's sad."

Mom paused, smoothing out my covers before she spoke again.

"It didn't crash, baby. Stars don't do that. What happened is it continued to sail through the sky like a big, old ship. It just kept going, round and round the Earth. It's still going, in fact. It always will be. It'll come around again someday and you can see for yourself."

"Really?" I said, growing happy now that everything made sense.

"Sure. And you're just like that star, Juliet. You'll always keep going, and soar high in the sky, no matter what. Life won't be without its problems, but it'll be wonderful for you. I know it."

As I carry my last box out of the house I once lived in with my ex-husband, I hope more than anything that Mom was right. Maybe some part of her is still sentient and can sense where I'm headed. Or maybe, like one of those trippy Christopher Nolan films, the shooting star was actually Mom in the future or something.

This is where my mind goes when there's a big, fat

unknown—deep into the murky past, clawing for signs of what should happen in the future.

"You sure you don't need a hand? An extra bungee cord or anything?" Matt says, coming to a stop a few feet behind me on the front walk. Lauren isn't around today. She knew I was coming, and I'm sure she would rather eat glass than repeat our last encounter. I have to give Matt credit, though. He had faithfully kept my boxed-up stuff untouched in the garage until I got around to picking it up.

"I'm good, thanks," I say, balancing the box on my thigh as I open the car door. I shove it into the backseat on top of two other banker's boxes loaded with books, totaling a weight that would rival a battleship. He saunters down the walk and stops a few feet in front of me, peers into the car.

"I'm surprised you kept so much, actually. And you've got space for all this in your new place?" He sees the look on my face, and holds up his hands. "Not trying to pry, honest. Just saying, I can keep some of this in the garage for a while if you need to. I know you had a lot over at your mom's."

"I did," I say. "But there's still room in the storage unit for all this. I didn't keep as much as I thought I would. Only the really meaningful stuff. The rest went to auction or was grabbed up at the estate sale."

I'd considered moving into Mom's and living there myself, but ultimately decided it's too soon. Maybe one day.

The process of emptying out her house for rent went far more smoothly than I'd imagined, mostly due to Colette's help. Without her, I wouldn't have survived any of this. I call or text her daily to check in. Not out of obligation, but because of the deep bond I've allowed myself to form with her. She's no longer just Mom's friend; she's also mine. Plus, she doesn't have kids, and I don't have a mother. We're kind of a perfect match.

Matt nods, rocks back on his heels. "And the new tenants aren't, like, serial killers, right?"

I snort. "I don't think so. But how well do you really know anyone?"

Our eyes meet and our smiles falter. Riding a wave of anxiety, I instinctively reach into my front pocket, only to find it empty. It takes me a second to register that I haven't refilled my Xanax prescription in weeks.

I haven't needed to.

"I also wanted to thank you for coming to Nana's funeral," I say, quickly moving on. "I don't know if I even said that to you the day of. I was so out of it, you know. All the people. And I was exhausted from the lead-up and planning and all that. It's just been a whirlwind of a few months. With everything."

I give a mirthless laugh as I think about everything that's happened. I lost my mother and grandmother, discovered the fifty-year-old murder of an American rock legend, as well as that of my own uncle. You know, the usual.

"I wouldn't have missed it," he says.

"Well, it meant a lot."

"I'm glad."

"It was a gorgeous day, wasn't it?" I think back to the startlingly blue sky and mild sun under which we laid Nana to rest next to Mom last month. The way the wind almost didn't dare to blow, for fear of disturbing even one flower petal on her casket, holding its breath until the service concluded. I miss them both with a longing that stretches to eternity. I wonder if this grief and loss will also travel around and around forever, just like my shooting star, but instead inside of me.

"She knows, you know," Matt says.

I screw up my face. "Huh?"

"That you figured out the truth about Henry; that it's resolved. She knows, even though you didn't get the chance to tell her. I really believe that."

Melancholy stings like nettles in my veins, as it always does when I think about how Nana never woke up. The gaping injustice of it. How, like everyone in my life up until now, I couldn't give her what she needed—in this case, resolution.

But what if Matt is right? Maybe she does know. In those final weeks of her life while she lay comatose, I sat by her side and told her everything. I recounted my entire journey to Italy as well as all I discovered about Henry's life. I held her hand and read aloud from Henry's journal, described to her in detail some of his best photographs, and told her about the book I'm writing. They say there's a good chance that coma patients continue to process events and sounds. I cling to the hope Nana heard it all.

"Thanks," I say with a wan smile and move to the driver's side door.

"Juliet." Matt walks over. He is quiet for a minute, looking past me at something on the horizon. Then back at me. "It wasn't all you, you know. I was wrong to put it all on you. How things ended between us. I was a dick. A lot of the time. I wasn't here for you, either, when you needed me. I don't know that either of us knew how to be here for anyone but ourselves. Does that even make sense?"

His eyes search mine. Without giving it a thought, I lean in and wrap my arms around him.

"More than you know," I say. After a few moments, we pull apart.

"Good luck with everything," he says, smiling, and starts walking away. I look at him and our house and can feel everything that seems like it happened in another lifetime. Because it did.

The me who lived in this house with him has come and gone, but her essence remains. Maybe that's what life after death really is. The resurrection of you, just bent to a different purpose. Over and over until you get it right.

"Matt?"

He turns. "Yeah?"

"I hope you two have a really good life together," I said. And I mean it.

❧

Airport Wi-Fi always sucks no matter where in the world you are, so I don't even bother. Instead of mindlessly browsing a million useless websites, I use my two-hour layover here in New York to review my dense book notes and the manuscript so far, all of which are all on my hard drive in addition to the cloud. Deidre, my agent, wants to see a completed first draft by three months from now. In fact, our publishing deal is contingent on its prompt delivery to her.

I get it. For anything to sell, it needs to be relevant. And at the pace our world now moves, Hank Elysian—and possibly Jim Morrison—will soon be distant memories, buried under whatever comes to dominate the news cycle next.

But for the first time in my life, the words come easy and steady. Unlike they ever have before. I write for hours at a time to tell Henry's story. Mornings see the bulk of my work. On an average day, I've got two chapters done by noon, then I spend the remainder of the day combing through the Hank Elysian email I set up for leads. I've encouraged anyone who interacted personally with Henry to connect with me through the quickie website I put together. It takes some wading though the spam and obnoxious requests to get to the good stuff, but it's there.

Just yesterday, an indie French journalist named Jacques Vacher, who interviewed Henry in the late '60s, reached out to me. Then there's an army corporal and two PFCs from the unit Henry traveled with in Vietnam. Another dude named Mobie claims to have been friends with both Henry and Jim at UCLA. I have upcoming video calls booked with all of them. And from the volume of unreads that continue to pile up in my inbox, I do not doubt that many more interviews will follow.

They've all come out of the woodwork, these humans who were in some way marked by Henry and his talents. Before I left for Rosanera, I feared I would never know my uncle. Now I have enough material to craft his robust biography, complete with a photographic catalogue of his works and select pages from his journals.

If I'm being honest, I'm terrified. I want to do Henry justice with this biography. To tell his astonishing story in a way that's true to who he was, without lionizing him into some cliched martyr or reducing him to this tortured artist stereotype. I don't know that I possess that capability. But at least I don't require the numbness of drink every single time I question it anymore. Just, you know, maybe every third or fourth time.

The thing that now brings me the most comfort I carry with me at all times.

I reach for my purse and peek into the secure zippered pocket, as if for confirmation. There it is—the original, creased mausoleum photo. Alessio was kind enough to mail it back to me. I run my fingertips across it and think back to my lucky star. Between what Mom and Nana left me and the advance for Henry's book, I would say I that I am, at least financially, very fortunate.

Yet in other respects, I am less prosperous. I have not one living relative left on this Earth. In that sense, in perhaps the most primitive, biological terms, I am alone.

But everything has a price. Even good fortune. And most of the time, I've now learned, we're tasked with making our own.

I jump as my phone alarm sounds, reminding me it's time to board my flight. As I turn it off, I see I got a new text.

Looks like your flight is on time. I'm counting the hours. I'll be there waiting for you. Bises.

I beam, warmth radiating through every inch of my body. I gather my things and pack them up, shrug into my backpack, and head to my gate. As I pass through the bustling crowd, amidst the joyful hellos and tearful goodbyes, all of us streaming through the vast corridor as one, like a mighty river, I feel anything but alone. Instead, I sense that I'm on the brink of something far bigger than myself. That the darkness has finally ushered me cautiously into the first tiny gradients of light.

I think I'll like calling Paris home.

Acknowledgments

It's fair to say that *Final Belongings* was at least 25 years in the making. There was a story brewing inside me that I couldn't quite articulate until recently, when I finally won my first major battle in the War of Art. As any writer knows, it's an interminable struggle but well worth the torment in the end.

I'd like to thank the San Diego Inkwells, my incredible writing group since 2017. Thank you, Will Barnes, Michelle Fogle, Dani Heinemeyer, David Hoffer, Ramona Josephs-Horton, Steve Nickell, Carol Pope, Valerie Power, and Ruth Roberts. Your keen insight and critique through both working drafts of the manuscript was invaluable.

I'm grateful to author T. Greenwood, under whose year-long tutelage I came to better understand the art and craft of novel writing.

Thank you to my dear friend and literary expert Dr. Jill Coste for her thorough copyediting of the manuscript and astute feedback.

My gratitude is also owed to author Jason Arnopp for his perceptive review and recommendations, all of which improved and clarified the direction of the novel.

A special thank you goes to my family for supporting

my creative writing endeavors throughout my life. Notably, Jeanne Mazess, who always believed I could do it.

Finally, this manuscript would never have met its completion if it weren't for the unconditional, loving support and endless encouragement of my husband, Jay. I love you more than words can say.

Hopefully, you, The Reader, found this story worthy of your time and attention. If you enjoyed the book, I invite you to leave a review and visit *www.sarahbeaucheminwriter.com*.

CPSIA information can be obtained
at www.ICGtesting.com
Printed in the USA
LVHW101048080423
743793LV00002BA/91